Love's not a Three Dollar Fare

More Stories from *Unsupervised Existance*

by Terry LaBan

FANTAGRAPHICS BOOKS

SEATTLE, WASHINGTON

FANTAGRAPHICS BOOKS

7563 Lake City Way NE, Seattle, WA 98115 USA

Editor: Gary Groth
Design, Production: Peppy White
Publishers: Gary Groth and Kim Thompson

First Fantagraphics Books edition: March, 1995

1 2 3 4 5 6 7 8 9

ISBN: 1-56097-165-7

TABLE OF CONTENTS

Acknowledgment

Thanks to my wife Patty,
who not only gave me love and support,
but also helped me write much of this stuff.

INTRODUCTION

The stories in this book originally comprised the bulk of a comic book which appeared sporadically between the fall of 1987 and the spring of 1992. The first two issues were self-published as minis, and the first two stories appeared in them. The rest were all published by Fantagraphics Books, publisher of the paperback you're holding now.

When I started writing these comics, I was young and ambitious. I wanted to portray the lives of the people around me and the things that were happening in my own life, in the manner of a novelist or a writer of short stories. The result was the more-or-less continuing saga of bohemian misfits I called *Unsupervised Existence,* a title I thought captured somewhat the ambivalent freedom of adulthood. There are certainly parallels between the events in my stories and my actual life, but none of it is, strictly speaking, autobiographical. I only say that because "autobiography" was only one of the genres my book was inappropriately lumped with; for years, people who actually met me were surprised that I wasn't a tall, gangly cabby with a scraggly beard and a nose the size of a watermelon.

Unsupervised Existence didn't break any sales records, at least at the high end. Certainly the fact that it was chronically late and that the size of the book kept changing didn't help; nor did the fact that no one seemed able to remember the name ("Excuse me Mr. Retailer — do you have the new... um... *Unsatisfied Exigency*?"). But I think the biggest problem was how difficult it was to describe. It was "realistic," but not really "slice of life," humorous, but not "funny," too confrontational and quirky to be "mainstream" and too good-natured to be "underground." After a couple years, tired of low sales and the stress of coming up with stories that took as much thought as these did, as well as changes in my own mind that made me eager to try other things, I ended the series and moved on.

Nonetheless, I'm awfully happy I did this stuff, and happier still you have a chance to read it. However you want to categorize them, I hope you find in these tales of love, angst, low rent and taxies things that amuse, entertain, and move you. If you end up caring about the characters as much as I do, this book will have a treasured place on your shelf long after anyone can recall ever seeing a comic book called *Unspecified Experience.* Or something like that.

— Terry LaBan, Chicago, 1994

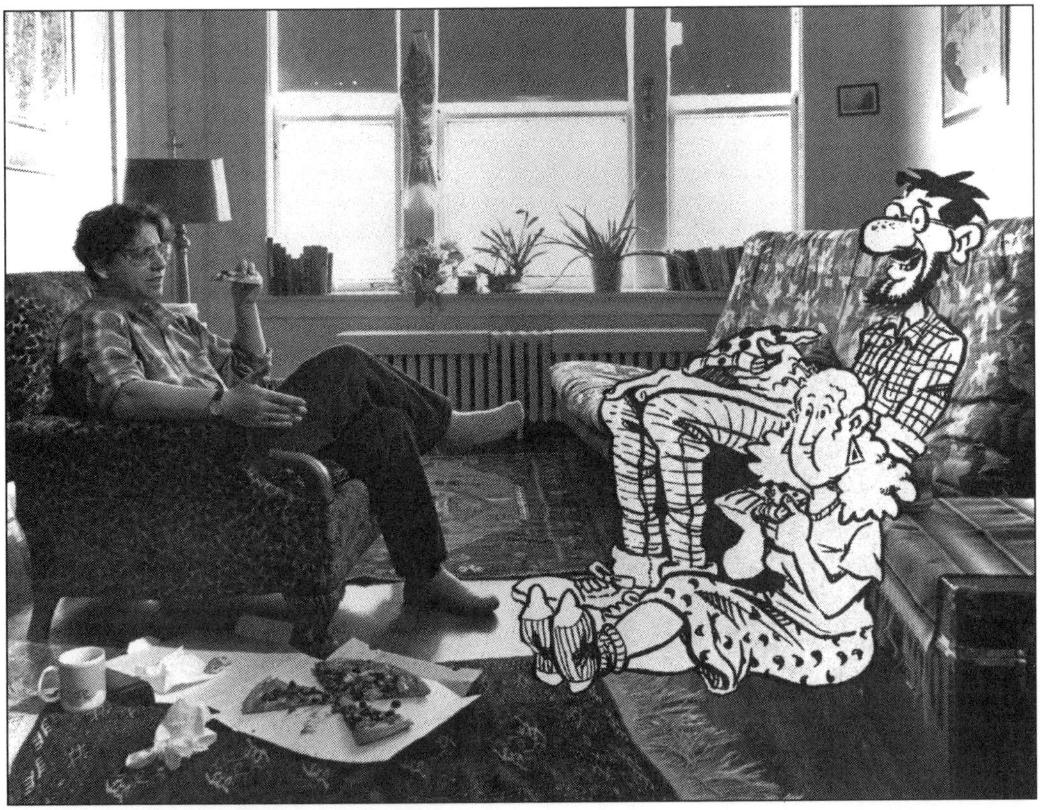

Photo by KEVIN HORAN

Terry LaBan and fictional creations, Chicago, 1990.

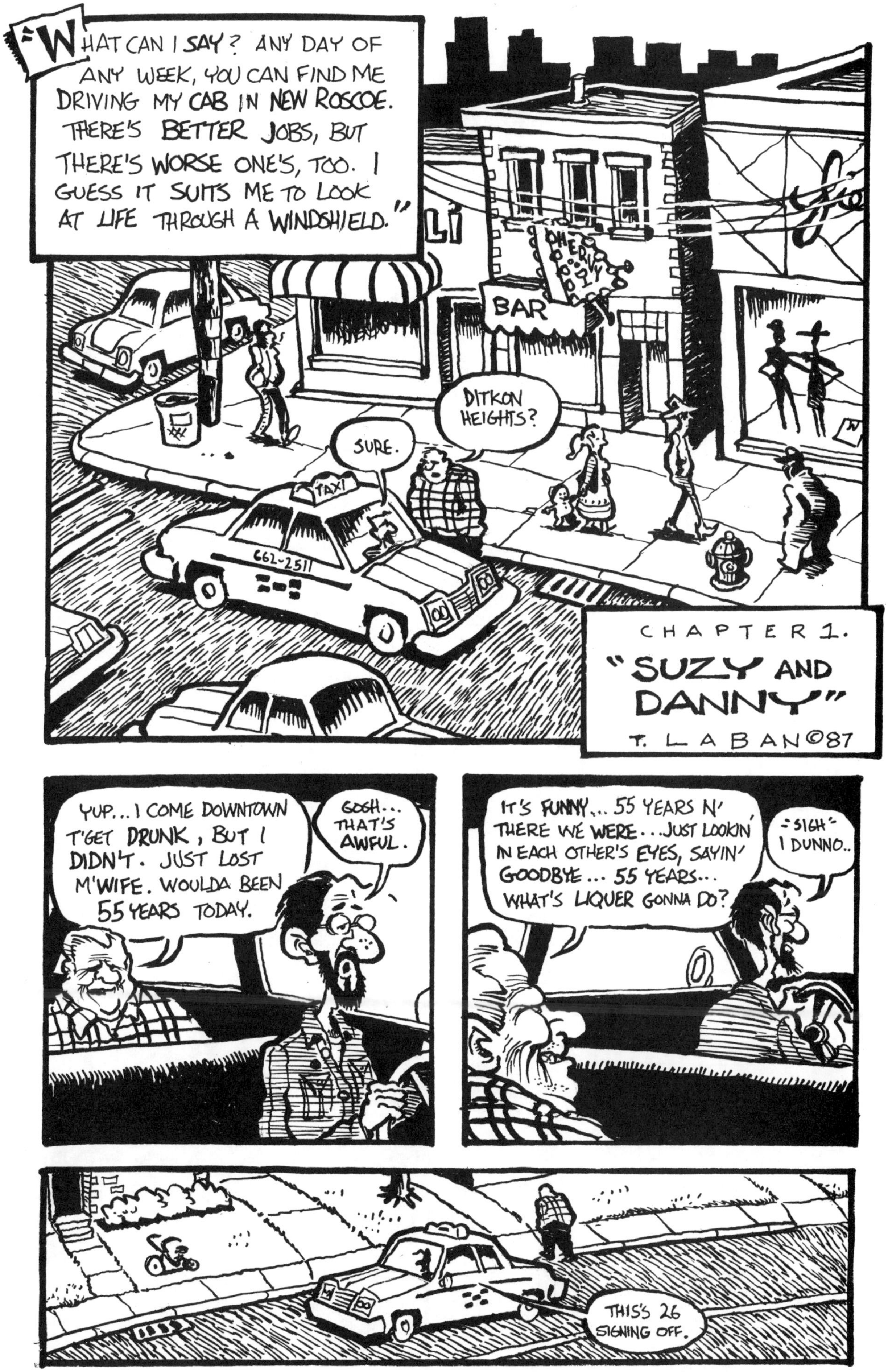
"WHAT CAN I SAY? ANY DAY OF ANY WEEK, YOU CAN FIND ME DRIVING MY CAB IN NEW ROSCOE. THERE'S BETTER JOBS, BUT THERE'S WORSE ONE'S, TOO. I GUESS IT SUITS ME TO LOOK AT LIFE THROUGH A WINDSHIELD."
BAR
TAXI
662-2511
DITKON HEIGHTS?
SURE.
CHAPTER 1.
"SUZY AND DANNY"
T. LABAN©87
YUP... I COME DOWNTOWN T'GET DRUNK, BUT I DIDN'T. JUST LOST M'WIFE. WOULDA BEEN 55 YEARS TODAY.
GOSH... THAT'S AWFUL.
IT'S FUNNY... 55 YEARS N' THERE WE WERE... JUST LOOKIN' IN EACH OTHER'S EYES, SAYIN' GOODBYE... 55 YEARS... WHAT'S LIQUER GONNA DO?
-SIGH- I DUNNO..
THIS'S 26 SIGNING OFF.

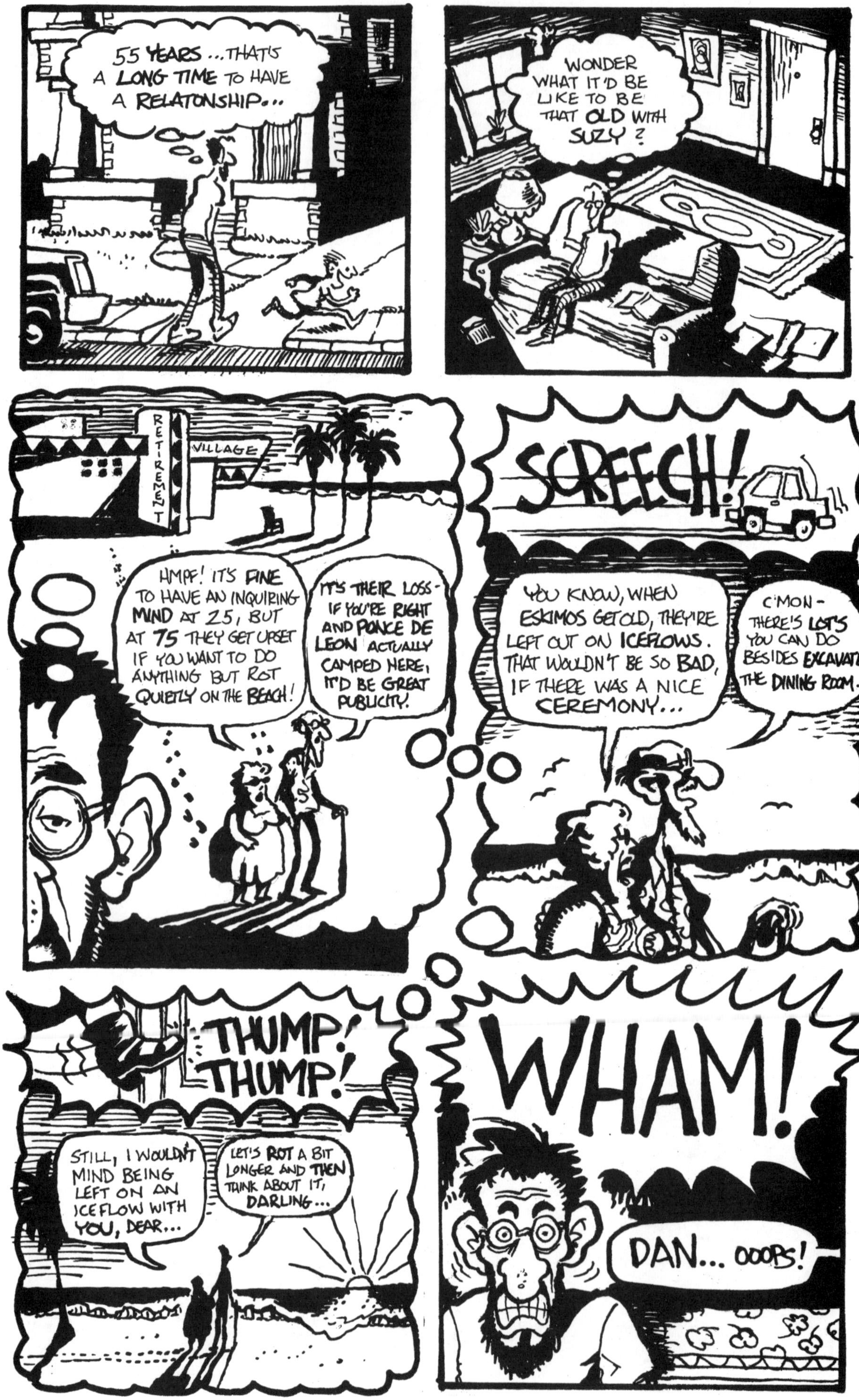
55 YEARS ...THAT'S A LONG TIME TO HAVE A RELATONSHIP...
WONDER WHAT IT'D BE LIKE TO BE THAT OLD WITH SUZY?
RETIREMENT
VILLAGE
HMPF! IT'S FINE TO HAVE AN INQUIRING MIND AT 25, BUT AT 75 THEY GET UPSET IF YOU WANT TO DO ANYTHING BUT ROT QUIETLY ON THE BEACH!
IT'S THEIR LOSS - IF YOU'RE RIGHT AND PONCE DE LEON ACTUALLY CAMPED HERE, IT'D BE GREAT PUBLICITY!
SCREECH!
YOU KNOW, WHEN ESKIMOS GET OLD, THEY'RE LEFT OUT ON ICEFLOWS. THAT WOULDN'T BE SO BAD, IF THERE WAS A NICE CEREMONY...
C'MON - THERE'S LOT'S YOU CAN DO BESIDES EXCAVATE THE DINING ROOM.
THUMP! THUMP!
STILL, I WOULDN'T MIND BEING LEFT ON AN ICEFLOW WITH YOU, DEAR...
LET'S ROT A BIT LONGER AND THEN THINK ABOUT IT, DARLING...
WHAM!
DAN... OOOPS!

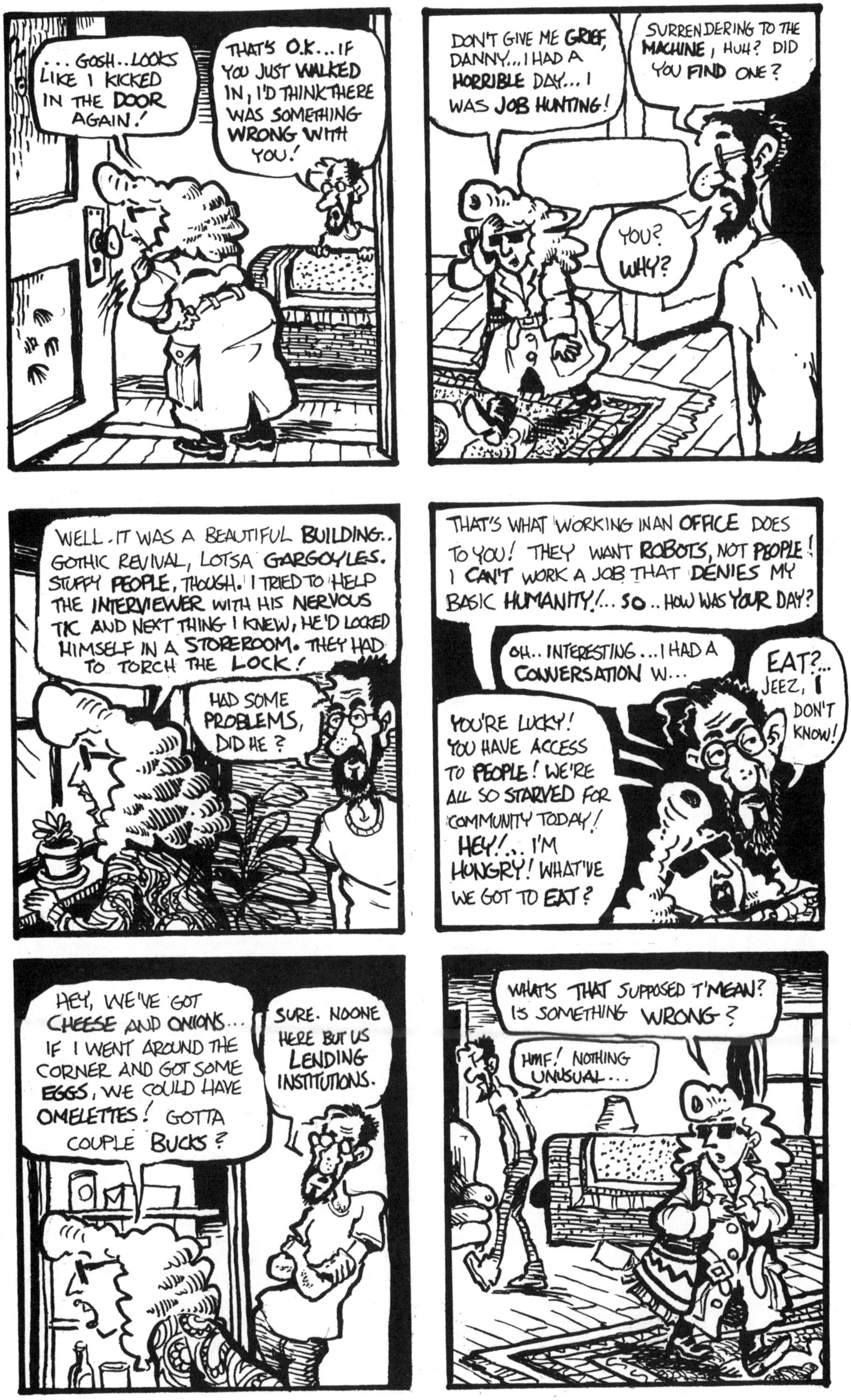
... GOSH.. LOOKS LIKE I KICKED IN THE DOOR AGAIN!
THAT'S O.K... IF YOU JUST WALKED IN, I'D THINK THERE WAS SOMETHING WRONG WITH YOU!
DON'T GIVE ME GRIEF, DANNY... I HAD A HORRIBLE DAY... I WAS JOB HUNTING!
SURRENDERING TO THE MACHINE, HUH? DID YOU FIND ONE?
YOU? WHY?
WELL. IT WAS A BEAUTIFUL BUILDING.. GOTHIC REVIVAL, LOTSA GARGOYLES. STUFFY PEOPLE, THOUGH. I TRIED TO HELP THE INTERVIEWER WITH HIS NERVOUS TIC AND NEXT THING I KNEW, HE'D LOCKED HIMSELF IN A STOREROOM. THEY HAD TO TORCH THE LOCK!
HAD SOME PROBLEMS, DID HE?
THAT'S WHAT WORKING IN AN OFFICE DOES TO YOU! THEY WANT ROBOTS, NOT PEOPLE! I CAN'T WORK A JOB THAT DENIES MY BASIC HUMANITY!... SO.. HOW WAS YOUR DAY?
OH.. INTERESTING... I HAD A CONVERSATION W...
YOU'RE LUCKY! YOU HAVE ACCESS TO PEOPLE! WE'RE ALL SO STARVED FOR COMMUNITY TODAY! HEY!... I'M HUNGRY! WHAT'VE WE GOT TO EAT?
EAT?... JEEZ, I DON'T KNOW!
HEY, WE'VE GOT CHEESE AND ONIONS... IF I WENT AROUND THE CORNER AND GOT SOME EGGS, WE COULD HAVE OMELETTES! GOTTA COUPLE BUCKS?
SURE. NOONE HERE BUT US LENDING INSTITUTIONS.
WHAT'S THAT SUPPOSED T'MEAN? IS SOMETHING WRONG?
HMF! NOTHING UNUSUAL...

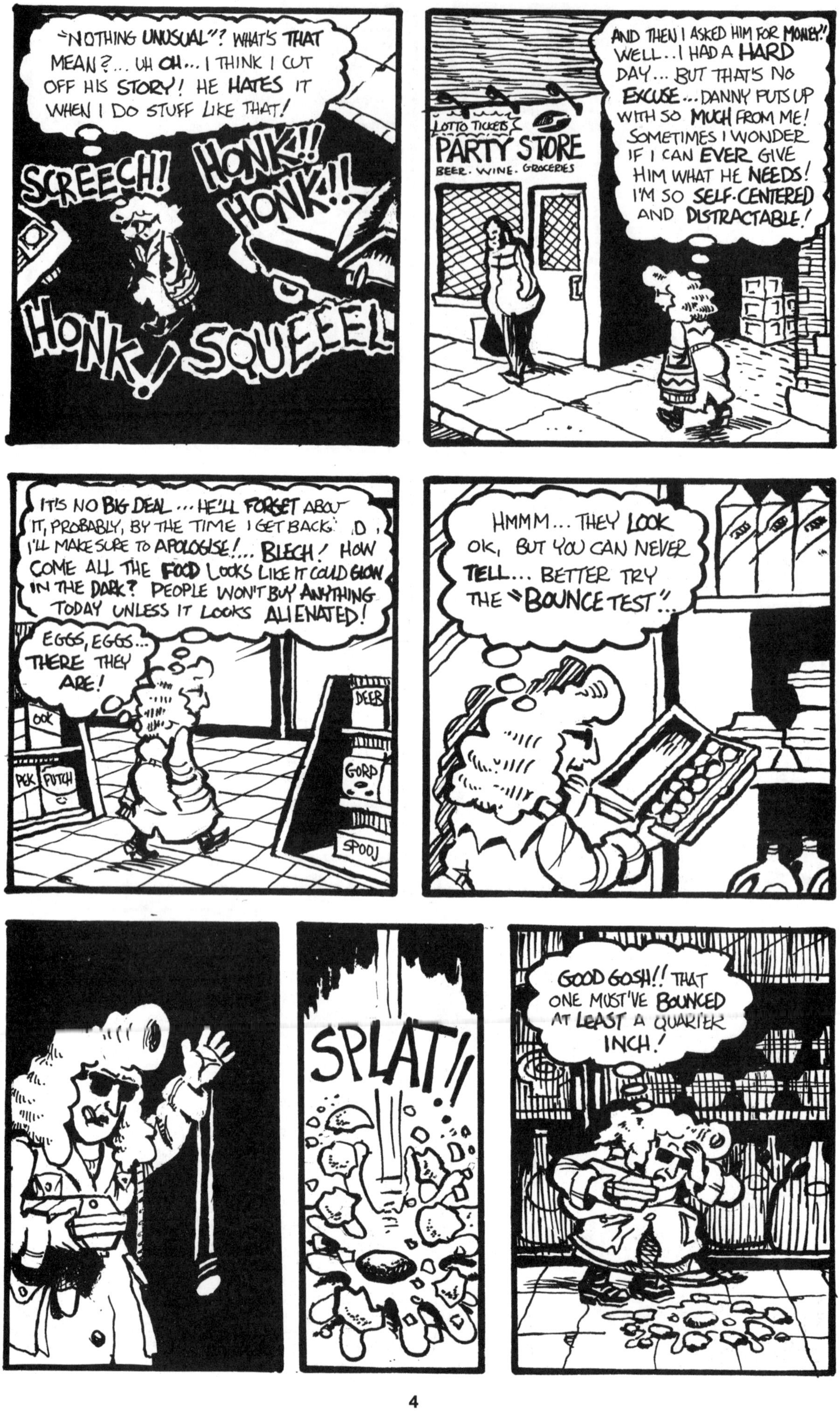
"NOTHING UNUSUAL"? WHAT'S THAT MEAN?... UH OH... I THINK I CUT OFF HIS STORY! HE HATES IT WHEN I DO STUFF LIKE THAT!
SCREECH! HONK!! HONK!!
HONK! SQUEEEL
LOTTO TICKETS
PARTY STORE
BEER · WINE · GROCERIES
AND THEN I ASKED HIM FOR MONEY! WELL.. I HAD A HARD DAY... BUT THAT'S NO EXCUSE... DANNY PUTS UP WITH SO MUCH FROM ME! SOMETIMES I WONDER IF I CAN EVER GIVE HIM WHAT HE NEEDS! I'M SO SELF-CENTERED AND DISTRACTABLE!
IT'S NO BIG DEAL... HE'LL FORGET ABOUT IT, PROBABLY, BY THE TIME I GET BACK... I'LL MAKE SURE TO APOLOGISE!... BLECH! HOW COME ALL THE FOOD LOOKS LIKE IT COULD GLOW IN THE DARK? PEOPLE WON'T BUY ANYTHING TODAY UNLESS IT LOOKS ALIENATED!
EGGS, EGGS... THERE THEY ARE!
OOK
PEK
PUTCH
DEEB
GORP
SPOOJ
HMMM... THEY LOOK OK, BUT YOU CAN NEVER TELL... BETTER TRY THE "BOUNCE TEST"...
SPLAT!!
GOOD GOSH!! THAT ONE MUST'VE BOUNCED AT LEAST A QUARTER INCH!

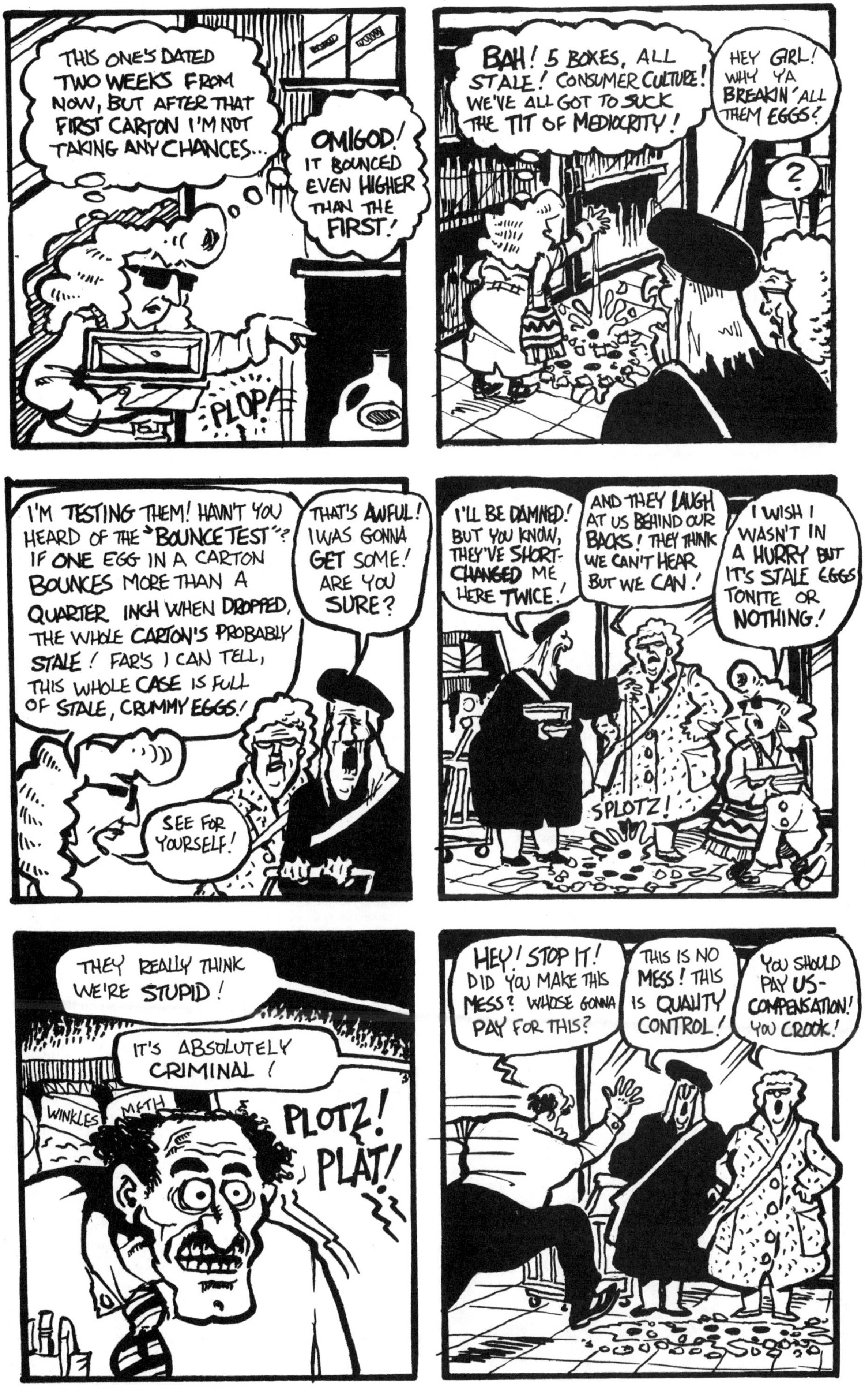
THIS ONE'S DATED TWO WEEKS FROM NOW, BUT AFTER THAT FIRST CARTON I'M NOT TAKING ANY CHANCES...
OMIGOD! IT BOUNCED EVEN HIGHER THAN THE FIRST!
PLOP!
BAH! 5 BOXES, ALL STALE! CONSUMER CULTURE! WE'VE ALL GOT TO SUCK THE TIT OF MEDIOCRITY!
HEY GIRL! WHY YA BREAKIN' ALL THEM EGGS?
?
I'M TESTING THEM! HAVN'T YOU HEARD OF THE "BOUNCE TEST"? IF ONE EGG IN A CARTON BOUNCES MORE THAN A QUARTER INCH WHEN DROPPED, THE WHOLE CARTON'S PROBABLY STALE! FAR'S I CAN TELL, THIS WHOLE CASE IS FULL OF STALE, CRUMMY EGGS!
THAT'S AWFUL! I WAS GONNA GET SOME! ARE YOU SURE?
SEE FOR YOURSELF!
I'LL BE DAMNED! BUT YOU KNOW, THEY'VE SHORT-CHANGED ME HERE TWICE!
AND THEY LAUGH AT US BEHIND OUR BACKS! THEY THINK WE CAN'T HEAR BUT WE CAN!
I WISH I WASN'T IN A HURRY BUT IT'S STALE EGGS TONITE OR NOTHING!
SPLOTZ!
THEY REALLY THINK WE'RE STUPID!
IT'S ABSOLUTELY CRIMINAL!
WINKLES
PLOTZ!
PLAT!
HEY! STOP IT! DID YOU MAKE THIS MESS? WHOSE GONNA PAY FOR THIS?
THIS IS NO MESS! THIS IS QUALITY CONTROL!
YOU SHOULD PAY US-COMPENSATION! YOU CROOK!

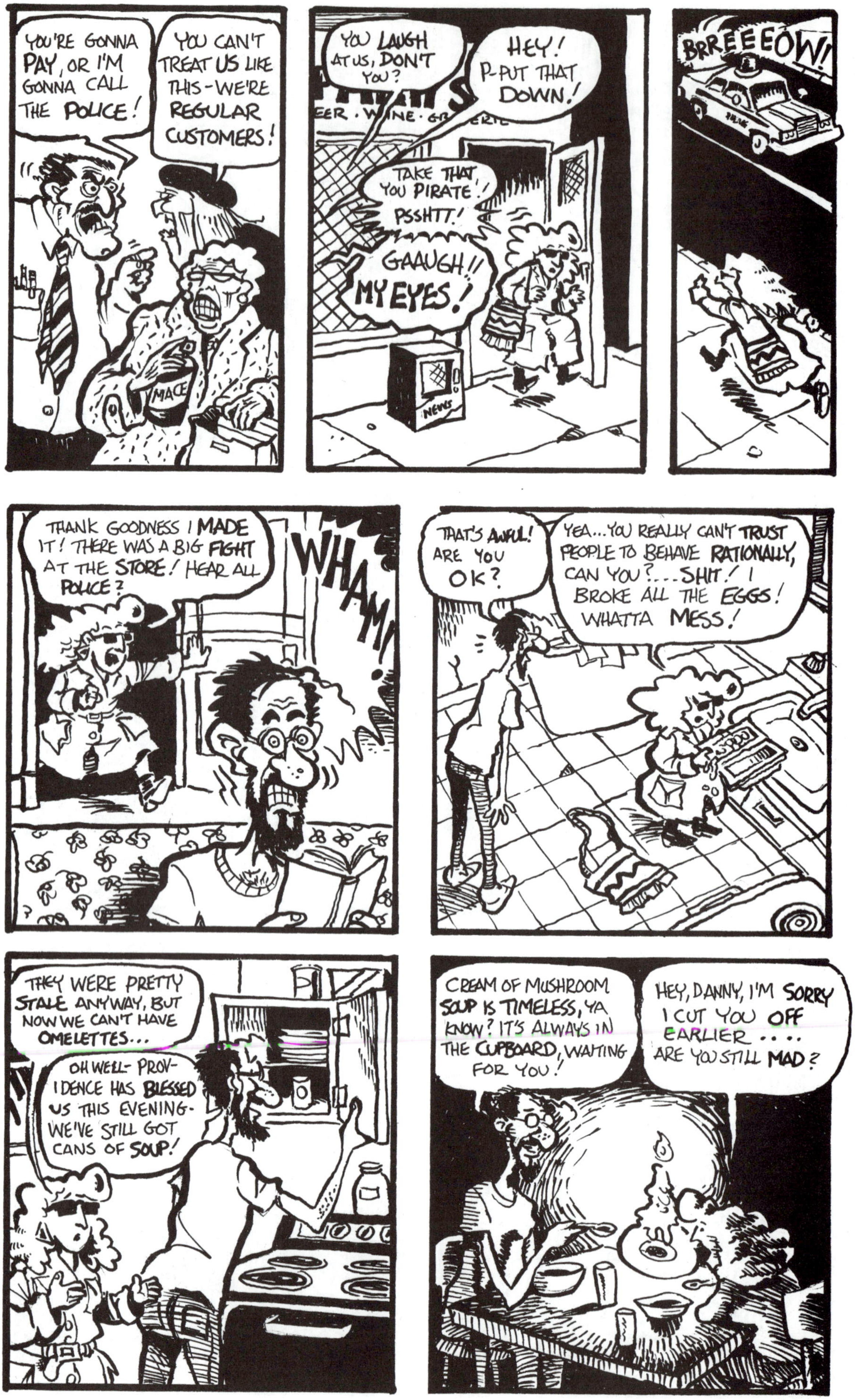

YOU'RE GONNA PAY, OR I'M GONNA CALL THE POLICE!
YOU CAN'T TREAT US LIKE THIS-WE'RE REGULAR CUSTOMERS!
MACE
YOU LAUGH AT US, DON'T YOU?
HEY! P-PUT THAT DOWN!
TAKE THAT, YOU PIRATE!
PSSHTT!
GAAUGH!! MY EYES!
NEWS
BRREEEOW!
THANK GOODNESS I MADE IT! THERE WAS A BIG FIGHT AT THE STORE! HEAR ALL POLICE?
WHAM!
THAT'S AWFUL! ARE YOU OK?
YEA...YOU REALLY CAN'T TRUST PEOPLE TO BEHAVE RATIONALLY, CAN YOU?...SHIT! I BROKE ALL THE EGGS! WHATTA MESS!
THEY WERE PRETTY STALE ANYWAY, BUT NOW WE CAN'T HAVE OMELETTES...
OH WELL- PROVIDENCE HAS BLESSED US THIS EVENING- WE'VE STILL GOT CANS OF SOUP!
CREAM OF MUSHROOM SOUP IS TIMELESS, YA KNOW? IT'S ALWAYS IN THE CUPBOARD, WAITING FOR YOU!
HEY, DANNY, I'M SORRY I CUT YOU OFF EARLIER.... ARE YOU STILL MAD?

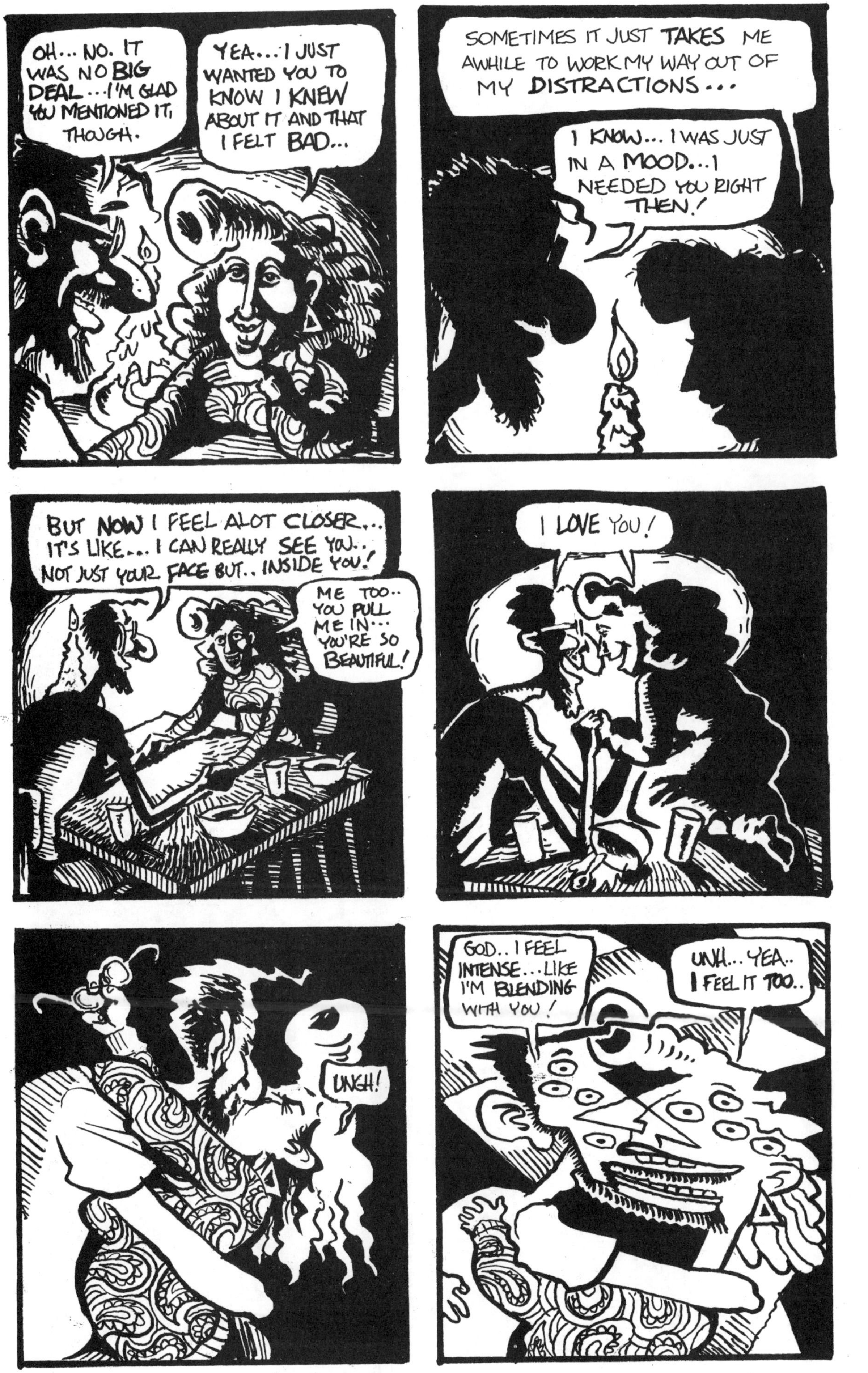

OH... NO. IT WAS NO BIG DEAL...I'M GLAD YOU MENTIONED IT, THOUGH.
YEA...I JUST WANTED YOU TO KNOW I KNEW ABOUT IT AND THAT I FELT BAD...
SOMETIMES IT JUST TAKES ME AWHILE TO WORK MY WAY OUT OF MY DISTRACTIONS...
I KNOW... I WAS JUST IN A MOOD...I NEEDED YOU RIGHT THEN!
BUT NOW I FEEL ALOT CLOSER... IT'S LIKE... I CAN REALLY SEE YOU.. NOT JUST YOUR FACE BUT.. INSIDE YOU!
ME TOO.. YOU PULL ME IN... YOU'RE SO BEAUTIFUL!
I LOVE YOU!
UNGH!
GOD.. I FEEL INTENSE... LIKE I'M BLENDING WITH YOU!
UNH... YEA.. I FEEL IT TOO..

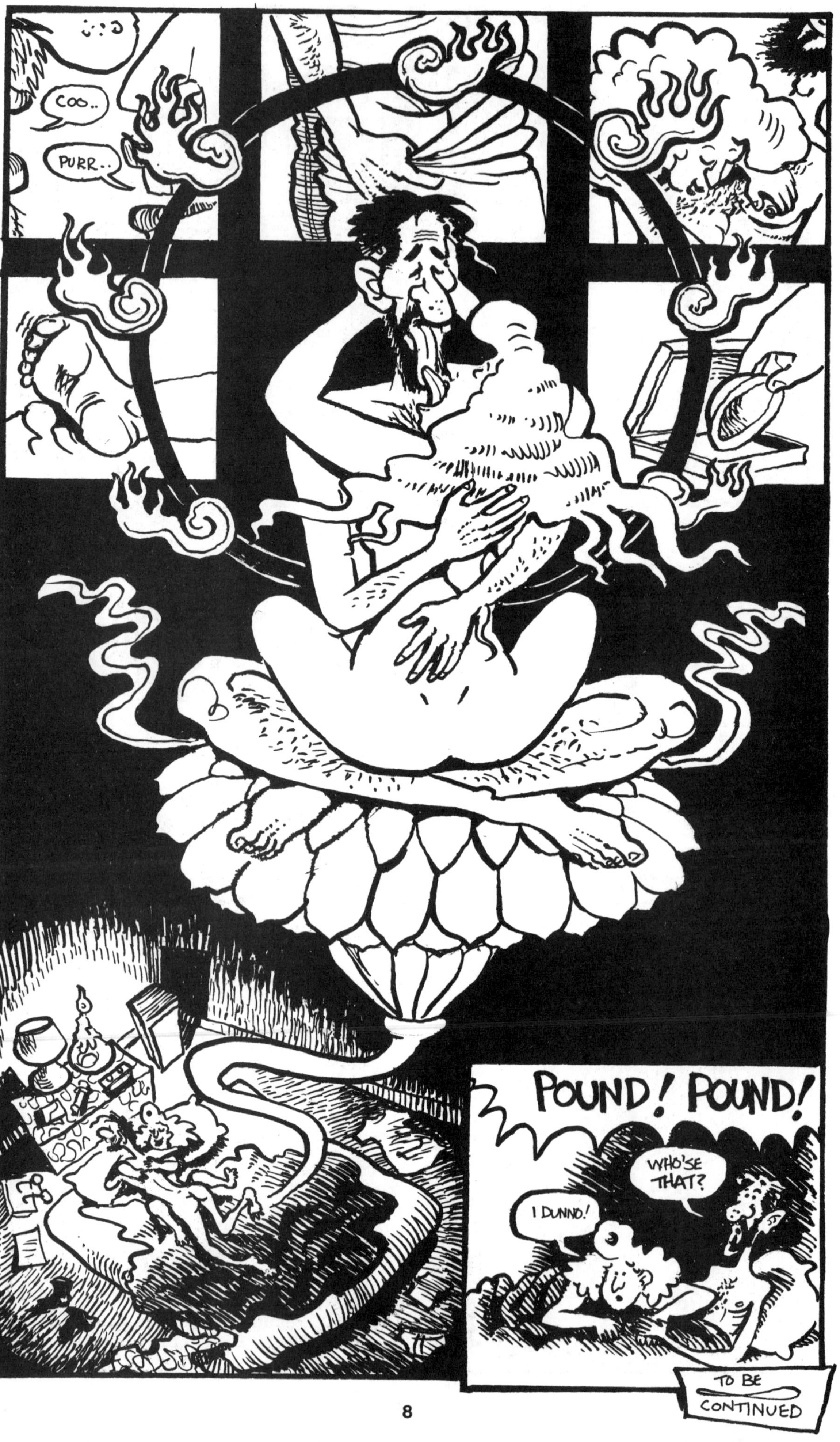
COO..
PURR..
POUND! POUND!
WHO'SE THAT?
I DUNNO!
TO BE CONTINUED

DINNER AT THE DREAMTIME!

T. LABAN
©1988

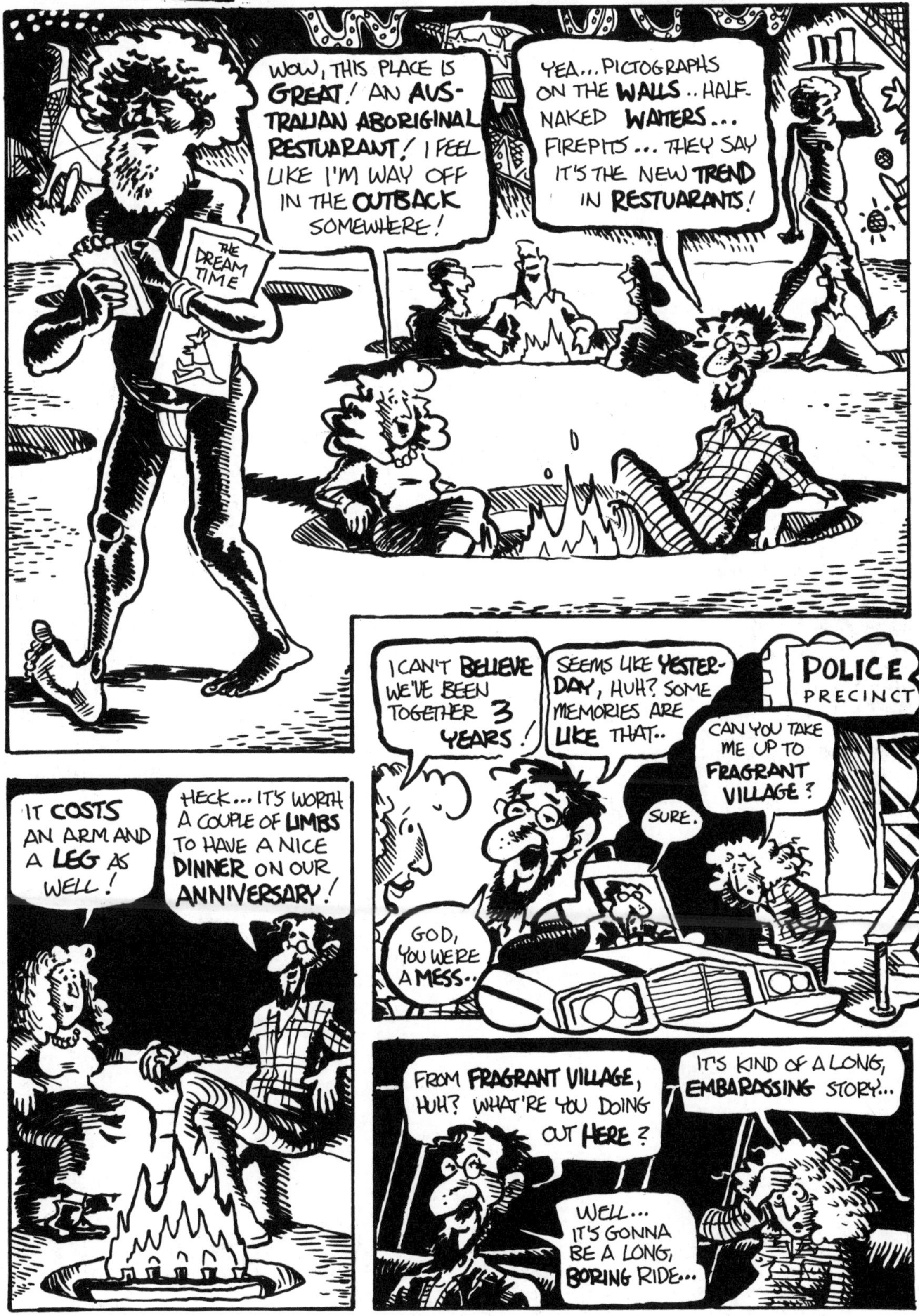
WOW, THIS PLACE IS GREAT! AN AUSTRALIAN ABORIGINAL RESTUARANT! I FEEL LIKE I'M WAY OFF IN THE OUTBACK SOMEWHERE!
YEA... PICTOGRAPHS ON THE WALLS.. HALF-NAKED WAITERS... FIREPITS... THEY SAY IT'S THE NEW TREND IN RESTUARANTS!
THE DREAM TIME
IT COSTS AN ARM AND A LEG AS WELL!
HECK... IT'S WORTH A COUPLE OF LIMBS TO HAVE A NICE DINNER ON OUR ANNIVERSARY!
I CAN'T BELIEVE WE'VE BEEN TOGETHER 3 YEARS!
SEEMS LIKE YESTERDAY, HUH? SOME MEMORIES ARE LIKE THAT..
POLICE PRECINCT
CAN YOU TAKE ME UP TO FRAGRANT VILLAGE?
SURE.
GOD, YOU WERE A MESS..
FROM FRAGRANT VILLAGE, HUH? WHAT'RE YOU DOING OUT HERE?
IT'S KIND OF A LONG, EMBARASSING STORY...
WELL... IT'S GONNA BE A LONG, BORING RIDE...

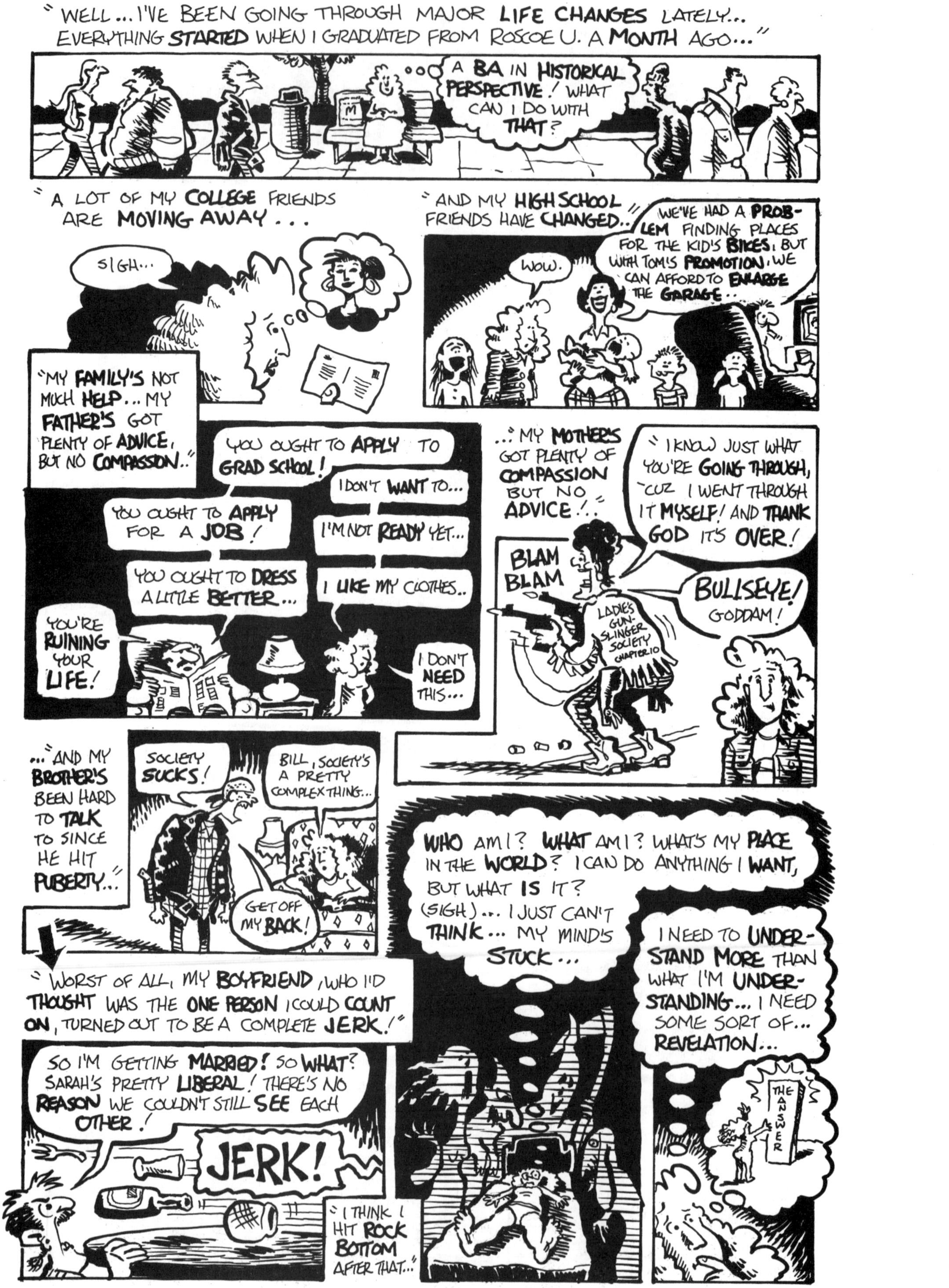
"WELL ... I'VE BEEN GOING THROUGH MAJOR LIFE CHANGES LATELY... EVERYTHING STARTED WHEN I GRADUATED FROM ROSCOE U. A MONTH AGO..."
A BA IN HISTORICAL PERSPECTIVE! WHAT CAN I DO WITH THAT?
"A LOT OF MY COLLEGE FRIENDS ARE MOVING AWAY . . .
SIGH...
"AND MY HIGH SCHOOL FRIENDS HAVE CHANGED..."
WE'VE HAD A PROBLEM FINDING PLACES FOR THE KID'S BIKES, BUT WITH TOM'S PROMOTION, WE CAN AFFORD TO ENLARGE THE GARAGE...
WOW.
"MY FAMILY'S NOT MUCH HELP... MY FATHER'S GOT PLENTY OF ADVICE, BUT NO COMPASSION..."
YOU OUGHT TO APPLY TO GRAD SCHOOL!
I DON'T WANT TO...
YOU OUGHT TO APPLY FOR A JOB!
I'M NOT READY YET...
YOU OUGHT TO DRESS A LITTLE BETTER...
I LIKE MY CLOTHES..
YOU'RE RUINING YOUR LIFE!
I DON'T NEED THIS...
..."MY MOTHER'S GOT PLENTY OF COMPASSION BUT NO ADVICE..."
"I KNOW JUST WHAT YOU'RE GOING THROUGH, 'CUZ I WENT THROUGH IT MYSELF! AND THANK GOD IT'S OVER!
BLAM BLAM
BULLSEYE! GODDAM!
LADIE'S GUN-SLINGER SOCIETY CHAPTER 10
..."AND MY BROTHER'S BEEN HARD TO TALK TO SINCE HE HIT PUBERTY..."
SOCIETY SUCKS!
BILL, SOCIETY'S A PRETTY COMPLEX THING...
GET OFF MY BACK!
"WORST OF ALL, MY BOYFRIEND, WHO I'D THOUGHT WAS THE ONE PERSON I COULD COUNT ON, TURNED OUT TO BE A COMPLETE JERK!"
SO I'M GETTING MARRIED! SO WHAT? SARAH'S PRETTY LIBERAL! THERE'S NO REASON WE COULDN'T STILL SEE EACH OTHER!
JERK!
"I THINK I HIT ROCK BOTTOM AFTER THAT..."
WHO AM I? WHAT AM I? WHAT'S MY PLACE IN THE WORLD? I CAN DO ANYTHING I WANT, BUT WHAT IS IT? (SIGH)... I JUST CAN'T THINK... MY MIND'S STUCK...
I NEED TO UNDERSTAND MORE THAN WHAT I'M UNDERSTANDING... I NEED SOME SORT OF... REVELATION...
THE ANSWER

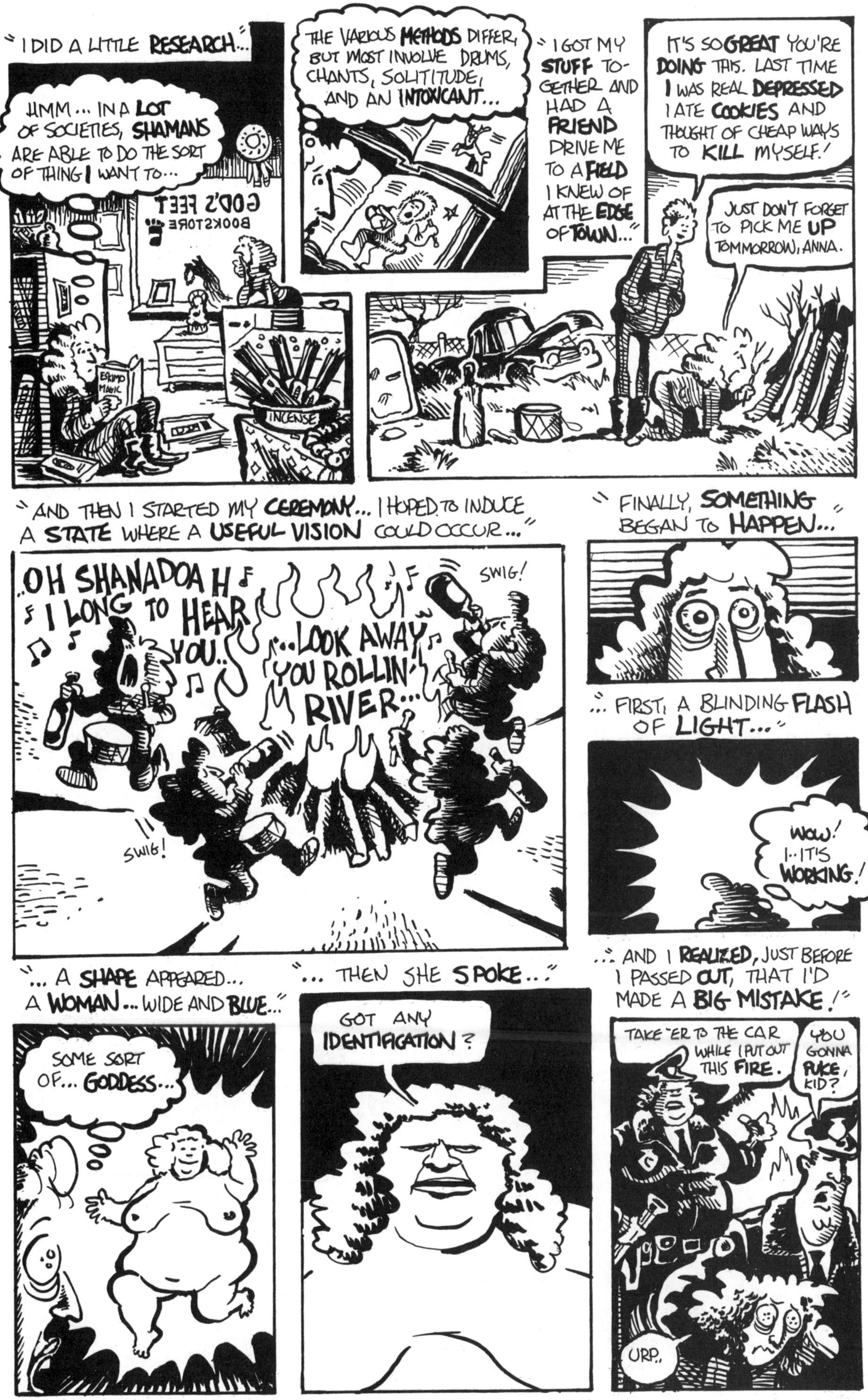
"I DID A LITTLE RESEARCH..."
HMM... IN A LOT OF SOCIETIES, SHAMANS ARE ABLE TO DO THE SORT OF THING I WANT TO...
GOD'S FEET BOOKSTORE
ESKIMO MAGIC
INCENSE
THE VARIOUS METHODS DIFFER, BUT MOST INVOLVE DRUMS, CHANTS, SOLITITUDE, AND AN INTOXICANT...
"I GOT MY STUFF TOGETHER AND HAD A FRIEND DRIVE ME TO A FIELD I KNEW OF AT THE EDGE OF TOWN..."
IT'S SO GREAT YOU'RE DOING THIS. LAST TIME I WAS REAL DEPRESSED I ATE COOKIES AND THOUGHT OF CHEAP WAYS TO KILL MYSELF!
JUST DON'T FORGET TO PICK ME UP TOMMORROW, ANNA.
"AND THEN I STARTED MY CEREMONY... I HOPED TO INDUCE A STATE WHERE A USEFUL VISION COULD OCCUR..."
..OH SHANADOAH I LONG TO HEAR YOU..
..LOOK AWAY YOU ROLLIN' RIVER...
SWIG!
SWIG!
"FINALLY, SOMETHING BEGAN TO HAPPEN..."
"...FIRST, A BLINDING FLASH OF LIGHT..."
WOW! I..IT'S WORKING!
"... A SHAPE APPEARED... A WOMAN... WIDE AND BLUE..."
SOME SORT OF... GODDESS...
"... THEN SHE SPOKE..."
GOT ANY IDENTIFICATION?
"...AND I REALIZED, JUST BEFORE I PASSED OUT, THAT I'D MADE A BIG MISTAKE!"
TAKE 'ER TO THE CAR WHILE I PUT OUT THIS FIRE.
YOU GONNA PUKE, KID?
URP..

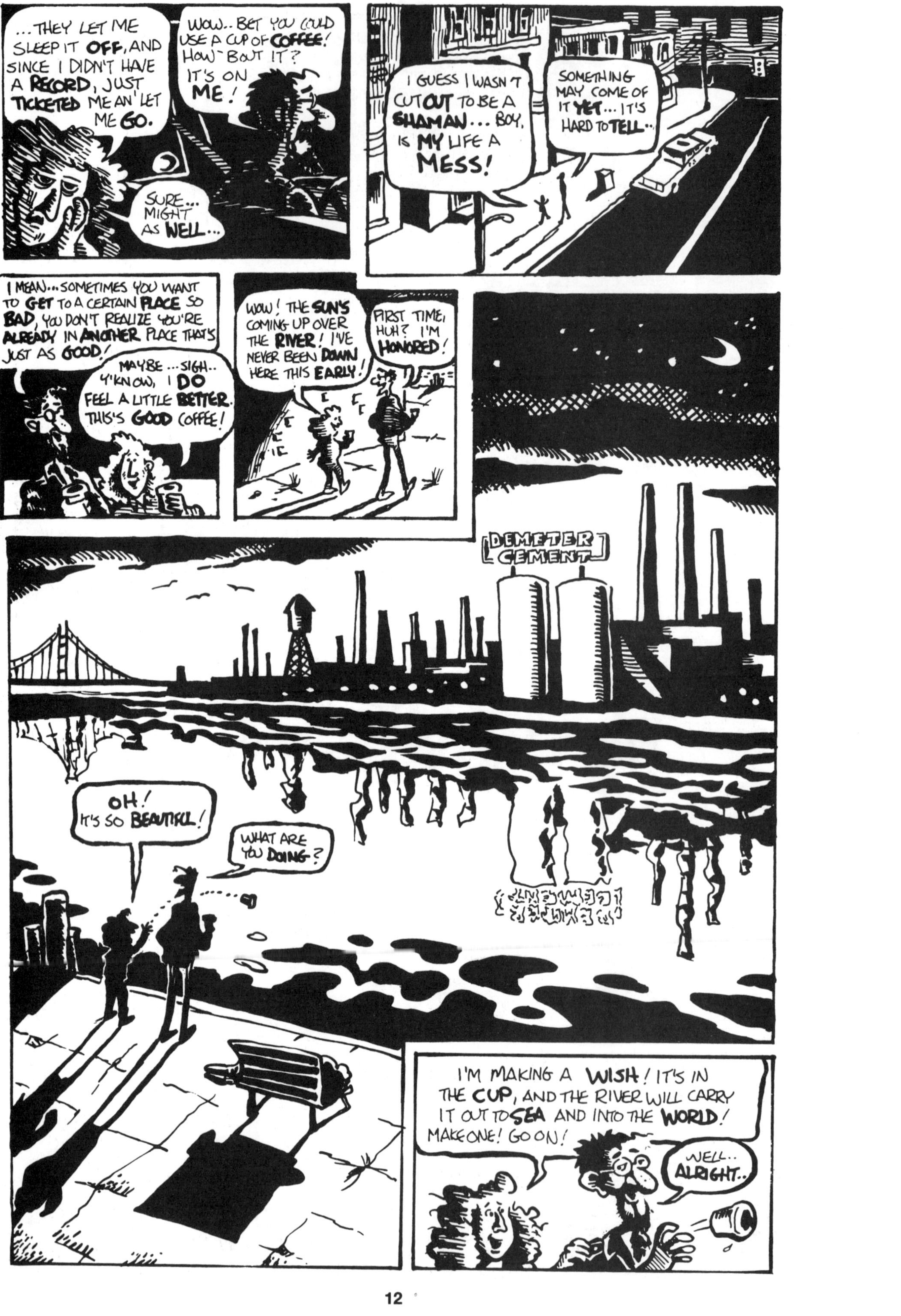
...THEY LET ME SLEEP IT OFF, AND SINCE I DIDN'T HAVE A RECORD, JUST TICKETED ME AN' LET ME GO.
WOW.. BET YOU COULD USE A CUP OF COFFEE! HOW 'BOUT IT? IT'S ON ME!
SURE... MIGHT AS WELL...
I GUESS I WASN'T CUT OUT TO BE A SHAMAN... BOY, IS MY LIFE A MESS!
SOMETHING MAY COME OF IT YET... IT'S HARD TO TELL...
I MEAN... SOMETIMES YOU WANT TO GET TO A CERTAIN PLACE SO BAD, YOU DON'T REALIZE YOU'RE ALREADY IN ANOTHER PLACE THAT'S JUST AS GOOD!
MAYBE ...SIGH.. Y'KNOW, I DO FEEL A LITTLE BETTER. THIS'S GOOD COFFEE!
WOW! THE SUN'S COMING UP OVER THE RIVER! I'VE NEVER BEEN DOWN HERE THIS EARLY!
FIRST TIME, HUH? I'M HONORED!
DEMETER CEMENT
OH! IT'S SO BEAUTIFUL!
WHAT ARE YOU DOING?
I'M MAKING A WISH! IT'S IN THE CUP, AND THE RIVER WILL CARRY IT OUT TO SEA AND INTO THE WORLD! MAKE ONE! GO ON!
WELL.. ALRIGHT..

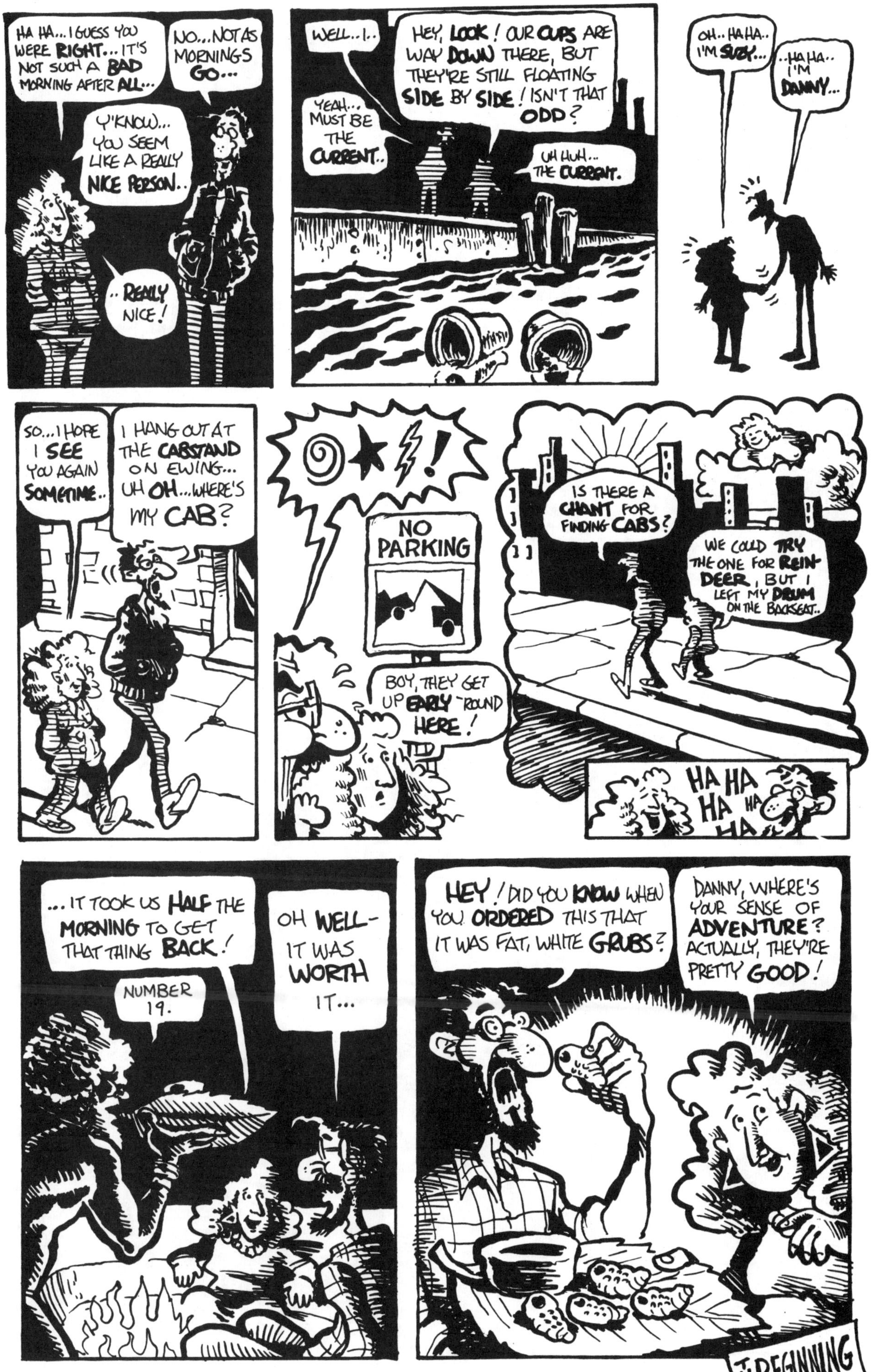
HA HA... I GUESS YOU WERE RIGHT... IT'S NOT SUCH A BAD MORNING AFTER ALL...
NO... NOT AS MORNINGS GO...
Y'KNOW... YOU SEEM LIKE A REALLY NICE PERSON...
...REALLY NICE!
WELL... I...
HEY, LOOK! OUR CUPS ARE WAY DOWN THERE, BUT THEY'RE STILL FLOATING SIDE BY SIDE! ISN'T THAT ODD?
YEAH... MUST BE THE CURRENT..
UH HUH... THE CURRENT.
OH.. HA HA.. I'M SUZY...
..HA HA.. I'M DANNY...
SO... I HOPE I SEE YOU AGAIN SOMETIME..
I HANG OUT AT THE CABSTAND ON EWING... UH OH... WHERE'S MY CAB?
NO PARKING
BOY, THEY GET UP EARLY 'ROUND HERE!
IS THERE A CHANT FOR FINDING CABS?
WE COULD TRY THE ONE FOR REINDEER, BUT I LEFT MY DRUM ON THE BACKSEAT..
HA HA HA HA HA
...IT TOOK US HALF THE MORNING TO GET THAT THING BACK!
NUMBER 19.
OH WELL- IT WAS WORTH IT...
HEY! DID YOU KNOW WHEN YOU ORDERED THIS THAT IT WAS FAT, WHITE GRUBS?
DANNY, WHERE'S YOUR SENSE OF ADVENTURE? ACTUALLY, THEY'RE PRETTY GOOD!
THE BEGINNING

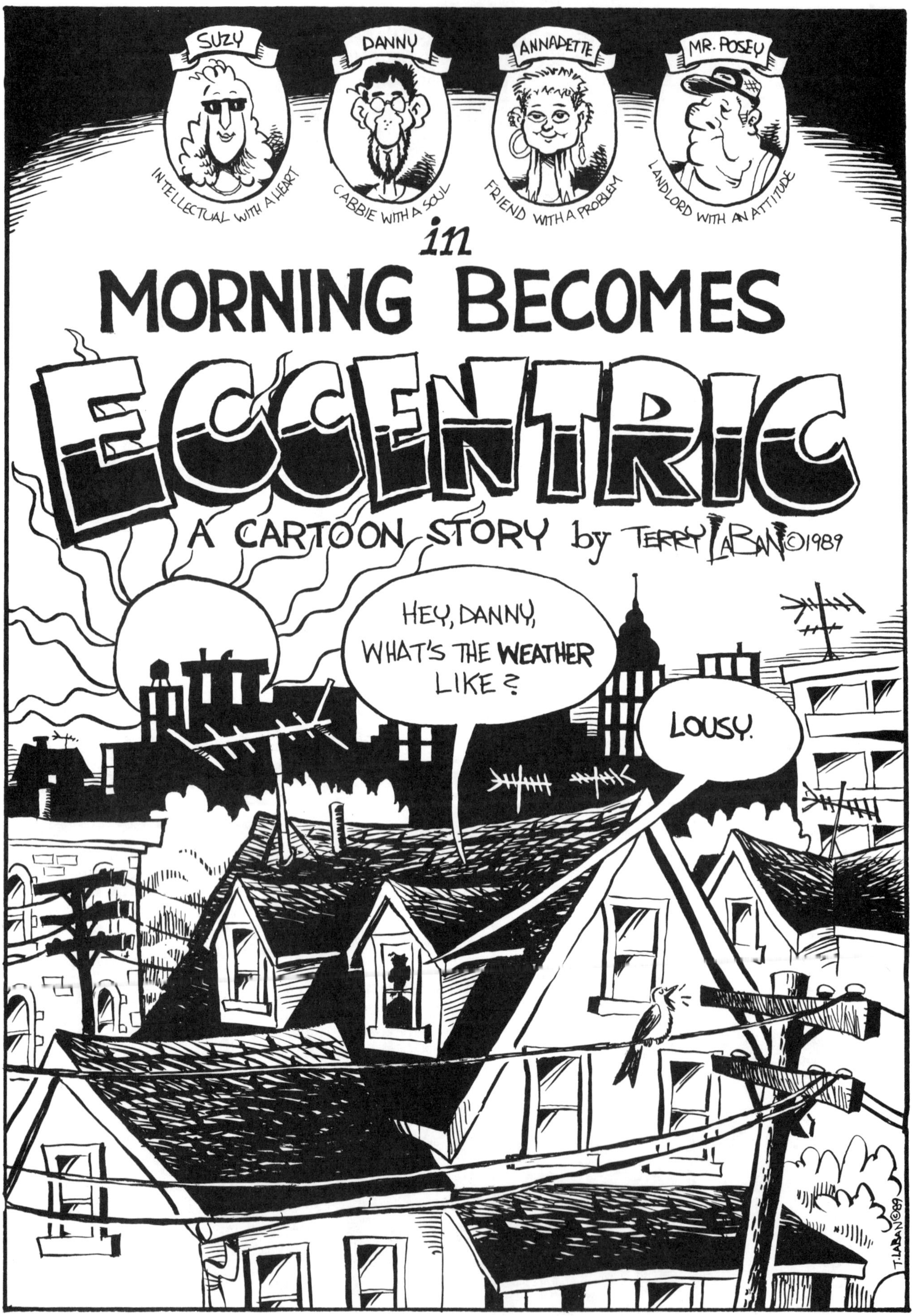

SUZY
INTELLECTUAL WITH A HEART
DANNY
CABBIE WITH A SOUL
ANNADETTE
FRIEND WITH A PROBLEM
MR. POSEY
LANDLORD WITH AN ATTITUDE
in
MORNING BECOMES
ECCENTRIC
A CARTOON STORY by TERRY LABAN ©1989
HEY, DANNY, WHAT'S THE WEATHER LIKE?
LOUSY.
T. LABAN ©89

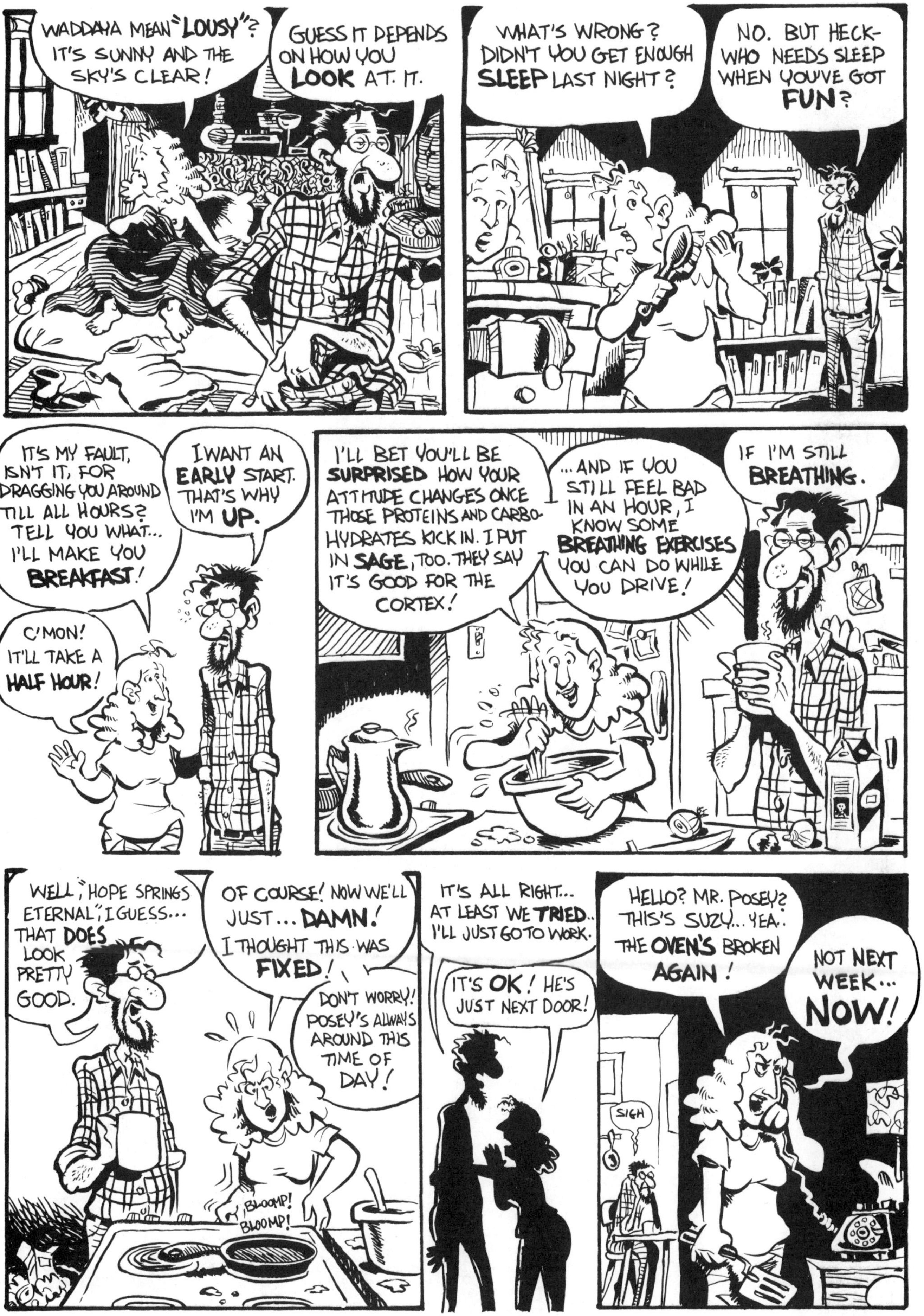
WADDAYA MEAN "LOUSY"? IT'S SUNNY AND THE SKY'S CLEAR!
GUESS IT DEPENDS ON HOW YOU LOOK AT IT.
WHAT'S WRONG? DIDN'T YOU GET ENOUGH SLEEP LAST NIGHT?
NO. BUT HECK- WHO NEEDS SLEEP WHEN YOU'VE GOT FUN?
IT'S MY FAULT, ISN'T IT, FOR DRAGGING YOU AROUND TILL ALL HOURS? TELL YOU WHAT... I'LL MAKE YOU BREAKFAST!
I WANT AN EARLY START. THAT'S WHY I'M UP.
C'MON! IT'LL TAKE A HALF HOUR!
I'LL BET YOU'LL BE SURPRISED HOW YOUR ATTITUDE CHANGES ONCE THOSE PROTEINS AND CARBO-HYDRATES KICK IN. I PUT IN SAGE, TOO. THEY SAY IT'S GOOD FOR THE CORTEX!
...AND IF YOU STILL FEEL BAD IN AN HOUR, I KNOW SOME BREATHING EXERCISES YOU CAN DO WHILE YOU DRIVE!
IF I'M STILL BREATHING.
WELL, "HOPE SPRINGS ETERNAL," I GUESS... THAT DOES LOOK PRETTY GOOD.
OF COURSE! NOW WE'LL JUST... DAMN! I THOUGHT THIS WAS FIXED!
DON'T WORRY! POSEY'S ALWAYS AROUND THIS TIME OF DAY!
BLOOMP! BLOOMP!
IT'S ALL RIGHT... AT LEAST WE TRIED.. I'LL JUST GO TO WORK.
IT'S OK! HE'S JUST NEXT DOOR!
HELLO? MR. POSEY? THIS'S SUZY... YEA.. THE OVEN'S BROKEN AGAIN!
NOT NEXT WEEK... NOW!
SIGH

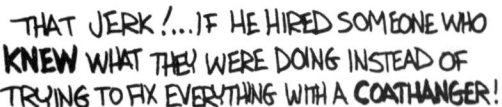

THAT JERK!...IF HE HIRED SOMEONE WHO **KNEW** WHAT THEY WERE DOING INSTEAD OF TRYING TO FIX EVERYTHING WITH A **COATHANGER**!

KNOCK! KNOCK!

ZZZT

H'LO. HAVIN' TROUBLE WITH TH' OVEN AGAIN? THOUGHT I JUST **FIXED** IT.

YUP. LET'S HAVE A LOOK.

SO DID **I**. OBVIOUSLY, WE WERE **WRONG**.

UMF...UMP... YA GOTTA LOOSE PART BACK THERE...I'LL JUST WIRE IT UP, AN' IT OUGHTA HOLD FOR A WHILE...

THAT'S WHAT YOU SAID **LAST TIME**.

DON'T YOU THINK IT'D BE A GOOD IDEA TO CALL A **REPAIRMAN**?

UH...WELL...LITTLE SHORT 'A MONEY RIGHT NOW. PROPERTY TAXES 'N ALL...MIGHTY TIGHT. BUT WE WANNA KEEP TH' **RENT DOWN**, Y'KNOW?

TELL YA WHAT, THOUGH—IF YA HAVE ANY MORE **TROUBLE**, I'LL CALL MY BROTHER. HE USED TA WORK FOR A STOVE COMPANY...TILL HE WENT **BLIND**...

GOTTA GOOD **PENSION**, THOUGH.

WHY DO WE PUT UP WITH HIM? THAT'S WHAT **I** WANNA KNOW!

BECAUSE EVEN WITH A CRETINOUS MISER FOR A LANDLORD, THIS PLACE IS STILL A GOOD **DEAL**.

OH WELL... IT'S WORKING NOW. THERE'S THE PHONE! WATCH THIS, OK?

RING! RING!

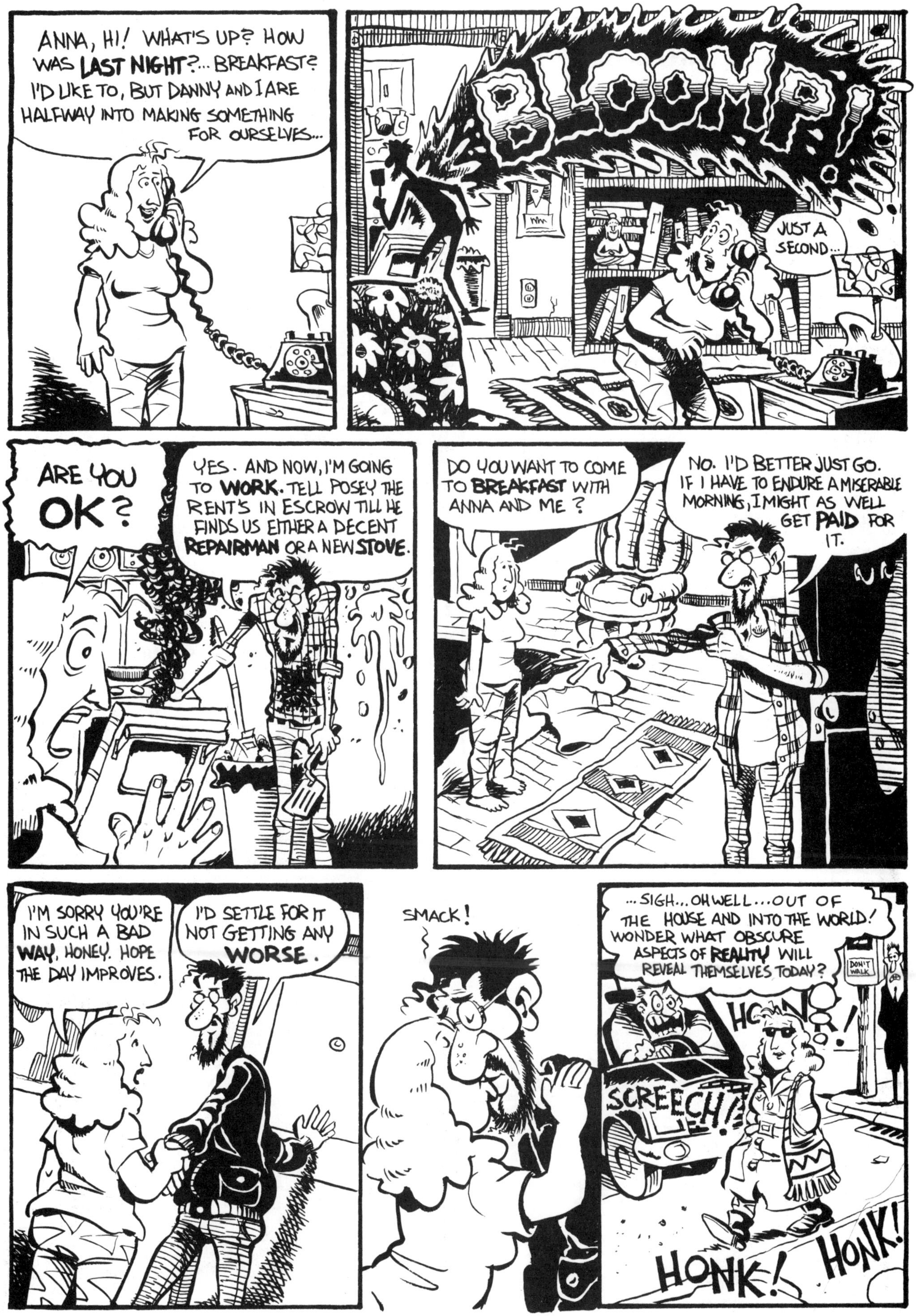

ANNA, HI! WHAT'S UP? HOW WAS LAST NIGHT?... BREAKFAST? I'D LIKE TO, BUT DANNY AND I ARE HALFWAY INTO MAKING SOMETHING FOR OURSELVES...
BLOOMP!
JUST A SECOND...
ARE YOU OK?
YES. AND NOW, I'M GOING TO WORK. TELL POSEY THE RENT'S IN ESCROW TILL HE FINDS US EITHER A DECENT REPAIRMAN OR A NEW STOVE.
DO YOU WANT TO COME TO BREAKFAST WITH ANNA AND ME?
NO. I'D BETTER JUST GO. IF I HAVE TO ENDURE A MISERABLE MORNING, I MIGHT AS WELL GET PAID FOR IT.
I'M SORRY YOU'RE IN SUCH A BAD WAY, HONEY. HOPE THE DAY IMPROVES.
I'D SETTLE FOR IT NOT GETTING ANY WORSE.
SMACK!
...SIGH...OH WELL...OUT OF THE HOUSE AND INTO THE WORLD! WONDER WHAT OBSCURE ASPECTS OF REALITY WILL REVEAL THEMSELVES TODAY?
DON'T WALK
SCREECH!
HONK!
HONK!

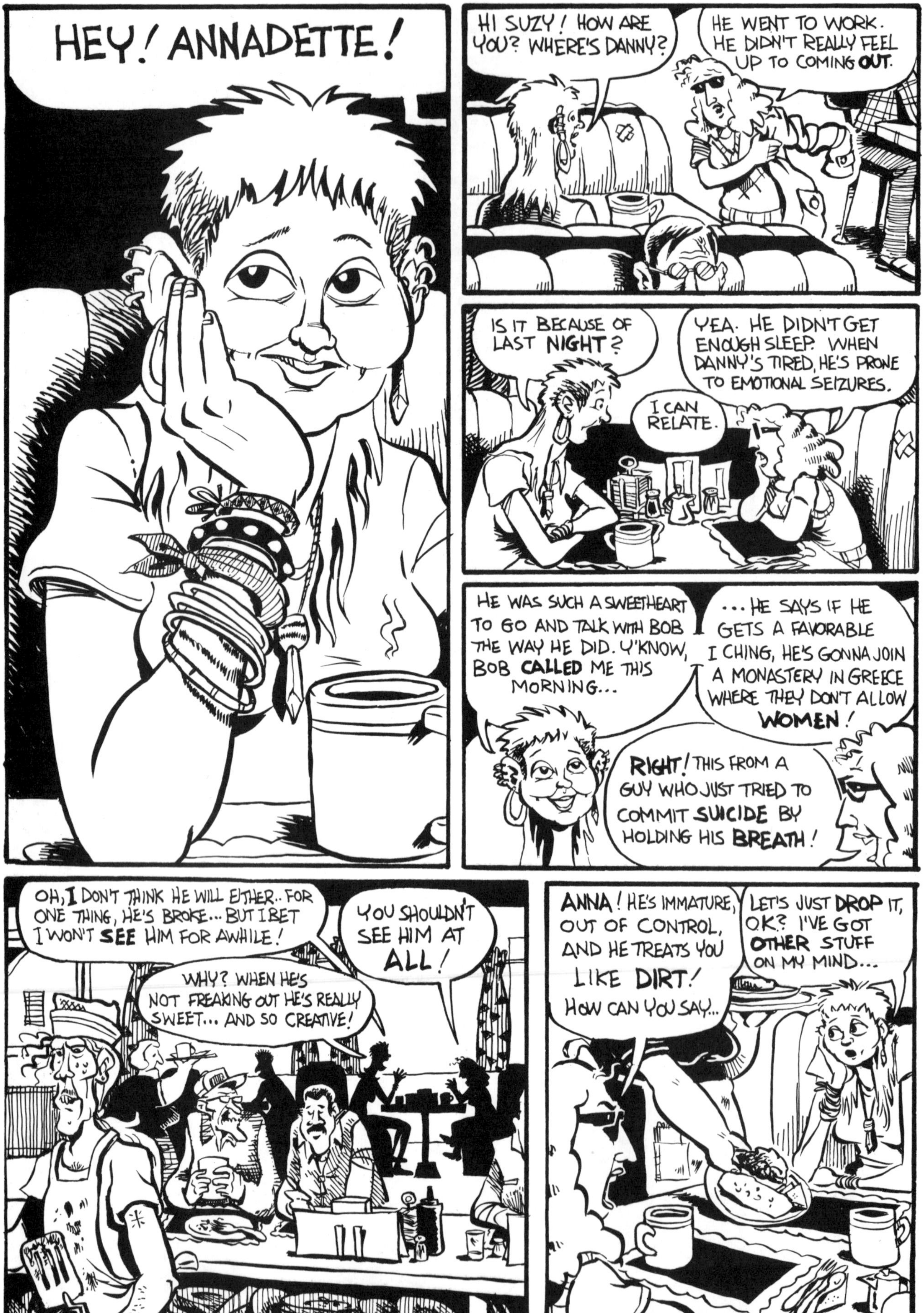
HEY! ANNADETTE!
HI SUZY! HOW ARE YOU? WHERE'S DANNY?
HE WENT TO WORK. HE DIDN'T REALLY FEEL UP TO COMING OUT.
IS IT BECAUSE OF LAST NIGHT?
YEA. HE DIDN'T GET ENOUGH SLEEP. WHEN DANNY'S TIRED, HE'S PRONE TO EMOTIONAL SEIZURES.
I CAN RELATE.
HE WAS SUCH A SWEETHEART TO GO AND TALK WITH BOB THE WAY HE DID. Y'KNOW, BOB CALLED ME THIS MORNING...
...HE SAYS IF HE GETS A FAVORABLE I CHING, HE'S GONNA JOIN A MONASTERY IN GREECE WHERE THEY DON'T ALLOW WOMEN!
RIGHT! THIS FROM A GUY WHO JUST TRIED TO COMMIT SUICIDE BY HOLDING HIS BREATH!
OH, I DON'T THINK HE WILL EITHER.. FOR ONE THING, HE'S BROKE... BUT I BET I WON'T SEE HIM FOR AWHILE!
YOU SHOULDN'T SEE HIM AT ALL!
WHY? WHEN HE'S NOT FREAKING OUT HE'S REALLY SWEET... AND SO CREATIVE!
ANNA! HE'S IMMATURE, OUT OF CONTROL, AND HE TREATS YOU LIKE DIRT! HOW CAN YOU SAY...
LET'S JUST DROP IT, OK? I'VE GOT OTHER STUFF ON MY MIND...

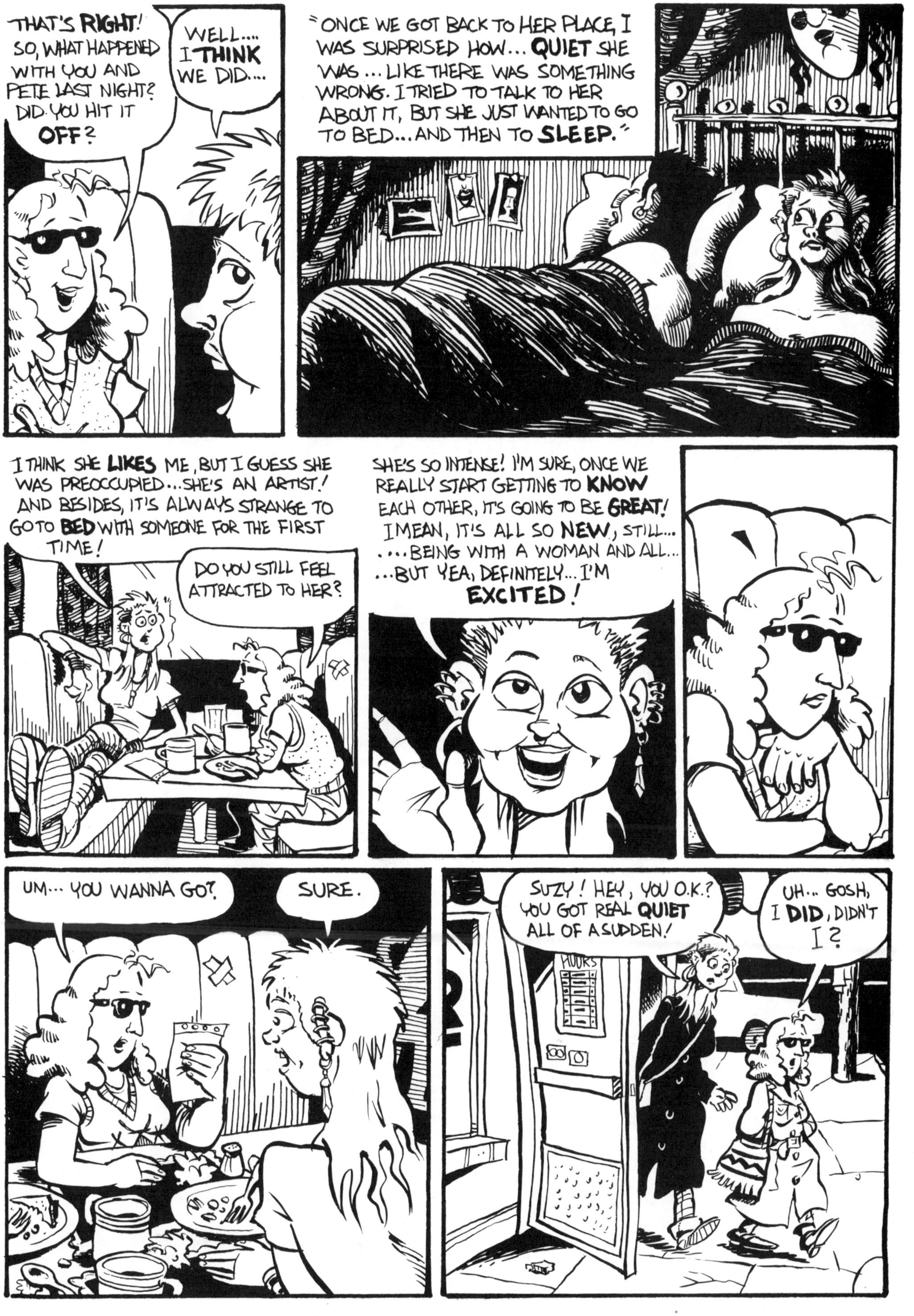
THAT'S RIGHT! SO, WHAT HAPPENED WITH YOU AND PETE LAST NIGHT? DID YOU HIT IT OFF?
WELL.... I THINK WE DID....
"ONCE WE GOT BACK TO HER PLACE, I WAS SURPRISED HOW... QUIET SHE WAS... LIKE THERE WAS SOMETHING WRONG. I TRIED TO TALK TO HER ABOUT IT, BUT SHE JUST WANTED TO GO TO BED... AND THEN TO SLEEP."
I THINK SHE LIKES ME, BUT I GUESS SHE WAS PREOCCUPIED... SHE'S AN ARTIST! AND BESIDES, IT'S ALWAYS STRANGE TO GO TO BED WITH SOMEONE FOR THE FIRST TIME!
DO YOU STILL FEEL ATTRACTED TO HER?
SHE'S SO INTENSE! I'M SURE, ONCE WE REALLY START GETTING TO KNOW EACH OTHER, IT'S GOING TO BE GREAT! I MEAN, IT'S ALL SO NEW, STILL... ....BEING WITH A WOMAN AND ALL... ...BUT YEA, DEFINITELY... I'M EXCITED!
UM... YOU WANNA GO?
SURE.
SUZY! HEY, YOU O.K.? YOU GOT REAL QUIET ALL OF A SUDDEN!
UH... GOSH, I DID, DIDN'T I?

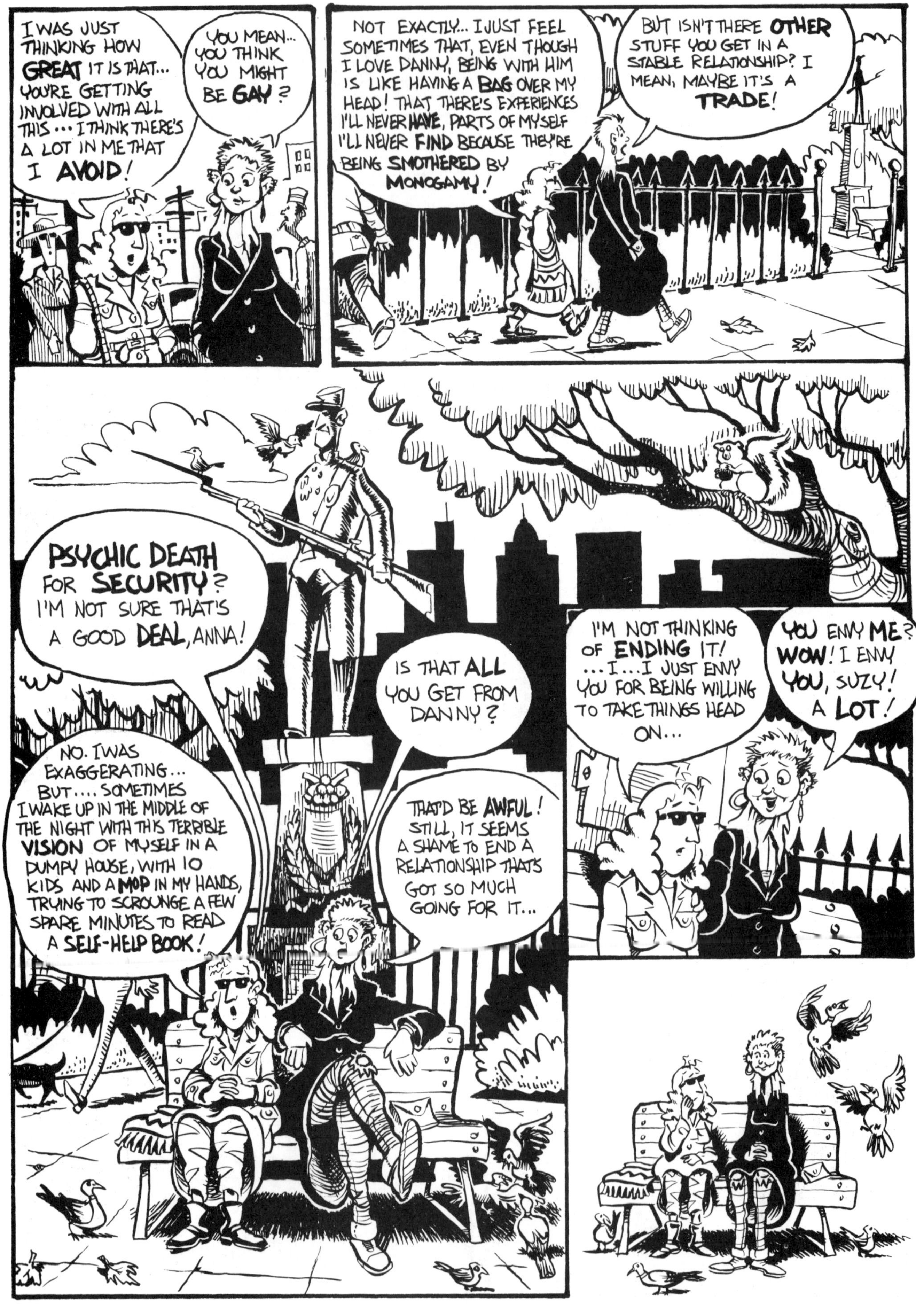
I WAS JUST THINKING HOW GREAT IT IS THAT... YOU'RE GETTING INVOLVED WITH ALL THIS... I THINK THERE'S A LOT IN ME THAT I AVOID!
YOU MEAN... YOU THINK YOU MIGHT BE GAY?
NOT EXACTLY... I JUST FEEL SOMETIMES THAT, EVEN THOUGH I LOVE DANNY, BEING WITH HIM IS LIKE HAVING A BAG OVER MY HEAD! THAT THERE'S EXPERIENCES I'LL NEVER HAVE, PARTS OF MYSELF I'LL NEVER FIND BECAUSE THEY'RE BEING SMOTHERED BY MONOGAMY!
BUT ISN'T THERE OTHER STUFF YOU GET IN A STABLE RELATIONSHIP? I MEAN, MAYBE IT'S A TRADE!
PSYCHIC DEATH FOR SECURITY? I'M NOT SURE THAT'S A GOOD DEAL, ANNA!
IS THAT ALL YOU GET FROM DANNY?
NO. I WAS EXAGGERATING... BUT.... SOMETIMES I WAKE UP IN THE MIDDLE OF THE NIGHT WITH THIS TERRIBLE VISION OF MYSELF IN A DUMPY HOUSE, WITH 10 KIDS AND A MOP IN MY HANDS, TRYING TO SCROUNGE A FEW SPARE MINUTES TO READ A SELF-HELP BOOK!
THAT'D BE AWFUL! STILL, IT SEEMS A SHAME TO END A RELATIONSHIP THAT'S GOT SO MUCH GOING FOR IT...
I'M NOT THINKING OF ENDING IT! ... I ... I JUST ENVY YOU FOR BEING WILLING TO TAKE THINGS HEAD ON...
YOU ENVY ME? WOW! I ENVY YOU, SUZY! A LOT!

CHAPTER 2

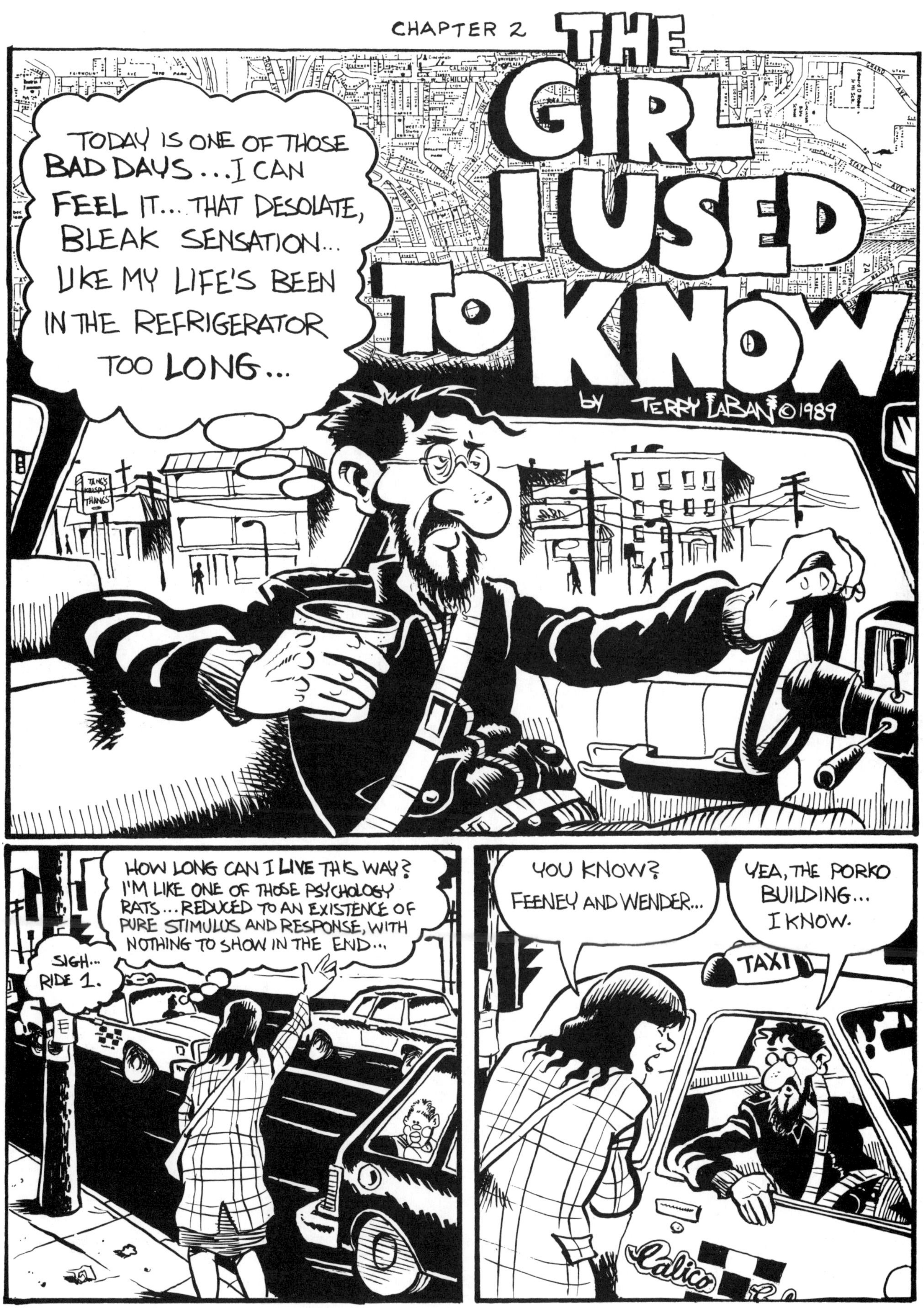
THE GIRL I USED TO KNOW
by TERRY LABAN ©1989
TODAY IS ONE OF THOSE BAD DAYS... I CAN FEEL IT... THAT DESOLATE, BLEAK SENSATION... LIKE MY LIFE'S BEEN IN THE REFRIGERATOR TOO LONG...
HOW LONG CAN I LIVE THIS WAY? I'M LIKE ONE OF THOSE PSYCHOLOGY RATS... REDUCED TO AN EXISTENCE OF PURE STIMULUS AND RESPONSE, WITH NOTHING TO SHOW IN THE END...
SIGH... RIDE 1.
YOU KNOW? FEENEY AND WENDER...
YEA, THE PORKO BUILDING... I KNOW.
TAXI
Calico

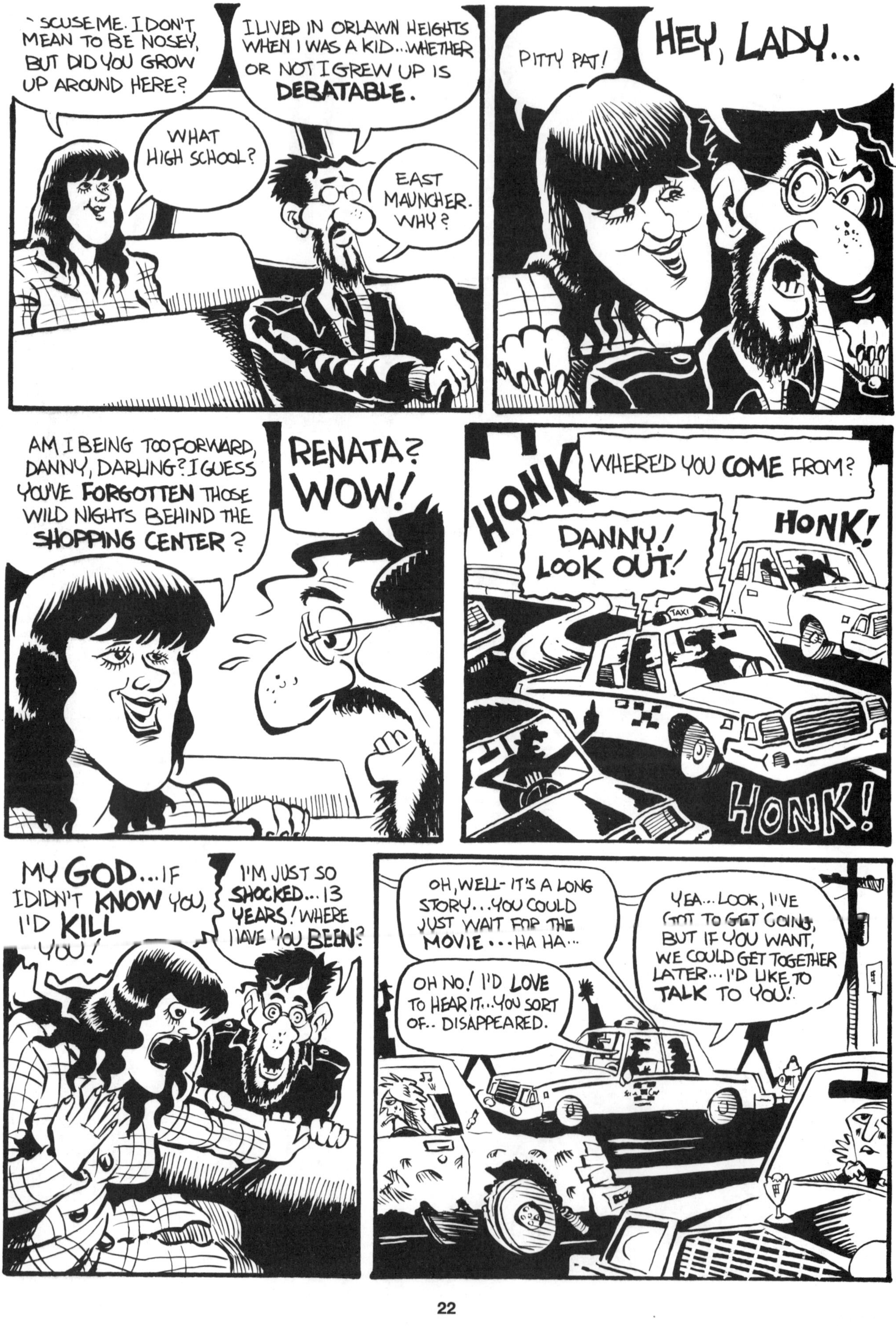

'SCUSE ME. I DON'T MEAN TO BE NOSEY, BUT DID YOU GROW UP AROUND HERE?
I LIVED IN ORLAWN HEIGHTS WHEN I WAS A KID... WHETHER OR NOT I GREW UP IS DEBATABLE.
WHAT HIGH SCHOOL?
EAST MAUNCHER. WHY?
PITTY PAT!
HEY, LADY...
AM I BEING TOO FORWARD, DANNY, DARLING? I GUESS YOU'VE FORGOTTEN THOSE WILD NIGHTS BEHIND THE SHOPPING CENTER?
RENATA? WOW!
HONK
WHERE'D YOU COME FROM?
DANNY! LOOK OUT!
HONK!
TAXI
HONK!
MY GOD... IF I DIDN'T KNOW YOU, I'D KILL YOU!
I'M JUST SO SHOCKED... 13 YEARS! WHERE HAVE YOU BEEN?
OH, WELL- IT'S A LONG STORY... YOU COULD JUST WAIT FOR THE MOVIE... HA HA...
OH NO! I'D LOVE TO HEAR IT... YOU SORT OF.. DISAPPEARED.
YEA... LOOK, I'VE GOT TO GET GOING, BUT IF YOU WANT, WE COULD GET TOGETHER LATER... I'D LIKE TO TALK TO YOU!

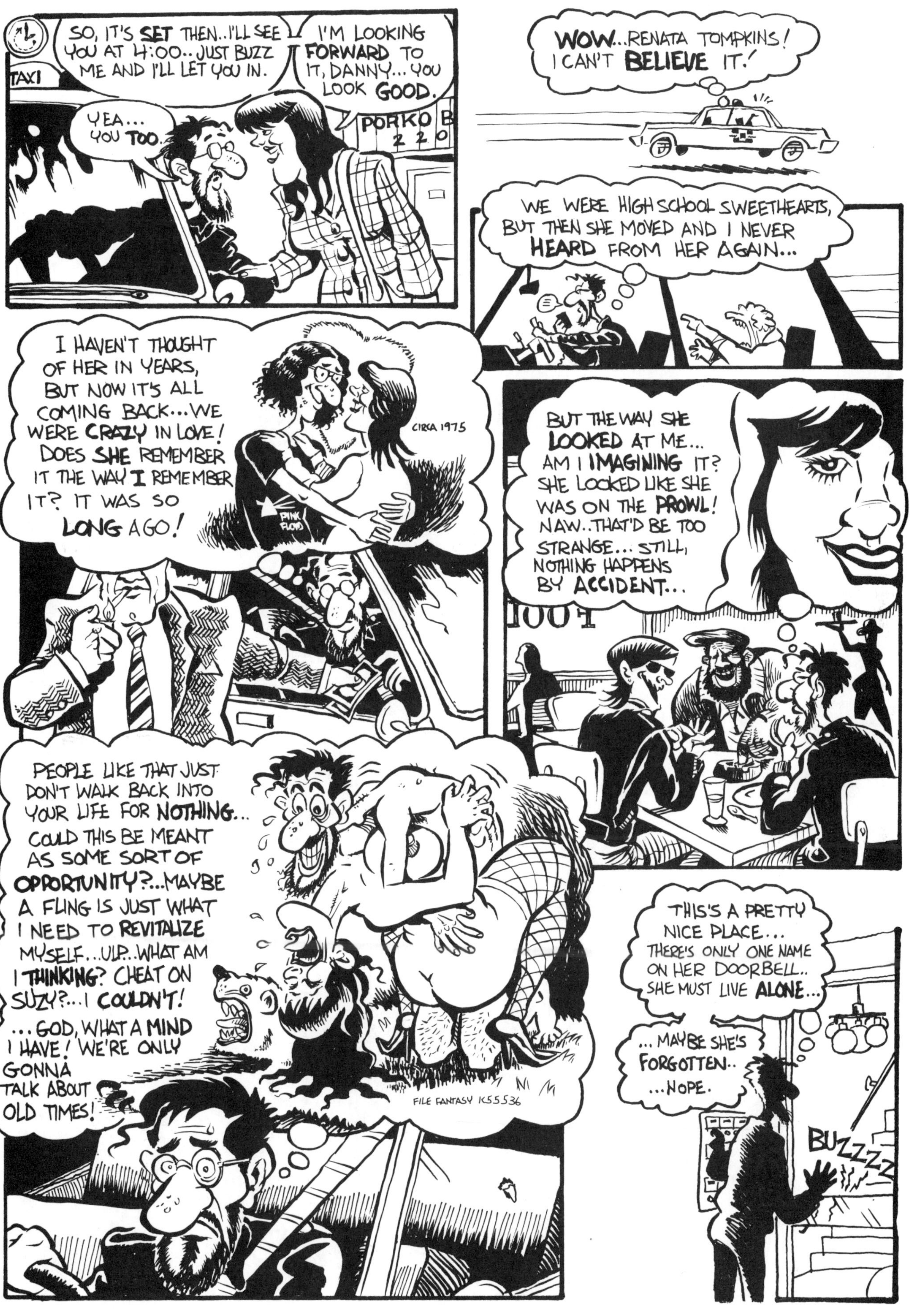
TAXI
SO, IT'S SET THEN.. I'LL SEE YOU AT 4:00.. JUST BUZZ ME AND I'LL LET YOU IN.
I'M LOOKING FORWARD TO IT, DANNY... YOU LOOK GOOD.
YEA... YOU TOO.
PORKO B 220
WOW...RENATA TOMPKINS! I CAN'T BELIEVE IT.!
WE WERE HIGH SCHOOL SWEETHEARTS, BUT THEN SHE MOVED AND I NEVER HEARD FROM HER AGAIN...
I HAVEN'T THOUGHT OF HER IN YEARS, BUT NOW IT'S ALL COMING BACK...WE WERE CRAZY IN LOVE! DOES SHE REMEMBER IT THE WAY I REMEMBER IT? IT WAS SO LONG AGO!
CIRCA 1975
PINK FLOYD
BUT THE WAY SHE LOOKED AT ME... AM I IMAGINING IT? SHE LOOKED LIKE SHE WAS ON THE PROWL! NAW..THAT'D BE TOO STRANGE... STILL, NOTHING HAPPENS BY ACCIDENT...
PEOPLE LIKE THAT JUST DON'T WALK BACK INTO YOUR LIFE FOR NOTHING... COULD THIS BE MEANT AS SOME SORT OF OPPORTUNITY?...MAYBE A FLING IS JUST WHAT I NEED TO REVITALIZE MYSELF...ULP..WHAT AM I THINKING? CHEAT ON SUZY?...I COULDN'T! ...GOD, WHAT A MIND I HAVE! WE'RE ONLY GONNA TALK ABOUT OLD TIMES!
FILE FANTASY K55536
THIS'S A PRETTY NICE PLACE... THERE'S ONLY ONE NAME ON HER DOORBELL.. SHE MUST LIVE ALONE...
...MAYBE SHE'S FORGOTTEN.. ...NOPE.
BUZZZZ

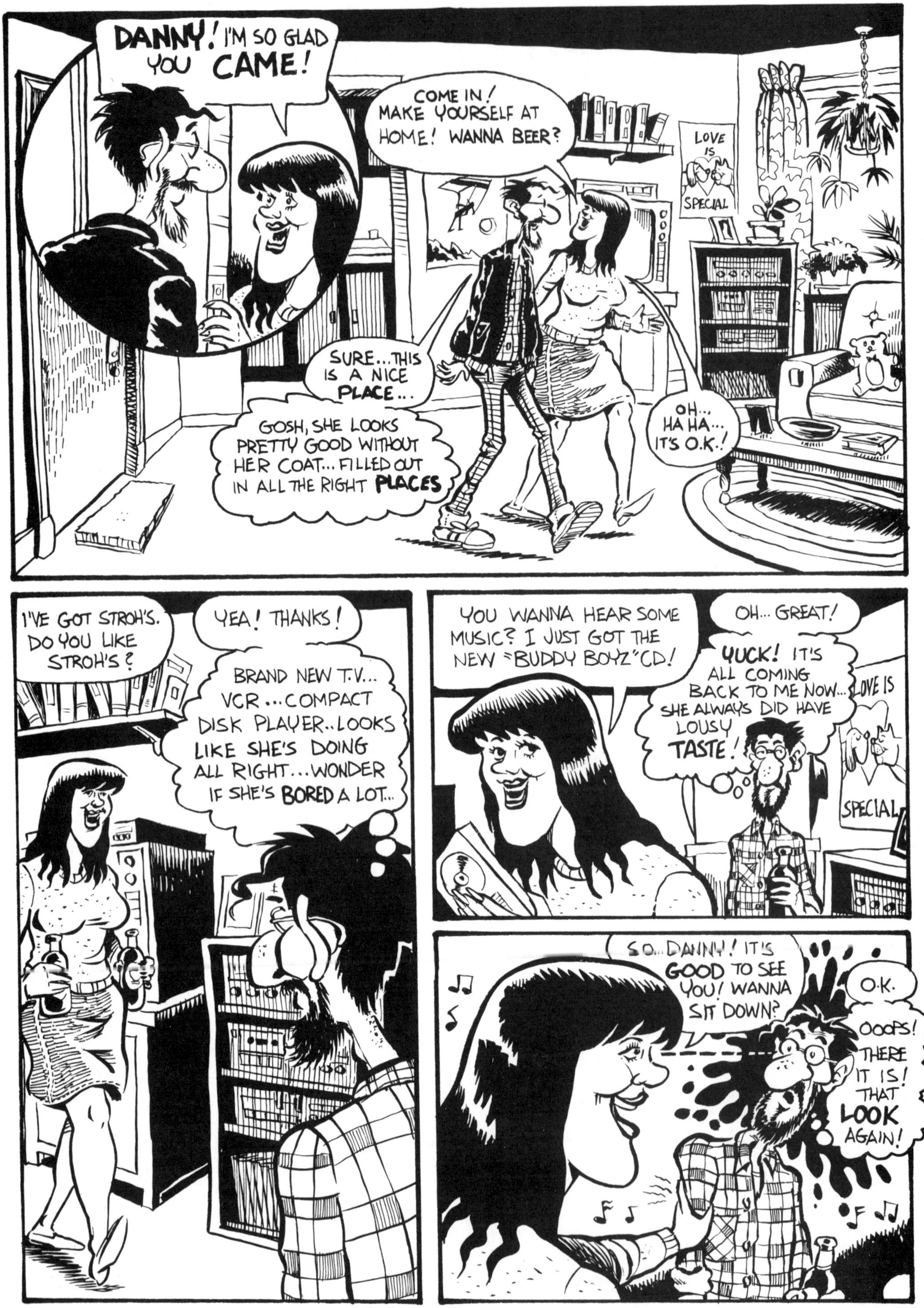
DANNY! I'M SO GLAD YOU CAME!
COME IN! MAKE YOURSELF AT HOME! WANNA BEER?
LOVE IS SPECIAL
SURE... THIS IS A NICE PLACE...
GOSH, SHE LOOKS PRETTY GOOD WITHOUT HER COAT... FILLED OUT IN ALL THE RIGHT PLACES
OH... HA HA... IT'S O.K.!
I'VE GOT STROH'S. DO YOU LIKE STROH'S?
YEA! THANKS!
BRAND NEW T.V... VCR... COMPACT DISK PLAYER.. LOOKS LIKE SHE'S DOING ALL RIGHT... WONDER IF SHE'S BORED A LOT...
YOU WANNA HEAR SOME MUSIC? I JUST GOT THE NEW "BUDDY BOYZ" CD!
OH... GREAT!
YUCK! IT'S ALL COMING BACK TO ME NOW... SHE ALWAYS DID HAVE LOUSY TASTE!
LOVE IS SPECIAL
SO.. DANNY! IT'S GOOD TO SEE YOU! WANNA SIT DOWN?
O.K.
OOOPS! THERE IT IS! THAT LOOK AGAIN!

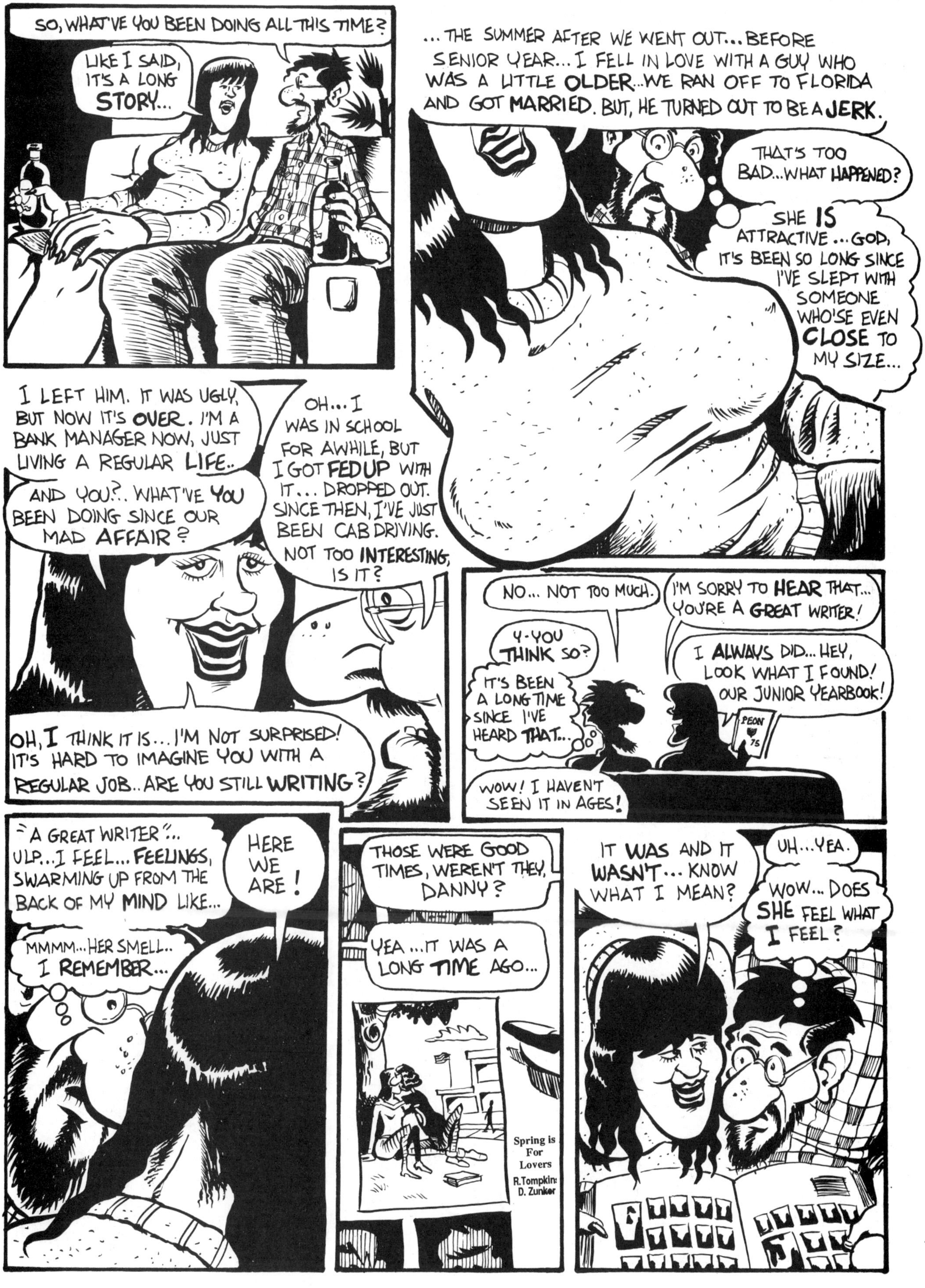
SO, WHAT'VE YOU BEEN DOING ALL THIS TIME?
LIKE I SAID, IT'S A LONG STORY...
... THE SUMMER AFTER WE WENT OUT... BEFORE SENIOR YEAR... I FELL IN LOVE WITH A GUY WHO WAS A LITTLE OLDER...WE RAN OFF TO FLORIDA AND GOT MARRIED. BUT, HE TURNED OUT TO BE A JERK.
THAT'S TOO BAD...WHAT HAPPENED?
SHE IS ATTRACTIVE...GOD, IT'S BEEN SO LONG SINCE I'VE SLEPT WITH SOMEONE WHO'SE EVEN CLOSE TO MY SIZE...
I LEFT HIM. IT WAS UGLY, BUT NOW IT'S OVER. I'M A BANK MANAGER NOW, JUST LIVING A REGULAR LIFE..
AND YOU?.. WHAT'VE YOU BEEN DOING SINCE OUR MAD AFFAIR?
OH... I WAS IN SCHOOL FOR AWHILE, BUT I GOT FED UP WITH IT... DROPPED OUT. SINCE THEN, I'VE JUST BEEN CAB DRIVING. NOT TOO INTERESTING, IS IT?
OH, I THINK IT IS... I'M NOT SURPRISED! IT'S HARD TO IMAGINE YOU WITH A REGULAR JOB.. ARE YOU STILL WRITING?
NO... NOT TOO MUCH.
I'M SORRY TO HEAR THAT... YOU'RE A GREAT WRITER!
Y-YOU THINK SO?
IT'S BEEN A LONG TIME SINCE I'VE HEARD THAT...
I ALWAYS DID... HEY, LOOK WHAT I FOUND! OUR JUNIOR YEARBOOK!
PEON 75
WOW! I HAVEN'T SEEN IT IN AGES!
"A GREAT WRITER"... ULP... I FEEL... FEELINGS, SWARMING UP FROM THE BACK OF MY MIND LIKE...
HERE WE ARE!
MMMM... HER SMELL.. I REMEMBER...
THOSE WERE GOOD TIMES, WEREN'T THEY, DANNY?
YEA... IT WAS A LONG TIME AGO...
Spring is For Lovers
R.Tompkins
D. Zunker
IT WAS AND IT WASN'T... KNOW WHAT I MEAN?
UH... YEA.
WOW... DOES SHE FEEL WHAT I FEEL?

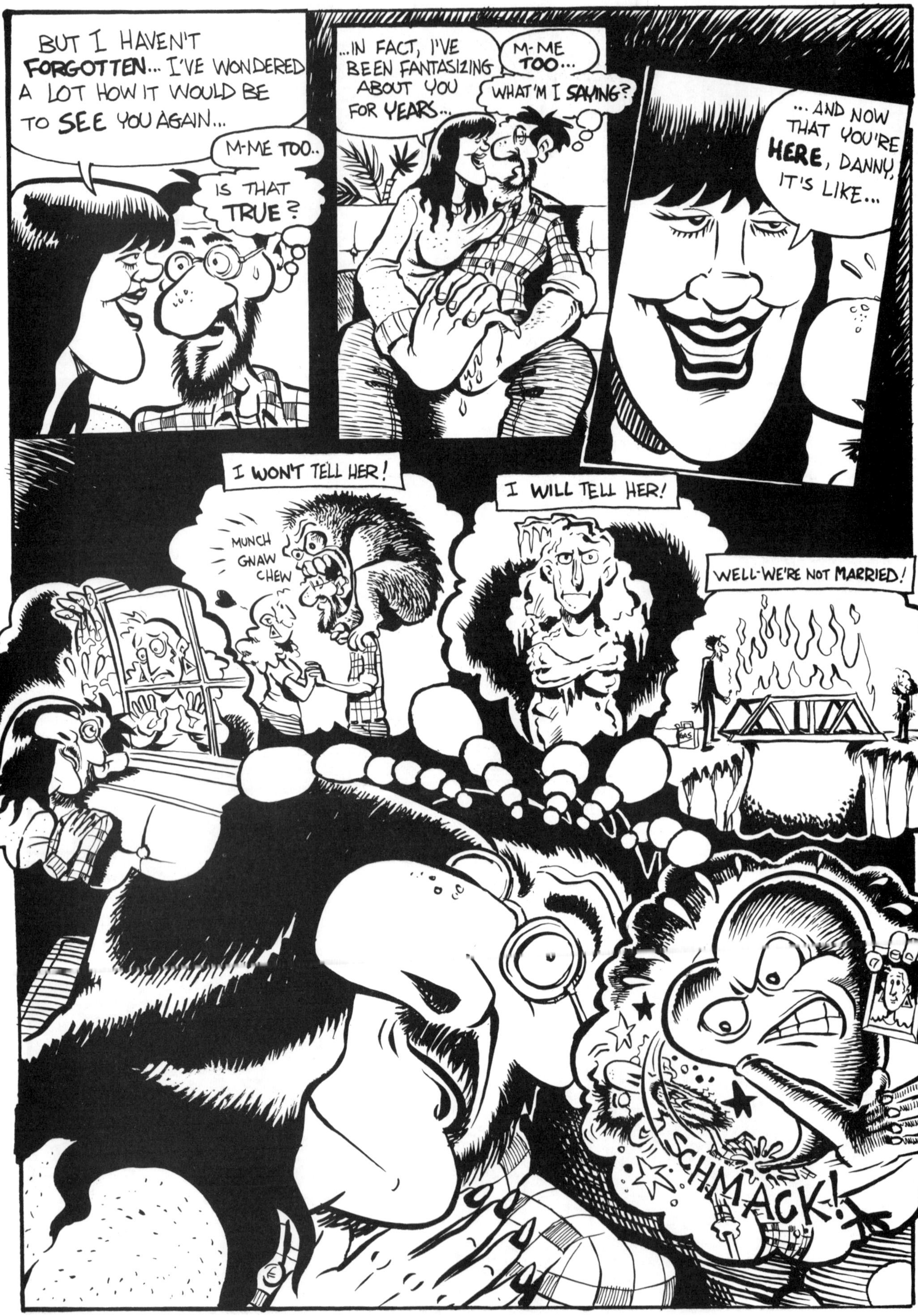

BUT I HAVEN'T FORGOTTEN... I'VE WONDERED A LOT HOW IT WOULD BE TO SEE YOU AGAIN...
M-ME TOO..
IS THAT TRUE?
...IN FACT, I'VE BEEN FANTASIZING ABOUT YOU FOR YEARS...
M-ME TOO...
WHAT'M I SAYING?
... AND NOW THAT YOU'RE HERE, DANNY, IT'S LIKE...
I WON'T TELL HER!
MUNCH GNAW CHEW
I WILL TELL HER!
WELL-WE'RE NOT MARRIED!
GAS
SCHMACK!

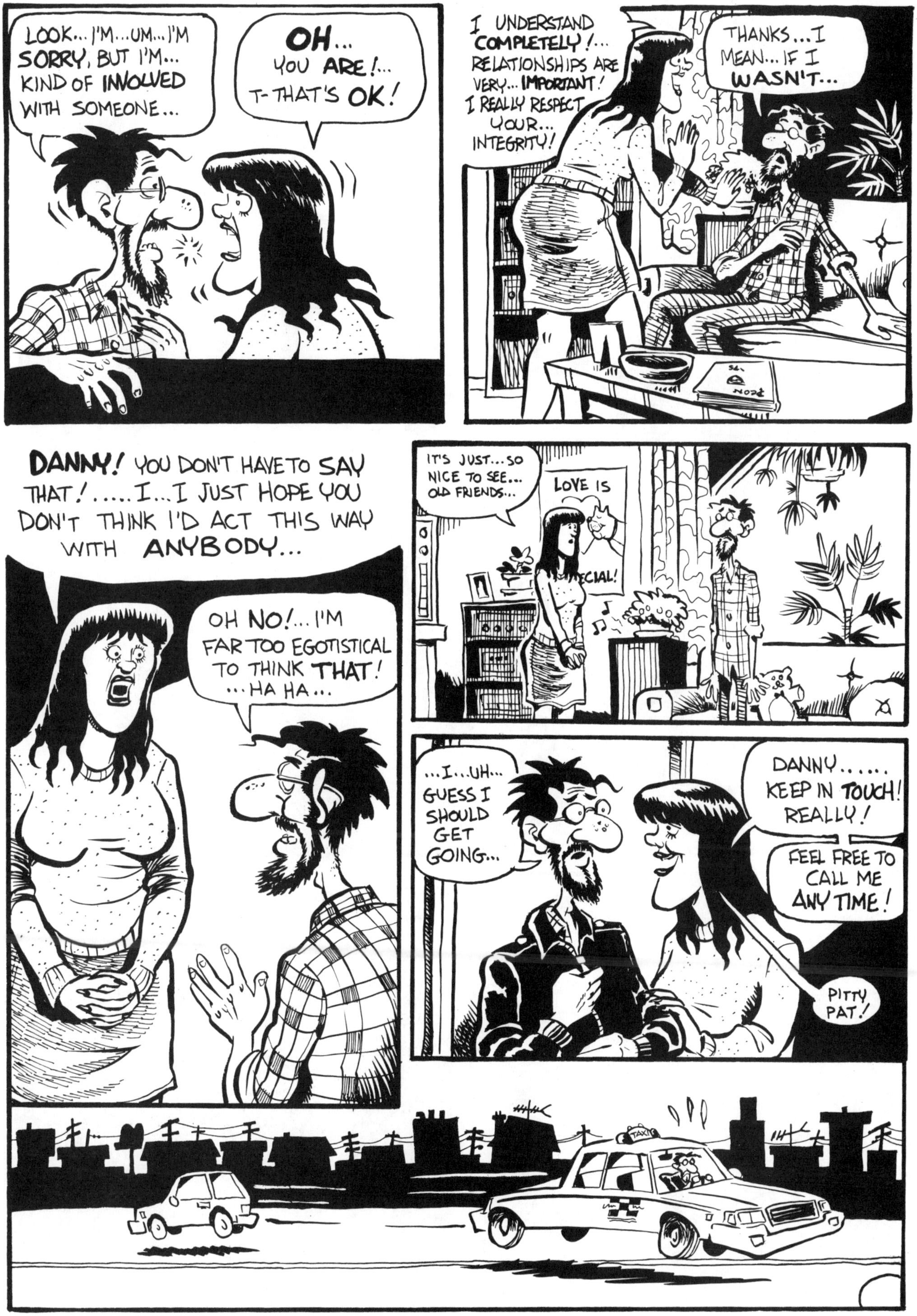

LOOK... I'M... UM... I'M SORRY, BUT I'M... KIND OF INVOLVED WITH SOMEONE...
OH... YOU ARE!... T-THAT'S OK!
I UNDERSTAND COMPLETELY!... RELATIONSHIPS ARE VERY... IMPORTANT! I REALLY RESPECT YOUR... INTEGRITY!
THANKS... I MEAN... IF I WASN'T...
DANNY! YOU DON'T HAVE TO SAY THAT!..... I... I JUST HOPE YOU DON'T THINK I'D ACT THIS WAY WITH ANYBODY...
OH NO!... I'M FAR TOO EGOTISTICAL TO THINK THAT! ...HA HA...
IT'S JUST... SO NICE TO SEE... OLD FRIENDS...
LOVE IS
...I... UH... GUESS I SHOULD GET GOING...
DANNY...... KEEP IN TOUCH! REALLY!
FEEL FREE TO CALL ME ANY TIME!
PITTY PAT!
TAXI

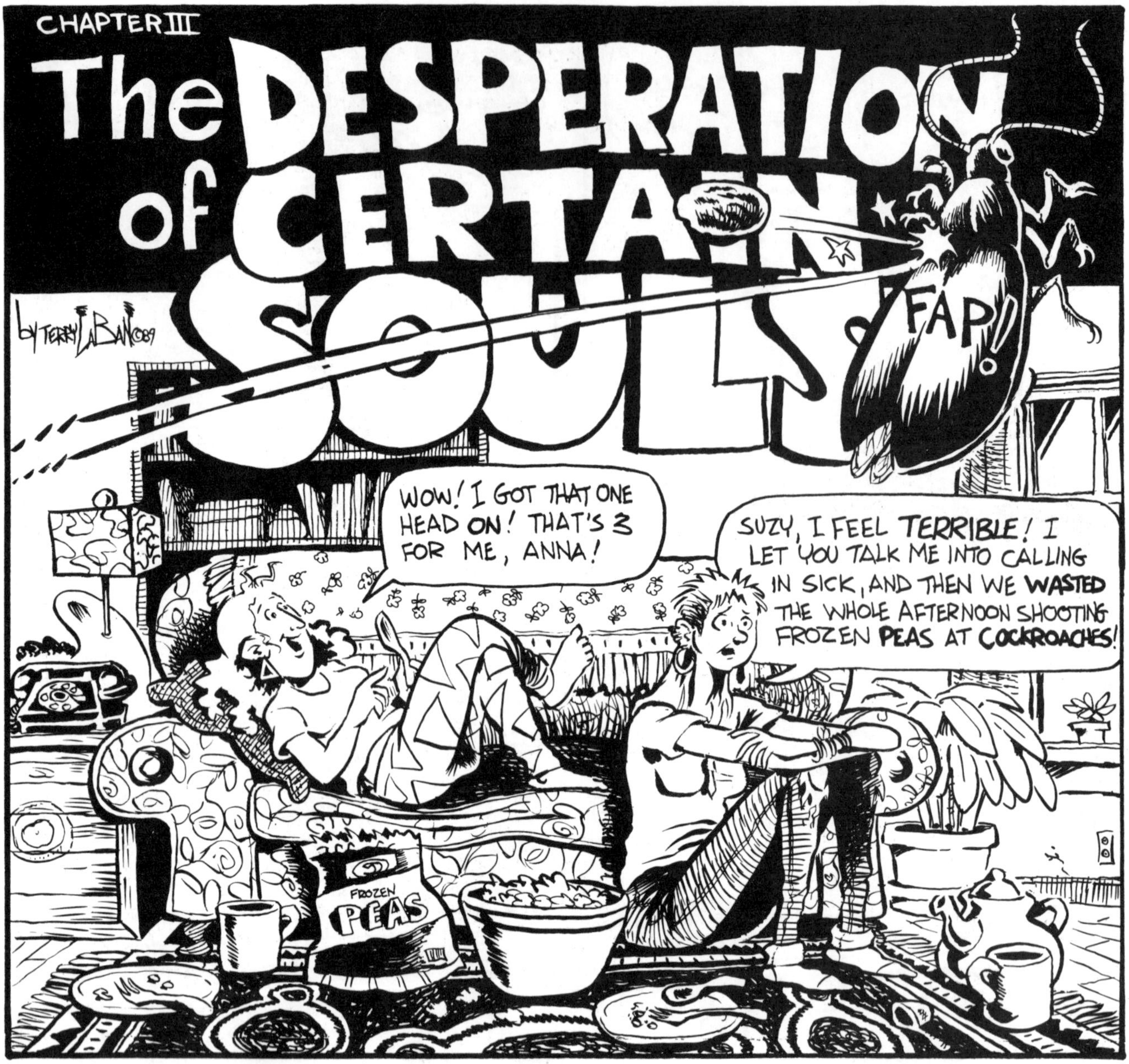
CHAPTER III
The DESPERATION of CERTAIN SOULS
by TERRY LaBAN ©89
FAP!
WOW! I GOT THAT ONE HEAD ON! THAT'S 3 FOR ME, ANNA!
SUZY, I FEEL TERRIBLE! I LET YOU TALK ME INTO CALLING IN SICK, AND THEN WE WASTED THE WHOLE AFTERNOON SHOOTING FROZEN PEAS AT COCKROACHES!
FROZEN PEAS

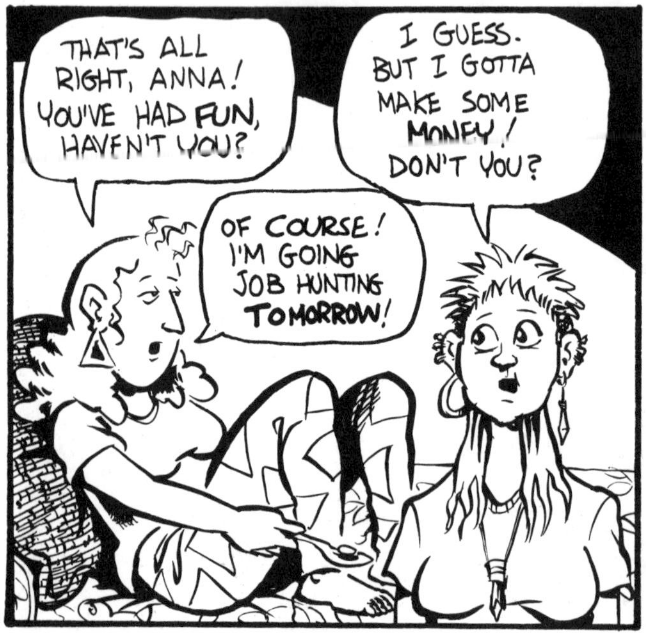
THAT'S ALL RIGHT, ANNA! YOU'VE HAD FUN, HAVEN'T YOU?
OF COURSE! I'M GOING JOB HUNTING TOMORROW!
I GUESS. BUT I GOTTA MAKE SOME MONEY! DON'T YOU?

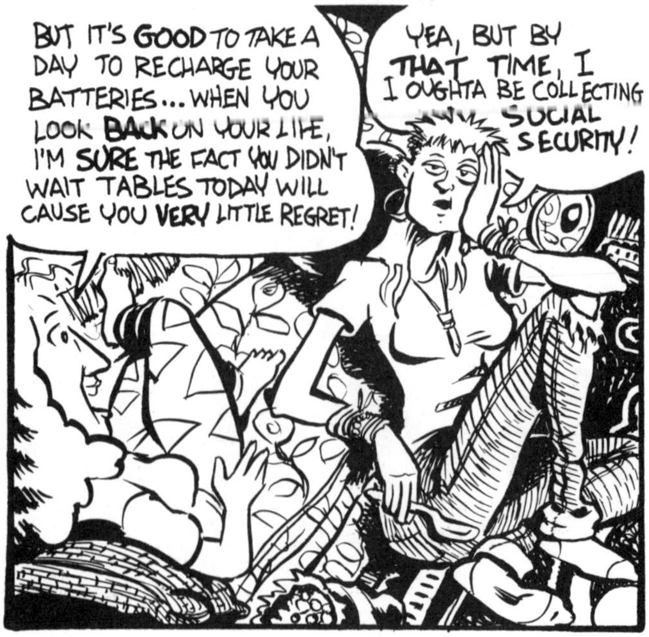
BUT IT'S GOOD TO TAKE A DAY TO RECHARGE YOUR BATTERIES... WHEN YOU LOOK BACK ON YOUR LIFE, I'M SURE THE FACT YOU DIDN'T WAIT TABLES TODAY WILL CAUSE YOU VERY LITTLE REGRET!
YEA, BUT BY THAT TIME, I I OUGHTA BE COLLECTING SOCIAL SECURITY!

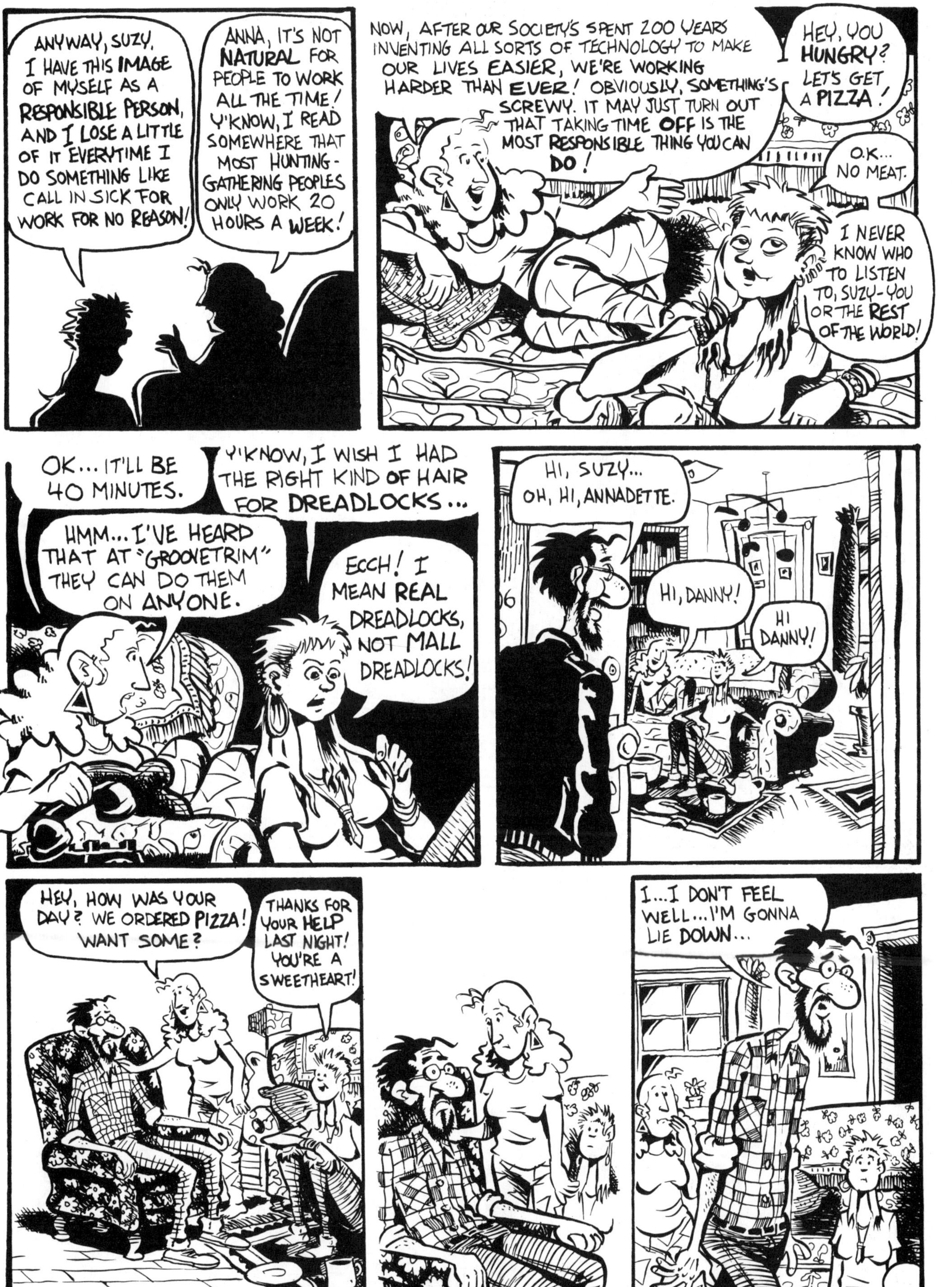
ANYWAY, SUZY, I HAVE THIS IMAGE OF MYSELF AS A RESPONSIBLE PERSON, AND I LOSE A LITTLE OF IT EVERYTIME I DO SOMETHING LIKE CALL IN SICK FOR WORK FOR NO REASON!
ANNA, IT'S NOT NATURAL FOR PEOPLE TO WORK ALL THE TIME! Y'KNOW, I READ SOMEWHERE THAT MOST HUNTING-GATHERING PEOPLES ONLY WORK 20 HOURS A WEEK!
NOW, AFTER OUR SOCIETY'S SPENT 200 YEARS INVENTING ALL SORTS OF TECHNOLOGY TO MAKE OUR LIVES EASIER, WE'RE WORKING HARDER THAN EVER! OBVIOUSLY, SOMETHING'S SCREWY. IT MAY JUST TURN OUT THAT TAKING TIME OFF IS THE MOST RESPONSIBLE THING YOU CAN DO!
HEY, YOU HUNGRY? LET'S GET A PIZZA!
O.K... NO MEAT.
I NEVER KNOW WHO TO LISTEN TO, SUZY- YOU OR THE REST OF THE WORLD!
OK... IT'LL BE 40 MINUTES.
Y'KNOW, I WISH I HAD THE RIGHT KIND OF HAIR FOR DREADLOCKS...
HMM... I'VE HEARD THAT AT "GROOVETRIM" THEY CAN DO THEM ON ANYONE.
ECCH! I MEAN REAL DREADLOCKS, NOT MALL DREADLOCKS!
HI, SUZY... OH, HI, ANNADETTE.
HI, DANNY!
HI DANNY!
HEY, HOW WAS YOUR DAY? WE ORDERED PIZZA! WANT SOME?
THANKS FOR YOUR HELP LAST NIGHT! YOU'RE A SWEETHEART!
I... I DON'T FEEL WELL... I'M GONNA LIE DOWN...

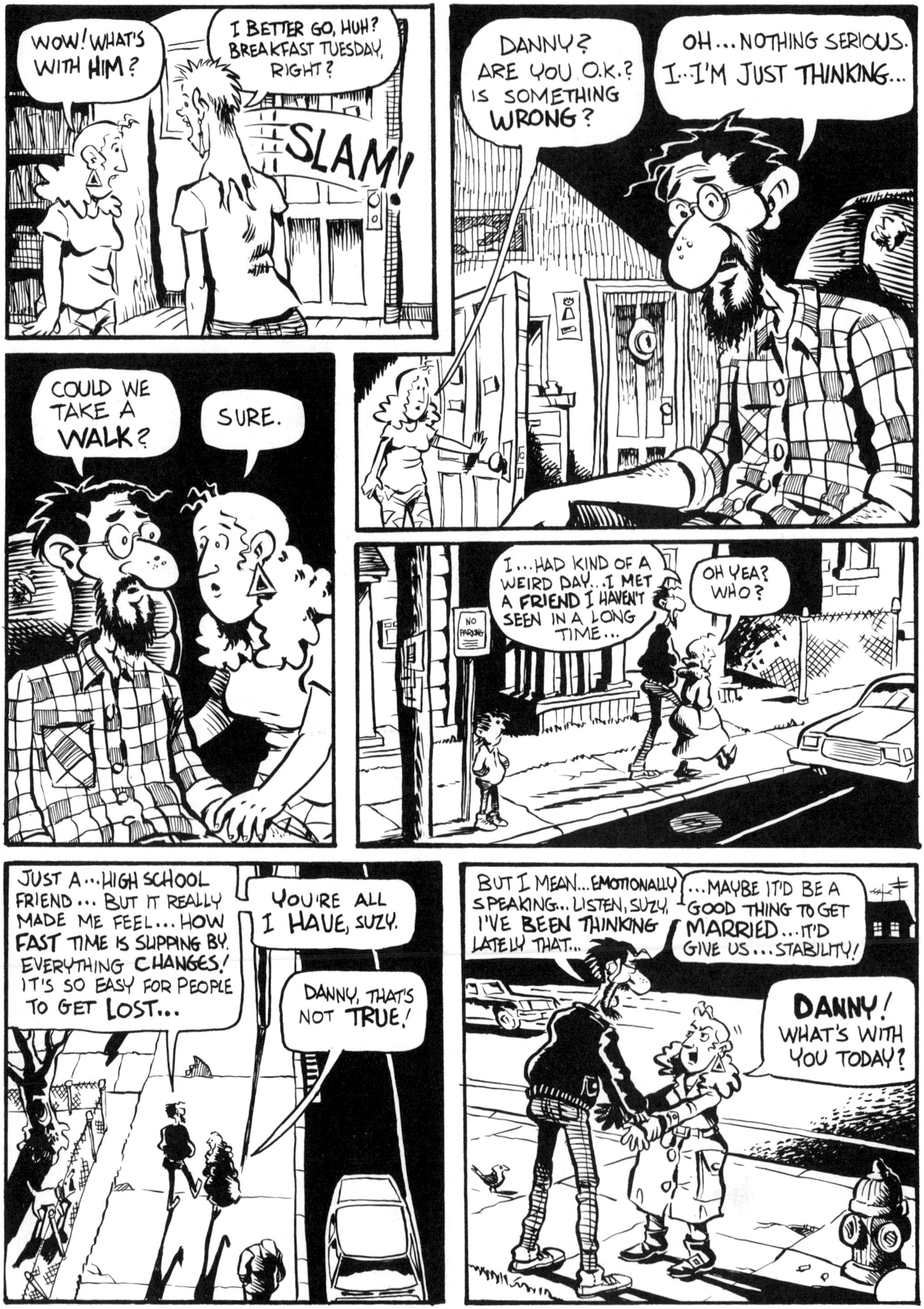
WOW! WHAT'S WITH HIM?
I BETTER GO, HUH? BREAKFAST TUESDAY, RIGHT?
SLAM!
DANNY? ARE YOU O.K.? IS SOMETHING WRONG?
OH... NOTHING SERIOUS. I.. I'M JUST THINKING...
COULD WE TAKE A WALK?
SURE.
I... HAD KIND OF A WEIRD DAY... I MET A FRIEND I HAVEN'T SEEN IN A LONG TIME...
OH YEA? WHO?
NO PARKING
JUST A... HIGH SCHOOL FRIEND... BUT IT REALLY MADE ME FEEL... HOW FAST TIME IS SLIPPING BY. EVERYTHING CHANGES! IT'S SO EASY FOR PEOPLE TO GET LOST...
YOU'RE ALL I HAVE, SUZY.
DANNY, THAT'S NOT TRUE!
BUT I MEAN... EMOTIONALLY SPEAKING... LISTEN, SUZY, I'VE BEEN THINKING LATELY THAT...
...MAYBE IT'D BE A GOOD THING TO GET MARRIED... IT'D GIVE US... STABILITY!
DANNY! WHAT'S WITH YOU TODAY?

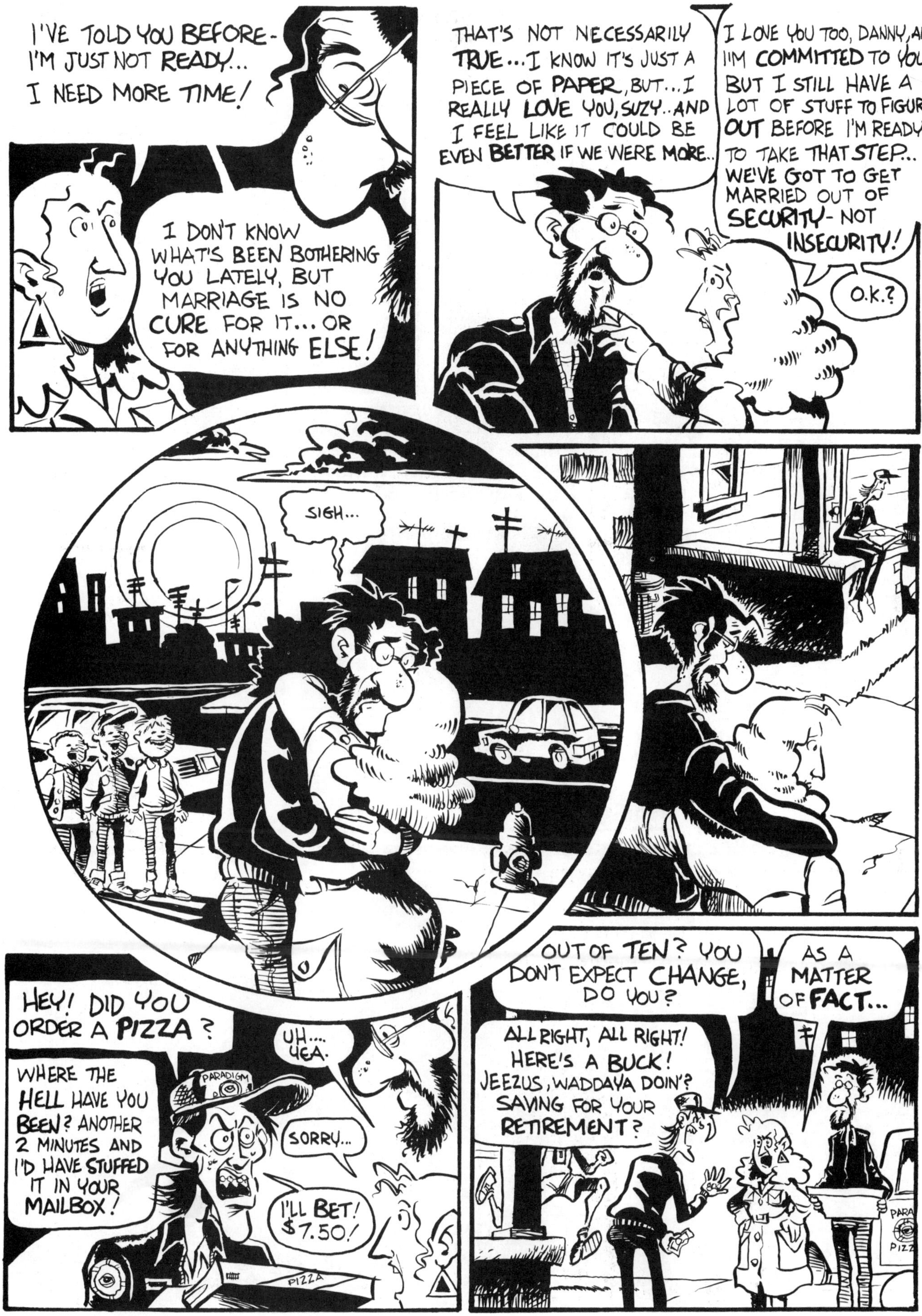
I'VE TOLD YOU BEFORE- I'M JUST NOT READY... I NEED MORE TIME!
I DON'T KNOW WHAT'S BEEN BOTHERING YOU LATELY, BUT MARRIAGE IS NO CURE FOR IT... OR FOR ANYTHING ELSE!
THAT'S NOT NECESSARILY TRUE... I KNOW IT'S JUST A PIECE OF PAPER, BUT... I REALLY LOVE YOU, SUZY.. AND I FEEL LIKE IT COULD BE EVEN BETTER IF WE WERE MORE..
I LOVE YOU TOO, DANNY, AND I'M COMMITTED TO YOU! BUT I STILL HAVE A LOT OF STUFF TO FIGURE OUT BEFORE I'M READY TO TAKE THAT STEP.. WE'VE GOT TO GET MARRIED OUT OF SECURITY- NOT INSECURITY!
O.K.?
SIGH...
HEY! DID YOU ORDER A PIZZA?
UH.... YEA.
WHERE THE HELL HAVE YOU BEEN? ANOTHER 2 MINUTES AND I'D HAVE STUFFED IT IN YOUR MAILBOX!
SORRY...
I'LL BET! $7.50!
PARADIGM
PIZZA
OUT OF TEN? YOU DON'T EXPECT CHANGE, DO YOU?
AS A MATTER OF FACT...
ALL RIGHT, ALL RIGHT! HERE'S A BUCK! JEEZUS, WADDAYA DOIN'? SAVING FOR YOUR RETIREMENT?

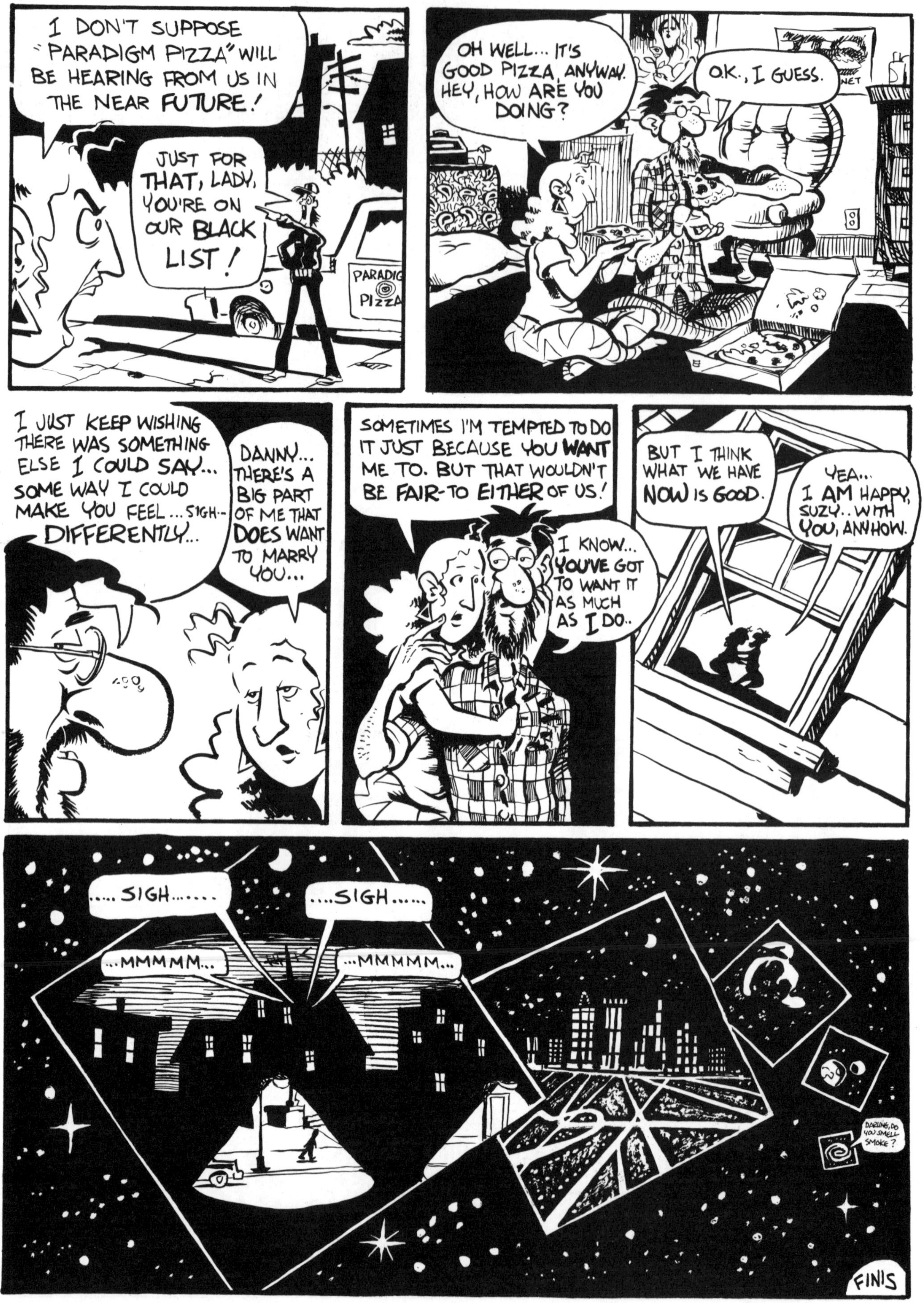

I DON'T SUPPOSE "PARADIGM PIZZA" WILL BE HEARING FROM US IN THE NEAR FUTURE!
JUST FOR THAT, LADY, YOU'RE ON OUR BLACK LIST!
PARADIGM PIZZA
OH WELL... IT'S GOOD PIZZA, ANYWAY. HEY, HOW ARE YOU DOING?
O.K., I GUESS.
I JUST KEEP WISHING THERE WAS SOMETHING ELSE I COULD SAY... SOME WAY I COULD MAKE YOU FEEL ...SIGH... DIFFERENTLY...
DANNY... THERE'S A BIG PART OF ME THAT DOES WANT TO MARRY YOU...
SOMETIMES I'M TEMPTED TO DO IT JUST BECAUSE YOU WANT ME TO. BUT THAT WOULDN'T BE FAIR-TO EITHER OF US!
I KNOW... YOU'VE GOT TO WANT IT AS MUCH AS I DO..
BUT I THINK WHAT WE HAVE NOW IS GOOD.
YEA... I AM HAPPY, SUZY.. WITH YOU, ANYHOW.
.....SIGH......
....SIGH......
...MMMMM...
...MMMMM...
DARLING, DO YOU SMELL SMOKE?
FINIS

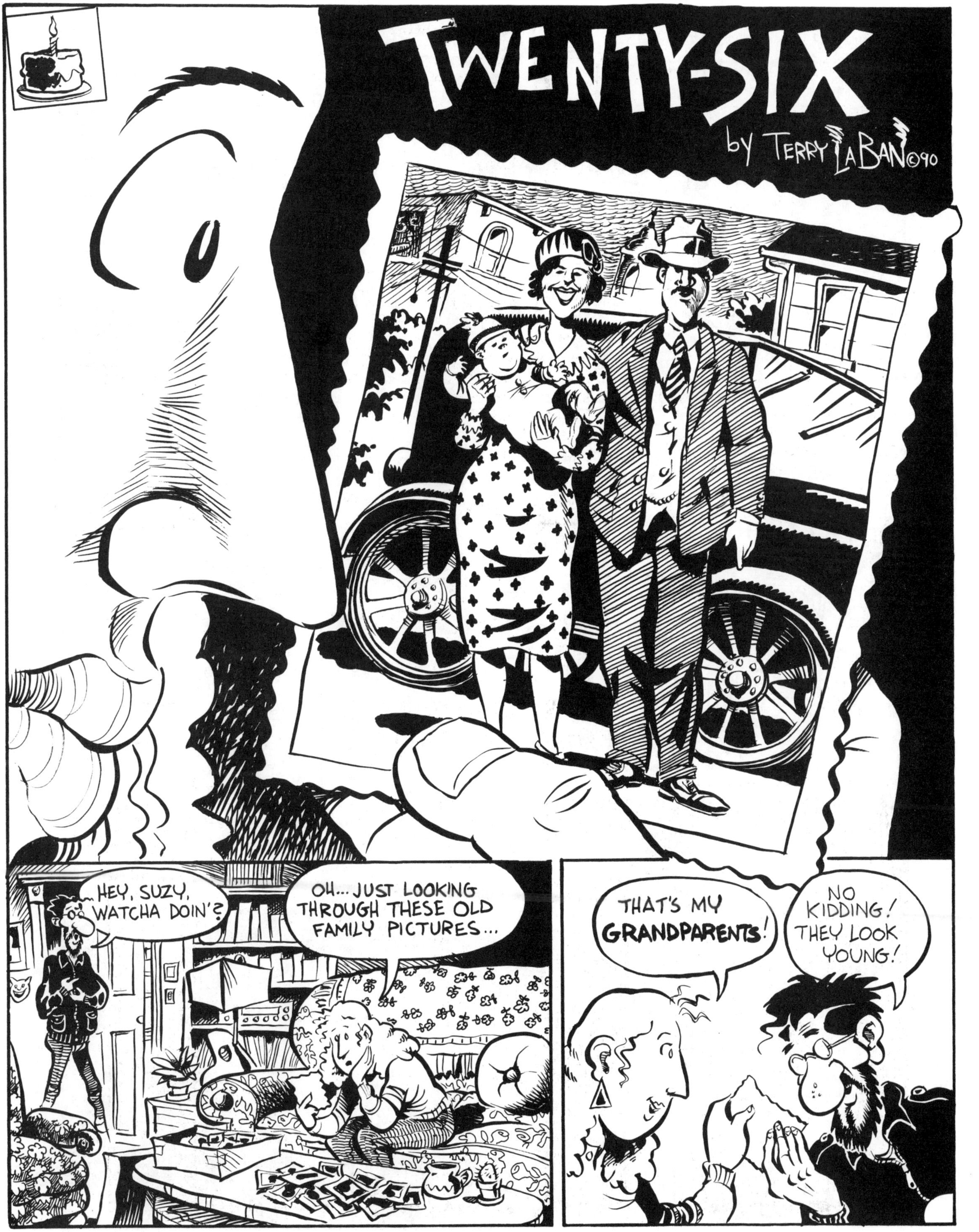
TWENTY-SIX
by TERRY LABAN ©90
HEY, SUZY, WATCHA DOIN'?
OH... JUST LOOKING THROUGH THESE OLD FAMILY PICTURES...
THAT'S MY GRANDPARENTS!
NO KIDDING! THEY LOOK YOUNG!

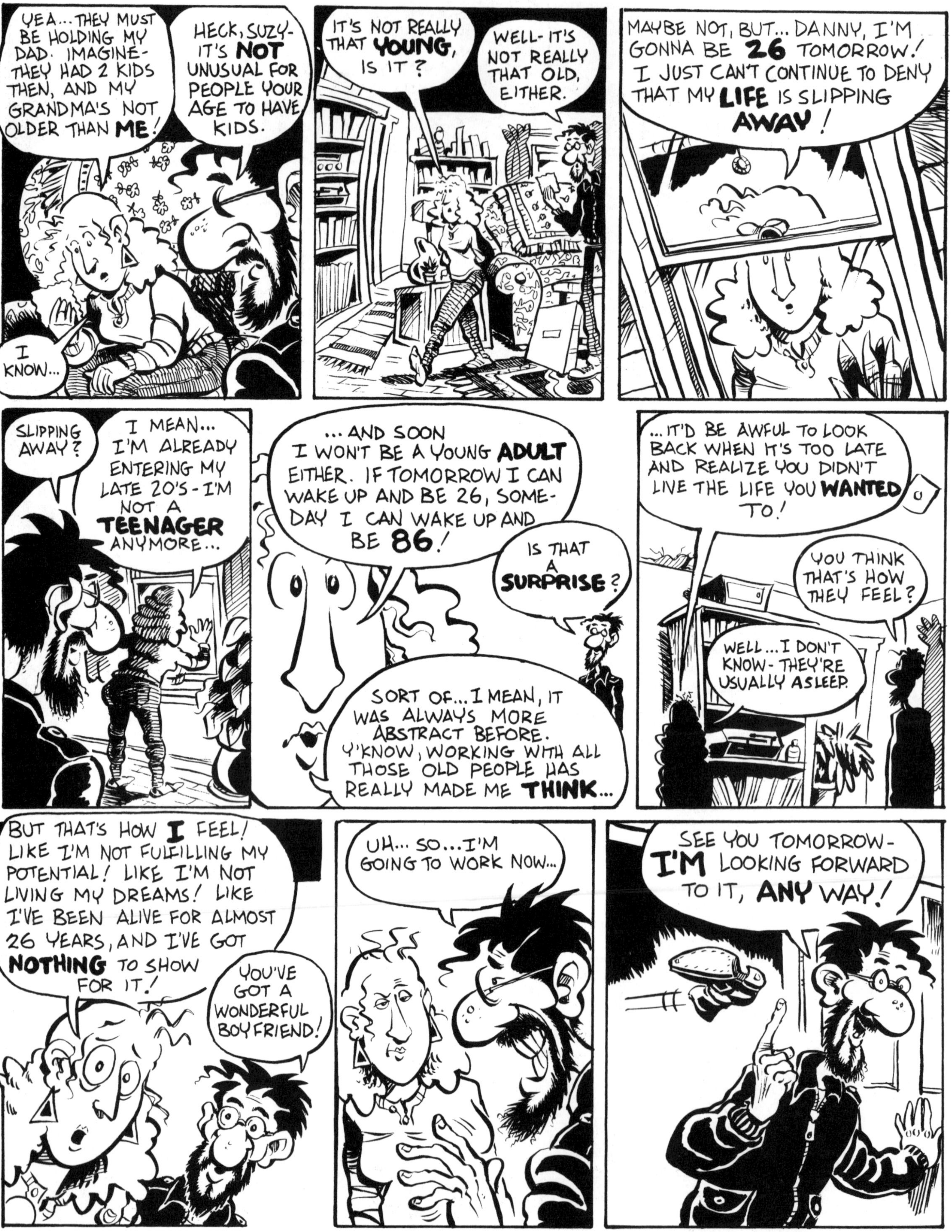
YEA... THEY MUST BE HOLDING MY DAD. IMAGINE- THEY HAD 2 KIDS THEN, AND MY GRANDMA'S NOT OLDER THAN ME!
HECK, SUZY- IT'S NOT UNUSUAL FOR PEOPLE YOUR AGE TO HAVE KIDS.
I KNOW...
IT'S NOT REALLY THAT YOUNG, IS IT?
WELL- IT'S NOT REALLY THAT OLD, EITHER.
MAYBE NOT, BUT... DANNY, I'M GONNA BE 26 TOMORROW! I JUST CAN'T CONTINUE TO DENY THAT MY LIFE IS SLIPPING AWAY!
SLIPPING AWAY?
I MEAN... I'M ALREADY ENTERING MY LATE 20'S - I'M NOT A TEENAGER ANYMORE...
...AND SOON I WON'T BE A YOUNG ADULT EITHER. IF TOMORROW I CAN WAKE UP AND BE 26, SOME-DAY I CAN WAKE UP AND BE 86!
IS THAT A SURPRISE?
SORT OF... I MEAN, IT WAS ALWAYS MORE ABSTRACT BEFORE. Y'KNOW, WORKING WITH ALL THOSE OLD PEOPLE HAS REALLY MADE ME THINK...
...IT'D BE AWFUL TO LOOK BACK WHEN IT'S TOO LATE AND REALIZE YOU DIDN'T LIVE THE LIFE YOU WANTED TO!
YOU THINK THAT'S HOW THEY FEEL?
WELL... I DON'T KNOW- THEY'RE USUALLY ASLEEP.
BUT THAT'S HOW I FEEL! LIKE I'M NOT FULFILLING MY POTENTIAL! LIKE I'M NOT LIVING MY DREAMS! LIKE I'VE BEEN ALIVE FOR ALMOST 26 YEARS, AND I'VE GOT NOTHING TO SHOW FOR IT!
YOU'VE GOT A WONDERFUL BOYFRIEND!
UH... SO... I'M GOING TO WORK NOW...
SEE YOU TOMORROW- I'M LOOKING FORWARD TO IT, ANY WAY!

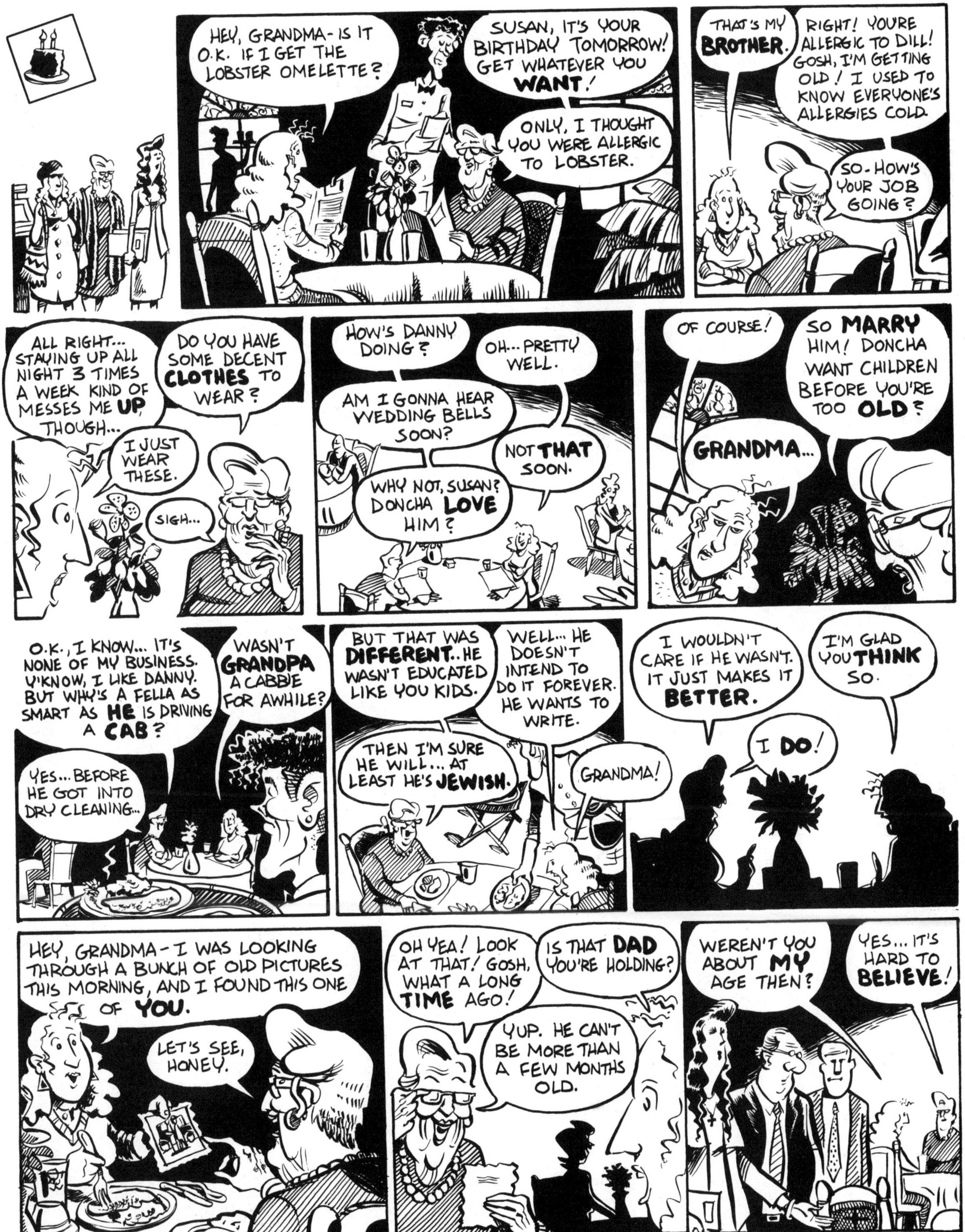
HEY, GRANDMA- IS IT O.K. IF I GET THE LOBSTER OMELETTE?
SUSAN, IT'S YOUR BIRTHDAY TOMORROW! GET WHATEVER YOU WANT!
ONLY, I THOUGHT YOU WERE ALLERGIC TO LOBSTER.
THAT'S MY BROTHER.
RIGHT! YOU'RE ALLERGIC TO DILL! GOSH, I'M GETTING OLD! I USED TO KNOW EVERYONE'S ALLERGIES COLD.
SO- HOW'S YOUR JOB GOING?
ALL RIGHT... STAYING UP ALL NIGHT 3 TIMES A WEEK KIND OF MESSES ME UP, THOUGH...
DO YOU HAVE SOME DECENT CLOTHES TO WEAR?
I JUST WEAR THESE.
SIGH...
HOW'S DANNY DOING?
OH... PRETTY WELL.
AM I GONNA HEAR WEDDING BELLS SOON?
NOT THAT SOON.
WHY NOT, SUSAN? DONCHA LOVE HIM?
OF COURSE!
SO MARRY HIM! DONCHA WANT CHILDREN BEFORE YOU'RE TOO OLD?
GRANDMA...
O.K., I KNOW... IT'S NONE OF MY BUSINESS. Y'KNOW, I LIKE DANNY. BUT WHY'S A FELLA AS SMART AS HE IS DRIVING A CAB?
WASN'T GRANDPA A CABBIE FOR AWHILE?
YES... BEFORE HE GOT INTO DRY CLEANING...
BUT THAT WAS DIFFERENT.. HE WASN'T EDUCATED LIKE YOU KIDS.
WELL... HE DOESN'T INTEND TO DO IT FOREVER. HE WANTS TO WRITE.
THEN I'M SURE HE WILL... AT LEAST HE'S JEWISH.
GRANDMA!
I WOULDN'T CARE IF HE WASN'T. IT JUST MAKES IT BETTER.
I DO!
I'M GLAD YOU THINK SO.
HEY, GRANDMA - I WAS LOOKING THROUGH A BUNCH OF OLD PICTURES THIS MORNING, AND I FOUND THIS ONE OF YOU.
LET'S SEE, HONEY.
OH YEA! LOOK AT THAT! GOSH, WHAT A LONG TIME AGO!
IS THAT DAD YOU'RE HOLDING?
YUP. HE CAN'T BE MORE THAN A FEW MONTHS OLD.
WEREN'T YOU ABOUT MY AGE THEN?
YES... IT'S HARD TO BELIEVE!

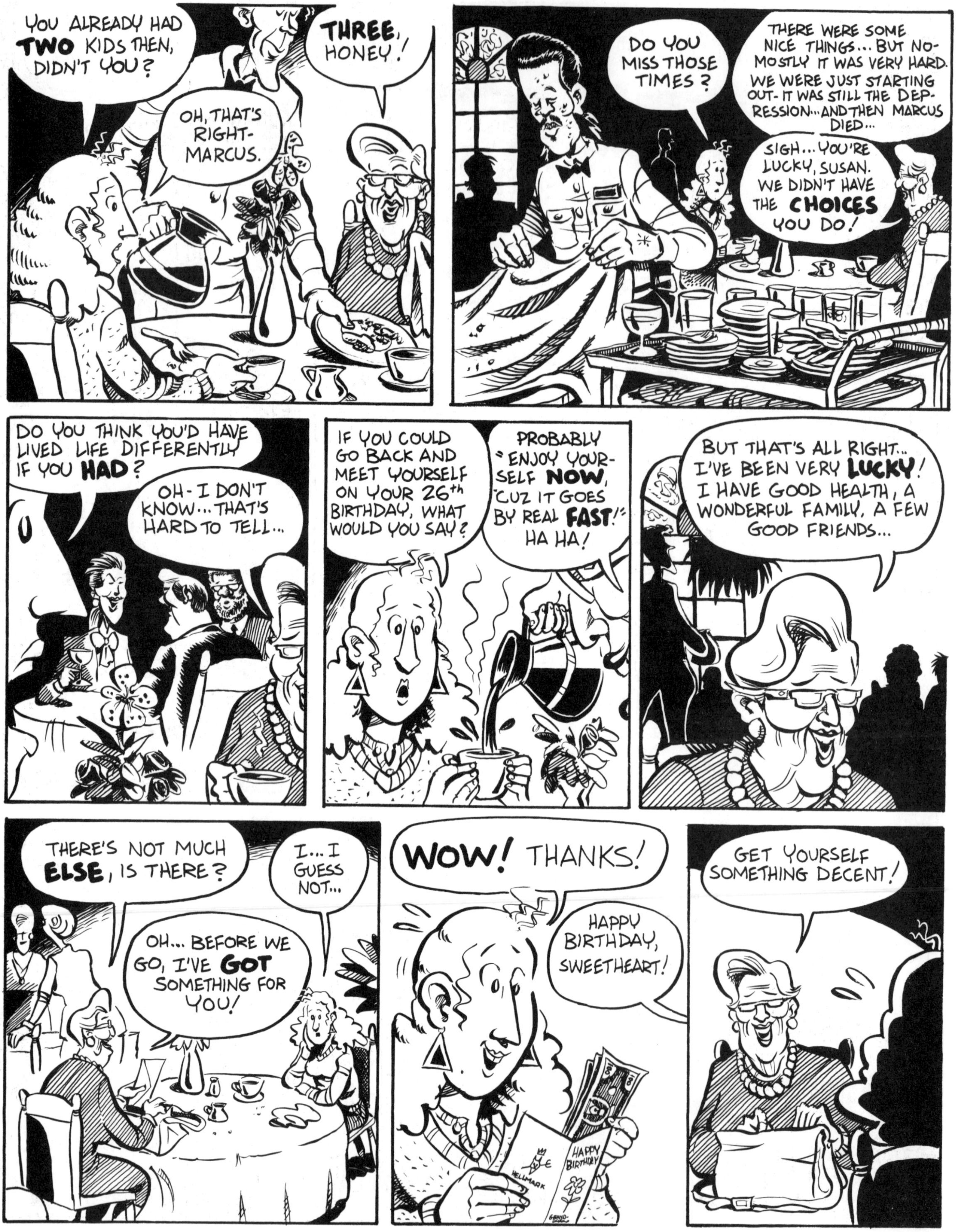
YOU ALREADY HAD TWO KIDS THEN, DIDN'T YOU?
THREE, HONEY!
OH, THAT'S RIGHT- MARCUS.
DO YOU MISS THOSE TIMES?
THERE WERE SOME NICE THINGS... BUT NO- MOSTLY IT WAS VERY HARD. WE WERE JUST STARTING OUT- IT WAS STILL THE DEP-RESSION... AND THEN MARCUS DIED...
SIGH... YOU'RE LUCKY, SUSAN. WE DIDN'T HAVE THE CHOICES YOU DO!
DO YOU THINK YOU'D HAVE LIVED LIFE DIFFERENTLY IF YOU HAD?
OH- I DON'T KNOW... THAT'S HARD TO TELL...
IF YOU COULD GO BACK AND MEET YOURSELF ON YOUR 26th BIRTHDAY, WHAT WOULD YOU SAY?
PROBABLY "ENJOY YOUR-SELF NOW, 'CUZ IT GOES BY REAL FAST!" HA HA!
BUT THAT'S ALL RIGHT... I'VE BEEN VERY LUCKY! I HAVE GOOD HEALTH, A WONDERFUL FAMILY, A FEW GOOD FRIENDS...
THERE'S NOT MUCH ELSE, IS THERE?
I... I GUESS NOT...
OH... BEFORE WE GO, I'VE GOT SOMETHING FOR YOU!
WOW! THANKS!
HAPPY BIRTHDAY, SWEETHEART!
HAPPY BIRTHDAY
HELLMARK
GET YOURSELF SOMETHING DECENT!

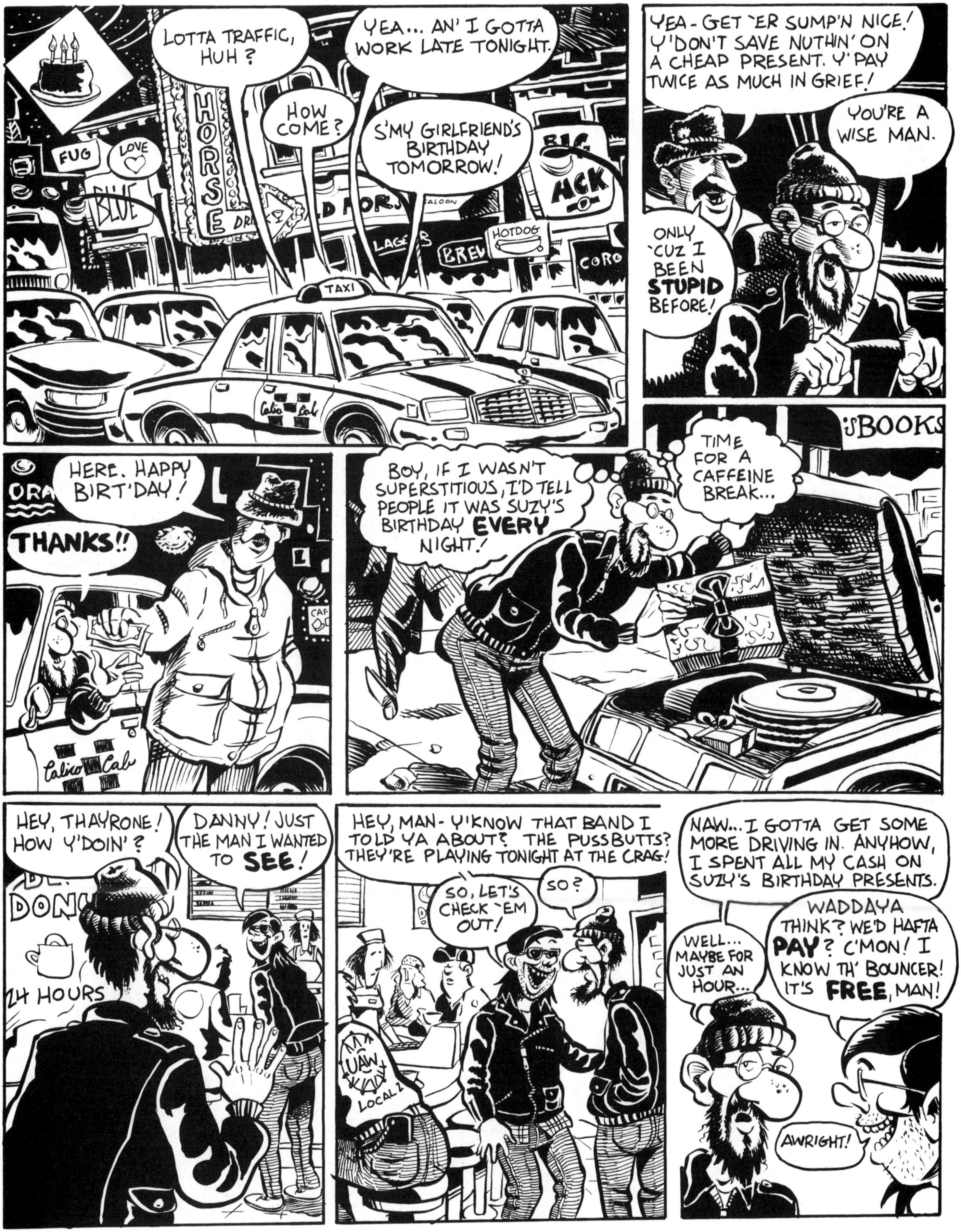
LOTTA TRAFFIC, HUH?
YEA... AN' I GOTTA WORK LATE TONIGHT.
HOW COME?
S'MY GIRLFRIEND'S BIRTHDAY TOMORROW!
HORSE
FUG
LOVE
BLUE
HOTDOG
BREW
LAGER
TAXI
Calico Cab
YEA - GET 'ER SUMP'N NICE! Y'DON'T SAVE NUTHIN' ON A CHEAP PRESENT. Y'PAY TWICE AS MUCH IN GRIEF!
YOU'RE A WISE MAN.
ONLY 'CUZ I BEEN STUPID BEFORE!
HERE. HAPPY BIRT'DAY!
THANKS!!
Calico Cab
BOOKS
BOY, IF I WASN'T SUPERSTITIOUS, I'D TELL PEOPLE IT WAS SUZY'S BIRTHDAY EVERY NIGHT!
TIME FOR A CAFFEINE BREAK...
HEY, THAYRONE! HOW Y'DOIN'?
DANNY! JUST THE MAN I WANTED TO SEE!
24 HOURS
HEY, MAN- Y'KNOW THAT BAND I TOLD YA ABOUT? THE PUSSBUTTS? THEY'RE PLAYING TONIGHT AT THE CRAG!
SO?
SO, LET'S CHECK 'EM OUT!
UAW LOCAL 2
NAW... I GOTTA GET SOME MORE DRIVING IN. ANYHOW, I SPENT ALL MY CASH ON SUZY'S BIRTHDAY PRESENTS.
WADDAYA THINK? WE'D HAFTA PAY? C'MON! I KNOW TH' BOUNCER! IT'S FREE, MAN!
WELL... MAYBE FOR JUST AN HOUR...
AWRIGHT!

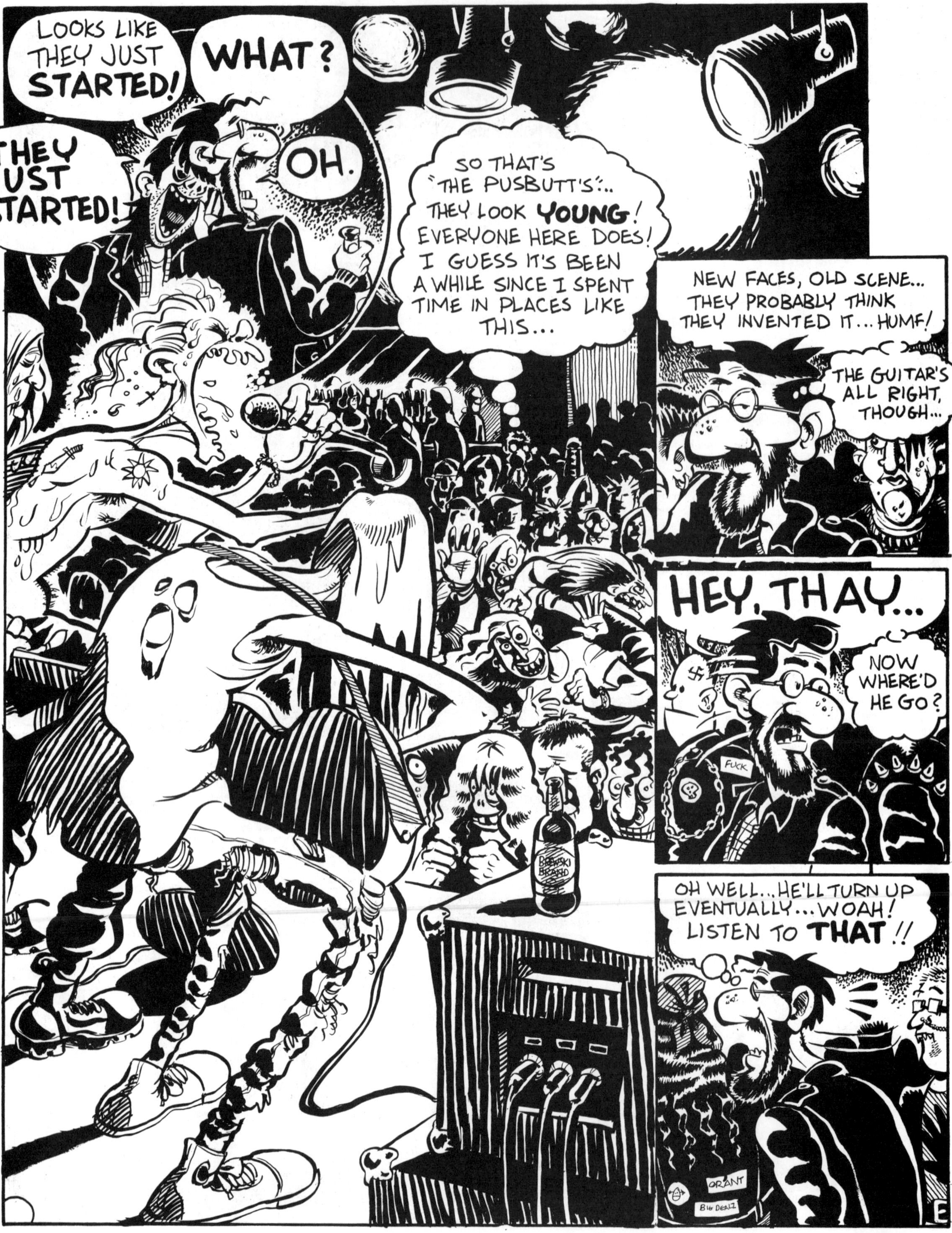
LOOKS LIKE THEY JUST STARTED!
WHAT?
THEY JUST STARTED!
OH.
SO THAT'S "THE PUSBUTT'S"... THEY LOOK YOUNG! EVERYONE HERE DOES! I GUESS IT'S BEEN A WHILE SINCE I SPENT TIME IN PLACES LIKE THIS...
NEW FACES, OLD SCENE... THEY PROBABLY THINK THEY INVENTED IT... HUMF!
THE GUITAR'S ALL RIGHT, THOUGH...
HEY, THAY...
NOW WHERE'D HE GO?
FUCK
OH WELL... HE'LL TURN UP EVENTUALLY... WOAH! LISTEN TO THAT!!
BREWSKI BRAND
GRANT
BIG DEAL

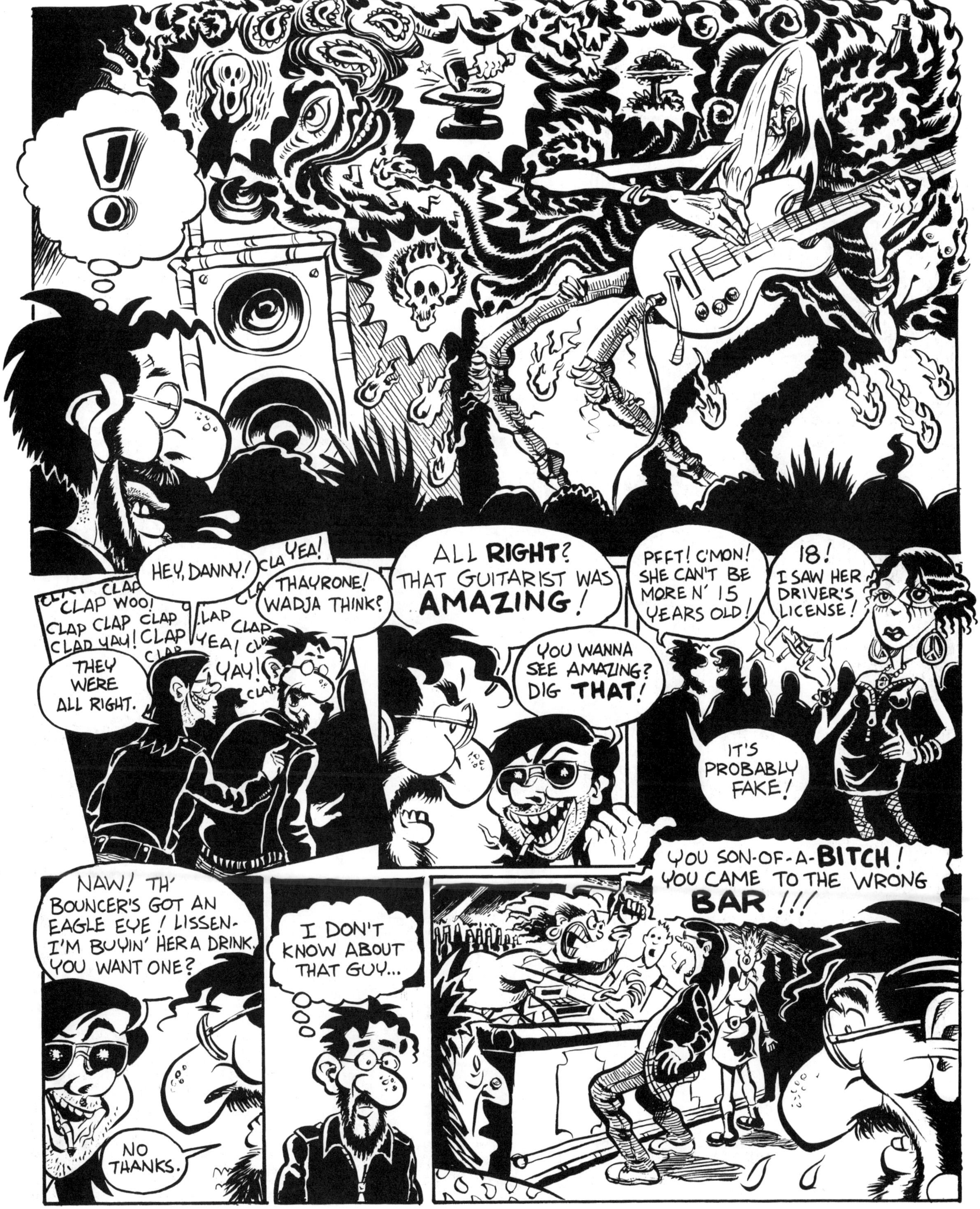
!
CLAP CLAP WOO! CLAP CLAP CLAP CLAP YAY! CLAP
HEY, DANNY!
CLA YEA!
CLAP YEA! YAY! CLAP
THAYRONE! WADJA THINK?
THEY WERE ALL RIGHT.
ALL RIGHT? THAT GUITARIST WAS AMAZING!
YOU WANNA SEE AMAZING? DIG THAT!
PFFT! C'MON! SHE CAN'T BE MORE N' 15 YEARS OLD!
18! I SAW HER DRIVER'S LICENSE!
IT'S PROBABLY FAKE!
NAW! TH' BOUNCER'S GOT AN EAGLE EYE! LISSEN- I'M BUYIN' HER A DRINK. YOU WANT ONE?
NO THANKS.
I DON'T KNOW ABOUT THAT GUY...
YOU SON-OF-A-BITCH! YOU CAME TO THE WRONG BAR!!!

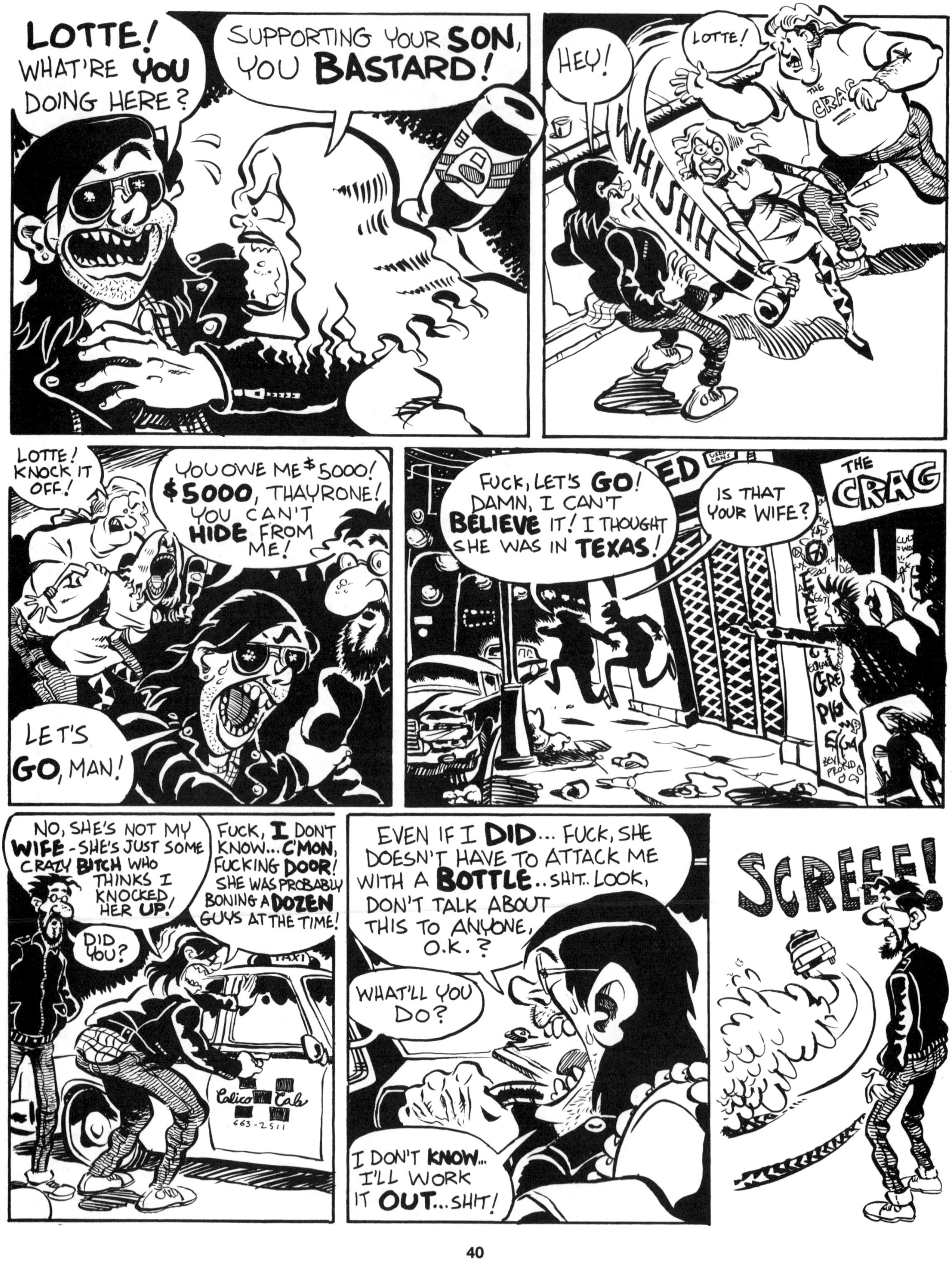
LOTTE! WHAT'RE YOU DOING HERE?
SUPPORTING YOUR SON, YOU BASTARD!
HEY!
LOTTE!
WHISHH
THE CRAG
LOTTE! KNOCK IT OFF!
YOU OWE ME $5000! $5000, THAYRONE! YOU CAN'T HIDE FROM ME!
LET'S GO, MAN!
FUCK, LET'S GO! DAMN, I CAN'T BELIEVE IT! I THOUGHT SHE WAS IN TEXAS!
IS THAT YOUR WIFE?
THE CRAG
NO, SHE'S NOT MY WIFE - SHE'S JUST SOME CRAZY BITCH WHO THINKS I KNOCKED HER UP!
FUCK, I DON'T KNOW... C'MON, FUCKING DOOR! SHE WAS PROBABLY BONING A DOZEN GUYS AT THE TIME!
DID YOU?
TAXI
Calico Cab
663-2511
EVEN IF I DID... FUCK, SHE DOESN'T HAVE TO ATTACK ME WITH A BOTTLE.. SHIT.. LOOK, DON'T TALK ABOUT THIS TO ANYONE, O.K.?
WHAT'LL YOU DO?
I DON'T KNOW.. I'LL WORK IT OUT...SHIT!
SCREEE!

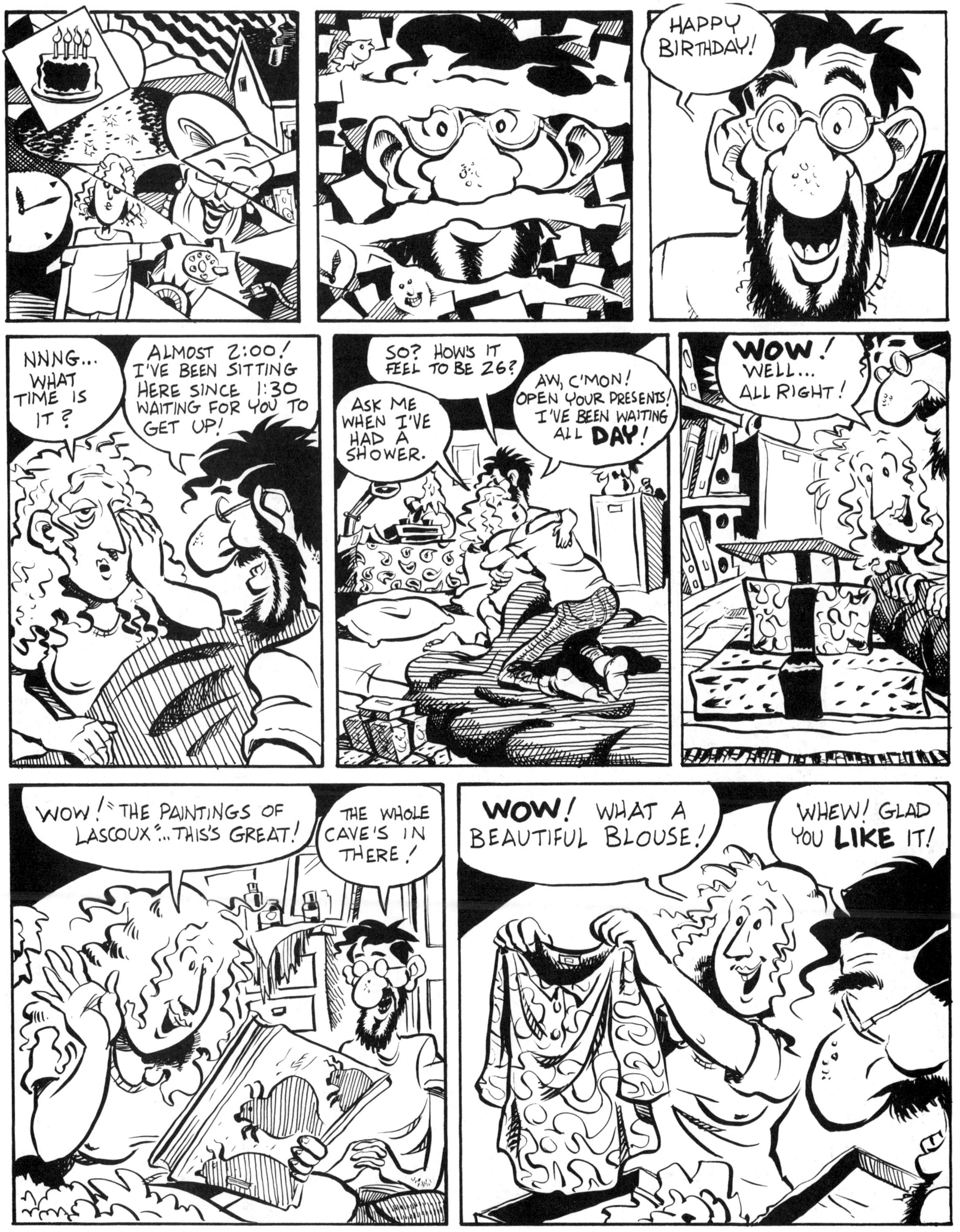
HAPPY BIRTHDAY!
NNNG... WHAT TIME IS IT?
ALMOST 2:00! I'VE BEEN SITTING HERE SINCE 1:30 WAITING FOR YOU TO GET UP!
SO? HOW'S IT FEEL TO BE 26?
ASK ME WHEN I'VE HAD A SHOWER.
AW, C'MON! OPEN YOUR PRESENTS! I'VE BEEN WAITING ALL DAY!
WOW! WELL... ALL RIGHT!
WOW! THE PAINTINGS OF LASCOUX... THIS'S GREAT!
THE WHOLE CAVE'S IN THERE!
WOW! WHAT A BEAUTIFUL BLOUSE!
WHEW! GLAD YOU LIKE IT!

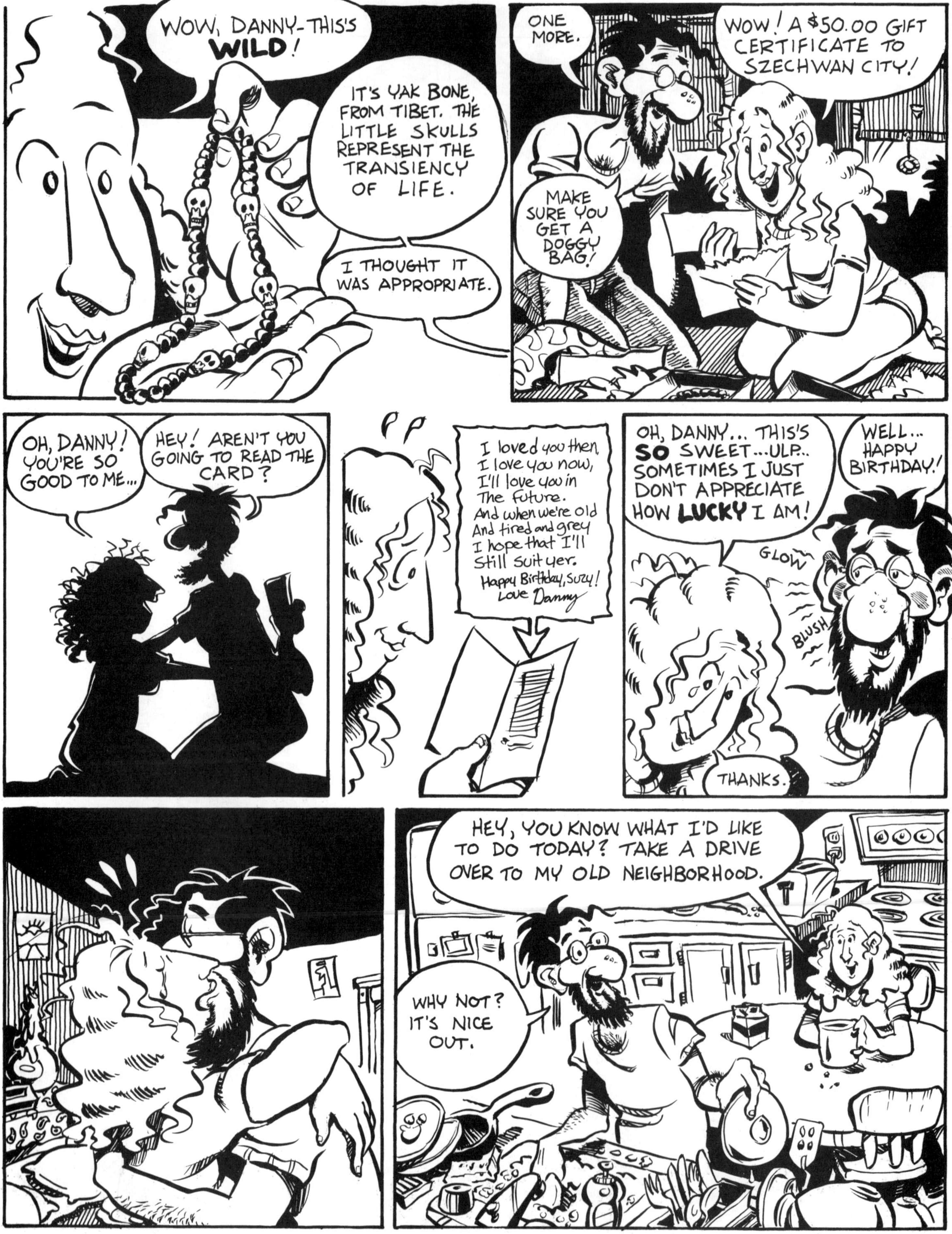
WOW, DANNY- THIS'S WILD!
IT'S YAK BONE, FROM TIBET. THE LITTLE SKULLS REPRESENT THE TRANSIENCY OF LIFE.
I THOUGHT IT WAS APPROPRIATE.
ONE MORE.
WOW! A $50.00 GIFT CERTIFICATE TO SZECHWAN CITY!
MAKE SURE YOU GET A DOGGY BAG!
OH, DANNY! YOU'RE SO GOOD TO ME...
HEY! AREN'T YOU GOING TO READ THE CARD?
I loved you then, I love you now, I'll love you in The future. And when we're old And tired and grey I hope that I'll Still suit yer. Happy Birthday, Suzy! Love Danny
OH, DANNY... THIS'S SO SWEET...ULP.. SOMETIMES I JUST DON'T APPRECIATE HOW LUCKY I AM!
WELL... HAPPY BIRTHDAY!
GLOW
BLUSH
THANKS.
HEY, YOU KNOW WHAT I'D LIKE TO DO TODAY? TAKE A DRIVE OVER TO MY OLD NEIGHBORHOOD.
WHY NOT? IT'S NICE OUT.

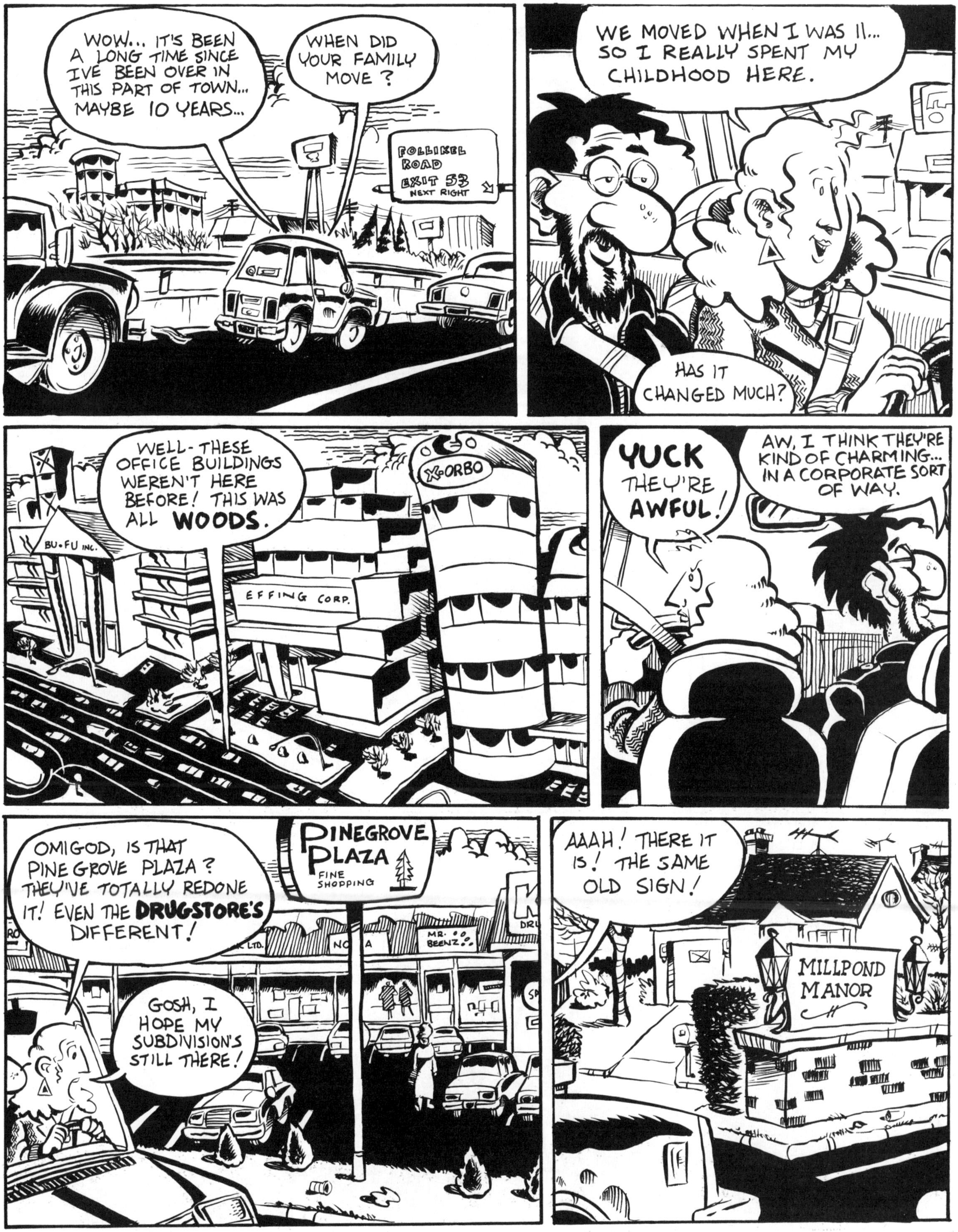
WOW... IT'S BEEN A LONG TIME SINCE I'VE BEEN OVER IN THIS PART OF TOWN... MAYBE 10 YEARS...
WHEN DID YOUR FAMILY MOVE ?
FOLLIKEL ROAD EXIT 53 NEXT RIGHT
WE MOVED WHEN I WAS 11... SO I REALLY SPENT MY CHILDHOOD HERE.
HAS IT CHANGED MUCH?
WELL- THESE OFFICE BUILDINGS WEREN'T HERE BEFORE! THIS WAS ALL WOODS.
BU•FU INC.
EFFING CORP.
X-ORBO
YUCK THEY'RE AWFUL!
AW, I THINK THEY'RE KIND OF CHARMING... IN A CORPORATE SORT OF WAY.
OMIGOD, IS THAT PINE GROVE PLAZA? THEY'VE TOTALLY REDONE IT! EVEN THE DRUGSTORE'S DIFFERENT!
PINEGROVE PLAZA FINE SHOPPING
MR. BEENZ
GOSH, I HOPE MY SUBDIVISION'S STILL THERE!
AAAH! THERE IT IS! THE SAME OLD SIGN!
MILLPOND MANOR

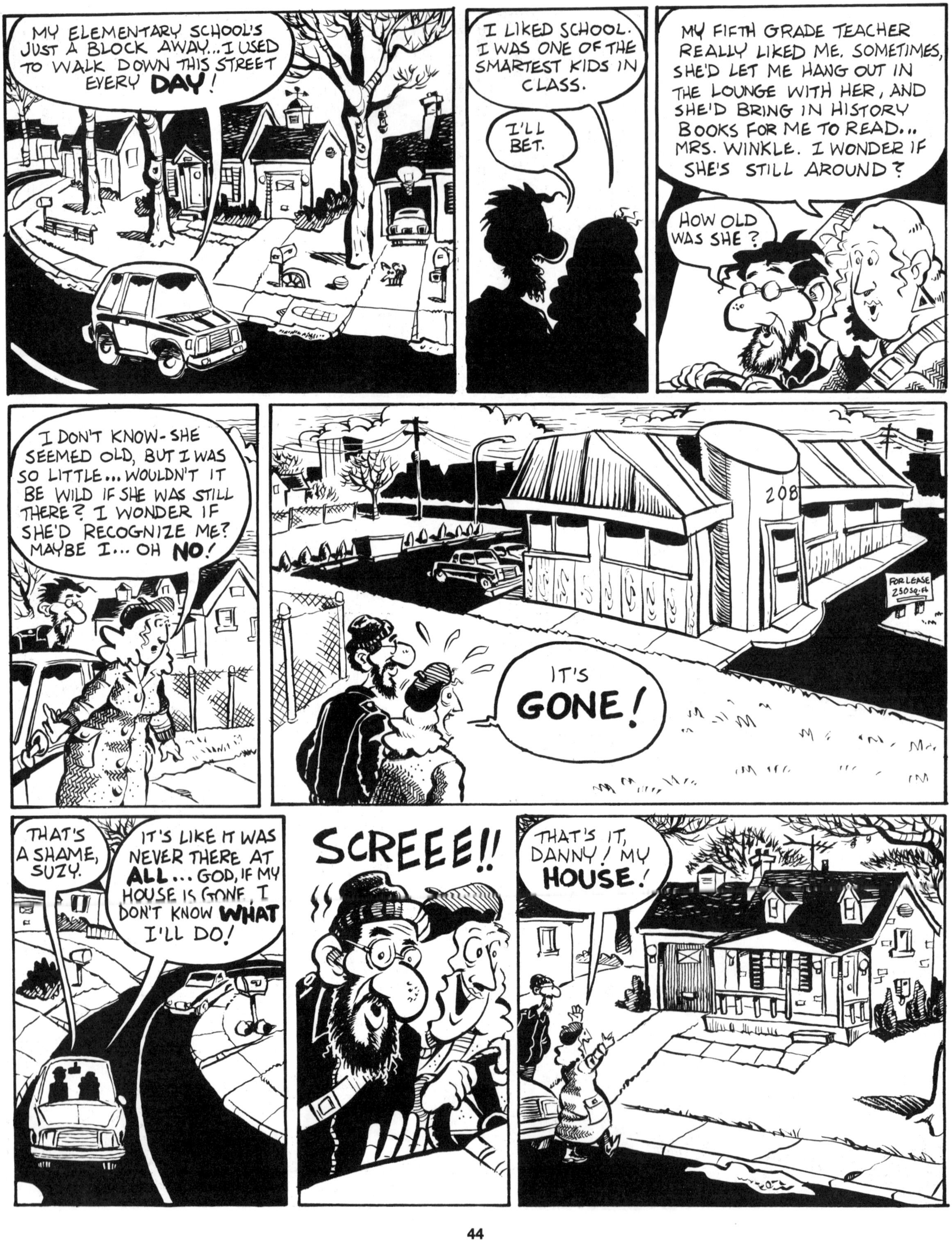
MY ELEMENTARY SCHOOL'S JUST A BLOCK AWAY... I USED TO WALK DOWN THIS STREET EVERY DAY!
I LIKED SCHOOL. I WAS ONE OF THE SMARTEST KIDS IN CLASS.
I'LL BET.
MY FIFTH GRADE TEACHER REALLY LIKED ME. SOMETIMES, SHE'D LET ME HANG OUT IN THE LOUNGE WITH HER, AND SHE'D BRING IN HISTORY BOOKS FOR ME TO READ... MRS. WINKLE. I WONDER IF SHE'S STILL AROUND?
HOW OLD WAS SHE?
I DON'T KNOW- SHE SEEMED OLD, BUT I WAS SO LITTLE... WOULDN'T IT BE WILD IF SHE WAS STILL THERE? I WONDER IF SHE'D RECOGNIZE ME? MAYBE I... OH NO!
208
FOR LEASE
IT'S GONE!
THAT'S A SHAME, SUZY.
IT'S LIKE IT WAS NEVER THERE AT ALL... GOD, IF MY HOUSE IS GONE, I DON'T KNOW WHAT I'LL DO!
SCREEEE!!
THAT'S IT, DANNY! MY HOUSE!

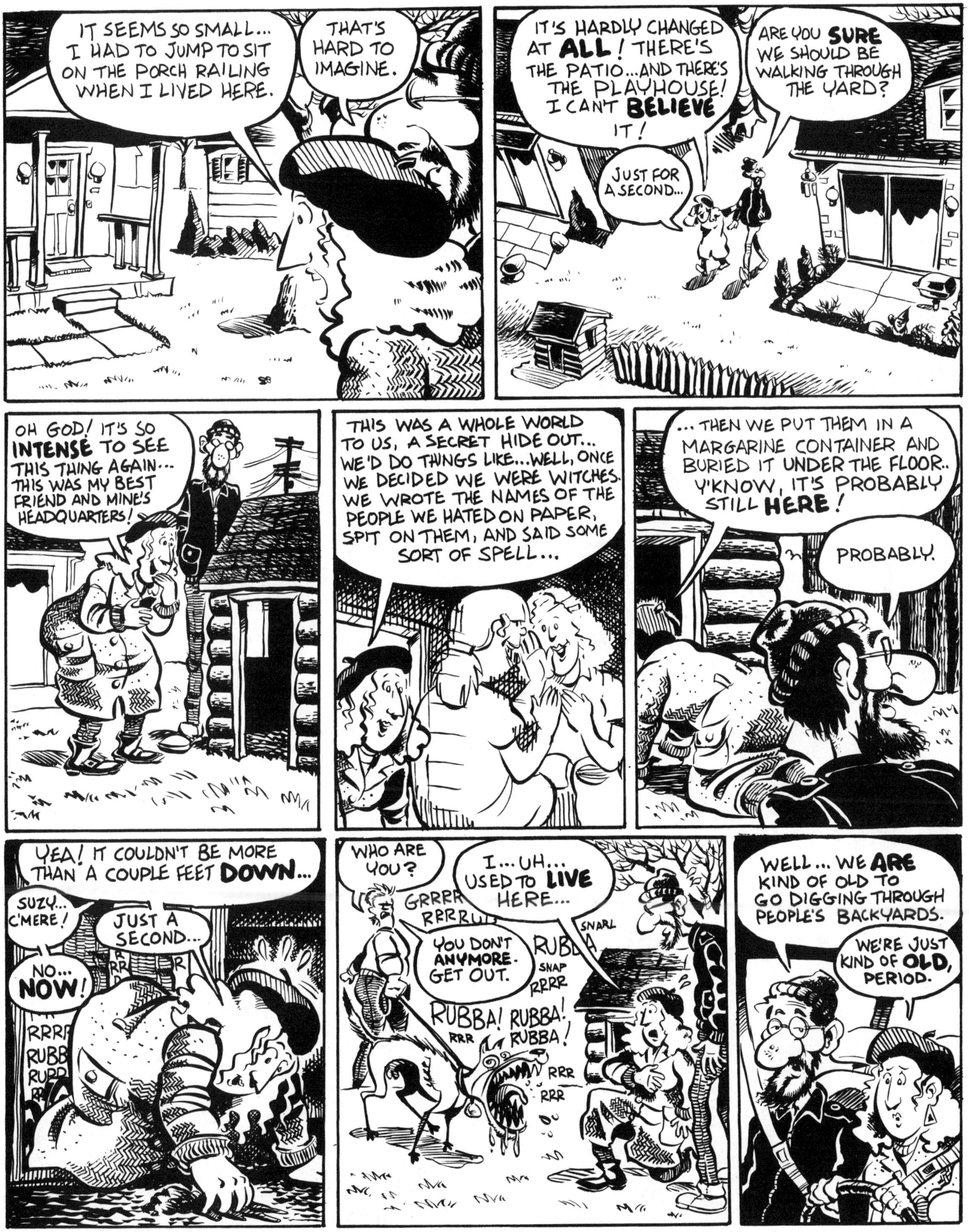
IT SEEMS SO SMALL... I HAD TO JUMP TO SIT ON THE PORCH RAILING WHEN I LIVED HERE.
THAT'S HARD TO IMAGINE.
IT'S HARDLY CHANGED AT ALL! THERE'S THE PATIO...AND THERE'S THE PLAYHOUSE! I CAN'T BELIEVE IT!
ARE YOU SURE WE SHOULD BE WALKING THROUGH THE YARD?
JUST FOR A SECOND...
OH GOD! IT'S SO INTENSE TO SEE THIS THING AGAIN... THIS WAS MY BEST FRIEND AND MINE'S HEADQUARTERS!
THIS WAS A WHOLE WORLD TO US, A SECRET HIDE OUT... WE'D DO THINGS LIKE...WELL, ONCE WE DECIDED WE WERE WITCHES. WE WROTE THE NAMES OF THE PEOPLE WE HATED ON PAPER, SPIT ON THEM, AND SAID SOME SORT OF SPELL...
... THEN WE PUT THEM IN A MARGARINE CONTAINER AND BURIED IT UNDER THE FLOOR.. Y'KNOW, IT'S PROBABLY STILL HERE!
PROBABLY.
YEA! IT COULDN'T BE MORE THAN A COUPLE FEET DOWN...
SUZY... C'MERE!
JUST A SECOND...
NO... NOW!
RRRR
RUBB
RUBB
WHO ARE YOU?
GRRRR RRRRU
I... UH... USED TO LIVE HERE...
SNARL
YOU DON'T ANYMORE. GET OUT.
RUBBA
SNAP
RRRR
RUBBA! RUBBA! RUBBA!
RRR
RRR
RRR
WELL... WE ARE KIND OF OLD TO GO DIGGING THROUGH PEOPLE'S BACKYARDS.
WE'RE JUST KIND OF OLD, PERIOD.

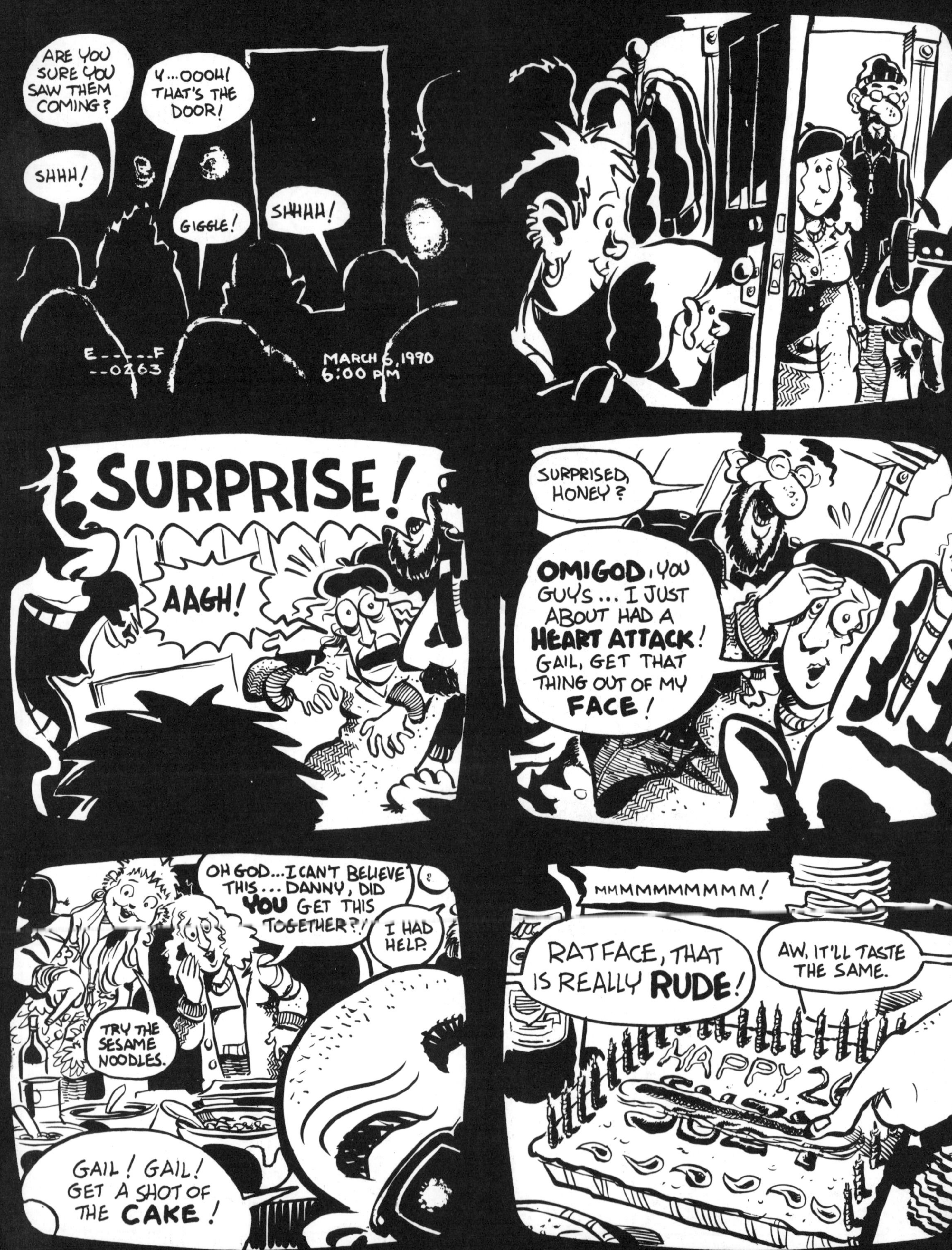
ARE YOU SURE YOU SAW THEM COMING?
Y...OOOH! THAT'S THE DOOR!
SHHH!
GIGGLE!
SHHHH!
E-----F --0263
MARCH 6, 1990 6:00 PM
SURPRISE!
AAGH!
SURPRISED, HONEY?
OMIGOD, YOU GUYS... I JUST ABOUT HAD A HEART ATTACK! GAIL, GET THAT THING OUT OF MY FACE!
OH GOD... I CAN'T BELIEVE THIS... DANNY, DID YOU GET THIS TOGETHER?!
I HAD HELP.
TRY THE SESAME NOODLES.
GAIL! GAIL! GET A SHOT OF THE CAKE!
MMMMMMMMMMM!
RATFACE, THAT IS REALLY RUDE!
AW, IT'LL TASTE THE SAME.
HAPPY 26

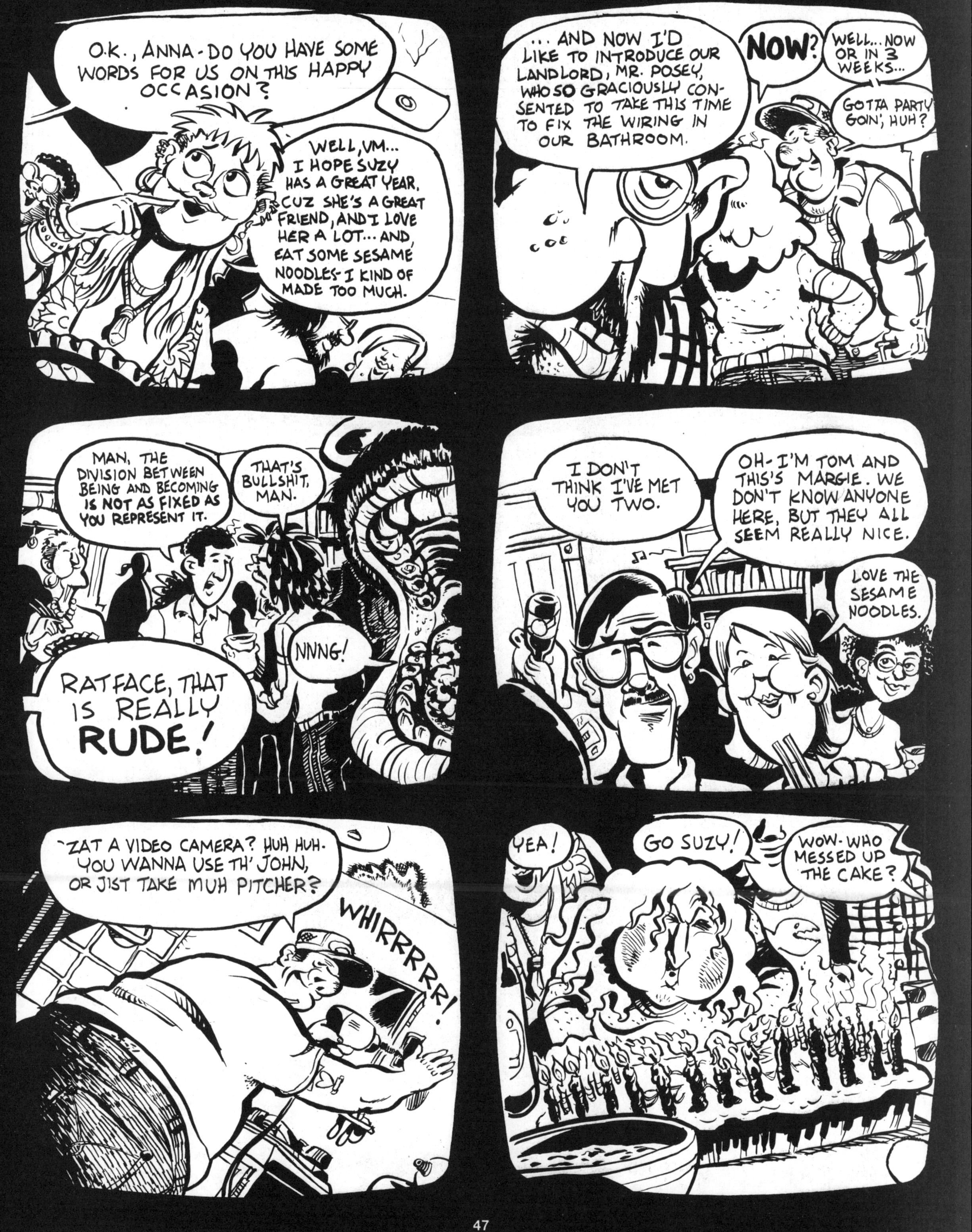
O.K., ANNA - DO YOU HAVE SOME WORDS FOR US ON THIS HAPPY OCCASION?
WELL, UM... I HOPE SUZY HAS A GREAT YEAR, CUZ SHE'S A GREAT FRIEND, AND I LOVE HER A LOT... AND, EAT SOME SESAME NOODLES- I KIND OF MADE TOO MUCH.
... AND NOW I'D LIKE TO INTRODUCE OUR LANDLORD, MR. POSEY, WHO SO GRACIOUSLY CONSENTED TO TAKE THIS TIME TO FIX THE WIRING IN OUR BATHROOM.
NOW?
WELL... NOW OR IN 3 WEEKS...
GOTTA PARTY GOIN', HUH?
MAN, THE DIVISION BETWEEN BEING AND BECOMING IS NOT AS FIXED AS YOU REPRESENT IT.
THAT'S BULLSHIT, MAN.
NNNG!
RATFACE, THAT IS REALLY RUDE!
I DON'T THINK I'VE MET YOU TWO.
OH- I'M TOM AND THIS'S MARGIE. WE DON'T KNOW ANYONE HERE, BUT THEY ALL SEEM REALLY NICE.
LOVE THE SESAME NOODLES.
'ZAT A VIDEO CAMERA? HUH HUH. YOU WANNA USE TH' JOHN, OR JIST TAKE MUH PITCHER?
WHIRRRRRR!
YEA!
GO SUZY!
WOW- WHO MESSED UP THE CAKE?

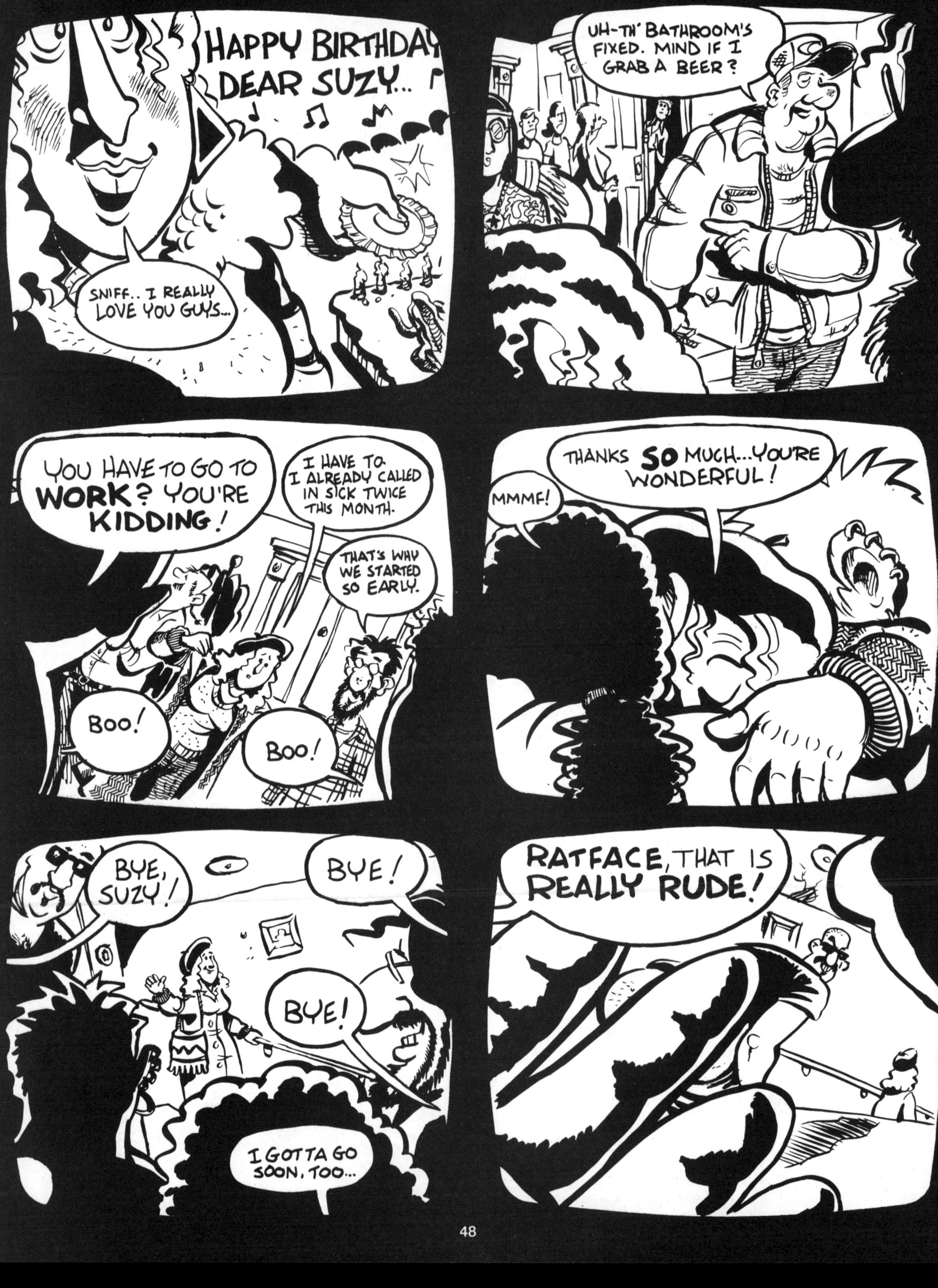
HAPPY BIRTHDAY DEAR SUZY...
SNIFF.. I REALLY LOVE YOU GUYS...
UH-TH' BATHROOM'S FIXED. MIND IF I GRAB A BEER?
YOU HAVE TO GO TO WORK? YOU'RE KIDDING!
I HAVE TO. I ALREADY CALLED IN SICK TWICE THIS MONTH.
THAT'S WHY WE STARTED SO EARLY.
BOO!
BOO!
MMMF!
THANKS SO MUCH...YOU'RE WONDERFUL!
BYE, SUZY!
BYE!
BYE!
I GOTTA GO SOON, TOO...
RATFACE, THAT IS REALLY RUDE!

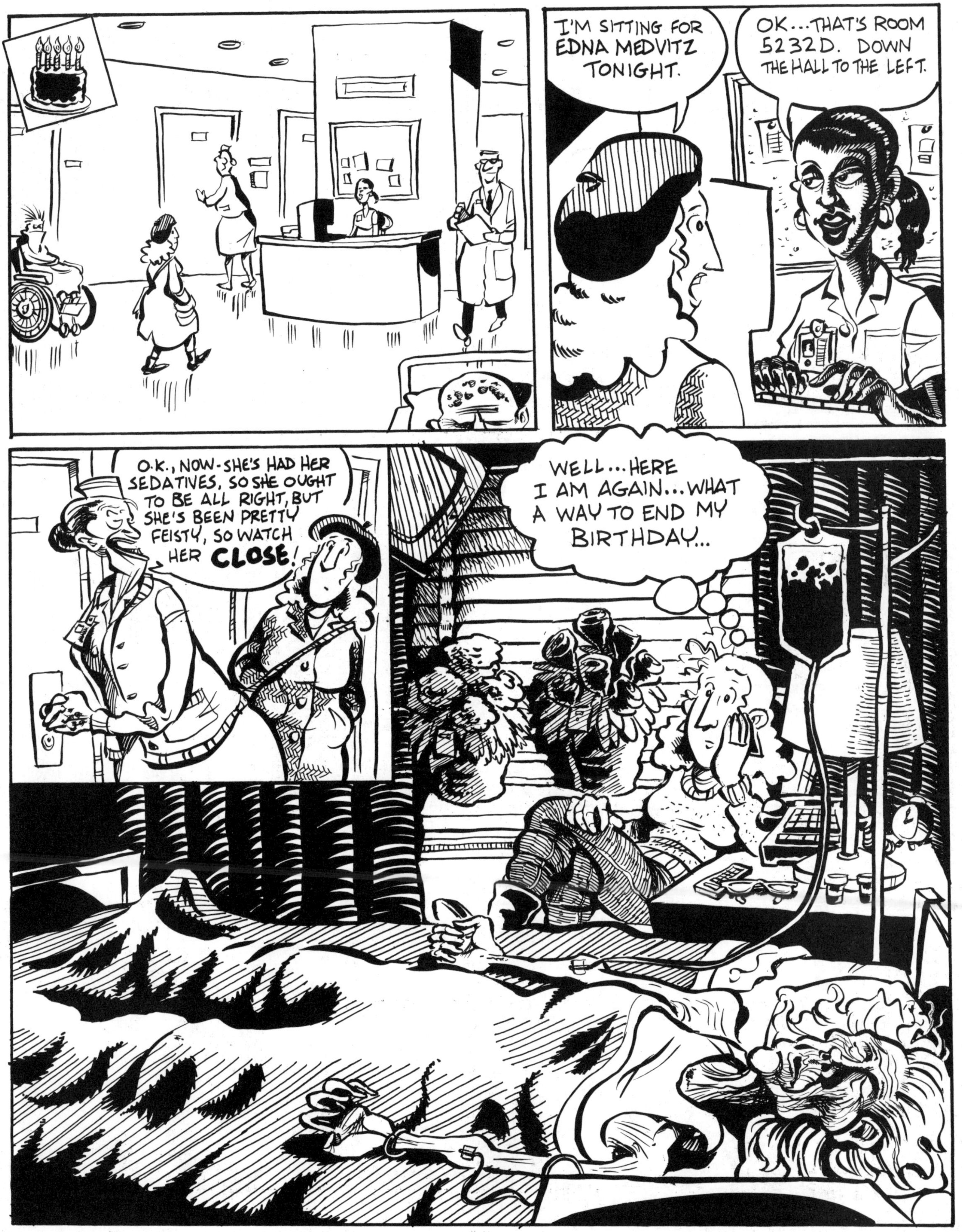
I'M SITTING FOR EDNA MEDVITZ TONIGHT.
OK...THAT'S ROOM 5232D. DOWN THE HALL TO THE LEFT.
O.K., NOW-SHE'S HAD HER SEDATIVES, SO SHE OUGHT TO BE ALL RIGHT, BUT SHE'S BEEN PRETTY FEISTY, SO WATCH HER CLOSE!
WELL...HERE I AM AGAIN...WHAT A WAY TO END MY BIRTHDAY...

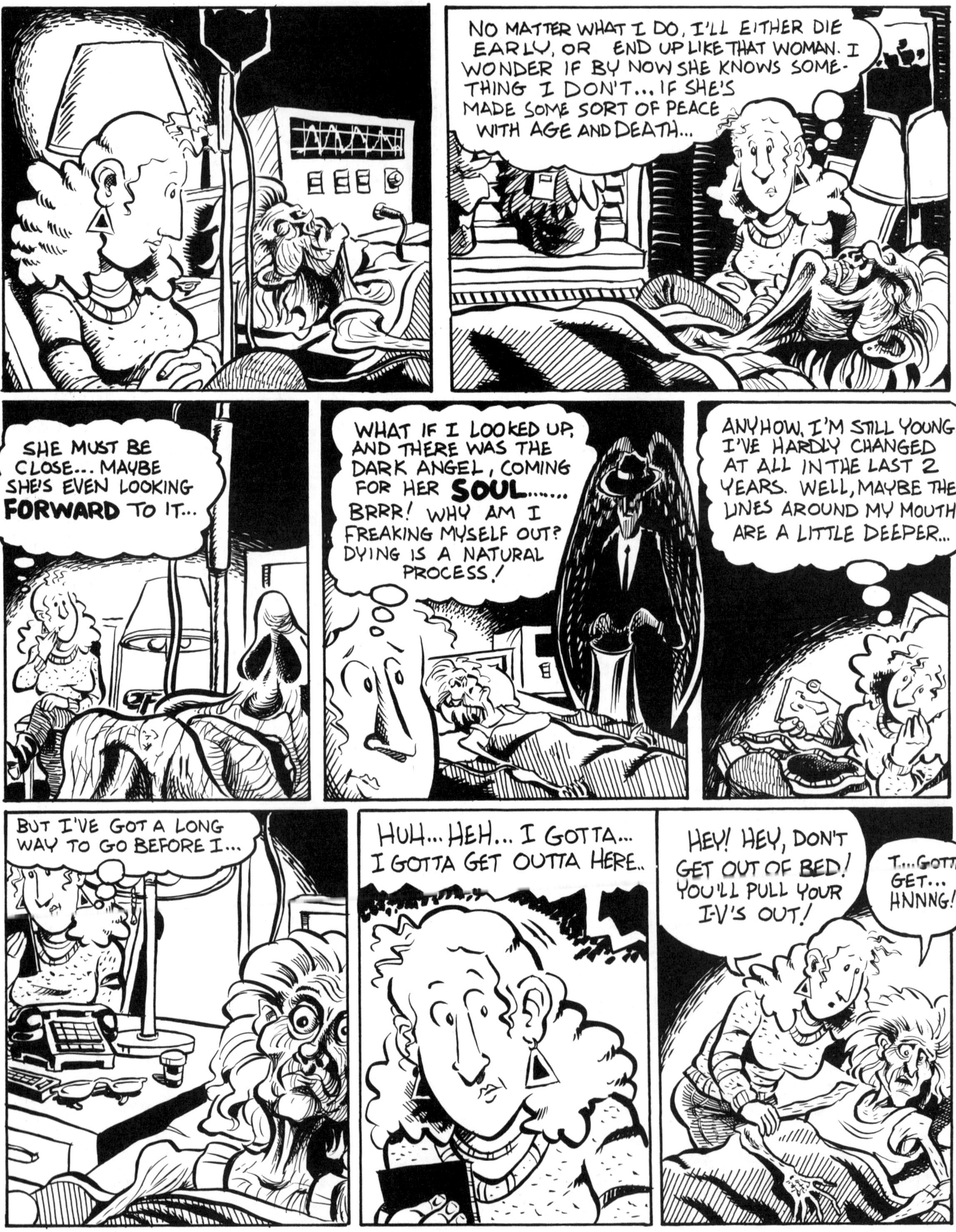
NO MATTER WHAT I DO, I'LL EITHER DIE EARLY, OR END UP LIKE THAT WOMAN. I WONDER IF BY NOW SHE KNOWS SOMETHING I DON'T... IF SHE'S MADE SOME SORT OF PEACE WITH AGE AND DEATH...
SHE MUST BE CLOSE... MAYBE SHE'S EVEN LOOKING **FORWARD** TO IT...
WHAT IF I LOOKED UP, AND THERE WAS THE DARK ANGEL, COMING FOR HER **SOUL**....... BRRR! WHY AM I FREAKING MYSELF OUT? DYING IS A NATURAL PROCESS!
ANYHOW, I'M STILL YOUNG. I'VE HARDLY CHANGED AT ALL IN THE LAST 2 YEARS. WELL, MAYBE THE LINES AROUND MY MOUTH ARE A LITTLE DEEPER...
BUT I'VE GOT A LONG WAY TO GO BEFORE I...
HUH... HEH... I GOTTA... I GOTTA GET OUTTA HERE..
HEY! HEY, DON'T GET OUT OF BED! YOU'LL PULL YOUR I-V'S OUT!
I... GOTTA GET... HNNNG!

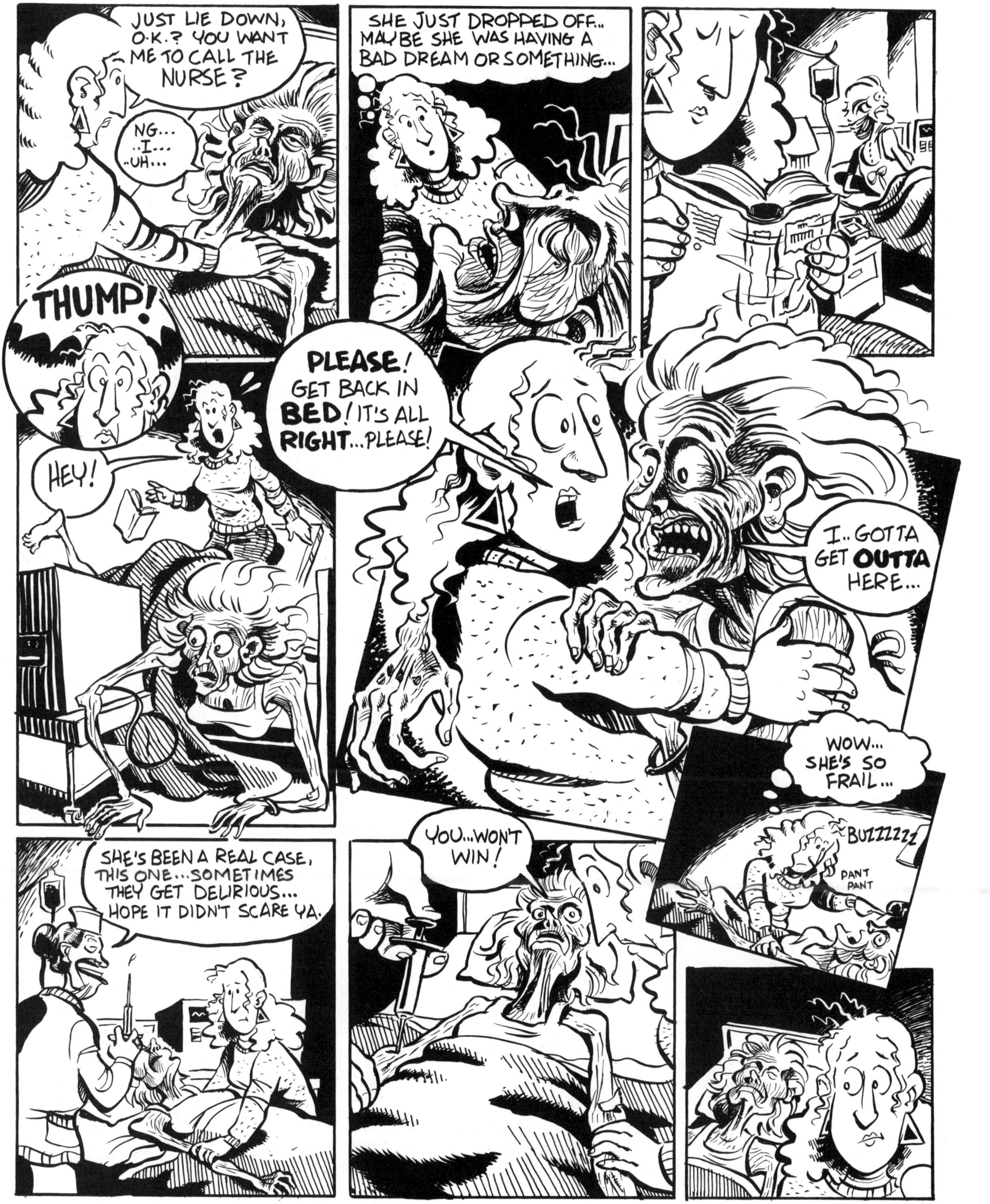
JUST LIE DOWN, O.K.? YOU WANT ME TO CALL THE NURSE?
NG... ..I... ..UH...
SHE JUST DROPPED OFF.. MAYBE SHE WAS HAVING A BAD DREAM OR SOMETHING...
THUMP!
HEY!
PLEASE! GET BACK IN BED! IT'S ALL RIGHT...PLEASE!
I.. GOTTA GET OUTTA HERE...
WOW... SHE'S SO FRAIL...
BUZZZZZZ
PANT PANT
SHE'S BEEN A REAL CASE, THIS ONE...SOMETIMES THEY GET DELIRIOUS... HOPE IT DIDN'T SCARE YA.
YOU...WON'T WIN!

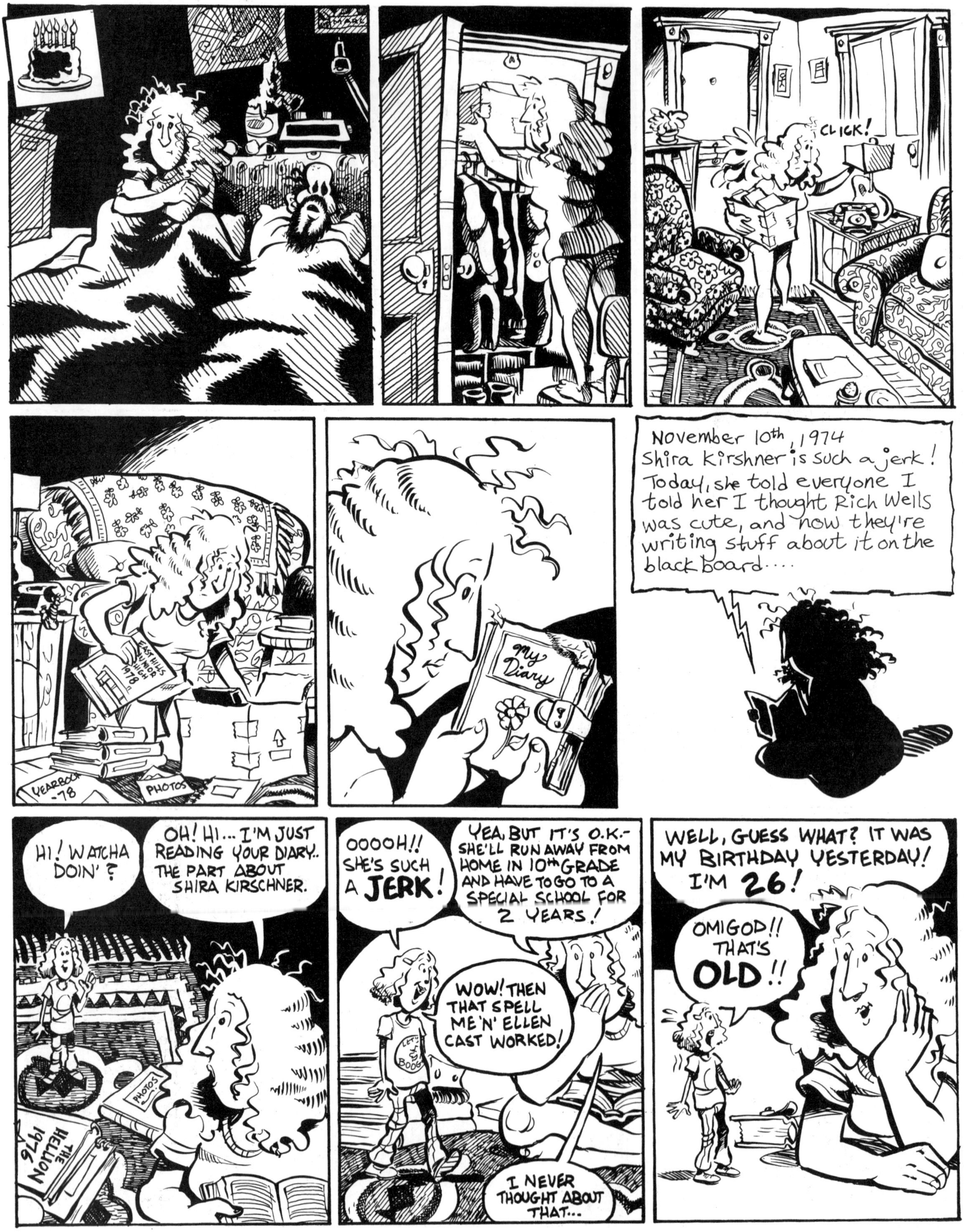

CLICK!
EAST HILLS JUNIOR HIGH 1978
YEARBOOK -78
PHOTOS
My Diary
November 10th, 1974
Shira Kirshner is such a jerk! Today, she told everyone I told her I thought Rich Wells was cute, and now they're writing stuff about it on the blackboard....
HI! WATCHA DOIN'?
OH! HI... I'M JUST READING YOUR DIARY.. THE PART ABOUT SHIRA KIRSCHNER.
PHOTOS
THE HELLION 1976
OOOOH!! SHE'S SUCH A JERK!
YEA, BUT IT'S O.K.- SHE'LL RUN AWAY FROM HOME IN 10th GRADE AND HAVE TO GO TO A SPECIAL SCHOOL FOR 2 YEARS!
WOW! THEN THAT SPELL ME 'N' ELLEN CAST WORKED!
I NEVER THOUGHT ABOUT THAT...
WELL, GUESS WHAT? IT WAS MY BIRTHDAY YESTERDAY! I'M 26!
OMIGOD!! THAT'S OLD!!

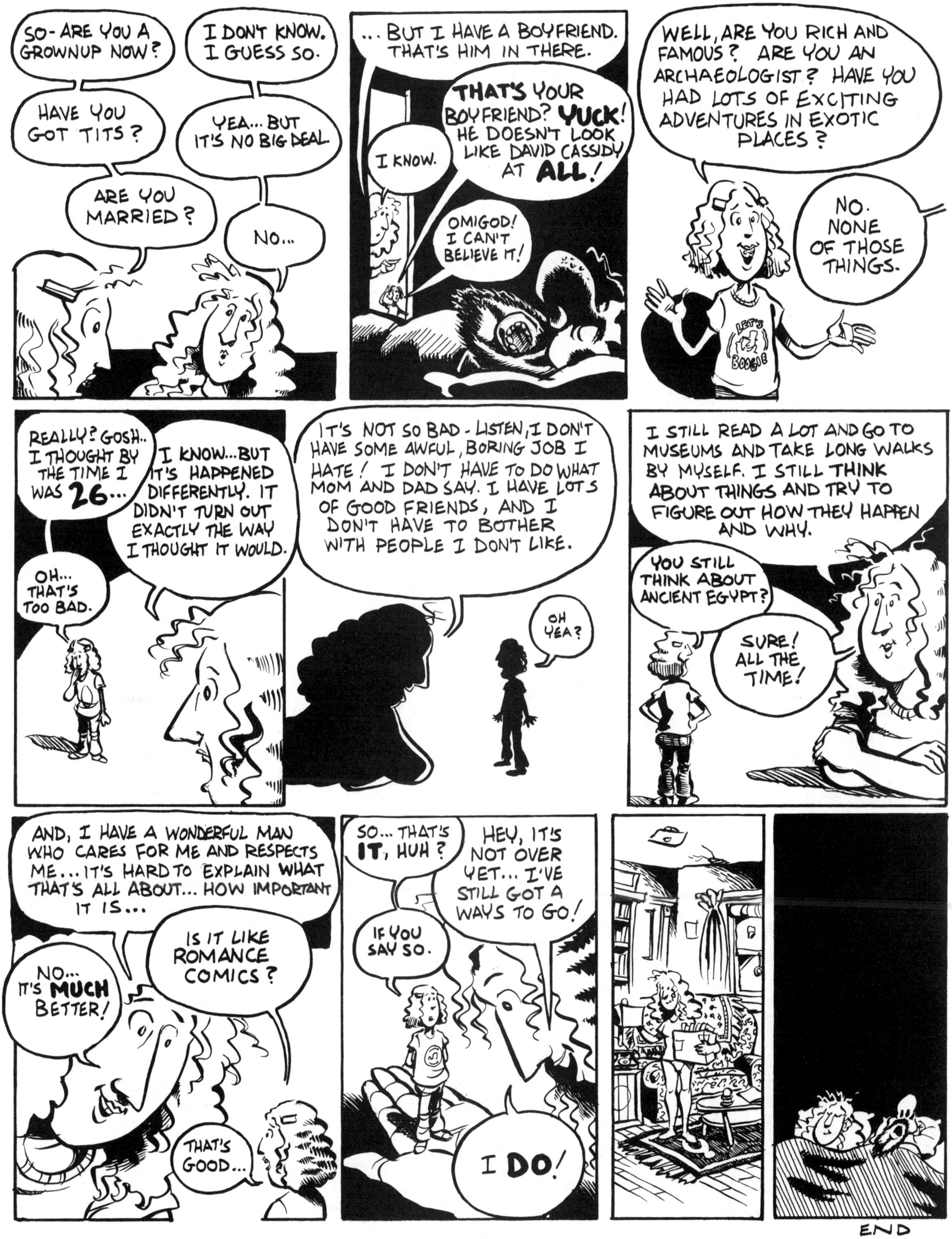
SO- ARE YOU A GROWNUP NOW?
I DON'T KNOW. I GUESS SO.
HAVE YOU GOT TITS?
YEA... BUT IT'S NO BIG DEAL.
ARE YOU MARRIED?
NO...
... BUT I HAVE A BOYFRIEND. THAT'S HIM IN THERE.
THAT'S YOUR BOYFRIEND? YUCK! HE DOESN'T LOOK LIKE DAVID CASSIDY AT ALL!
I KNOW.
OMIGOD! I CAN'T BELIEVE IT!
WELL, ARE YOU RICH AND FAMOUS? ARE YOU AN ARCHAEOLOGIST? HAVE YOU HAD LOTS OF EXCITING ADVENTURES IN EXOTIC PLACES?
NO. NONE OF THOSE THINGS.
LET'S BOOGIE
REALLY? GOSH.. I THOUGHT BY THE TIME I WAS 26...
I KNOW...BUT IT'S HAPPENED DIFFERENTLY. IT DIDN'T TURN OUT EXACTLY THE WAY I THOUGHT IT WOULD.
OH... THAT'S TOO BAD.
IT'S NOT SO BAD - LISTEN, I DON'T HAVE SOME AWFUL, BORING JOB I HATE! I DON'T HAVE TO DO WHAT MOM AND DAD SAY. I HAVE LOTS OF GOOD FRIENDS, AND I DON'T HAVE TO BOTHER WITH PEOPLE I DON'T LIKE.
OH YEA?
I STILL READ A LOT AND GO TO MUSEUMS AND TAKE LONG WALKS BY MYSELF. I STILL THINK ABOUT THINGS AND TRY TO FIGURE OUT HOW THEY HAPPEN AND WHY.
YOU STILL THINK ABOUT ANCIENT EGYPT?
SURE! ALL THE TIME!
AND, I HAVE A WONDERFUL MAN WHO CARES FOR ME AND RESPECTS ME... IT'S HARD TO EXPLAIN WHAT THAT'S ALL ABOUT... HOW IMPORTANT IT IS...
IS IT LIKE ROMANCE COMICS?
NO... IT'S MUCH BETTER!
THAT'S GOOD...
SO... THAT'S IT, HUH?
HEY, IT'S NOT OVER YET... I'VE STILL GOT A WAYS TO GO!
IF YOU SAY SO.
I DO!
END

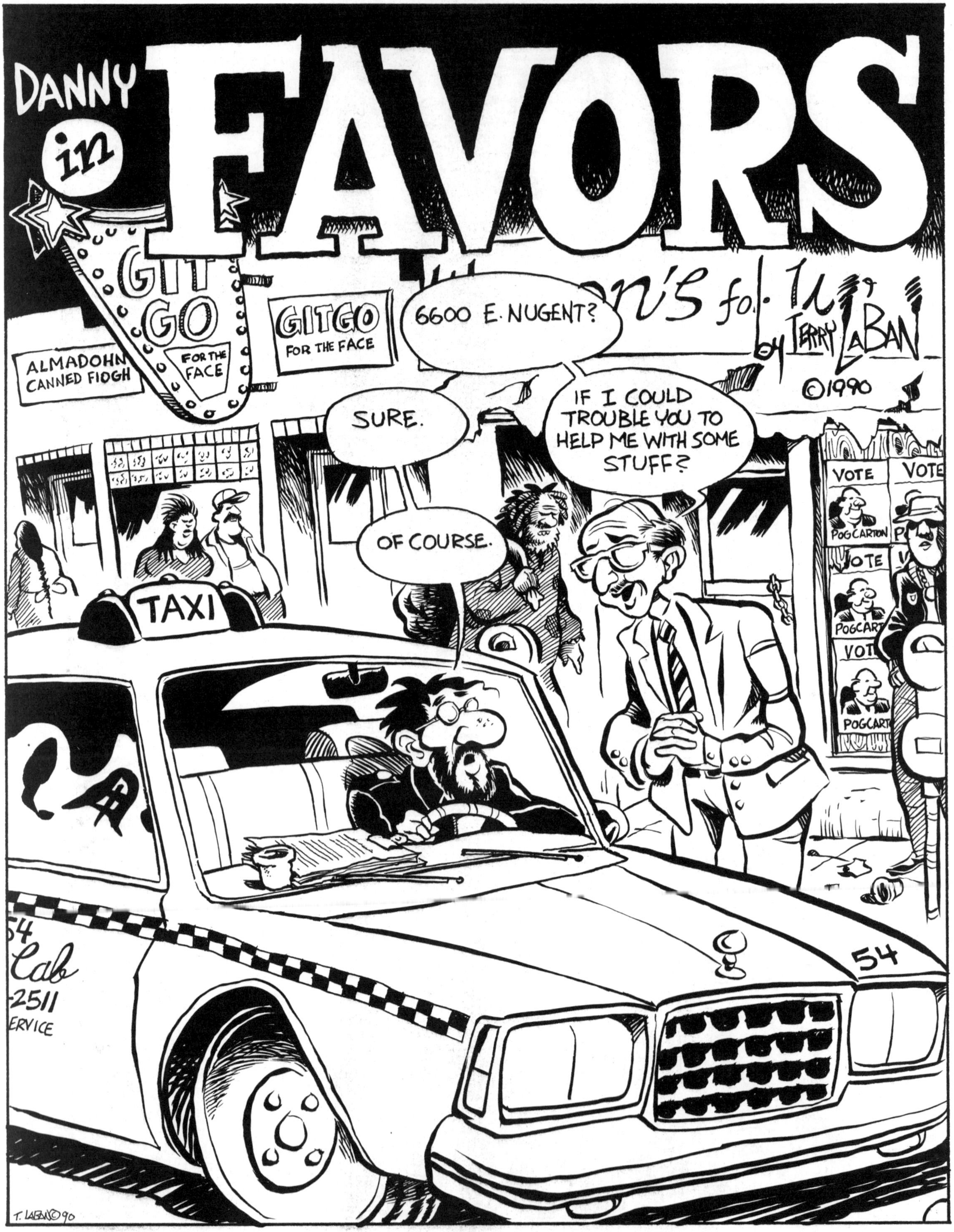
DANNY in FAVORS
by TERRY LABAN
©1990
GIT GO FOR THE FACE
GITGO FOR THE FACE
ALMADOHN CANNED FIOGH
6600 E. NUGENT?
SURE.
IF I COULD TROUBLE YOU TO HELP ME WITH SOME STUFF?
OF COURSE.
VOTE POGCARTON
TAXI
54
T. LABAN©90

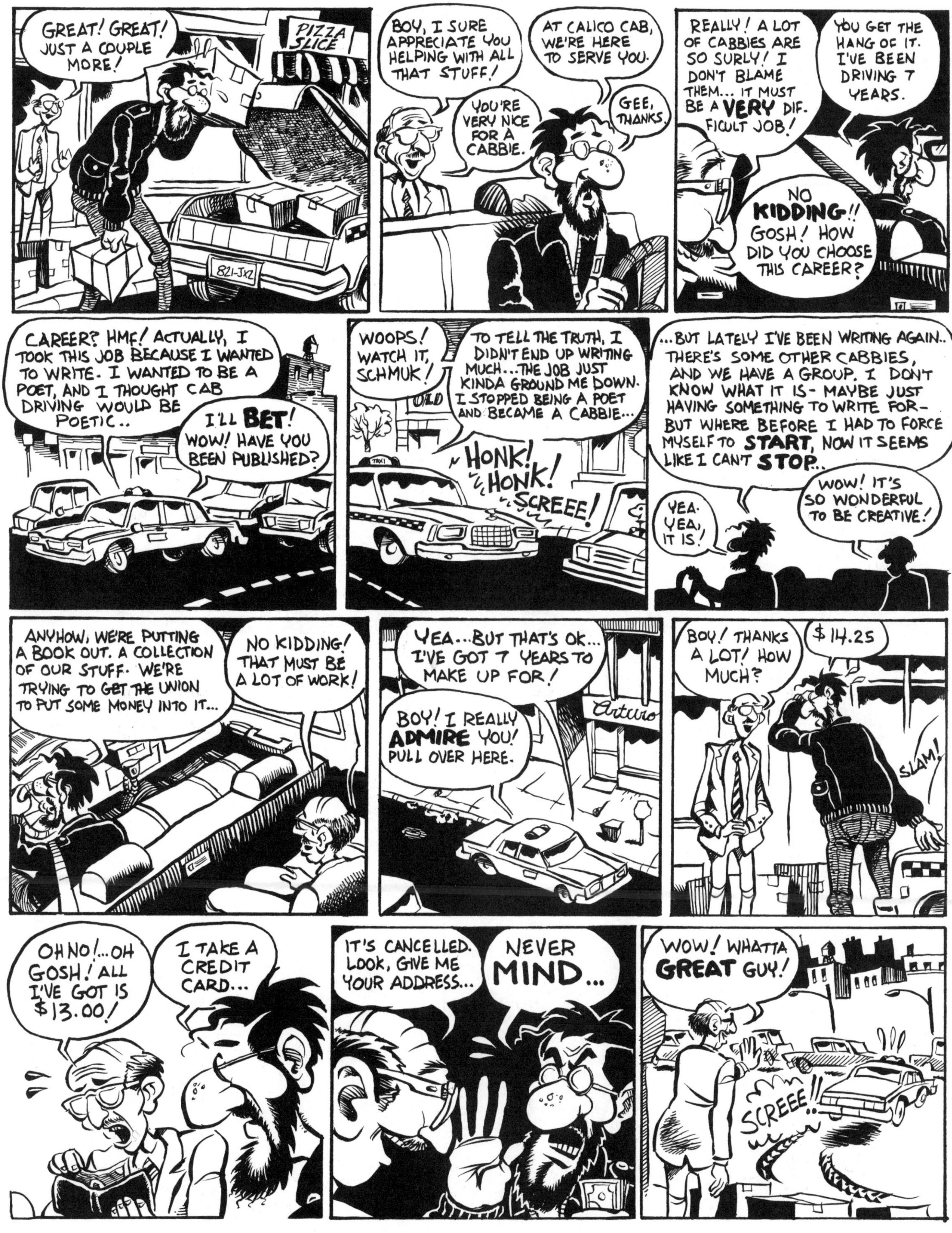
GREAT! GREAT! JUST A COUPLE MORE!
PIZZA SLICE
821-JXZ
BOY, I SURE APPRECIATE YOU HELPING WITH ALL THAT STUFF!
AT CALICO CAB, WE'RE HERE TO SERVE YOU.
YOU'RE VERY NICE FOR A CABBIE.
GEE, THANKS.
REALLY! A LOT OF CABBIES ARE SO SURLY! I DON'T BLAME THEM... IT MUST BE A VERY DIFFICULT JOB!
YOU GET THE HANG OF IT. I'VE BEEN DRIVING 7 YEARS.
NO KIDDING!! GOSH! HOW DID YOU CHOOSE THIS CAREER?
CAREER? HMF! ACTUALLY, I TOOK THIS JOB BECAUSE I WANTED TO WRITE. I WANTED TO BE A POET, AND I THOUGHT CAB DRIVING WOULD BE POETIC..
I'LL BET! WOW! HAVE YOU BEEN PUBLISHED?
WOOPS! WATCH IT, SCHMUK!
TO TELL THE TRUTH, I DIDN'T END UP WRITING MUCH... THE JOB JUST KINDA GROUND ME DOWN. I STOPPED BEING A POET AND BECAME A CABBIE...
HONK! HONK! SCREEE!
...BUT LATELY I'VE BEEN WRITING AGAIN.. THERE'S SOME OTHER CABBIES, AND WE HAVE A GROUP. I DON'T KNOW WHAT IT IS - MAYBE JUST HAVING SOMETHING TO WRITE FOR - BUT WHERE BEFORE I HAD TO FORCE MYSELF TO START, NOW IT SEEMS LIKE I CAN'T STOP..
YEA. YEA, IT IS!
WOW! IT'S SO WONDERFUL TO BE CREATIVE!
ANYHOW, WE'RE PUTTING A BOOK OUT. A COLLECTION OF OUR STUFF. WE'RE TRYING TO GET THE UNION TO PUT SOME MONEY INTO IT...
NO KIDDING! THAT MUST BE A LOT OF WORK!
YEA...BUT THAT'S OK... I'VE GOT 7 YEARS TO MAKE UP FOR!
BOY! I REALLY ADMIRE YOU! PULL OVER HERE.
Arturo
BOY! THANKS A LOT! HOW MUCH?
$14.25
SLAM!
OH NO!...OH GOSH! ALL I'VE GOT IS $13.00!
I TAKE A CREDIT CARD...
IT'S CANCELLED. LOOK, GIVE ME YOUR ADDRESS...
NEVER MIND...
WOW! WHATTA GREAT GUY!
SCREEE!!

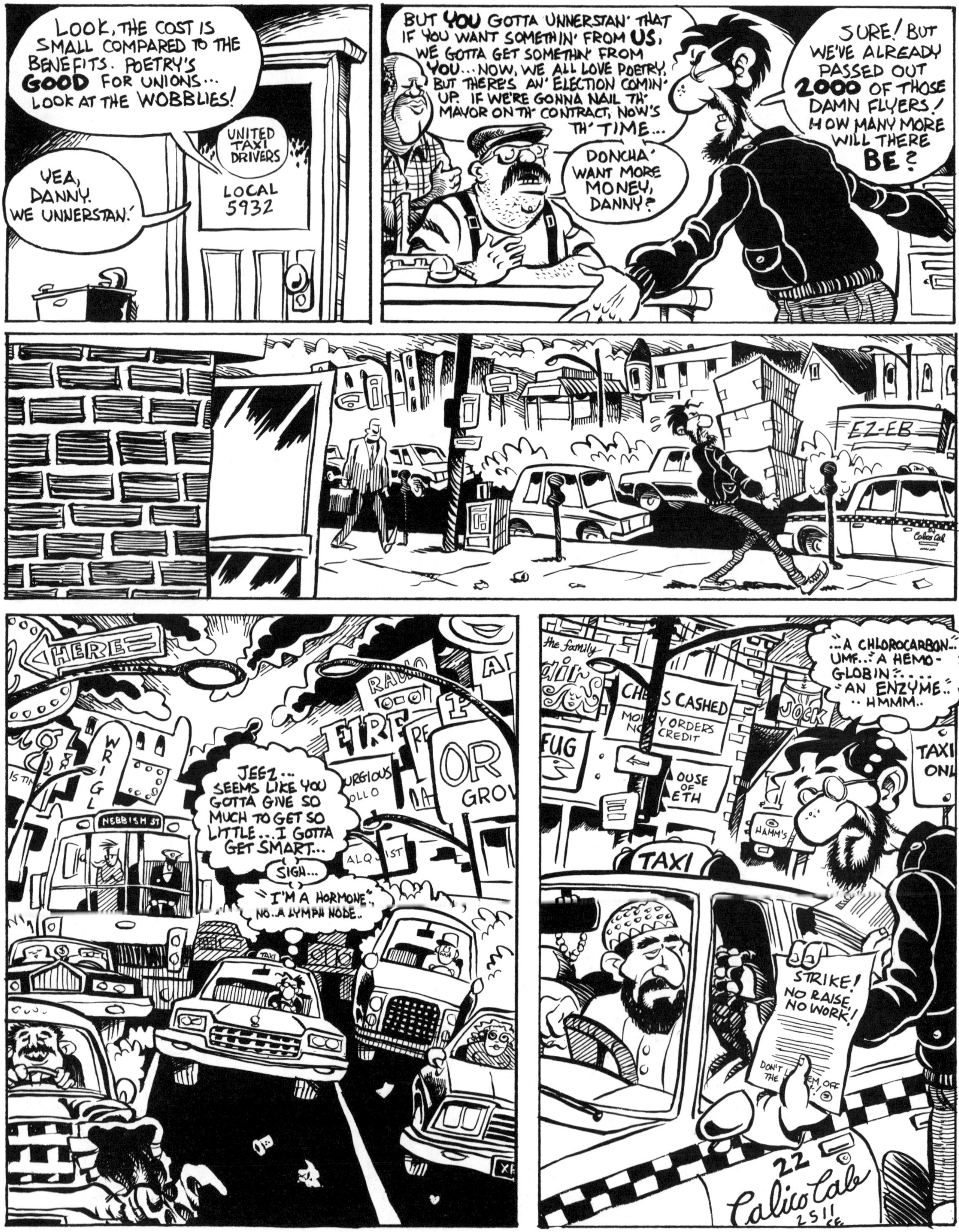
LOOK, THE COST IS SMALL COMPARED TO THE BENEFITS. POETRY'S GOOD FOR UNIONS... LOOK AT THE WOBBLIES!
YEA, DANNY. WE UNNERSTAN'
UNITED TAXI DRIVERS
LOCAL 5932
BUT YOU GOTTA UNNERSTAN' THAT IF YOU WANT SOMETHIN' FROM US, WE GOTTA GET SOMETHIN' FROM YOU... NOW, WE ALL LOVE POETRY, BUT THERE'S AN' ELECTION COMIN' UP. IF WE'RE GONNA NAIL TH' MAYOR ON TH' CONTRACT, NOW'S TH' TIME...
DONCHA' WANT MORE MONEY, DANNY?
SURE! BUT WE'VE ALREADY PASSED OUT 2000 OF THOSE DAMN FLYERS! HOW MANY MORE WILL THERE BE?
EZ-EB
JEEZ... SEEMS LIKE YOU GOTTA GIVE SO MUCH TO GET SO LITTLE... I GOTTA GET SMART...
SIGH...
I'M A HORMONE... NO.. A LYMPH NODE..
NEBBISH ST
HERE
...A CHLOROCARBON... UMF... A HEMO-GLOBIN... AN ENZYME... HMMM..
CHECKS CASHED
TAXI
STRIKE! NO RAISE, NO WORK!
22
Calico Cab

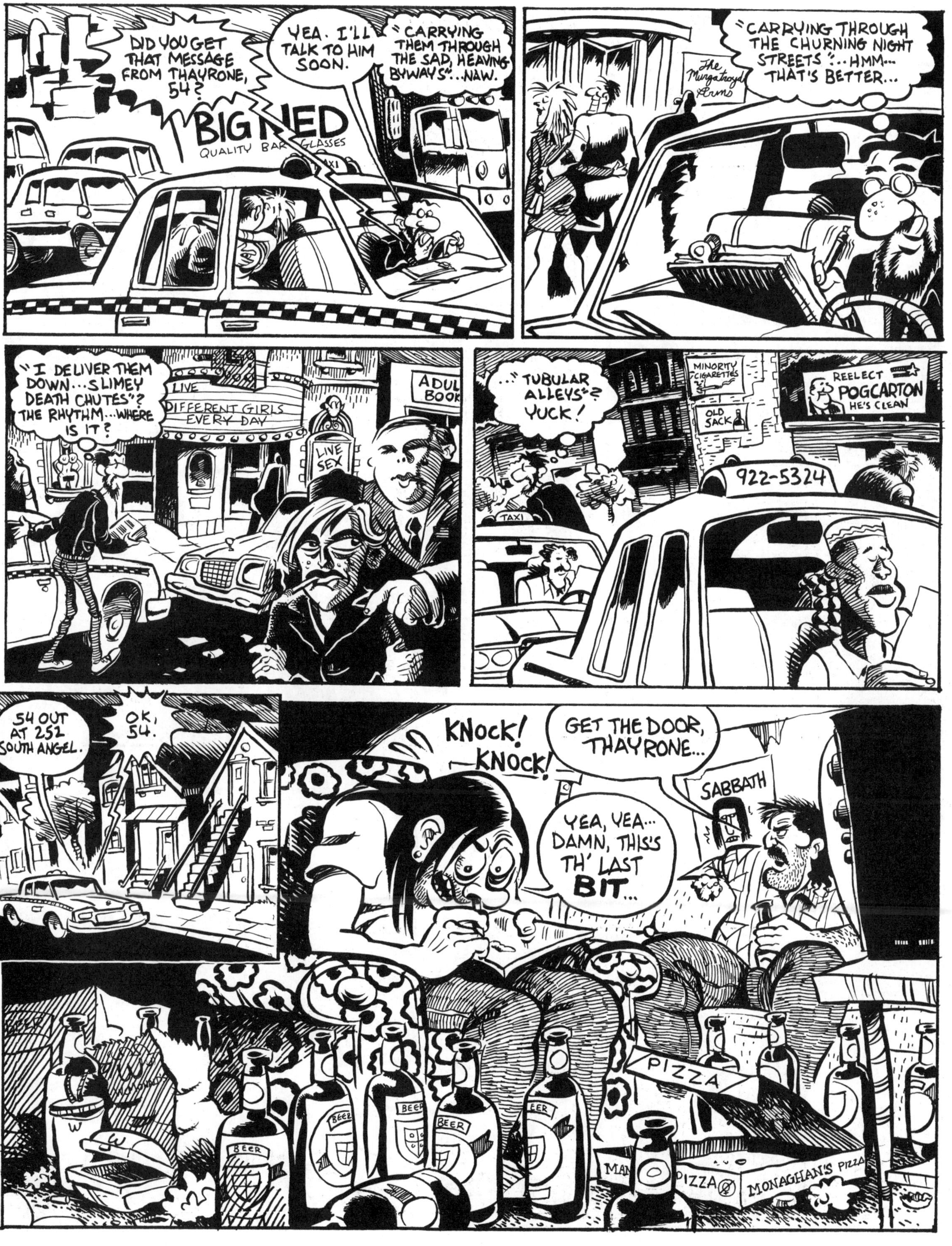
DID YOU GET THAT MESSAGE FROM THAYRONE, 54?
YEA. I'LL TALK TO HIM SOON.
"CARRYING THEM THROUGH THE SAD, HEAVING BYWAYS"...NAW.
QUALITY BAR GLASSES
TAXI
"CARRYING THROUGH THE CHURNING NIGHT STREETS"...HMM... THAT'S BETTER...
The Murgatroyd Arms
"I DELIVER THEM DOWN...SLIMEY DEATH CHUTES"? THE RHYTHM...WHERE IS IT?
LIVE
DIFFERENT GIRLS EVERY DAY
ADUL BOOK
LIVE SEX
..."TUBULAR ALLEYS"? YUCK!
MINORITY CIGARETTES
OLD SACK
REELECT POGCARTON HE'S CLEAN
922-5324
TAXI
54 OUT AT 252 SOUTH ANGEL.
OK, 54.
KNOCK! KNOCK!
GET THE DOOR, THAYRONE...
SABBATH
YEA, YEA... DAMN, THIS'S TH' LAST BIT...
PIZZA
BEER
MONAGHAN'S PIZZA

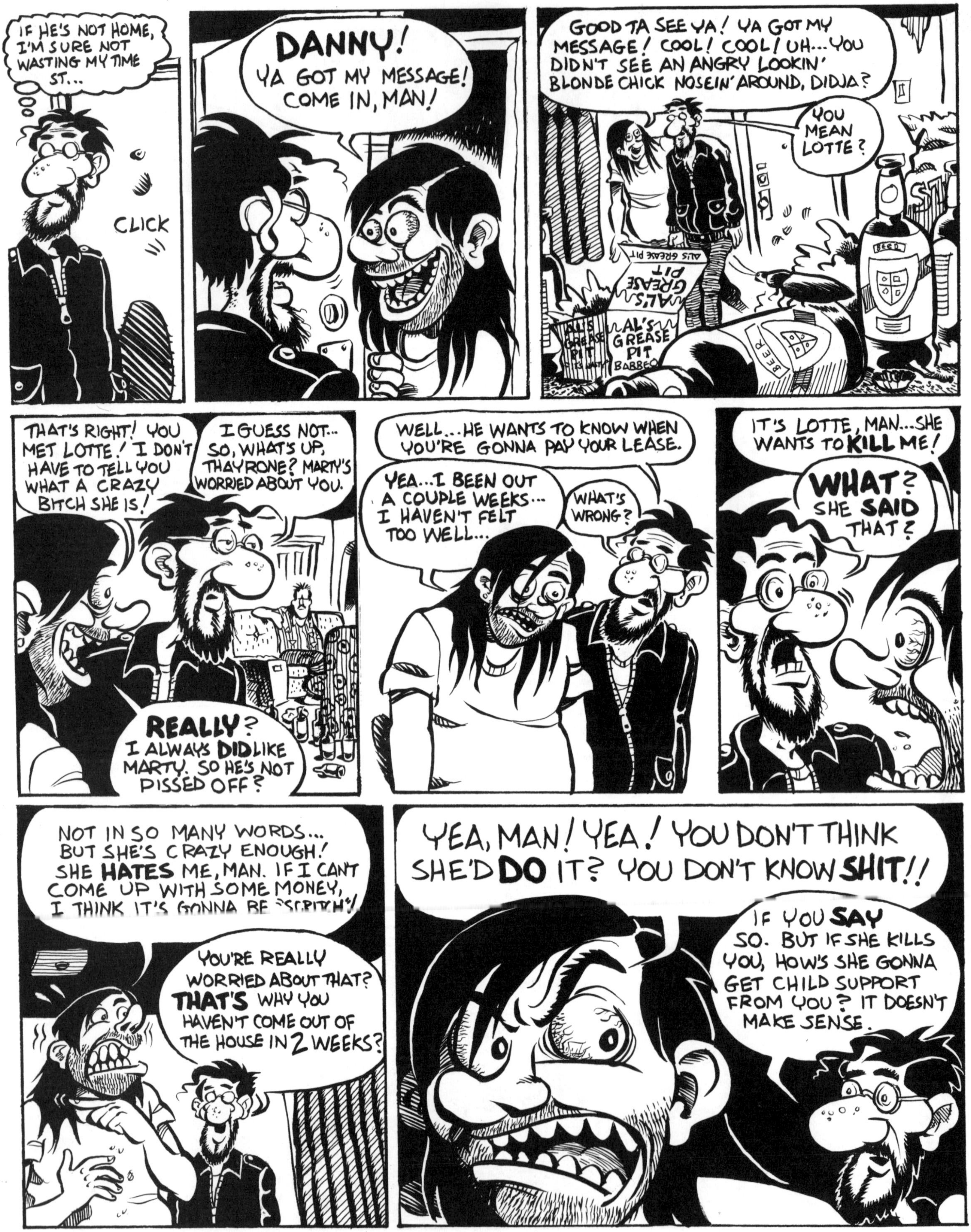
IF HE'S NOT HOME, I'M SURE NOT WASTING MY TIME ST...
CLICK
DANNY! YA GOT MY MESSAGE! COME IN, MAN!
GOOD TA SEE YA! YA GOT MY MESSAGE! COOL! COOL! UH... YOU DIDN'T SEE AN ANGRY LOOKIN' BLONDE CHICK NOSEIN' AROUND, DIDJA?
YOU MEAN LOTTE?
AL'S GREASE PIT
BEER
THAT'S RIGHT! YOU MET LOTTE! I DON'T HAVE TO TELL YOU WHAT A CRAZY BITCH SHE IS!
I GUESS NOT... SO, WHAT'S UP, THAYRONE? MARTY'S WORRIED ABOUT YOU.
REALLY? I ALWAYS DID LIKE MARTY. SO HE'S NOT PISSED OFF?
WELL... HE WANTS TO KNOW WHEN YOU'RE GONNA PAY YOUR LEASE.
YEA... I BEEN OUT A COUPLE WEEKS... I HAVEN'T FELT TOO WELL...
WHAT'S WRONG?
IT'S LOTTE, MAN... SHE WANTS TO KILL ME!
WHAT? SHE SAID THAT?
NOT IN SO MANY WORDS... BUT SHE'S CRAZY ENOUGH! SHE HATES ME, MAN. IF I CAN'T COME UP WITH SOME MONEY, I THINK IT'S GONNA BE "SCRITCH"!
YOU'RE REALLY WORRIED ABOUT THAT? THAT'S WHY YOU HAVEN'T COME OUT OF THE HOUSE IN 2 WEEKS?
YEA, MAN! YEA! YOU DON'T THINK SHE'D DO IT? YOU DON'T KNOW SHIT!!
IF YOU SAY SO. BUT IF SHE KILLS YOU, HOW'S SHE GONNA GET CHILD SUPPORT FROM YOU? IT DOESN'T MAKE SENSE.

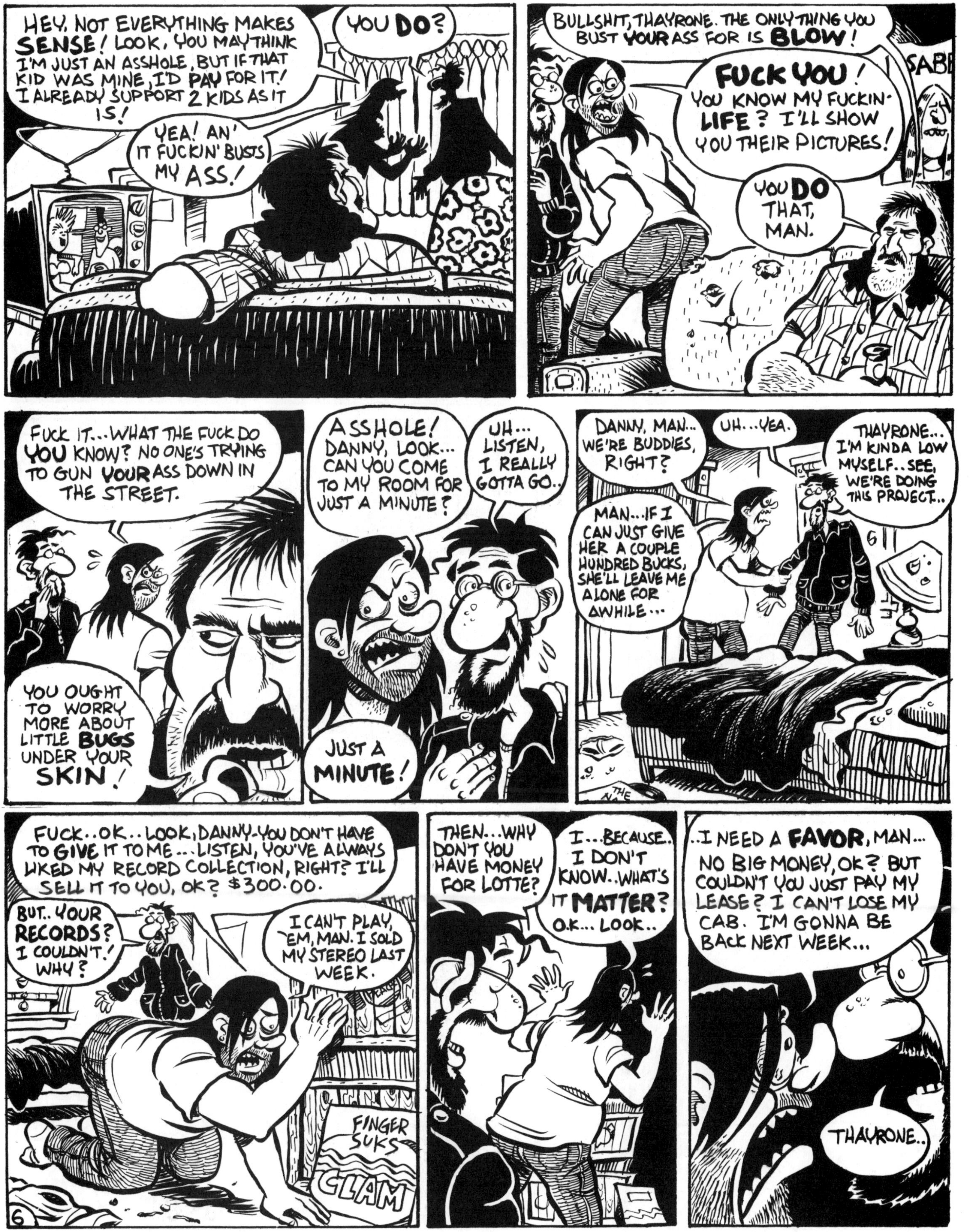
HEY, NOT EVERYTHING MAKES SENSE! LOOK, YOU MAY THINK I'M JUST AN ASSHOLE, BUT IF THAT KID WAS MINE, I'D PAY FOR IT! I ALREADY SUPPORT 2 KIDS AS IT IS!
YOU DO?
YEA! AN' IT FUCKIN' BUSTS MY ASS!
BULLSHIT, THAYRONE. THE ONLY THING YOU BUST YOUR ASS FOR IS BLOW!
FUCK YOU! YOU KNOW MY FUCKIN' LIFE? I'LL SHOW YOU THEIR PICTURES!
YOU DO THAT, MAN.
FUCK IT... WHAT THE FUCK DO YOU KNOW? NO ONE'S TRYING TO GUN YOUR ASS DOWN IN THE STREET.
YOU OUGHT TO WORRY MORE ABOUT LITTLE BUGS UNDER YOUR SKIN!
ASSHOLE! DANNY, LOOK... CAN YOU COME TO MY ROOM FOR JUST A MINUTE?
UH... LISTEN, I REALLY GOTTA GO..
JUST A MINUTE!
DANNY, MAN... WE'RE BUDDIES, RIGHT?
UH... YEA.
THAYRONE... I'M KINDA LOW MYSELF.. SEE, WE'RE DOING THIS PROJECT...
MAN... IF I CAN JUST GIVE HER A COUPLE HUNDRED BUCKS, SHE'LL LEAVE ME ALONE FOR AWHILE...
FUCK.. OK.. LOOK, DANNY-YOU DON'T HAVE TO GIVE IT TO ME... LISTEN, YOU'VE ALWAYS LIKED MY RECORD COLLECTION, RIGHT? I'LL SELL IT TO YOU, OK? $300.00.
BUT.. YOUR RECORDS? I COULDN'T! WHY?
I CAN'T PLAY 'EM, MAN. I SOLD MY STEREO LAST WEEK.
FINGER SUKS
CLAM
6
THEN... WHY DON'T YOU HAVE MONEY FOR LOTTE?
I... BECAUSE.. I DON'T KNOW.. WHAT'S IT MATTER? O.K... LOOK..
..I NEED A FAVOR, MAN... NO BIG MONEY, OK? BUT COULDN'T YOU JUST PAY MY LEASE? I CAN'T LOSE MY CAB. I'M GONNA BE BACK NEXT WEEK...
THAYRONE..

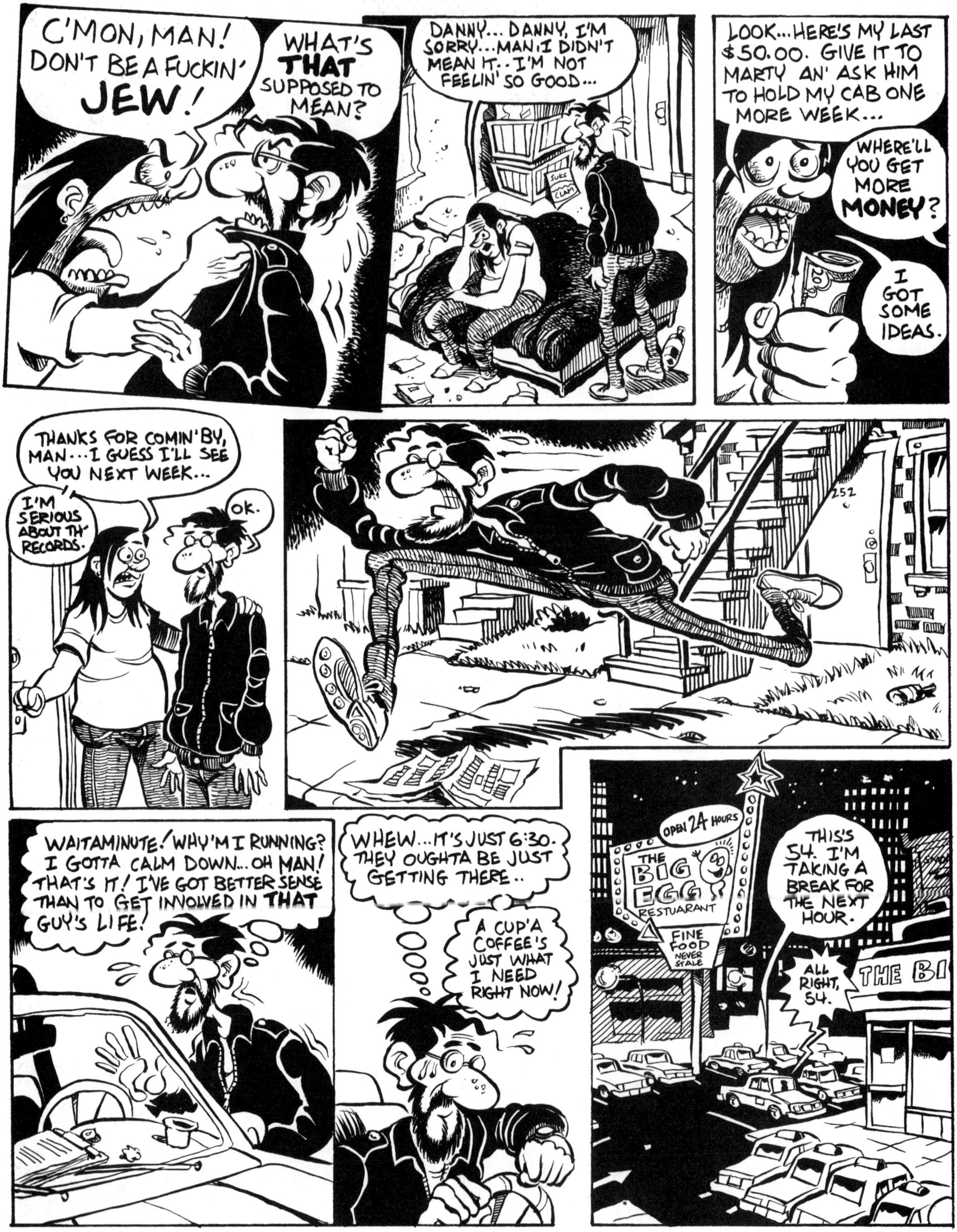

C'MON, MAN! DON'T BE A FUCKIN' JEW!
WHAT'S THAT SUPPOSED TO MEAN?
DANNY... DANNY, I'M SORRY... MAN, I DIDN'T MEAN IT.. I'M NOT FEELIN' SO GOOD...
LOOK... HERE'S MY LAST $50.00. GIVE IT TO MARTY AN' ASK HIM TO HOLD MY CAB ONE MORE WEEK...
WHERE'LL YOU GET MORE MONEY?
I GOT SOME IDEAS.
THANKS FOR COMIN' BY, MAN... I GUESS I'LL SEE YOU NEXT WEEK...
I'M SERIOUS ABOUT TH' RECORDS.
OK.
252
WAITAMINUTE! WHY'M I RUNNING? I GOTTA CALM DOWN... OH MAN! THAT'S IT! I'VE GOT BETTER SENSE THAN TO GET INVOLVED IN THAT GUY'S LIFE!
WHEW... IT'S JUST 6:30. THEY OUGHTA BE JUST GETTING THERE..
A CUP'A COFFEE'S JUST WHAT I NEED RIGHT NOW!
OPEN 24 HOURS
THE BIG EGG RESTAURANT
FINE FOOD NEVER STALE
THIS'S 54. I'M TAKING A BREAK FOR THE NEXT HOUR.
ALL RIGHT, 54.
THE BI

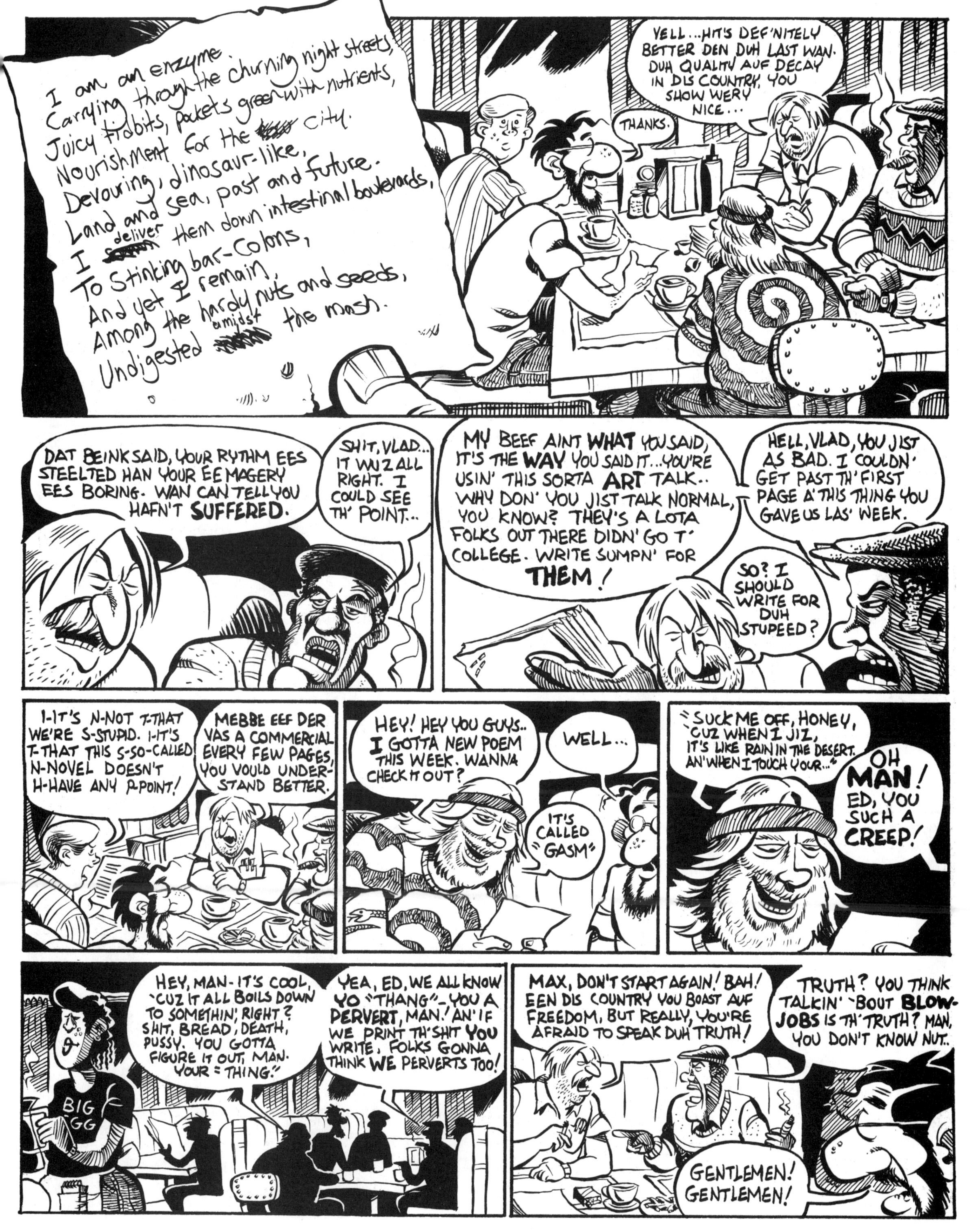
I am an enzyme.
Carrying through the churning night streets,
Juicy tidbits, pockets green with nutrients,
Nourishment for the city.
Devouring, dinosaur-like,
Land and sea, past and future.
I deliver them down intestinal boulevards,
To Stinking bar-colons,
And yet I remain,
Among the hardy nuts and seeds,
Undigested amidst the mash.
THANKS.
YELL...HIT'S DEF'NITELY BETTER DEN DUH LAST WAN. DUH QUALITY AUF DECAY IN DIS COUNTRY, YOU SHOW WERY NICE...
DAT BEINK SAID, YOUR RYTHM EES STEELTED HAN YOUR EE MAGERY EES BORING. WAN CAN TELL YOU HAFN'T SUFFERED.
SHIT, VLAD... IT WUZ ALL RIGHT. I COULD SEE TH' POINT...
MY BEEF AINT WHAT YOU SAID, IT'S THE WAY YOU SAID IT...YOU'RE USIN' THIS SORTA ART TALK.. WHY DON' YOU JIST TALK NORMAL, YOU KNOW? THEY'S A LOTA FOLKS OUT THERE DIDN' GO T' COLLEGE. WRITE SUMPN' FOR THEM!
HELL, VLAD, YOU JIST AS BAD. I COULDN' GET PAST TH' FIRST PAGE A' THIS THING YOU GAVE US LAS' WEEK.
SO? I SHOULD WRITE FOR DUH STUPEED?
I-IT'S N-NOT T-THAT WE'RE S-STUPID. I-IT'S T-THAT THIS S-SO-CALLED N-NOVEL DOESN'T H-HAVE ANY P-POINT!
MEBBE EEF DER VAS A COMMERCIAL EVERY FEW PAGES, YOU VOULD UNDERSTAND BETTER.
HEY! HEY YOU GUYS.. I GOTTA NEW POEM THIS WEEK. WANNA CHECK IT OUT?
WELL...
IT'S CALLED "GASM"
"SUCK ME OFF, HONEY, 'CUZ WHEN I JIZ, IT'S LIKE RAIN IN THE DESERT. AN' WHEN I TOUCH YOUR..."
OH MAN! ED, YOU SUCH A CREEP!
HEY, MAN-IT'S COOL, 'CUZ IT ALL BOILS DOWN TO SOMETHIN', RIGHT? SHIT, BREAD, DEATH, PUSSY. YOU GOTTA FIGURE IT OUT, MAN. YOUR "THING."
YEA, ED, WE ALL KNOW YO "THANG"-YOU A PERVERT, MAN! AN' IF WE PRINT TH' SHIT YOU WRITE, FOLKS GONNA THINK WE PERVERTS TOO!
BIG GG
MAX, DON'T START AGAIN! BAH! EEN DIS COUNTRY YOU BOAST AUF FREEDOM, BUT REALLY, YOU'RE AFRAID TO SPEAK DUH TRUTH!
TRUTH? YOU THINK TALKIN' 'BOUT BLOW-JOBS IS TH' TRUTH? MAN, YOU DON'T KNOW NUT..
GENTLEMEN! GENTLEMEN!

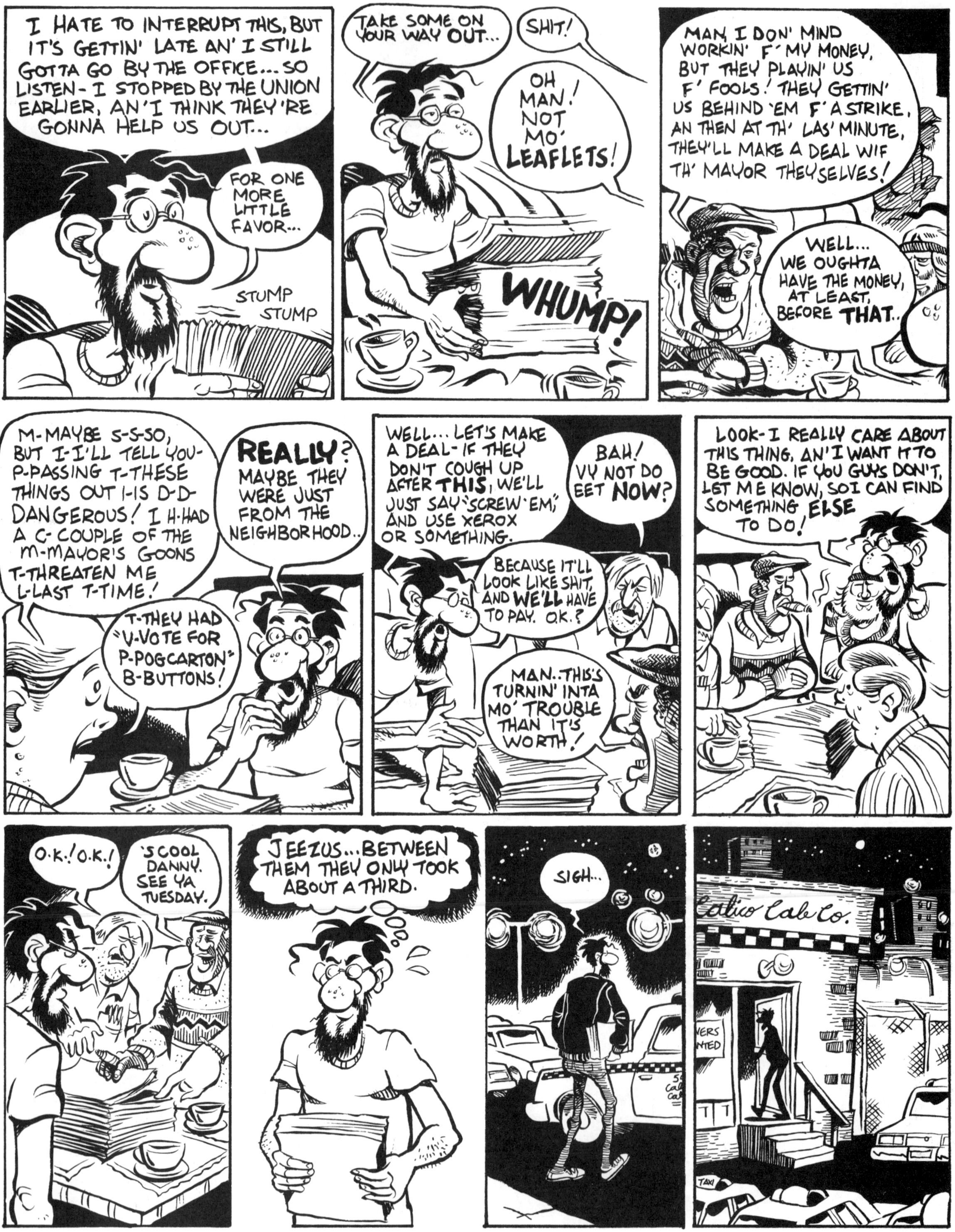
I HATE TO INTERRUPT THIS, BUT IT'S GETTIN' LATE AN' I STILL GOTTA GO BY THE OFFICE... SO LISTEN- I STOPPED BY THE UNION EARLIER, AN' I THINK THEY'RE GONNA HELP US OUT...
FOR ONE MORE LITTLE FAVOR...
STUMP STUMP
TAKE SOME ON YOUR WAY OUT...
SHIT!
OH MAN! NOT MO' LEAFLETS!
WHUMP!
MAN, I DON' MIND WORKIN' F' MY MONEY, BUT THEY PLAYIN' US F' FOOLS! THEY GETTIN' US BEHIND 'EM F' A STRIKE, AN THEN AT TH' LAS' MINUTE, THEY'LL MAKE A DEAL WIF TH' MAYOR THEYSELVES!
WELL... WE OUGHTA HAVE THE MONEY, AT LEAST, BEFORE THAT...
M-MAYBE S-S-SO, BUT I-I'LL TELL YOU- P-PASSING T-THESE THINGS OUT I-IS D-D-DANGEROUS! I H-HAD A C-COUPLE OF THE M-MAYOR'S GOONS T-THREATEN ME L-LAST T-TIME!
REALLY? MAYBE THEY WERE JUST FROM THE NEIGHBORHOOD..
T-THEY HAD "V-VOTE FOR P-POGCARTON" B-BUTTONS!
WELL... LET'S MAKE A DEAL- IF THEY DON'T COUGH UP AFTER THIS, WE'LL JUST SAY "SCREW 'EM," AND USE XEROX OR SOMETHING.
BAH! VY NOT DO EET NOW?
BECAUSE IT'LL LOOK LIKE SHIT, AND WE'LL HAVE TO PAY. O.K.?
MAN.. THIS'S TURNIN' INTA MO' TROUBLE THAN IT'S WORTH!
LOOK- I REALLY CARE ABOUT THIS THING, AN' I WANT IT TO BE GOOD. IF YOU GUYS DON'T, LET ME KNOW, SO I CAN FIND SOMETHING ELSE TO DO!
O.K.! O.K.!
'S COOL DANNY. SEE YA TUESDAY.
JEEZUS... BETWEEN THEM THEY ONLY TOOK ABOUT A THIRD.
SIGH...
Calico Cab Co.
TAXI

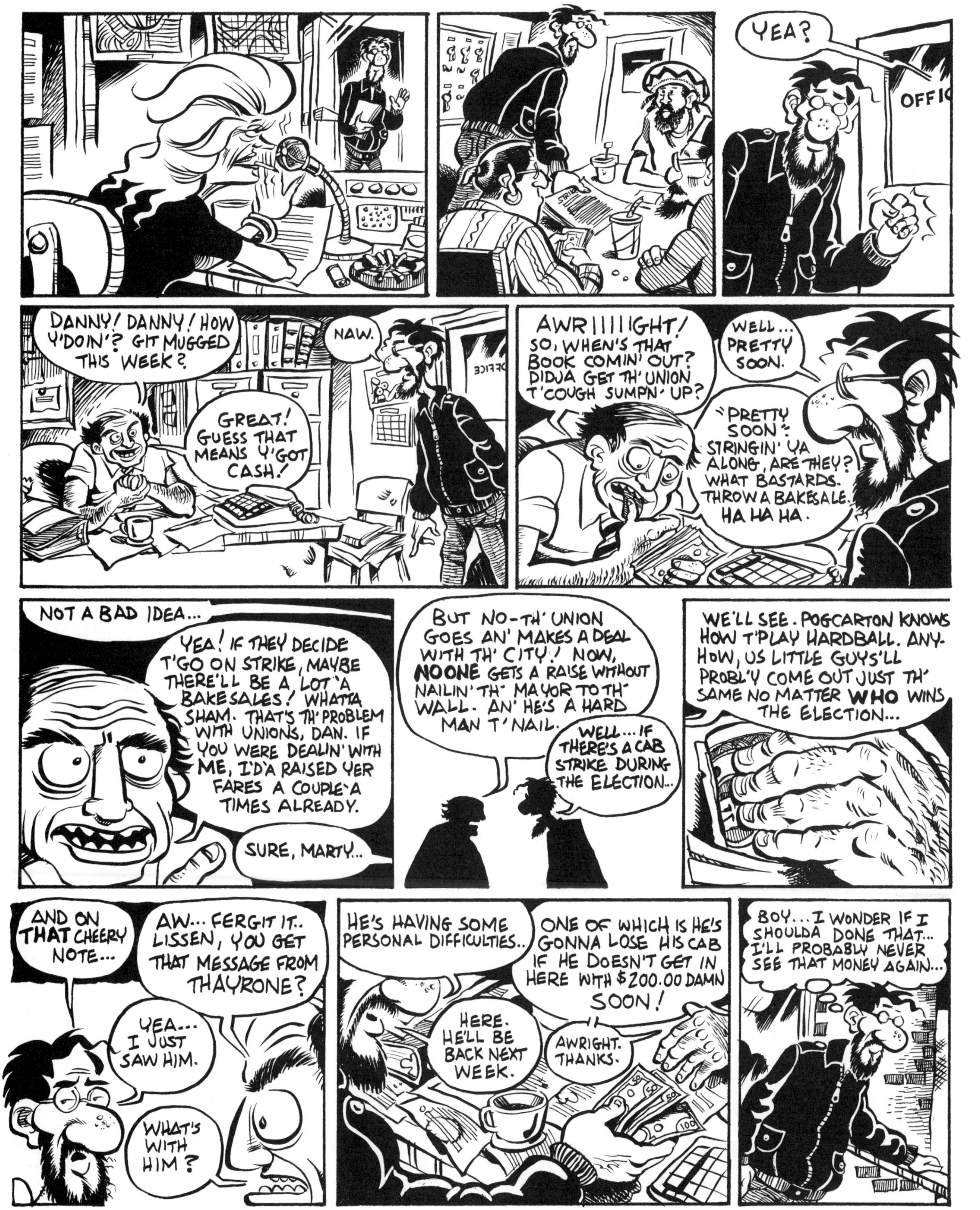
YEA?
OFFIC
DANNY! DANNY! HOW Y'DOIN'? GIT MUGGED THIS WEEK?
NAW.
GREAT! GUESS THAT MEANS Y'GOT CASH!
OFFICE
AWRIIIIIGHT! SO, WHEN'S THAT BOOK COMIN' OUT? DIDJA GET TH' UNION T'COUGH SUMP'N' UP?
WELL... PRETTY SOON.
"PRETTY SOON". STRINGIN' YA ALONG, ARE THEY? WHAT BASTARDS. THROW A BAKESALE. HA HA HA.
NOT A BAD IDEA...
YEA! IF THEY DECIDE T'GO ON STRIKE, MAYBE THERE'LL BE A LOT'A BAKESALES! WHATTA SHAM. THAT'S TH' PROBLEM WITH UNIONS, DAN. IF YOU WERE DEALIN' WITH ME, I'D'A RAISED YER FARES A COUPLE'A TIMES ALREADY.
SURE, MARTY...
BUT NO-TH' UNION GOES AN' MAKES A DEAL WITH TH' CITY! NOW, NO ONE GETS A RAISE WITHOUT NAILIN' TH' MAYOR TO TH' WALL. AN' HE'S A HARD MAN T'NAIL.
WELL... IF THERE'S A CAB STRIKE DURING THE ELECTION...
WE'LL SEE. POGCARTON KNOWS HOW T'PLAY HARDBALL. ANYHOW, US LITTLE GUYS'LL PROBL'Y COME OUT JUST TH' SAME NO MATTER WHO WINS THE ELECTION...
AND ON THAT CHEERY NOTE...
AW... FERGIT IT.. LISSEN, YOU GET THAT MESSAGE FROM THAYRONE?
YEA... I JUST SAW HIM.
WHAT'S WITH HIM?
HE'S HAVING SOME PERSONAL DIFFICULTIES..
ONE OF WHICH IS HE'S GONNA LOSE HIS CAB IF HE DOESN'T GET IN HERE WITH $200.00 DAMN SOON!
HERE. HE'LL BE BACK NEXT WEEK.
AWRIGHT. THANKS.
BOY... I WONDER IF I SHOULDA DONE THAT... I'LL PROBABLY NEVER SEE THAT MONEY AGAIN...

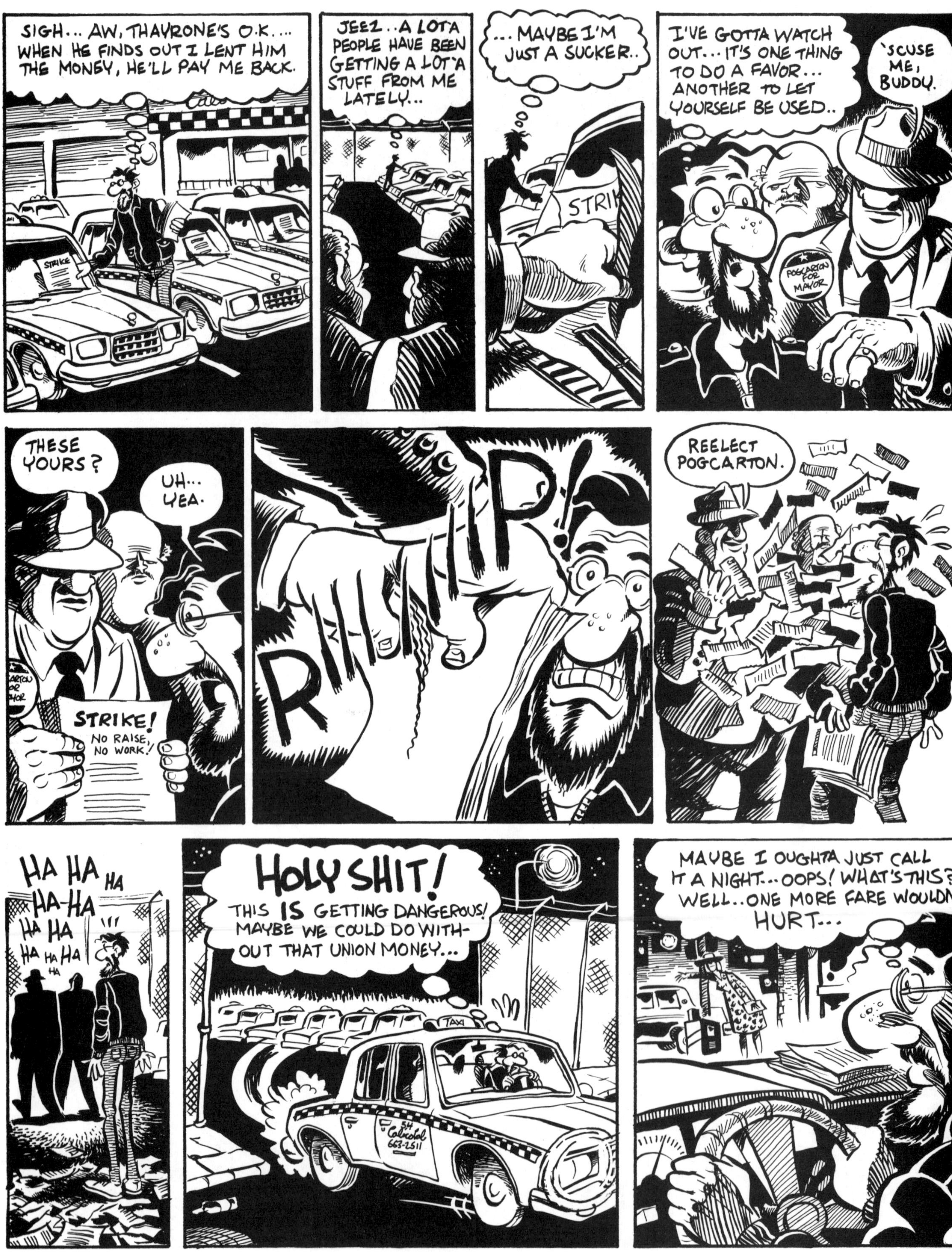
SIGH... AW, THAYRONE'S O.K.... WHEN HE FINDS OUT I LENT HIM THE MONEY, HE'LL PAY ME BACK.
STRIKE
JEEZ..A LOT'A PEOPLE HAVE BEEN GETTING A LOT'A STUFF FROM ME LATELY...
...MAYBE I'M JUST A SUCKER..
STRIK
I'VE GOTTA WATCH OUT... IT'S ONE THING TO DO A FAVOR... ANOTHER TO LET YOURSELF BE USED..
'SCUSE ME, BUDDY.
POGCARTON FOR MAYOR
THESE YOURS?
UH... YEA.
STRIKE! NO RAISE, NO WORK!
RIIIIIP!
REELECT POGCARTON.
HA HA HA HA-HA HA HA HA HA HA HA
HOLY SHIT! THIS IS GETTING DANGEROUS! MAYBE WE COULD DO WITHOUT THAT UNION MONEY...
TAXI
663-2511
MAYBE I OUGHTA JUST CALL IT A NIGHT... OOPS! WHAT'S THIS? WELL..ONE MORE FARE WOULDN'T HURT...

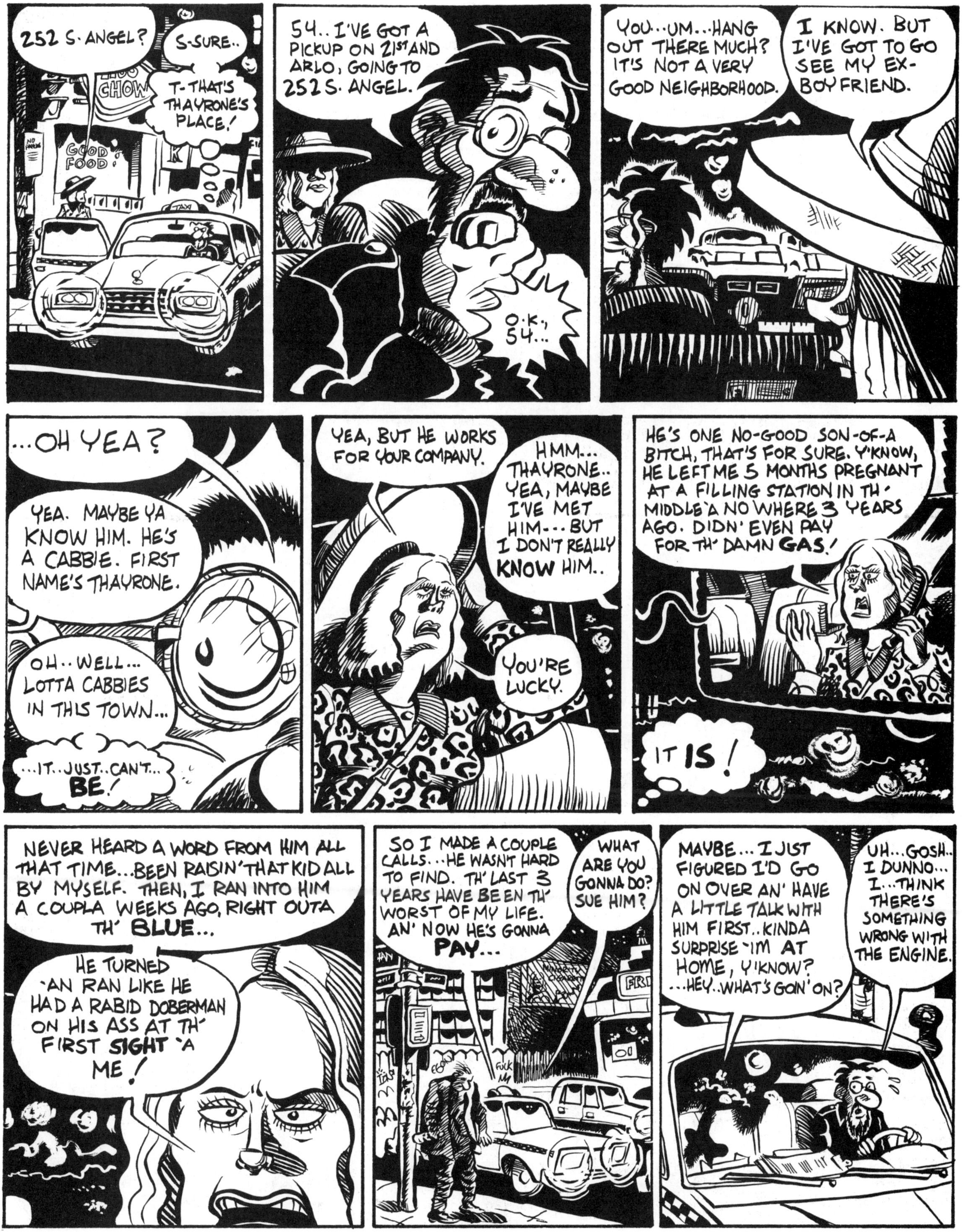
252 S. ANGEL?
S-SURE..
T-THAT'S THAYRONE'S PLACE!
GOOD FOOD
54.. I'VE GOT A PICKUP ON 21ST AND ARLO, GOING TO 252 S. ANGEL.
O.K., 54...
YOU...UM...HANG OUT THERE MUCH? IT'S NOT A VERY GOOD NEIGHBORHOOD.
I KNOW. BUT I'VE GOT TO GO SEE MY EX-BOYFRIEND.
...OH YEA?
YEA. MAYBE YA KNOW HIM. HE'S A CABBIE. FIRST NAME'S THAYRONE.
OH.. WELL... LOTTA CABBIES IN THIS TOWN...
...IT.. JUST.. CAN'T... BE!
YEA, BUT HE WORKS FOR YOUR COMPANY.
HMM... THAYRONE.. YEA, MAYBE I'VE MET HIM--- BUT I DON'T REALLY KNOW HIM..
YOU'RE LUCKY.
HE'S ONE NO-GOOD SON-OF-A BITCH, THAT'S FOR SURE. Y'KNOW, HE LEFT ME 5 MONTHS PREGNANT AT A FILLING STATION IN TH' MIDDLE 'A NO WHERE 3 YEARS AGO. DIDN' EVEN PAY FOR TH' DAMN GAS!
IT IS!
NEVER HEARD A WORD FROM HIM ALL THAT TIME... BEEN RAISIN' THAT KID ALL BY MYSELF. THEN, I RAN INTO HIM A COUPLA WEEKS AGO, RIGHT OUTA TH' BLUE...
HE TURNED 'AN RAN LIKE HE HAD A RABID DOBERMAN ON HIS ASS AT TH' FIRST SIGHT 'A ME!
SO I MADE A COUPLE CALLS... HE WASN'T HARD TO FIND. TH' LAST 3 YEARS HAVE BEEN TH' WORST OF MY LIFE. AN' NOW HE'S GONNA PAY...
WHAT ARE YOU GONNA DO? SUE HIM?
MAYBE... I JUST FIGURED I'D GO ON OVER AN' HAVE A LITTLE TALK WITH HIM FIRST.. KINDA SURPRISE 'IM AT HOME, Y'KNOW? ...HEY.. WHAT'S GOIN' ON?
UH... GOSH.. I DUNNO... I... THINK THERE'S SOMETHING WRONG WITH THE ENGINE.

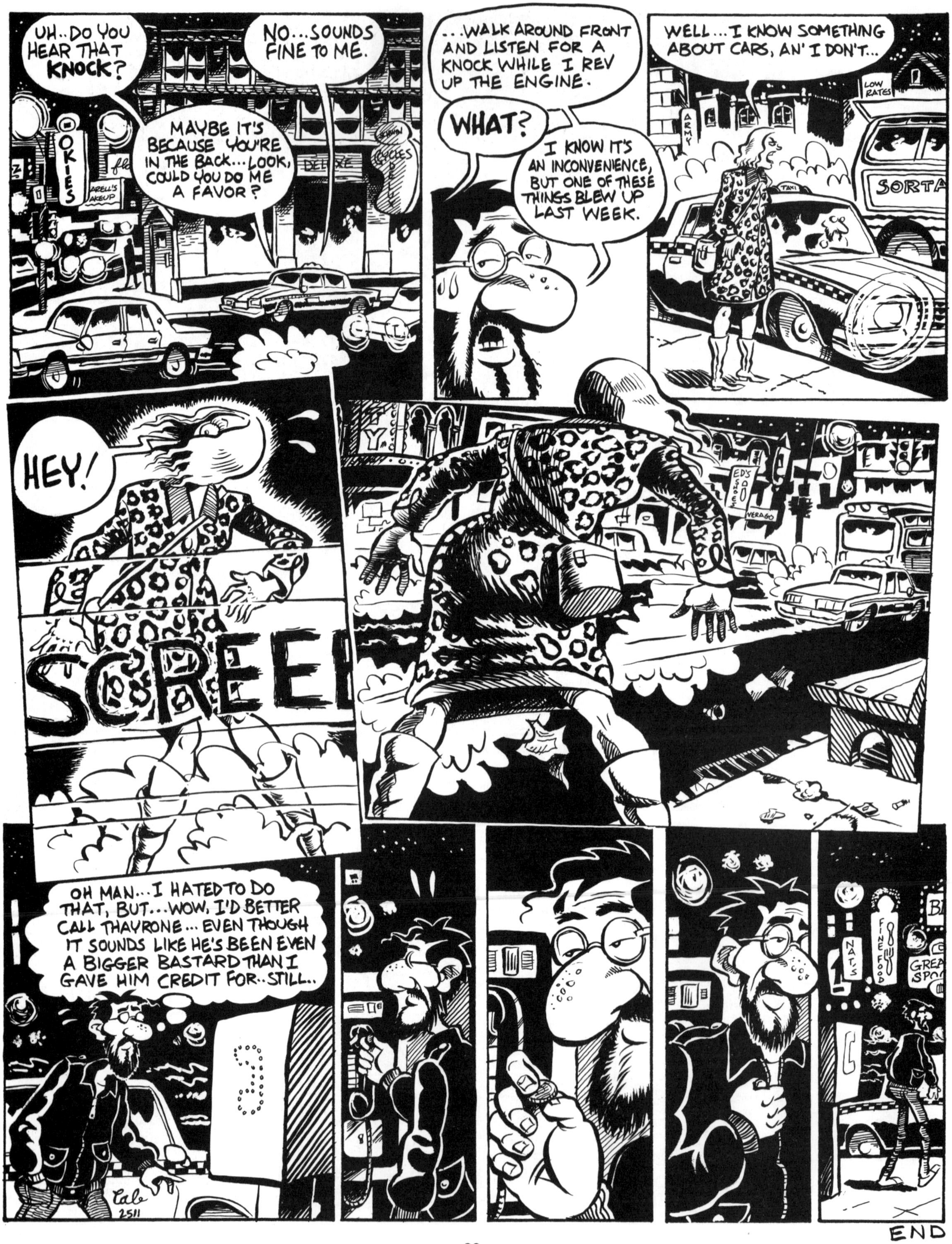
UH.. DO YOU HEAR THAT KNOCK?
NO... SOUNDS FINE TO ME.
MAYBE IT'S BECAUSE YOU'RE IN THE BACK... LOOK, COULD YOU DO ME A FAVOR?
...WALK AROUND FRONT AND LISTEN FOR A KNOCK WHILE I REV UP THE ENGINE.
WHAT?
I KNOW IT'S AN INCONVENIENCE, BUT ONE OF THESE THINGS BLEW UP LAST WEEK.
WELL... I KNOW SOMETHING ABOUT CARS, AN' I DON'T...
HEY!
SCREEE
OH MAN... I HATED TO DO THAT, BUT... WOW, I'D BETTER CALL THAYRONE... EVEN THOUGH IT SOUNDS LIKE HE'S BEEN EVEN A BIGGER BASTARD THAN I GAVE HIM CREDIT FOR.. STILL..
END

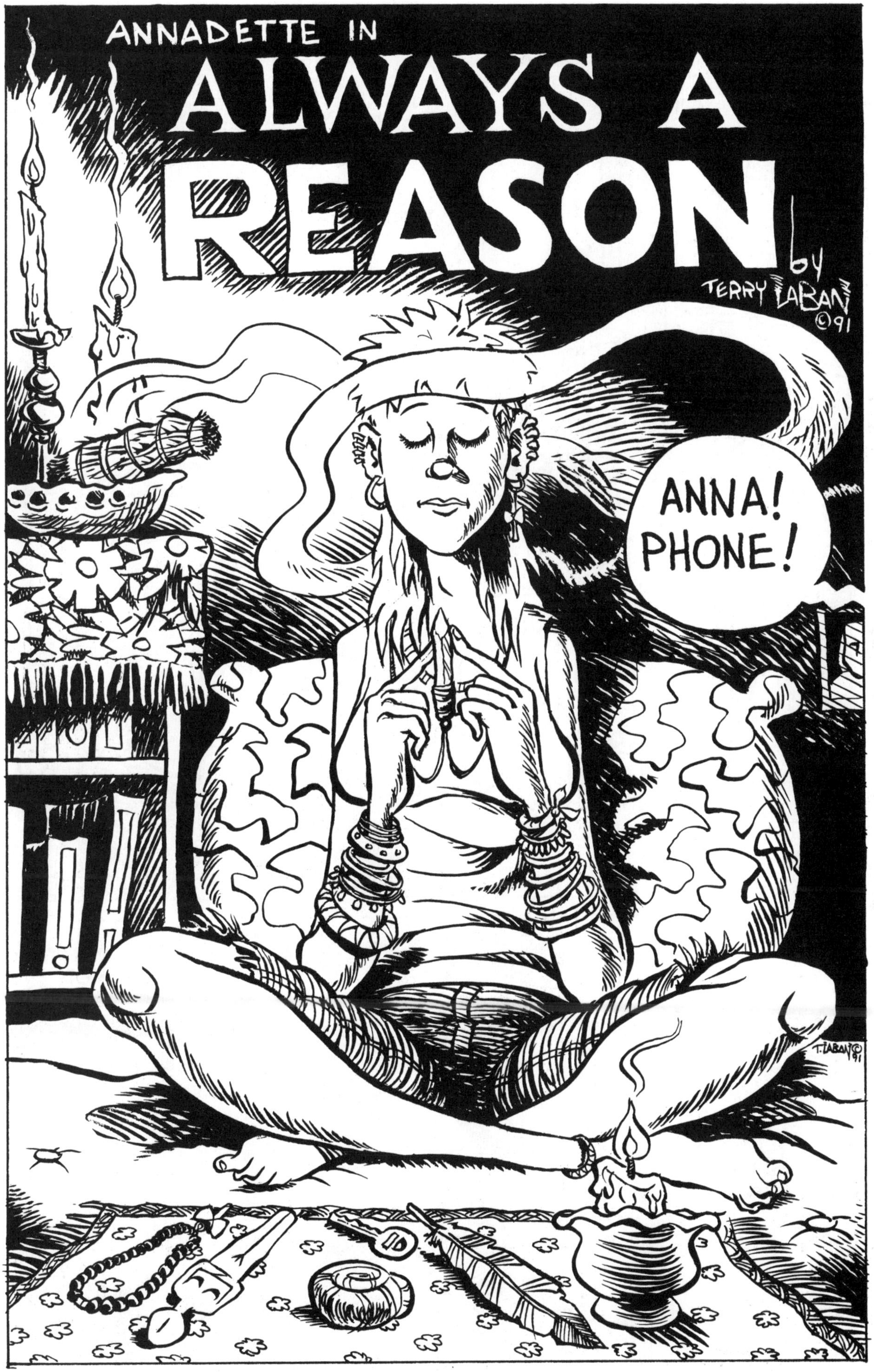

ANNADETTE IN
ALWAYS A
REASON
by
TERRY LABAN
©91
ANNA! PHONE!
T. LABAN © 91

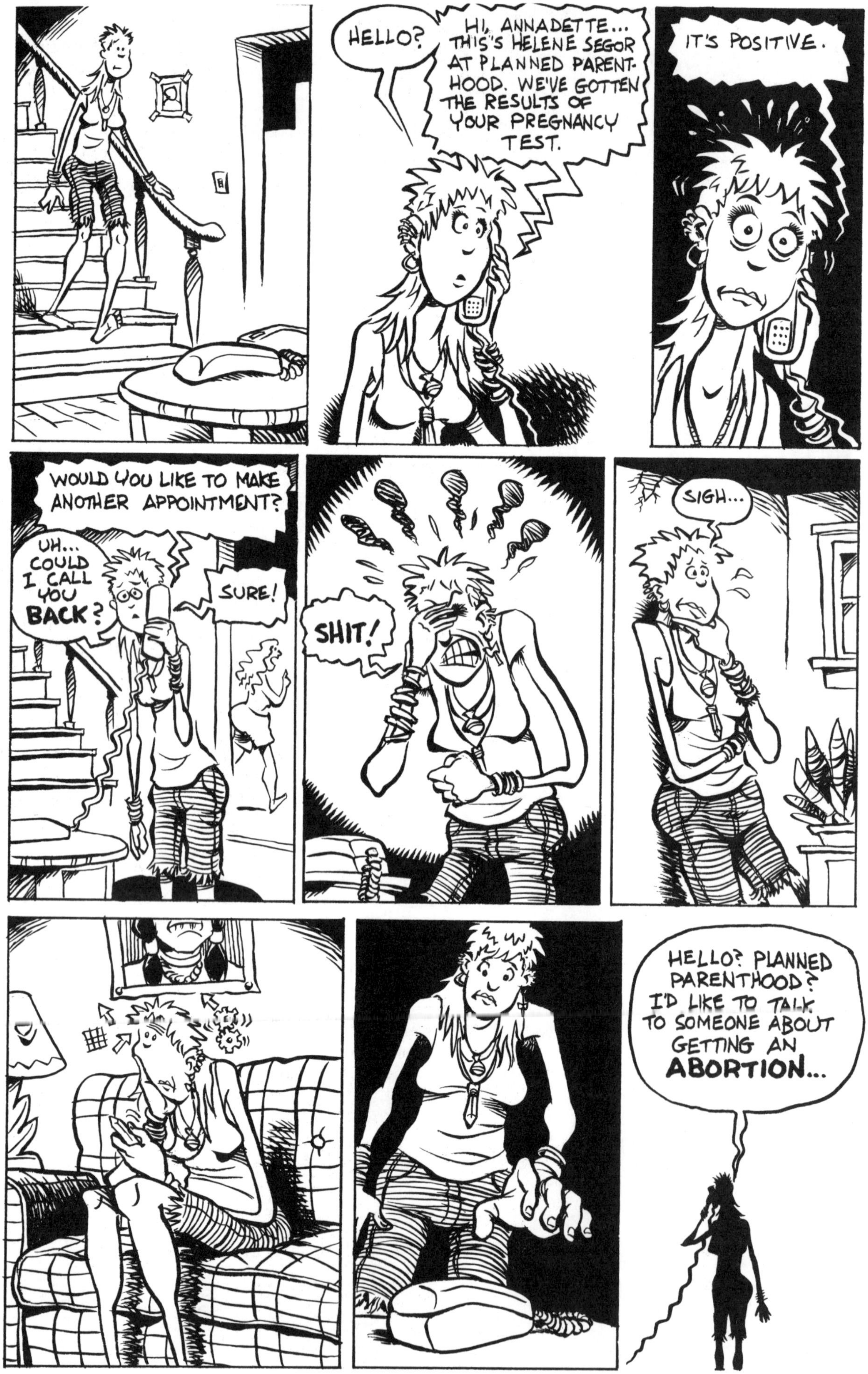
HELLO?
HI, ANNADETTE... THIS'S HELENE SEGOR AT PLANNED PARENT-HOOD. WE'VE GOTTEN THE RESULTS OF YOUR PREGNANCY TEST.
IT'S POSITIVE.
WOULD YOU LIKE TO MAKE ANOTHER APPOINTMENT?
UH... COULD I CALL YOU BACK?
SURE!
SHIT!
SIGH...
HELLO? PLANNED PARENTHOOD? I'D LIKE TO TALK TO SOMEONE ABOUT GETTING AN ABORTION...

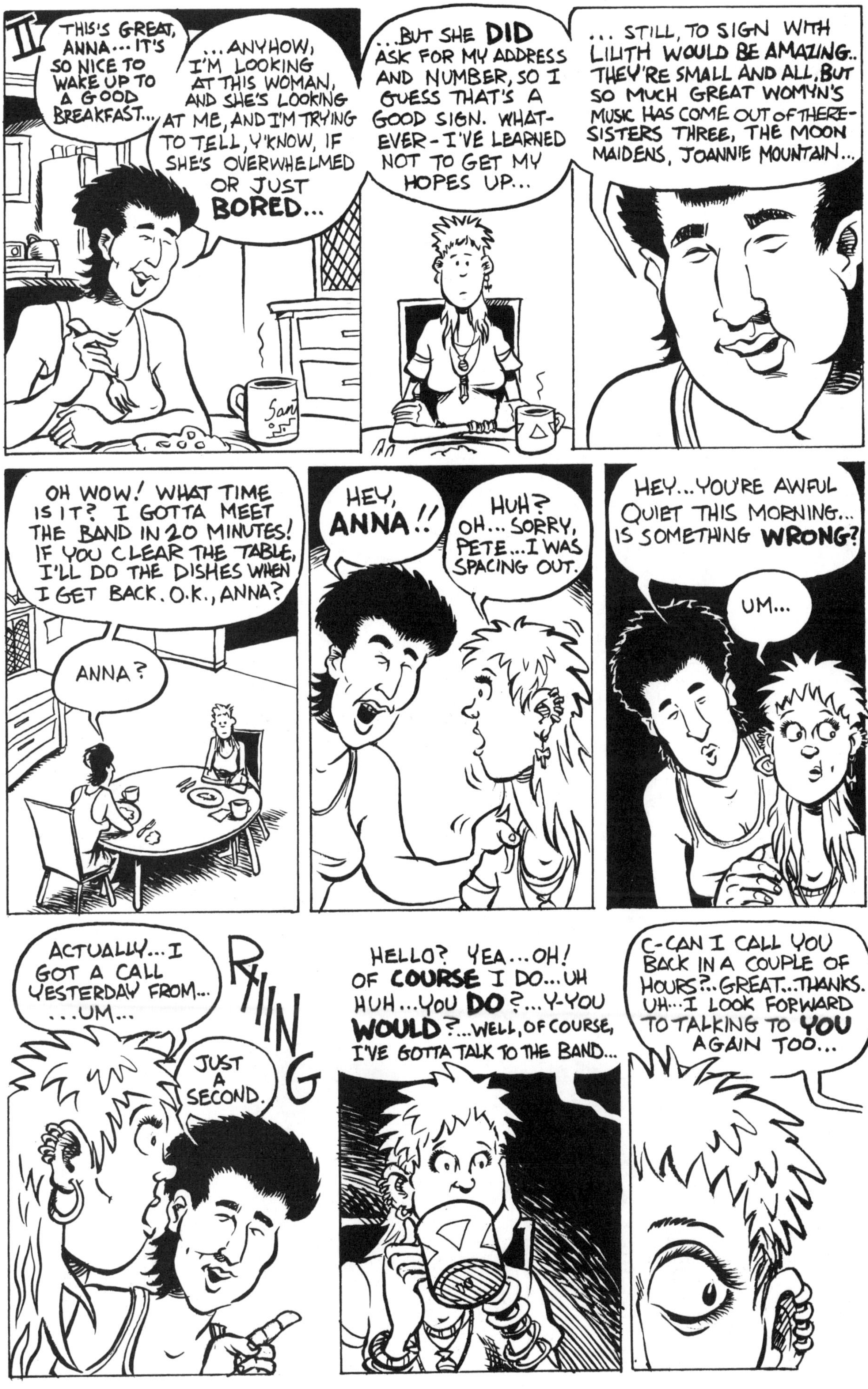
II
THIS'S GREAT, ANNA... IT'S SO NICE TO WAKE UP TO A GOOD BREAKFAST...
...ANYHOW, I'M LOOKING AT THIS WOMAN, AND SHE'S LOOKING AT ME, AND I'M TRYING TO TELL, Y'KNOW, IF SHE'S OVERWHELMED OR JUST BORED...
...BUT SHE DID ASK FOR MY ADDRESS AND NUMBER, SO I GUESS THAT'S A GOOD SIGN. WHATEVER - I'VE LEARNED NOT TO GET MY HOPES UP...
... STILL, TO SIGN WITH LILITH WOULD BE AMAZING.. THEY'RE SMALL AND ALL, BUT SO MUCH GREAT WOMYN'S MUSIC HAS COME OUT OF THERE - SISTERS THREE, THE MOON MAIDENS, JOANNIE MOUNTAIN...
OH WOW! WHAT TIME IS IT? I GOTTA MEET THE BAND IN 20 MINUTES! IF YOU CLEAR THE TABLE, I'LL DO THE DISHES WHEN I GET BACK. O.K., ANNA?
ANNA?
HEY, ANNA!!
HUH? OH... SORRY, PETE... I WAS SPACING OUT.
HEY... YOU'RE AWFUL QUIET THIS MORNING... IS SOMETHING WRONG?
UM...
ACTUALLY... I GOT A CALL YESTERDAY FROM... ...UM...
RHIING
JUST A SECOND.
HELLO? YEA... OH! OF COURSE I DO... UH HUH... YOU DO?... Y-YOU WOULD?... WELL, OF COURSE, I'VE GOTTA TALK TO THE BAND...
C-CAN I CALL YOU BACK IN A COUPLE OF HOURS?.. GREAT... THANKS. UH... I LOOK FORWARD TO TALKING TO YOU AGAIN TOO...

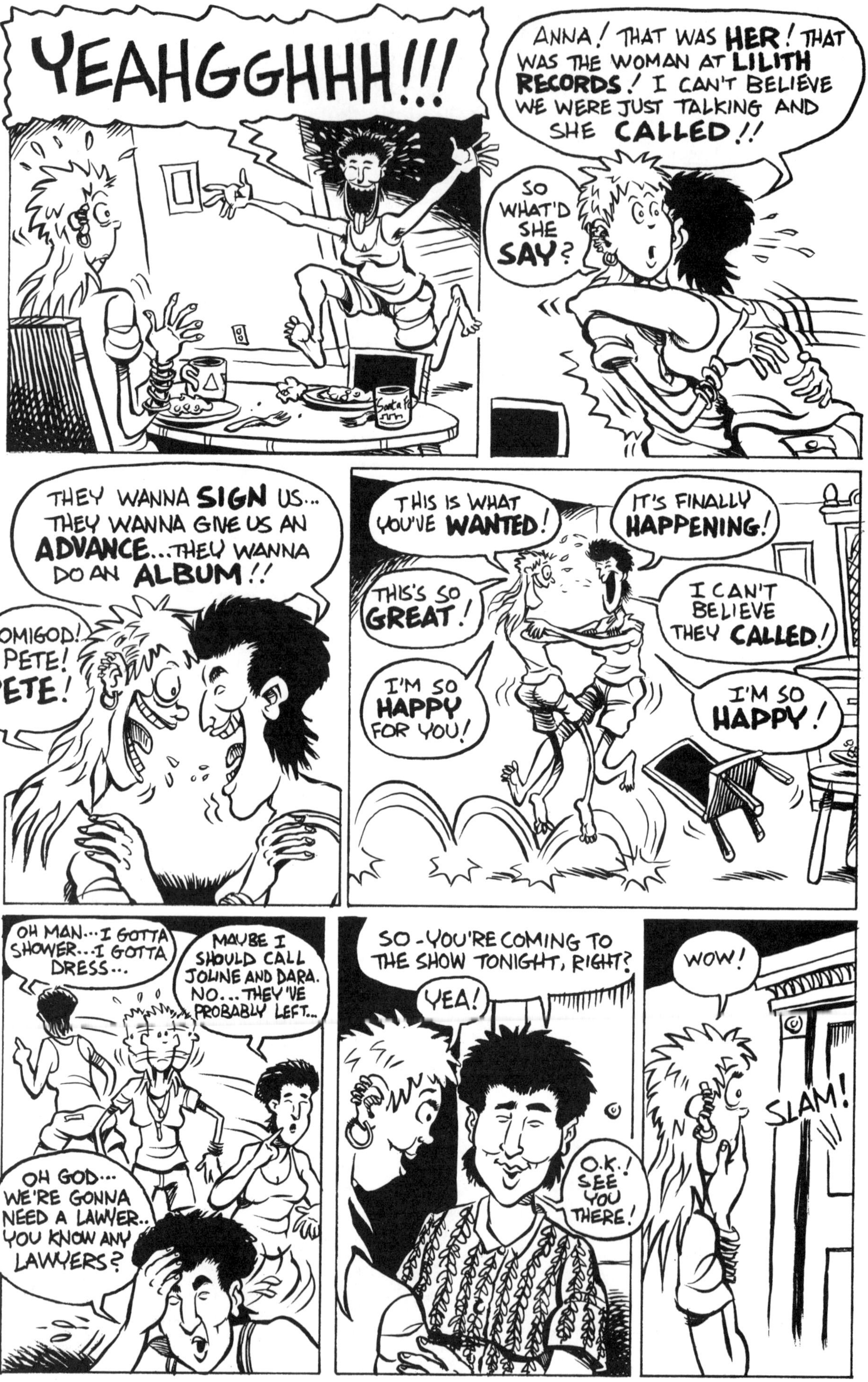

YEAHGGHHH!!!
ANNA! THAT WAS **HER**! THAT WAS THE WOMAN AT **LILITH RECORDS**! I CAN'T BELIEVE WE WERE JUST TALKING AND SHE **CALLED**!!
SO WHAT'D SHE **SAY**?
THEY WANNA **SIGN** US... THEY WANNA GIVE US AN **ADVANCE**...THEY WANNA DO AN **ALBUM**!!
OMIGOD! PETE! **PETE**!
THIS IS WHAT YOU'VE **WANTED**!
IT'S FINALLY **HAPPENING**!
THIS'S SO **GREAT**!
I CAN'T BELIEVE THEY **CALLED**!
I'M SO **HAPPY** FOR YOU!
I'M SO **HAPPY**!
OH MAN... I GOTTA SHOWER... I GOTTA DRESS...
MAYBE I SHOULD CALL JOLINE AND DARA. NO... THEY'VE PROBABLY LEFT...
OH GOD... WE'RE GONNA NEED A LAWYER.. YOU KNOW ANY LAWYERS?
SO - YOU'RE COMING TO THE SHOW TONIGHT, RIGHT?
YEA!
O.K.! SEE YOU THERE!
WOW!
SLAM!

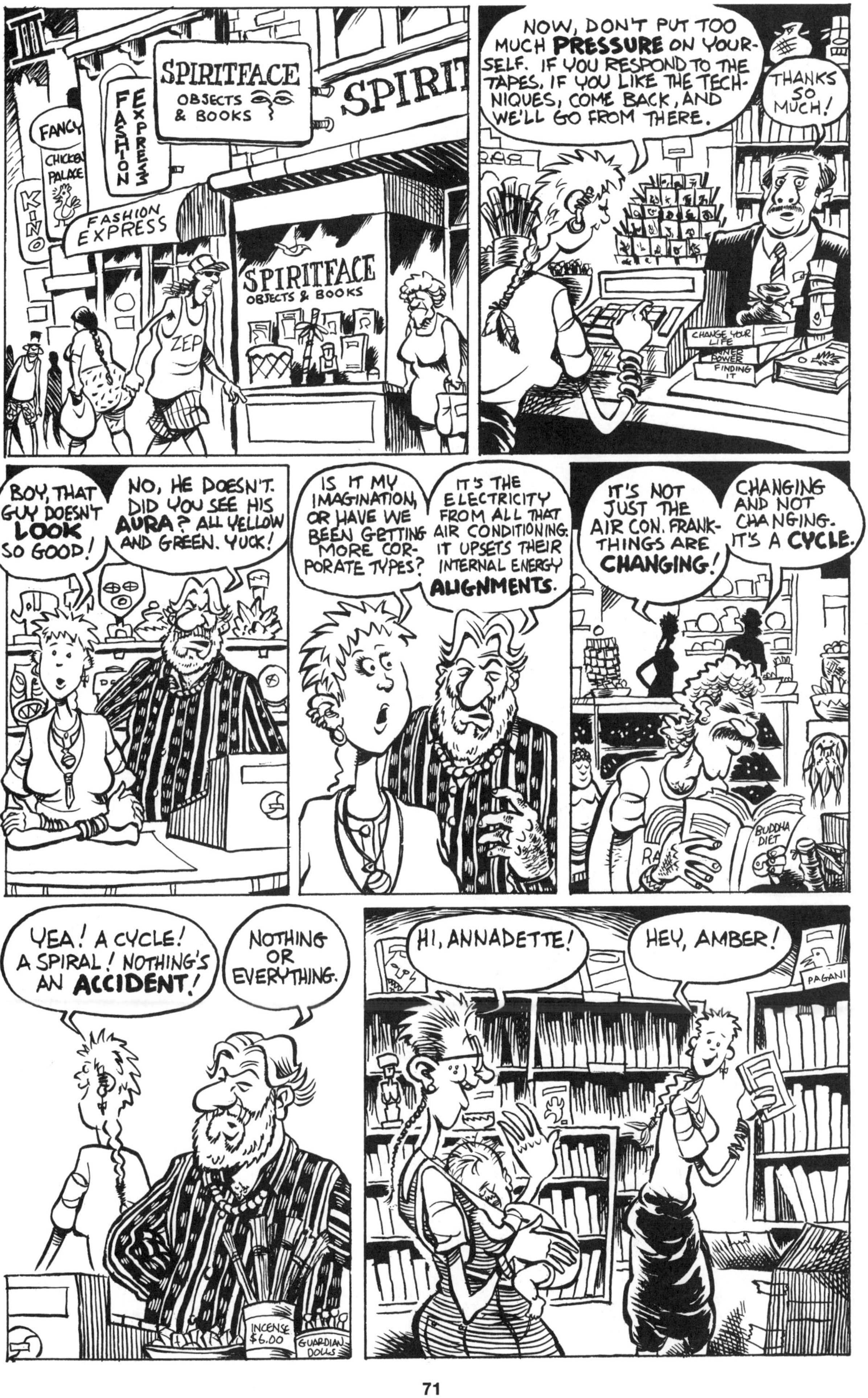
FANCY CHICKEN PALACE
KINO
FASHION EXPRESS
SPIRITFACE OBJECTS & BOOKS
FASHION EXPRESS
SPIRIT
SPIRITFACE OBJECTS & BOOKS
ZEP
NOW, DON'T PUT TOO MUCH PRESSURE ON YOURSELF. IF YOU RESPOND TO THE TAPES, IF YOU LIKE THE TECHNIQUES, COME BACK, AND WE'LL GO FROM THERE.
THANKS SO MUCH!
CHANGE YOUR LIFE
INNER POWER
FINDING IT
BOY, THAT GUY DOESN'T LOOK SO GOOD!
NO, HE DOESN'T. DID YOU SEE HIS AURA? ALL YELLOW AND GREEN. YUCK!
IS IT MY IMAGINATION, OR HAVE WE BEEN GETTING MORE CORPORATE TYPES?
IT'S THE ELECTRICITY FROM ALL THAT AIR CONDITIONING. IT UPSETS THEIR INTERNAL ENERGY ALIGNMENTS.
IT'S NOT JUST THE AIR CON. FRANK- THINGS ARE CHANGING!
CHANGING AND NOT CHANGING. IT'S A CYCLE.
BUDDHA DIET
YEA! A CYCLE! A SPIRAL! NOTHING'S AN ACCIDENT!
NOTHING OR EVERYTHING.
INCENSE $6.00
GUARDIAN DOLLS
HI, ANNADETTE!
HEY, AMBER!
PAGAN

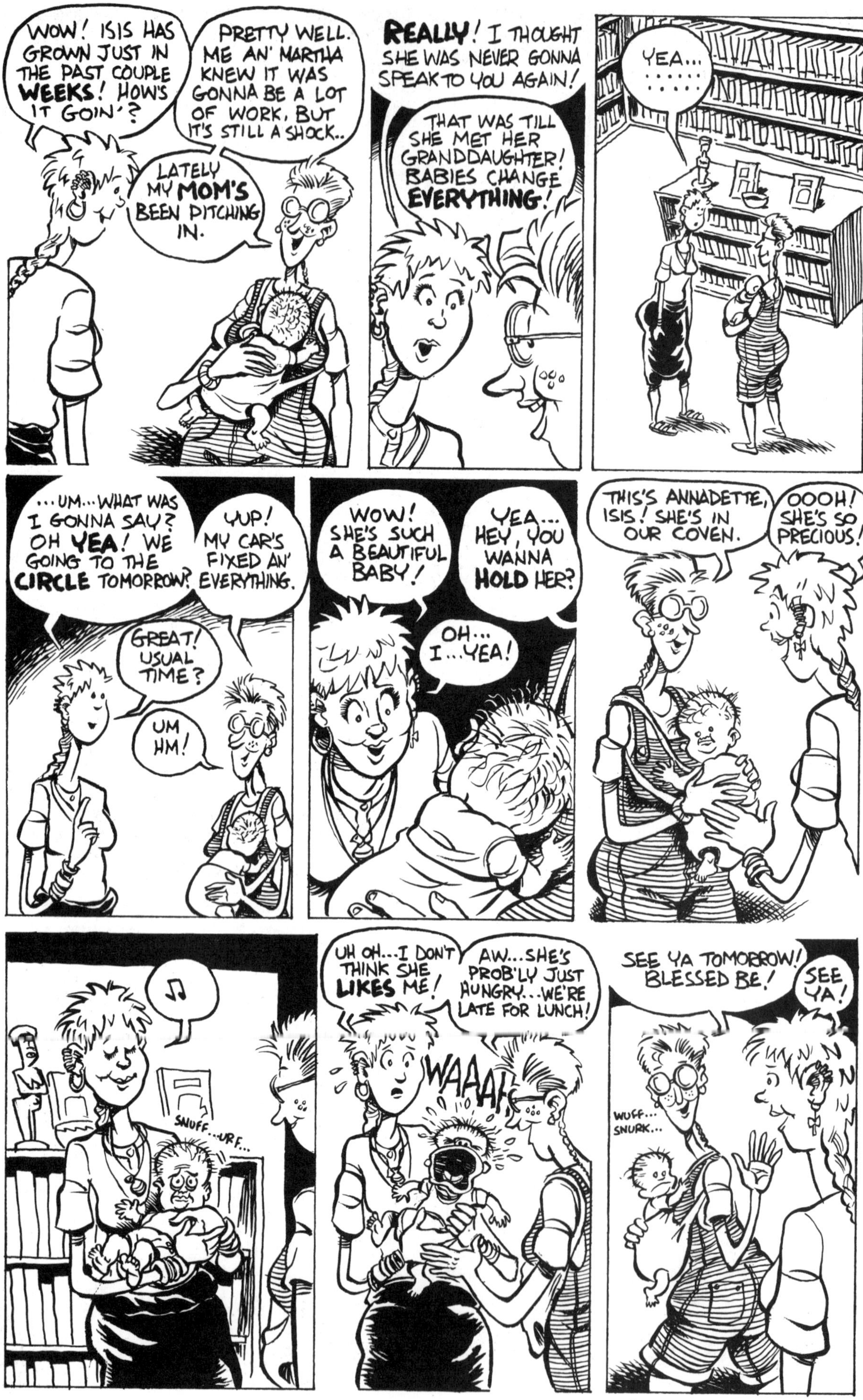
WOW! ISIS HAS GROWN JUST IN THE PAST COUPLE WEEKS! HOW'S IT GOIN'?
PRETTY WELL. ME AN' MARTHA KNEW IT WAS GONNA BE A LOT OF WORK, BUT IT'S STILL A SHOCK..
LATELY MY MOM'S BEEN PITCHING IN.
REALLY! I THOUGHT SHE WAS NEVER GONNA SPEAK TO YOU AGAIN!
THAT WAS TILL SHE MET HER GRANDDAUGHTER! BABIES CHANGE EVERYTHING!
YEA...
...UM...WHAT WAS I GONNA SAY? OH YEA! WE GOING TO THE CIRCLE TOMORROW?
YUP! MY CAR'S FIXED AN' EVERYTHING.
GREAT! USUAL TIME?
UM HM!
WOW! SHE'S SUCH A BEAUTIFUL BABY!
YEA... HEY, YOU WANNA HOLD HER?
OH... I...YEA!
THIS'S ANNADETTE, ISIS! SHE'S IN OUR COVEN.
OOOH! SHE'S SO PRECIOUS!
♫
SNUFF...URF...
UH OH...I DON'T THINK SHE LIKES ME!
AW...SHE'S PROB'LY JUST HUNGRY...WE'RE LATE FOR LUNCH!
WAAAH
SEE YA TOMORROW! BLESSED BE!
SEE YA!
WUFF... SNURK...

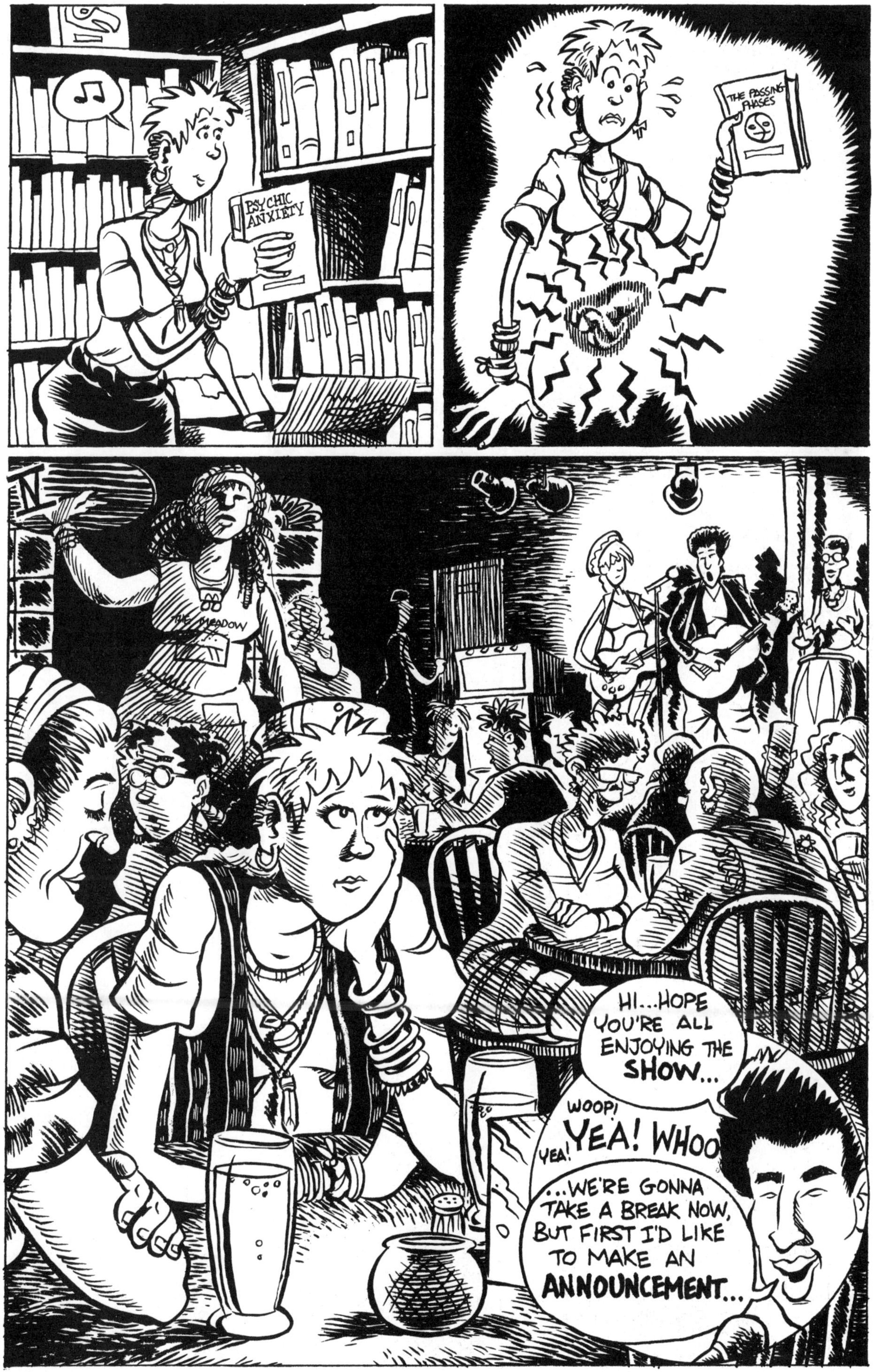
PSYCHIC ANXIETY
THE PASSING PHASES
THE MEADOW
HI...HOPE YOU'RE ALL ENJOYING THE **SHOW**...
WOOP!
YEA! YEA! WHOO
...WE'RE GONNA TAKE A BREAK NOW, BUT FIRST I'D LIKE TO MAKE AN **ANNOUNCEMENT**...

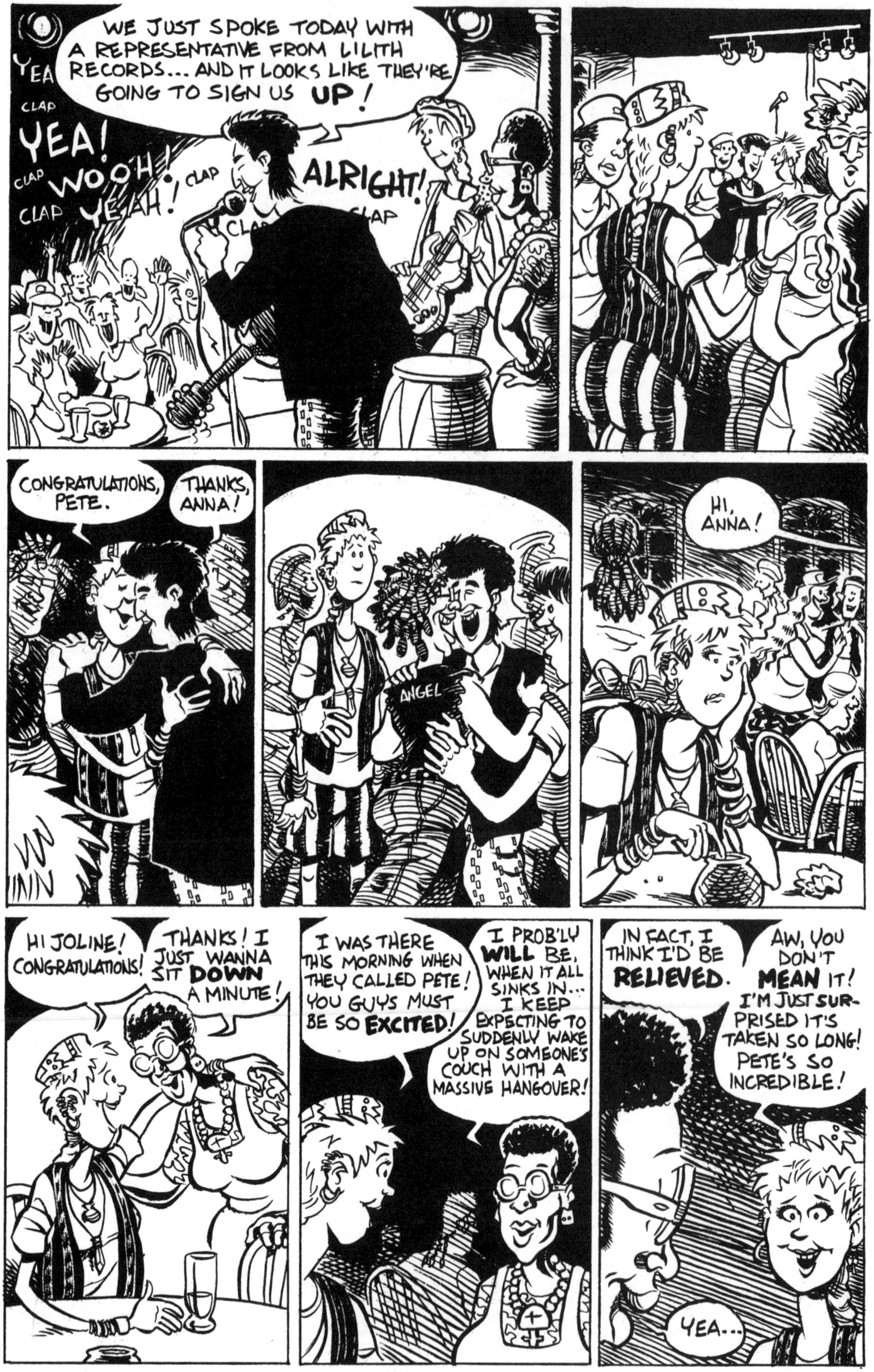
WE JUST SPOKE TODAY WITH A REPRESENTATIVE FROM LILITH RECORDS... AND IT LOOKS LIKE THEY'RE GOING TO SIGN US UP!
YEA
CLAP
YEA!
CLAP WOO'H!
CLAP YEAH!
CLAP
ALRIGHT!
CLAP
CLAP
CONGRATULATIONS, PETE.
THANKS, ANNA!
ANGEL
HI, ANNA!
HI JOLINE! CONGRATULATIONS!
THANKS! I JUST WANNA SIT DOWN A MINUTE!
I WAS THERE THIS MORNING WHEN THEY CALLED PETE! YOU GUYS MUST BE SO EXCITED!
I PROB'LY WILL BE, WHEN IT ALL SINKS IN... I KEEP EXPECTING TO SUDDENLY WAKE UP ON SOMEONE'S COUCH WITH A MASSIVE HANGOVER!
IN FACT, I THINK I'D BE RELIEVED.
AW, YOU DON'T MEAN IT! I'M JUST SURPRISED IT'S TAKEN SO LONG! PETE'S SO INCREDIBLE!
YEA...

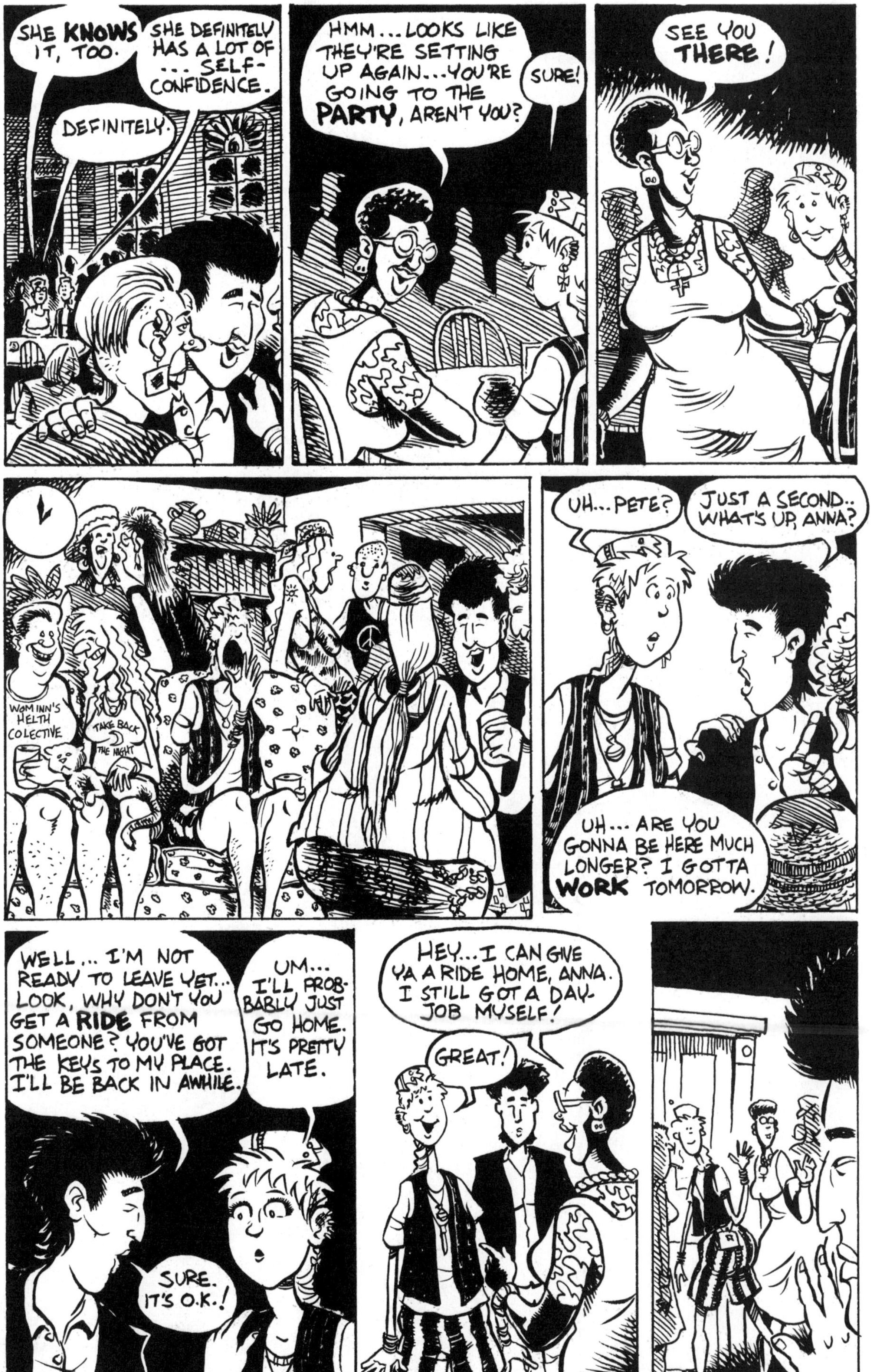
SHE KNOWS IT, TOO.
SHE DEFINITELY HAS A LOT OF ... SELF-CONFIDENCE.
DEFINITELY.
HMM... LOOKS LIKE THEY'RE SETTING UP AGAIN... YOU'RE GOING TO THE PARTY, AREN'T YOU?
SURE!
SEE YOU THERE!
WOM INN'S HELTH COLECTIVE
TAKE BACK THE NIGHT
UH... PETE?
JUST A SECOND.. WHAT'S UP, ANNA?
UH... ARE YOU GONNA BE HERE MUCH LONGER? I GOTTA WORK TOMORROW.
WELL... I'M NOT READY TO LEAVE YET... LOOK, WHY DON'T YOU GET A RIDE FROM SOMEONE? YOU'VE GOT THE KEYS TO MY PLACE. I'LL BE BACK IN AWHILE.
UM... I'LL PROB-BABLY JUST GO HOME. IT'S PRETTY LATE.
SURE. IT'S O.K.!
HEY... I CAN GIVE YA A RIDE HOME, ANNA. I STILL GOT A DAY-JOB MYSELF!
GREAT!

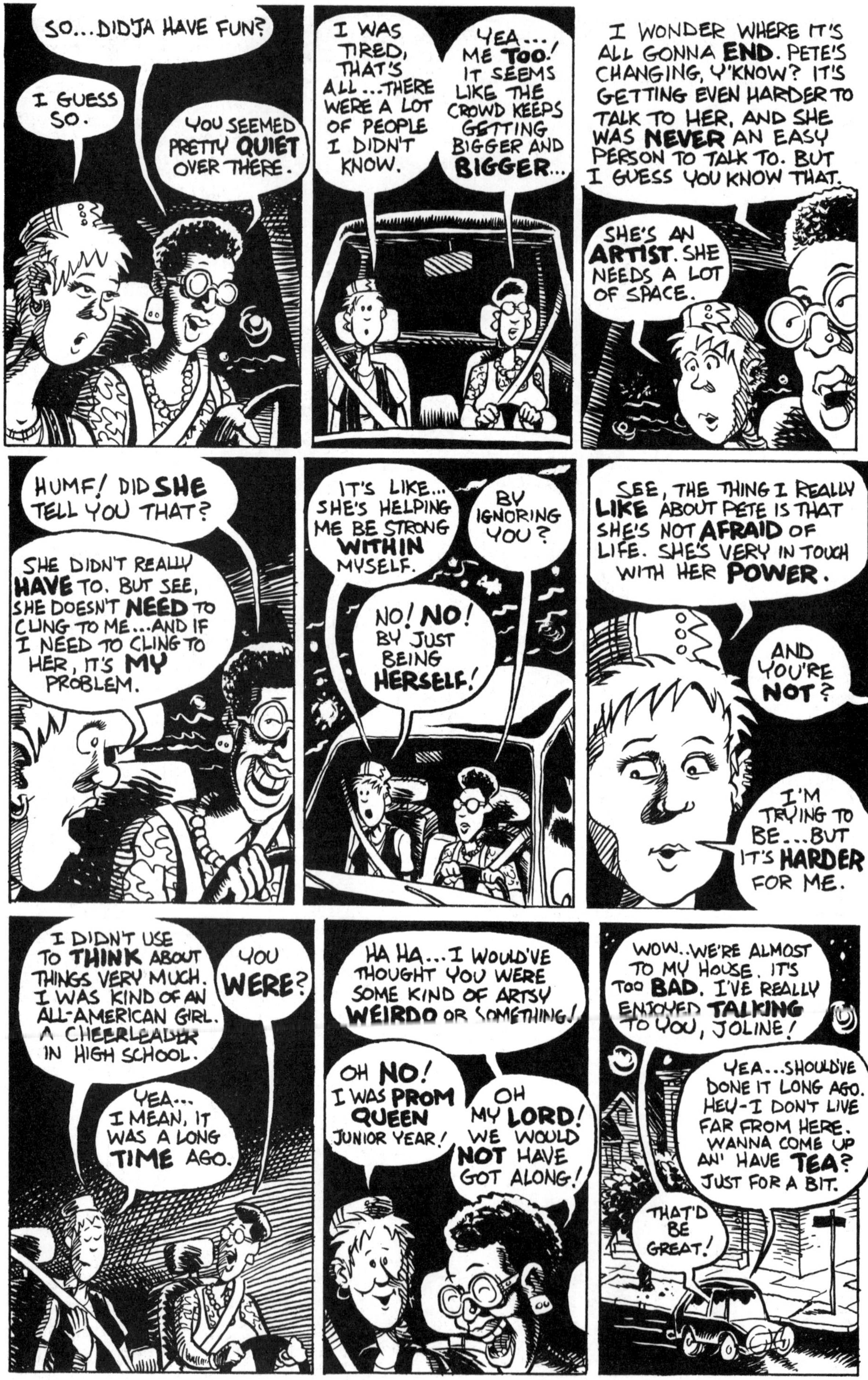
SO... DID'JA HAVE FUN?
I GUESS SO.
YOU SEEMED PRETTY QUIET OVER THERE.
I WAS TIRED, THAT'S ALL... THERE WERE A LOT OF PEOPLE I DIDN'T KNOW.
YEA... ME TOO! IT SEEMS LIKE THE CROWD KEEPS GETTING BIGGER AND BIGGER...
I WONDER WHERE IT'S ALL GONNA END. PETE'S CHANGING, Y'KNOW? IT'S GETTING EVEN HARDER TO TALK TO HER, AND SHE WAS NEVER AN EASY PERSON TO TALK TO. BUT I GUESS YOU KNOW THAT.
SHE'S AN ARTIST. SHE NEEDS A LOT OF SPACE.
HUMF! DID SHE TELL YOU THAT?
SHE DIDN'T REALLY HAVE TO. BUT SEE, SHE DOESN'T NEED TO CLING TO ME... AND IF I NEED TO CLING TO HER, IT'S MY PROBLEM.
IT'S LIKE... SHE'S HELPING ME BE STRONG WITHIN MYSELF.
BY IGNORING YOU?
NO! NO! BY JUST BEING HERSELF!
SEE, THE THING I REALLY LIKE ABOUT PETE IS THAT SHE'S NOT AFRAID OF LIFE. SHE'S VERY IN TOUCH WITH HER POWER.
AND YOU'RE NOT?
I'M TRYING TO BE... BUT IT'S HARDER FOR ME.
I DIDN'T USE TO THINK ABOUT THINGS VERY MUCH. I WAS KIND OF AN ALL-AMERICAN GIRL. A CHEERLEADER IN HIGH SCHOOL.
YOU WERE?
YEA... I MEAN, IT WAS A LONG TIME AGO.
HA HA... I WOULD'VE THOUGHT YOU WERE SOME KIND OF ARTSY WEIRDO OR SOMETHING!
OH NO! I WAS PROM QUEEN JUNIOR YEAR!
OH MY LORD! WE WOULD NOT HAVE GOT ALONG!
WOW.. WE'RE ALMOST TO MY HOUSE. IT'S TOO BAD. I'VE REALLY ENJOYED TALKING TO YOU, JOLINE!
YEA... SHOULD'VE DONE IT LONG AGO. HEY- I DON'T LIVE FAR FROM HERE. WANNA COME UP AN' HAVE TEA? JUST FOR A BIT.
THAT'D BE GREAT!

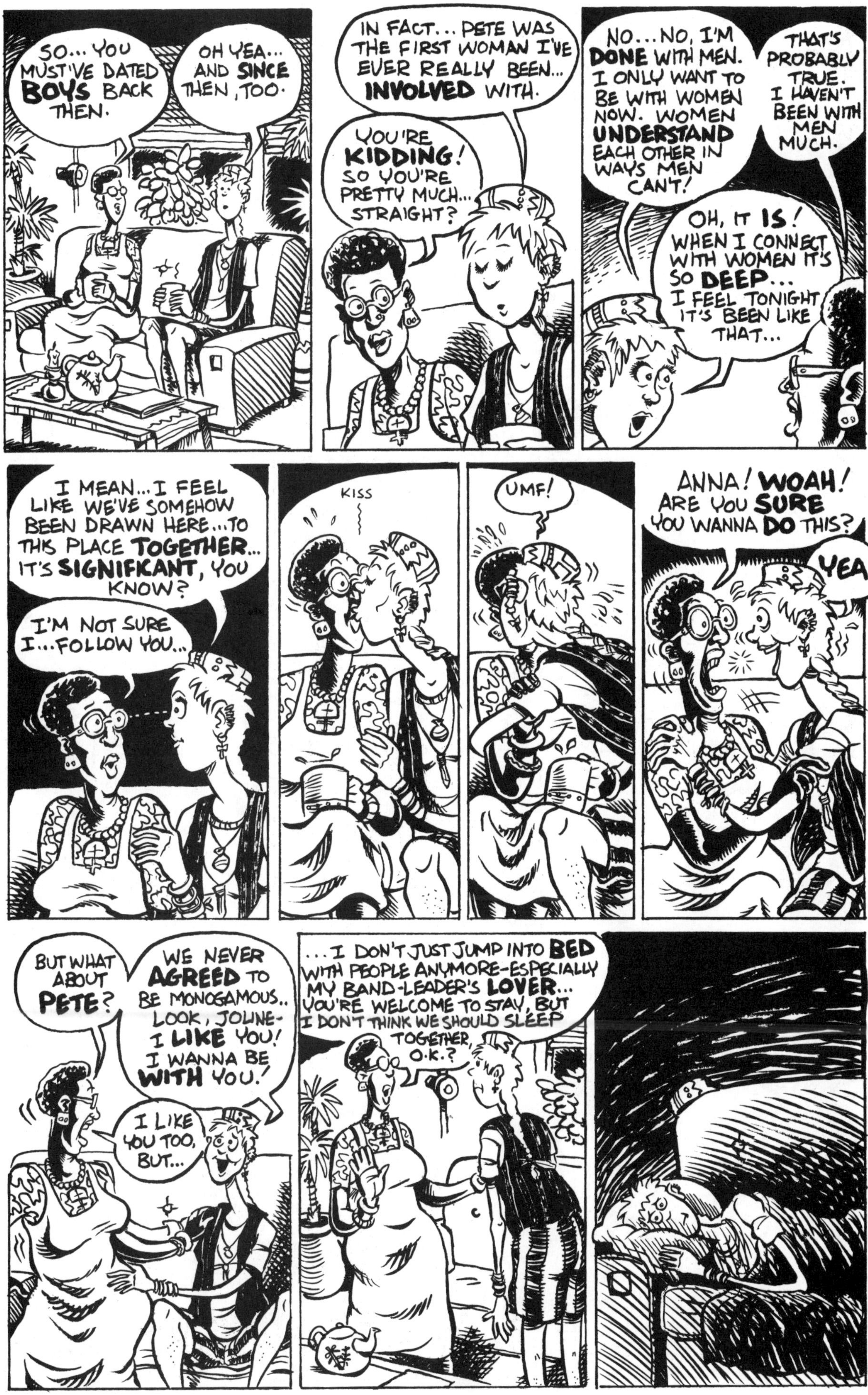

SO... YOU MUST'VE DATED BOYS BACK THEN.
OH YEA... AND SINCE THEN, TOO.
IN FACT... PETE WAS THE FIRST WOMAN I'VE EVER REALLY BEEN... INVOLVED WITH.
YOU'RE KIDDING! SO YOU'RE PRETTY MUCH... STRAIGHT?
NO... NO, I'M DONE WITH MEN. I ONLY WANT TO BE WITH WOMEN NOW. WOMEN UNDERSTAND EACH OTHER IN WAYS MEN CAN'T!
THAT'S PROBABLY TRUE. I HAVEN'T BEEN WITH MEN MUCH.
OH, IT IS! WHEN I CONNECT WITH WOMEN IT'S SO DEEP... I FEEL TONIGHT IT'S BEEN LIKE THAT...
I MEAN... I FEEL LIKE WE'VE SOMEHOW BEEN DRAWN HERE... TO THIS PLACE TOGETHER... IT'S SIGNIFICANT, YOU KNOW?
I'M NOT SURE I... FOLLOW YOU...
KISS
UMF!
ANNA! WOAH! ARE YOU SURE YOU WANNA DO THIS?
YEA!
BUT WHAT ABOUT PETE?
WE NEVER AGREED TO BE MONOGAMOUS.. LOOK, JOLINE- I LIKE YOU! I WANNA BE WITH YOU!
I LIKE YOU TOO, BUT...
...I DON'T JUST JUMP INTO BED WITH PEOPLE ANYMORE-ESPECIALLY MY BAND-LEADER'S LOVER... YOU'RE WELCOME TO STAY, BUT I DON'T THINK WE SHOULD SLEEP TOGETHER, O.K.?

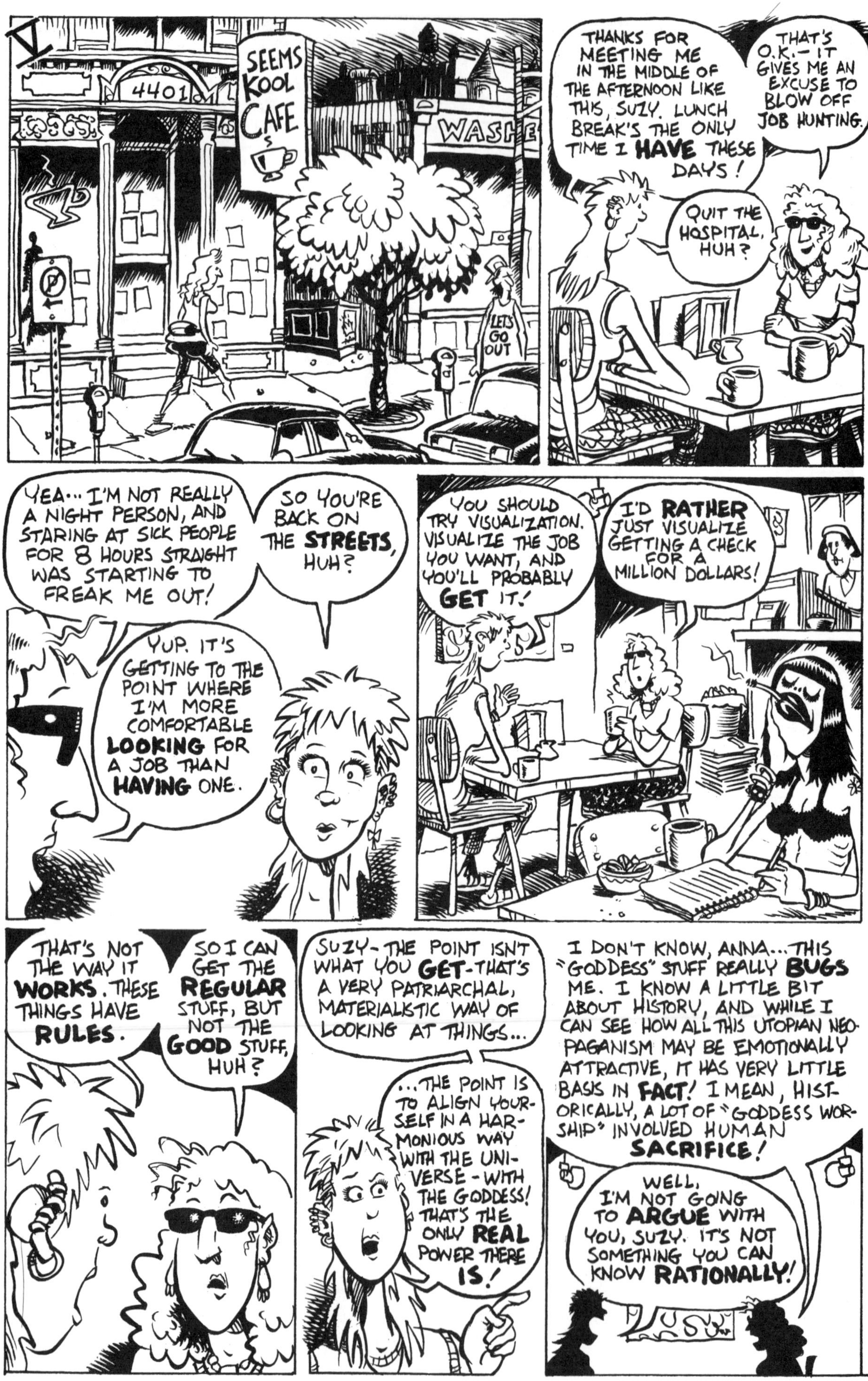

4401
SEEMS KOOL CAFE
WASH
LET'S GO OUT
THANKS FOR MEETING ME IN THE MIDDLE OF THE AFTERNOON LIKE THIS, SUZY. LUNCH BREAK'S THE ONLY TIME I HAVE THESE DAYS!
THAT'S O.K.–IT GIVES ME AN EXCUSE TO BLOW OFF JOB HUNTING.
QUIT THE HOSPITAL, HUH?
YEA... I'M NOT REALLY A NIGHT PERSON, AND STARING AT SICK PEOPLE FOR 8 HOURS STRAIGHT WAS STARTING TO FREAK ME OUT!
SO YOU'RE BACK ON THE STREETS, HUH?
YUP. IT'S GETTING TO THE POINT WHERE I'M MORE COMFORTABLE LOOKING FOR A JOB THAN HAVING ONE.
YOU SHOULD TRY VISUALIZATION. VISUALIZE THE JOB YOU WANT, AND YOU'LL PROBABLY GET IT!
I'D RATHER JUST VISUALIZE GETTING A CHECK FOR A MILLION DOLLARS!
THAT'S NOT THE WAY IT WORKS. THESE THINGS HAVE RULES.
SO I CAN GET THE REGULAR STUFF, BUT NOT THE GOOD STUFF, HUH?
SUZY–THE POINT ISN'T WHAT YOU GET–THAT'S A VERY PATRIARCHAL, MATERIALISTIC WAY OF LOOKING AT THINGS...
...THE POINT IS TO ALIGN YOURSELF IN A HARMONIOUS WAY WITH THE UNIVERSE–WITH THE GODDESS! THAT'S THE ONLY REAL POWER THERE IS!
I DON'T KNOW, ANNA... THIS "GODDESS" STUFF REALLY BUGS ME. I KNOW A LITTLE BIT ABOUT HISTORY, AND WHILE I CAN SEE HOW ALL THIS UTOPIAN NEO-PAGANISM MAY BE EMOTIONALLY ATTRACTIVE, IT HAS VERY LITTLE BASIS IN FACT! I MEAN, HISTORICALLY, A LOT OF "GODDESS WORSHIP" INVOLVED HUMAN SACRIFICE!
WELL, I'M NOT GOING TO ARGUE WITH YOU, SUZY. IT'S NOT SOMETHING YOU CAN KNOW RATIONALLY!

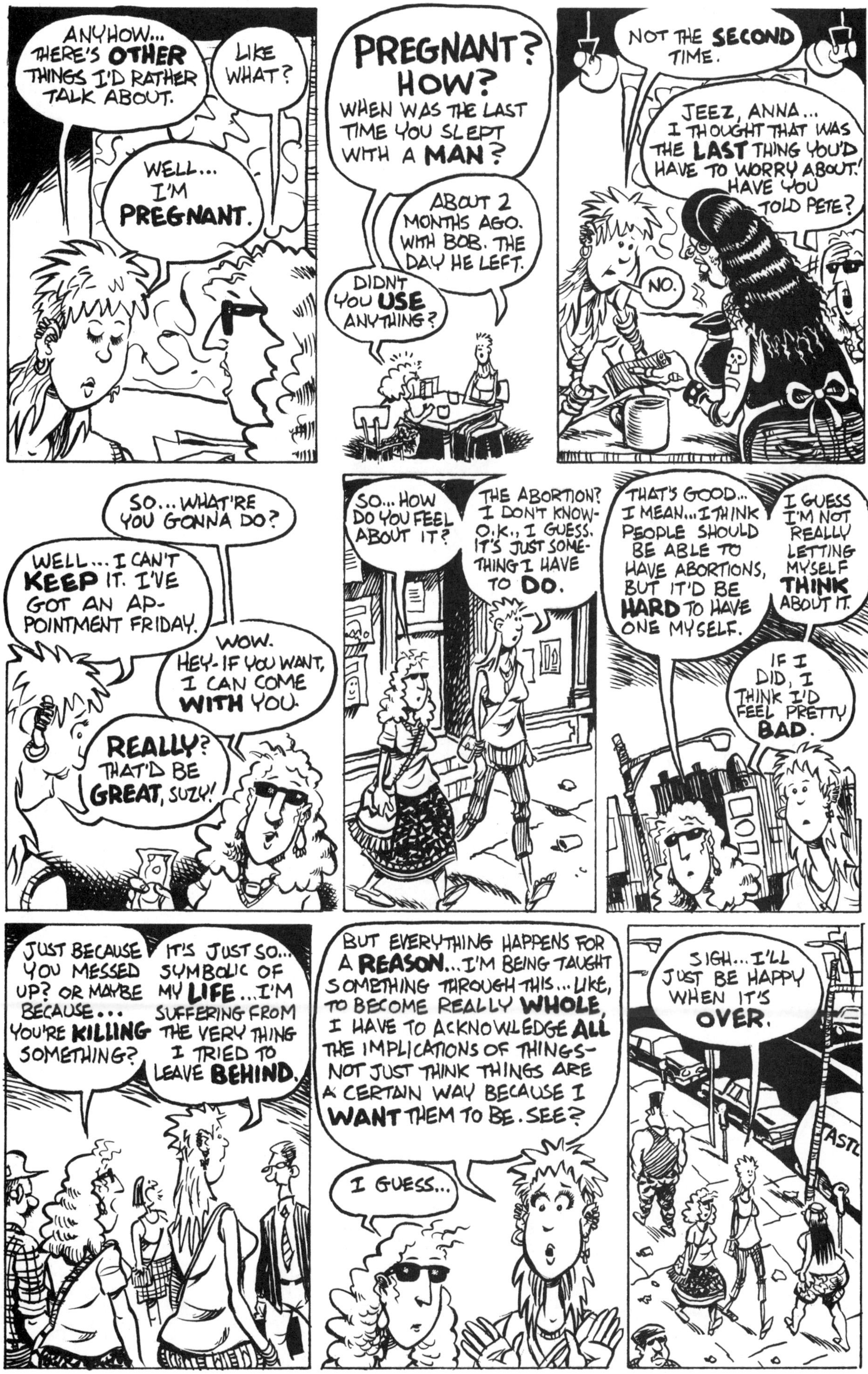
ANYHOW... THERE'S OTHER THINGS I'D RATHER TALK ABOUT.
LIKE WHAT?
WELL... I'M PREGNANT.
PREGNANT? HOW? WHEN WAS THE LAST TIME YOU SLEPT WITH A MAN?
ABOUT 2 MONTHS AGO. WITH BOB. THE DAY HE LEFT.
DIDN'T YOU USE ANYTHING?
NOT THE SECOND TIME.
JEEZ, ANNA... I THOUGHT THAT WAS THE LAST THING YOU'D HAVE TO WORRY ABOUT! HAVE YOU TOLD PETE?
NO.
SO... WHAT'RE YOU GONNA DO?
WELL... I CAN'T KEEP IT. I'VE GOT AN AP-POINTMENT FRIDAY.
WOW. HEY- IF YOU WANT, I CAN COME WITH YOU.
REALLY? THAT'D BE GREAT, SUZY!
SO... HOW DO YOU FEEL ABOUT IT?
THE ABORTION? I DON'T KNOW- O.K., I GUESS. IT'S JUST SOME-THING I HAVE TO DO.
THAT'S GOOD... I MEAN... I THINK PEOPLE SHOULD BE ABLE TO HAVE ABORTIONS, BUT IT'D BE HARD TO HAVE ONE MYSELF.
I GUESS I'M NOT REALLY LETTING MYSELF THINK ABOUT IT.
IF I DID, I THINK I'D FEEL PRETTY BAD.
JUST BECAUSE YOU MESSED UP? OR MAYBE BECAUSE... YOU'RE KILLING SOMETHING?
IT'S JUST SO... SYMBOLIC OF MY LIFE... I'M SUFFERING FROM THE VERY THING I TRIED TO LEAVE BEHIND.
BUT EVERYTHING HAPPENS FOR A REASON... I'M BEING TAUGHT SOMETHING THROUGH THIS... LIKE, TO BECOME REALLY WHOLE, I HAVE TO ACKNOWLEDGE ALL THE IMPLICATIONS OF THINGS- NOT JUST THINK THINGS ARE A CERTAIN WAY BECAUSE I WANT THEM TO BE. SEE?
I GUESS...
SIGH... I'LL JUST BE HAPPY WHEN IT'S OVER.

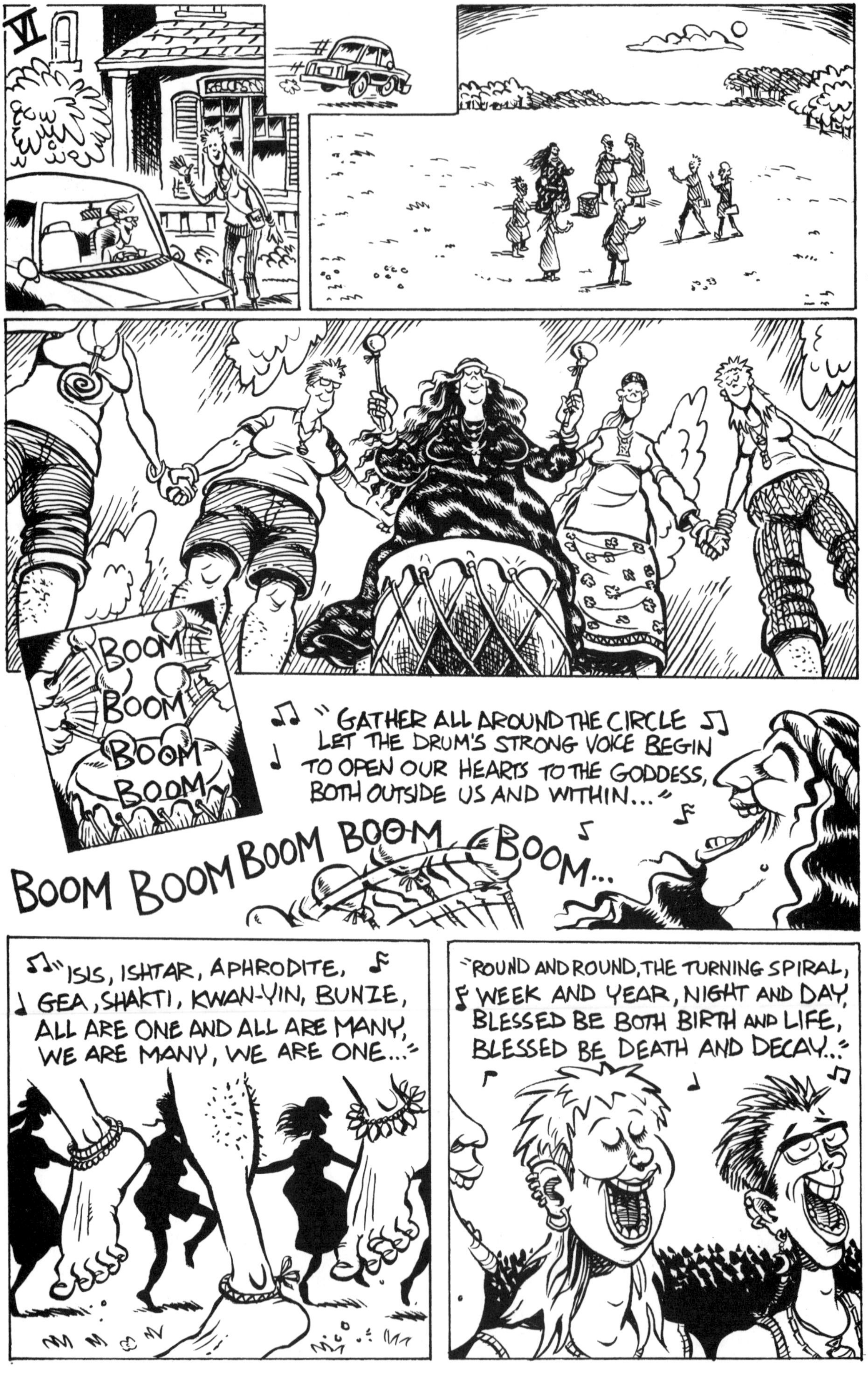
VI
BOOM BOOM BOOM BOOM
"GATHER ALL AROUND THE CIRCLE
LET THE DRUM'S STRONG VOICE BEGIN
TO OPEN OUR HEARTS TO THE GODDESS,
BOTH OUTSIDE US AND WITHIN..."
BOOM BOOM BOOM BOOM BOOM...
"ISIS, ISHTAR, APHRODITE,
GEA, SHAKTI, KWAN-YIN, BUNZE,
ALL ARE ONE AND ALL ARE MANY,
WE ARE MANY, WE ARE ONE..."
"ROUND AND ROUND, THE TURNING SPIRAL,
WEEK AND YEAR, NIGHT AND DAY,
BLESSED BE BOTH BIRTH AND LIFE,
BLESSED BE DEATH AND DECAY..."

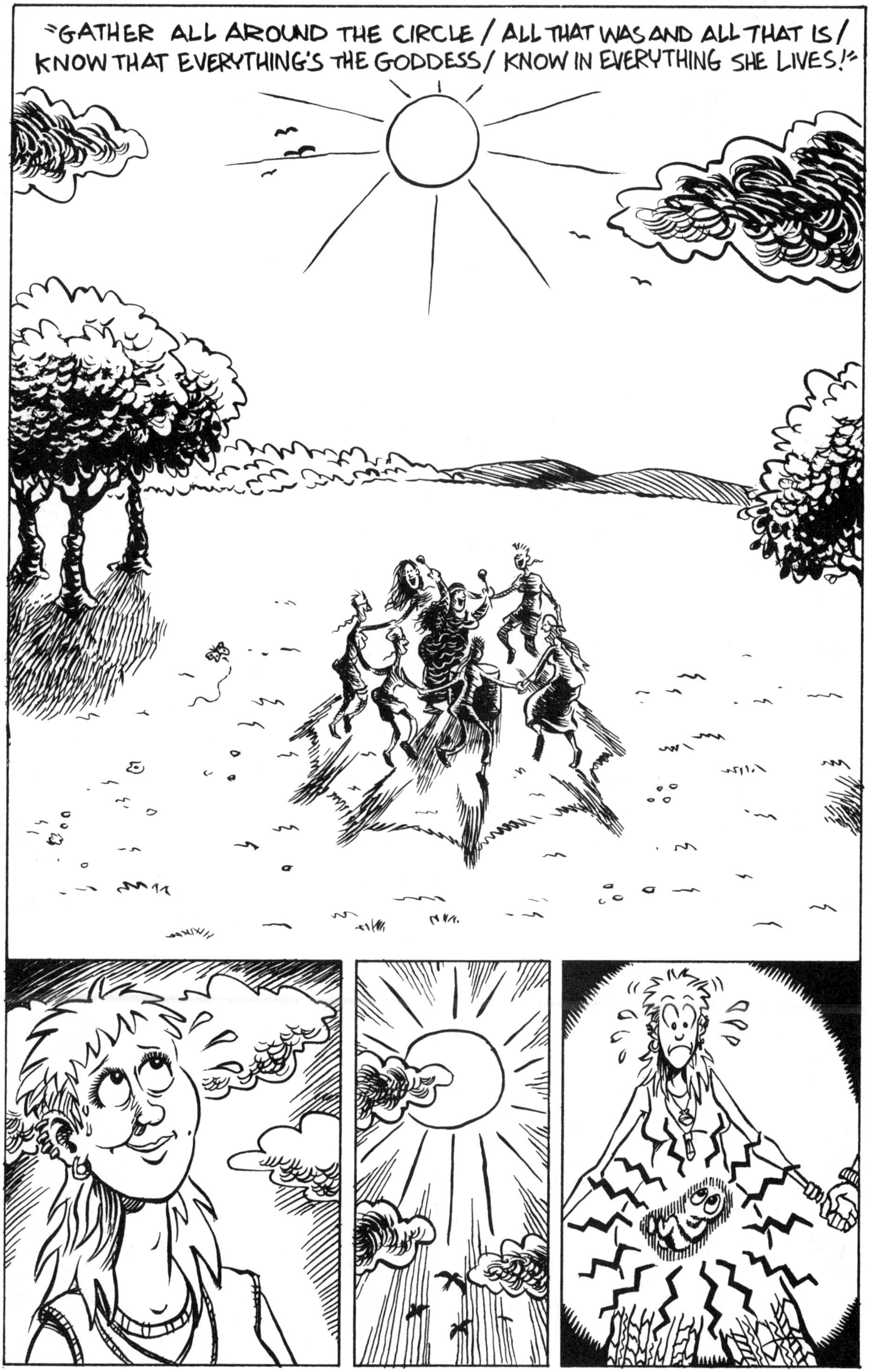
"GATHER ALL AROUND THE CIRCLE / ALL THAT WAS AND ALL THAT IS / KNOW THAT EVERYTHING'S THE GODDESS / KNOW IN EVERYTHING SHE LIVES!"

HI, PETE!

HI.

YOU AND JOLINE HAVE **FUN** LAST NIGHT?

HUH?

YOU'RE **NOT** GOING TO TELL ME YOU DIDN'T SPEND THE NIGHT WITH HER, **ARE** YOU?

N-NO! BUT WE DIDN'T **SLEEP** TOGETHER!

WOMYN'S MUSIC FESTIVAL

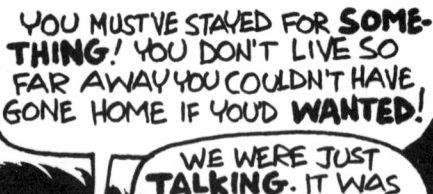

YOU MUST'VE STAYED FOR **SOME-THING**! YOU DON'T LIVE SO FAR AWAY YOU COULDN'T HAVE GONE HOME IF YOU'D **WANTED**!

WE WERE JUST **TALKING**. IT WAS LATE, AND I DIDN'T FEEL LIKE LEAVING!

"TALKING," RIGHT.

IT'S **TRUE**! THAT'S ALL WE DID! I... I WAS JUST REALLY HAPPY TO BE **TALKING** WITH SOMEONE...

I MEAN... AFTER A WHILE IT GETS KIND OF **HARD** SITTING THERE ALL BY MYSELF, WATCHING **YOU** TALK...

POOR LITTLE **ANNA**...

...HEY, I'M **SORRY** IF I HAVE MORE **PRESSING** THINGS TO DO THAN HOLD YOUR **HAND** 24 HOURS A **DAY**! I'M **SORRY** IF EVERYTHING I'VE WORKED FOR FOR **YEARS** IS FINALLY BEARING SOME **FRUIT** AND IT DISTRACTS ME FROM NOTICING YOU'RE **BORED** AT A **PARTY**..

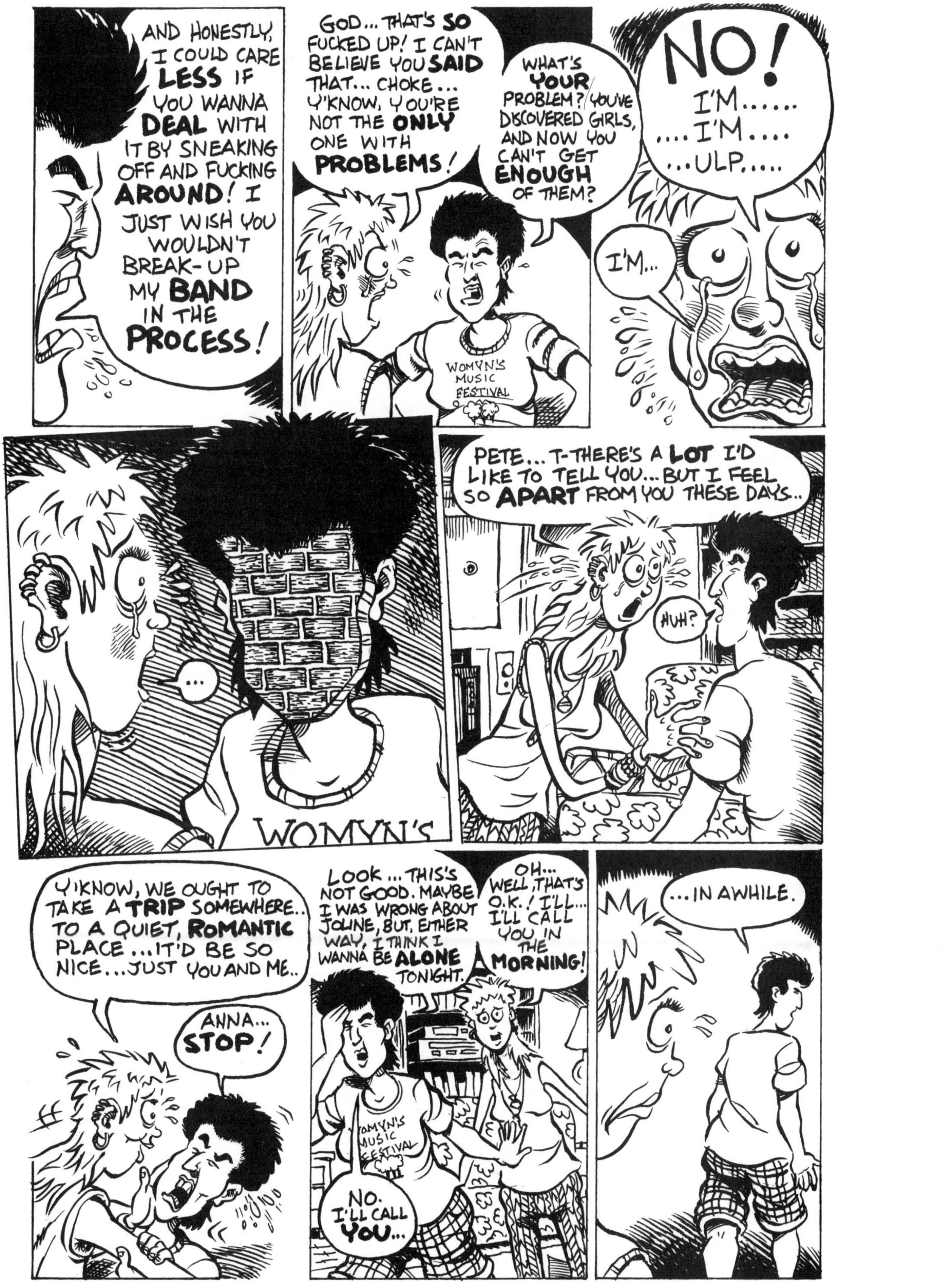

AND HONESTLY, I COULD CARE LESS IF YOU WANNA DEAL WITH IT BY SNEAKING OFF AND FUCKING AROUND! I JUST WISH YOU WOULDN'T BREAK-UP MY BAND IN THE PROCESS!
GOD... THAT'S SO FUCKED UP! I CAN'T BELIEVE YOU SAID THAT... CHOKE... Y'KNOW, YOU'RE NOT THE ONLY ONE WITH PROBLEMS!
WHAT'S YOUR PROBLEM? YOU'VE DISCOVERED GIRLS, AND NOW YOU CAN'T GET ENOUGH OF THEM?
WOMYN'S MUSIC FESTIVAL
NO! I'M...... ....I'M.... ...ULP.....
I'M...
...
WOMYN'S
PETE... T-THERE'S A LOT I'D LIKE TO TELL YOU... BUT I FEEL SO APART FROM YOU THESE DAYS...
HUH?
Y'KNOW, WE OUGHT TO TAKE A TRIP SOMEWHERE.. TO A QUIET, ROMANTIC PLACE... IT'D BE SO NICE... JUST YOU AND ME..
ANNA... STOP!
LOOK... THIS'S NOT GOOD. MAYBE I WAS WRONG ABOUT JOLINE, BUT, EITHER WAY, I THINK I WANNA BE ALONE TONIGHT.
OH... WELL, THAT'S O.K.! I'LL... I'LL CALL YOU IN THE MORNING!
WOMYN'S MUSIC FESTIVAL
NO. I'LL CALL YOU...
...IN AWHILE.

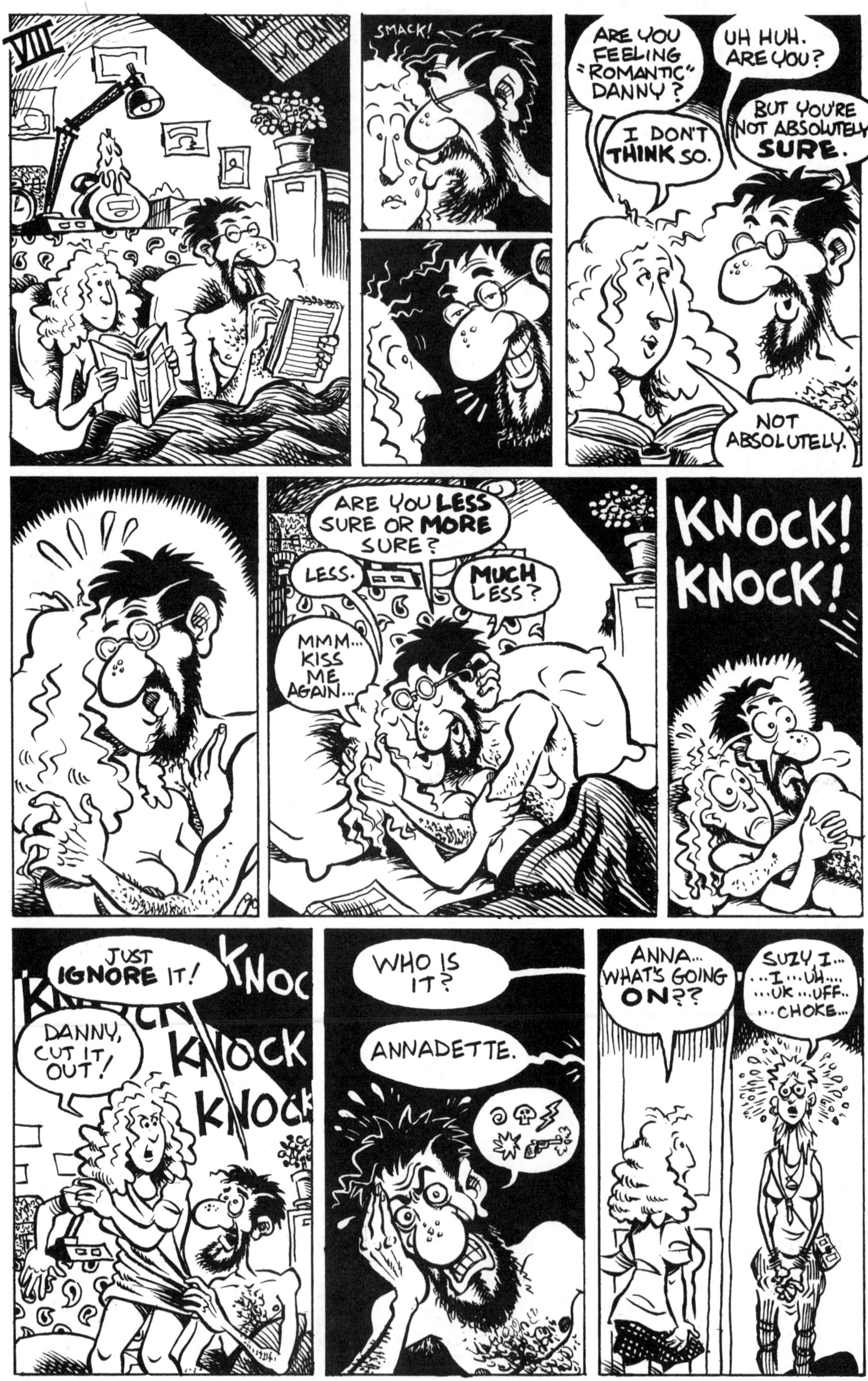
VIII
MON
SMACK!
ARE YOU FEELING "ROMANTIC" DANNY?
I DON'T THINK SO.
UH HUH. ARE YOU?
BUT YOU'RE NOT ABSOLUTELY SURE.
NOT ABSOLUTELY.
ARE YOU LESS SURE OR MORE SURE?
LESS.
MUCH LESS?
MMM... KISS ME AGAIN...
KNOCK! KNOCK!
JUST IGNORE IT!
DANNY, CUT IT OUT!
KNOCK
KNOCK
KNOCK
WHO IS IT?
ANNADETTE.
ANNA... WHAT'S GOING ON??
SUZY I... ...I...UH.... ...UK ...UFF.. ...CHOKE...

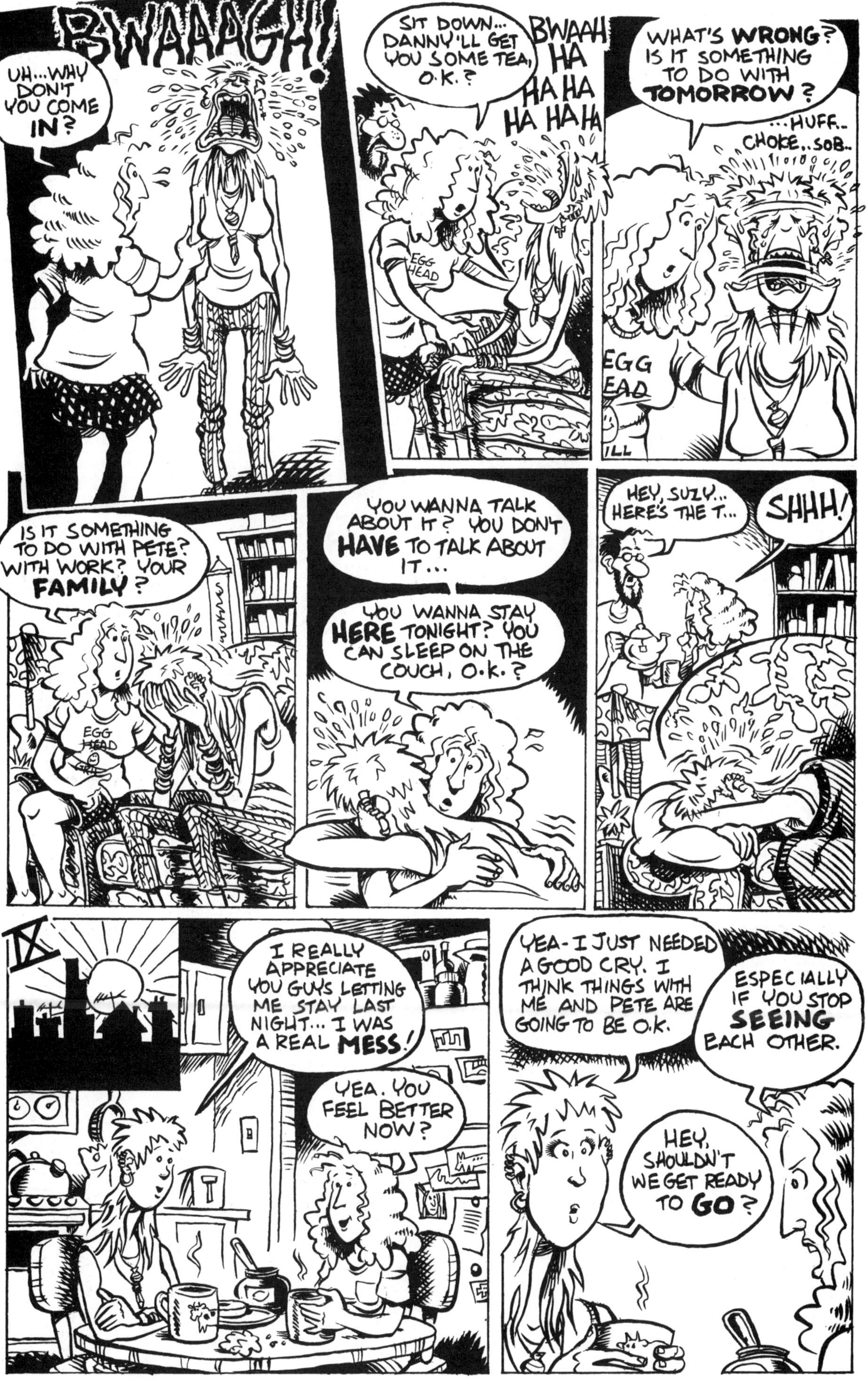
BWAAAGH!
UH...WHY DON'T YOU COME IN?
SIT DOWN... DANNY'LL GET YOU SOME TEA, O.K.?
BWAAH HA HA HA HA HA HA
WHAT'S WRONG? IS IT SOMETHING TO DO WITH TOMORROW?
...HUFF.. CHOKE..SOB..
EGG HEAD
IS IT SOMETHING TO DO WITH PETE? WITH WORK? YOUR FAMILY?
EGG HEAD
YOU WANNA TALK ABOUT IT? YOU DON'T HAVE TO TALK ABOUT IT...
YOU WANNA STAY HERE TONIGHT? YOU CAN SLEEP ON THE COUCH, O.K.?
HEY, SUZY... HERE'S THE T...
SHHH!
IX
I REALLY APPRECIATE YOU GUYS LETTING ME STAY LAST NIGHT... I WAS A REAL MESS!
YEA. YOU FEEL BETTER NOW?
YEA- I JUST NEEDED A GOOD CRY. I THINK THINGS WITH ME AND PETE ARE GOING TO BE O.K.
ESPECIALLY IF YOU STOP SEEING EACH OTHER.
HEY, SHOULDN'T WE GET READY TO GO?

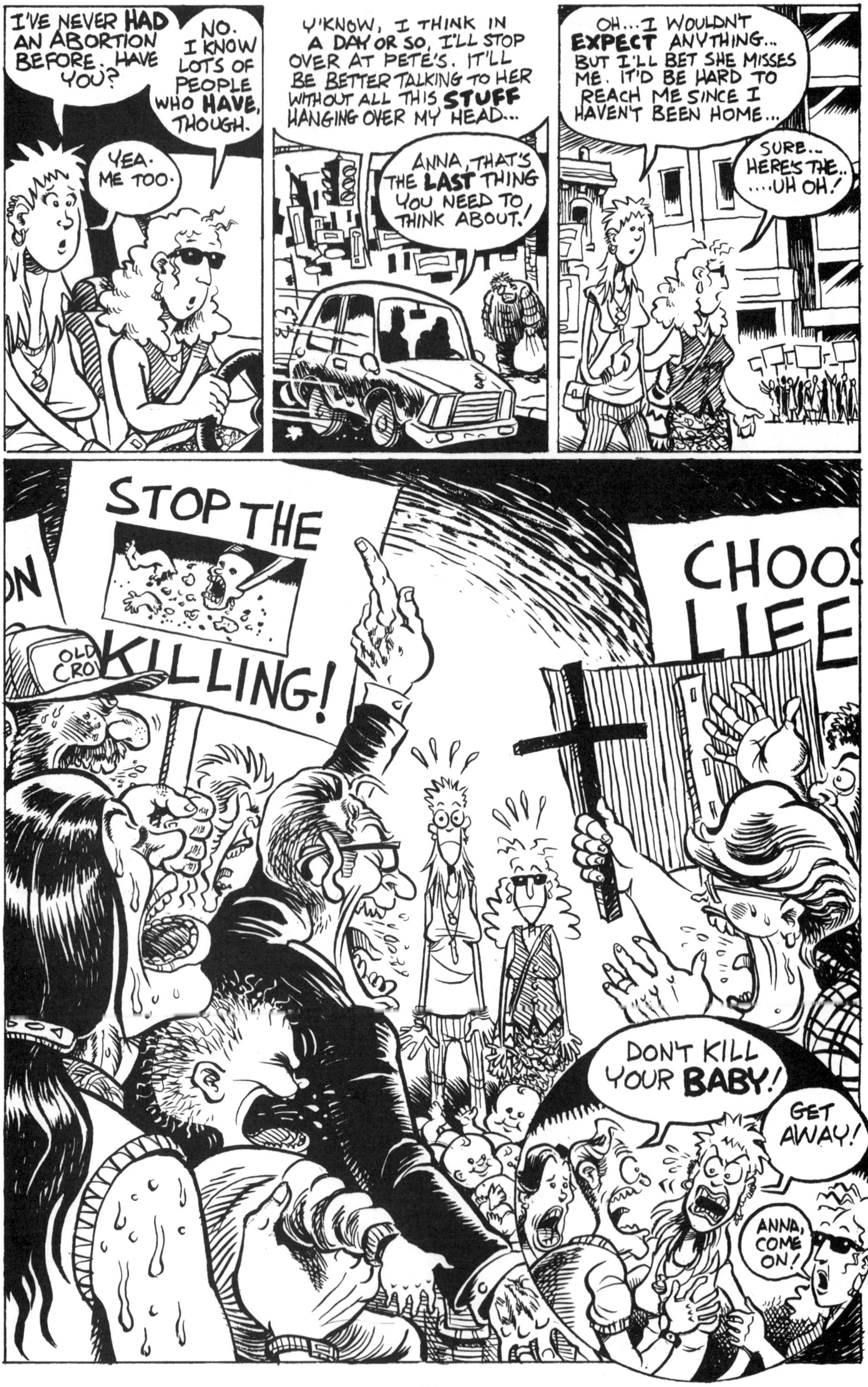

I'VE NEVER HAD AN ABORTION BEFORE. HAVE YOU?
NO. I KNOW LOTS OF PEOPLE WHO HAVE, THOUGH.
YEA. ME TOO.
Y'KNOW, I THINK IN A DAY OR SO, I'LL STOP OVER AT PETE'S. IT'LL BE BETTER TALKING TO HER WITHOUT ALL THIS STUFF HANGING OVER MY HEAD...
ANNA, THAT'S THE LAST THING YOU NEED TO THINK ABOUT!
OH... I WOULDN'T EXPECT ANYTHING... BUT I'LL BET SHE MISSES ME. IT'D BE HARD TO REACH ME SINCE I HAVEN'T BEEN HOME...
SURE... HERE'S THE... ...UH OH!
STOP THE KILLING!
OLD CRO
ON
CHOOS LIFE
DON'T KILL YOUR BABY!
GET AWAY!
ANNA, COME ON!

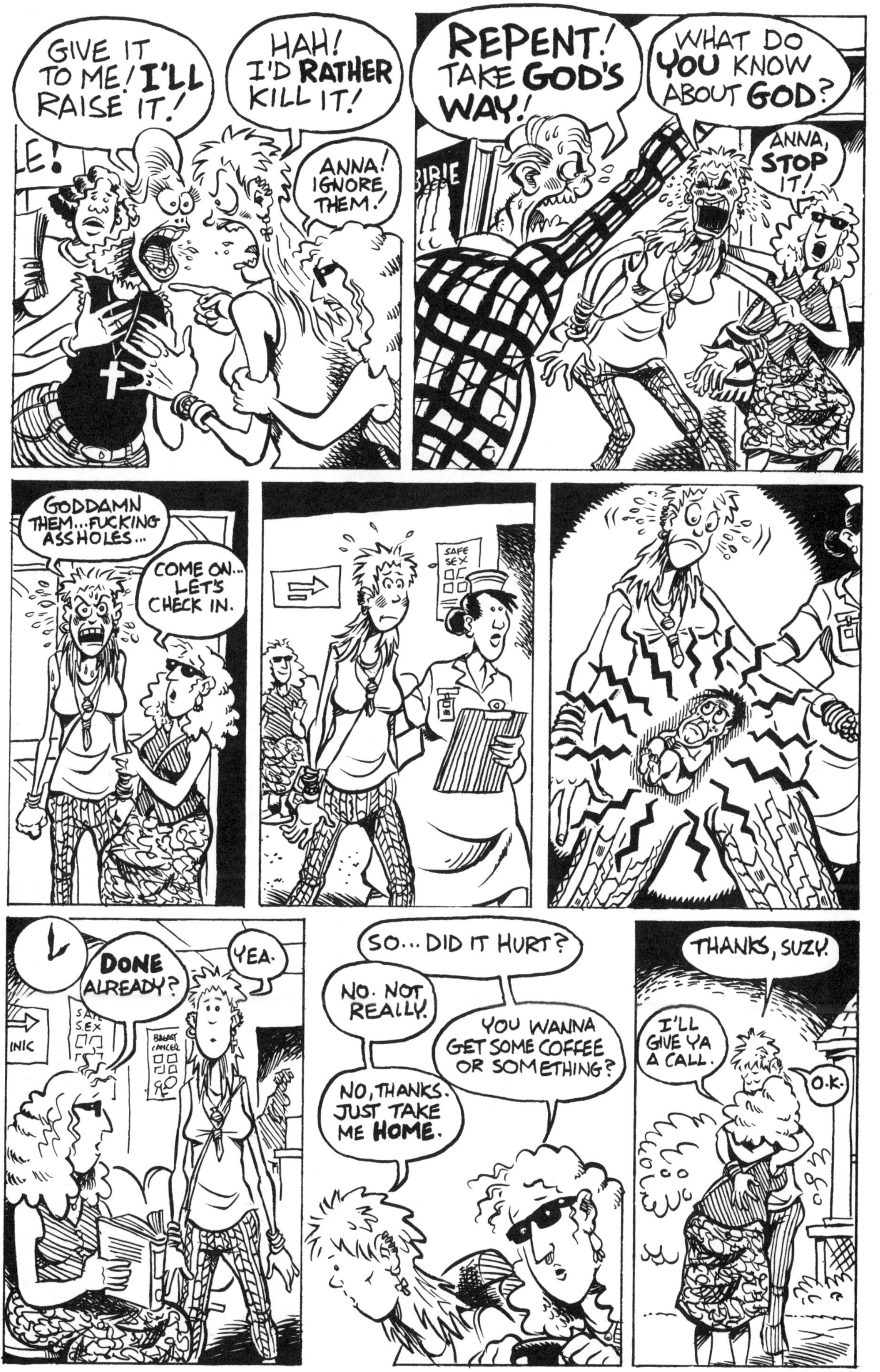
GIVE IT TO ME! I'LL RAISE IT!
HAH! I'D RATHER KILL IT!
ANNA! IGNORE THEM!
REPENT! TAKE GOD'S WAY!
WHAT DO YOU KNOW ABOUT GOD?
ANNA, STOP IT!
GODDAMN THEM... FUCKING ASSHOLES...
COME ON... LET'S CHECK IN.
SAFE SEX
DONE ALREADY?
YEA.
THANKS, SUZY.
SO... DID IT HURT?
NO. NOT REALLY.
YOU WANNA GET SOME COFFEE OR SOMETHING?
NO, THANKS. JUST TAKE ME HOME.
I'LL GIVE YA A CALL.
O.K.

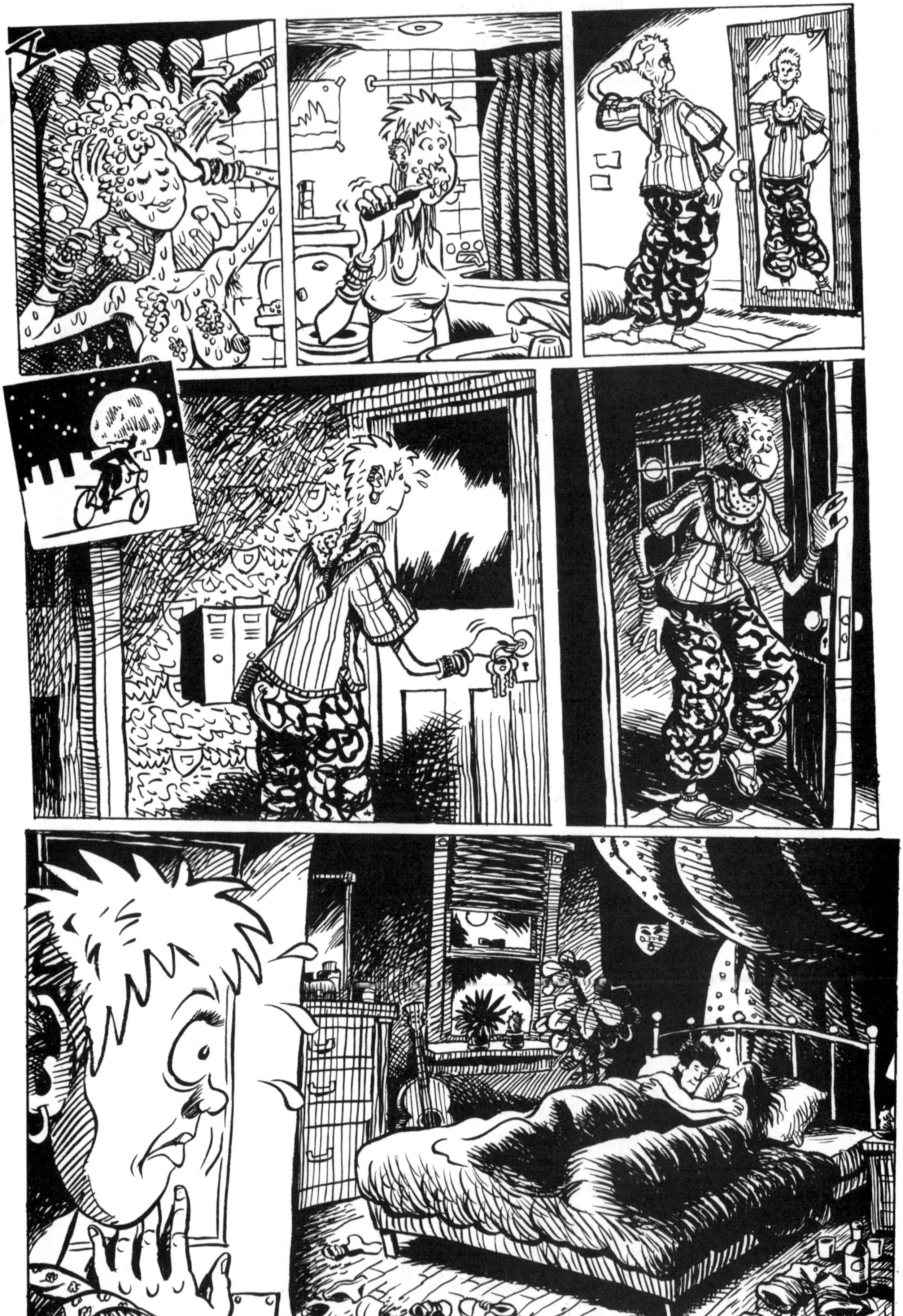

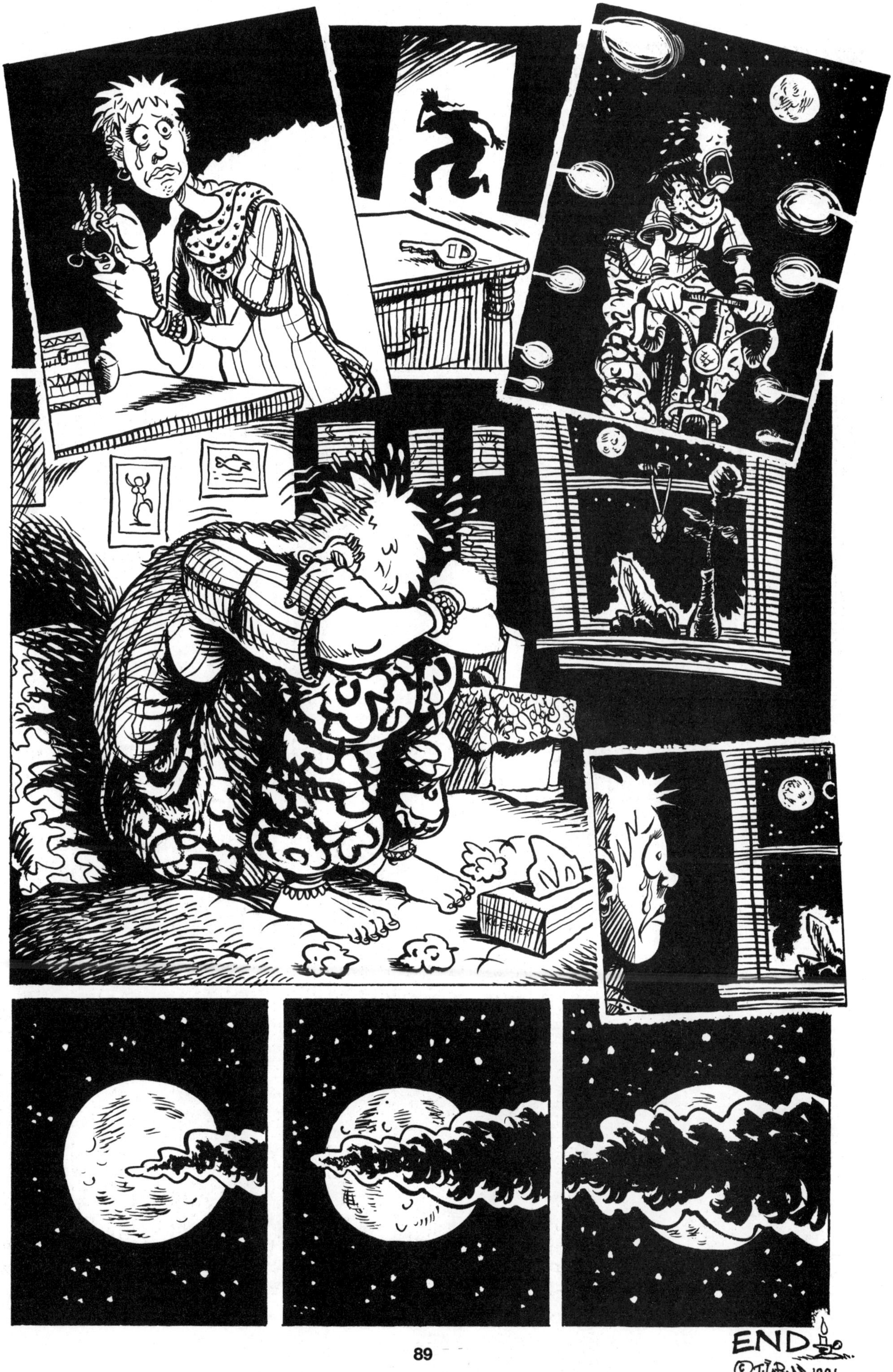
END
© T. LaBan 1991

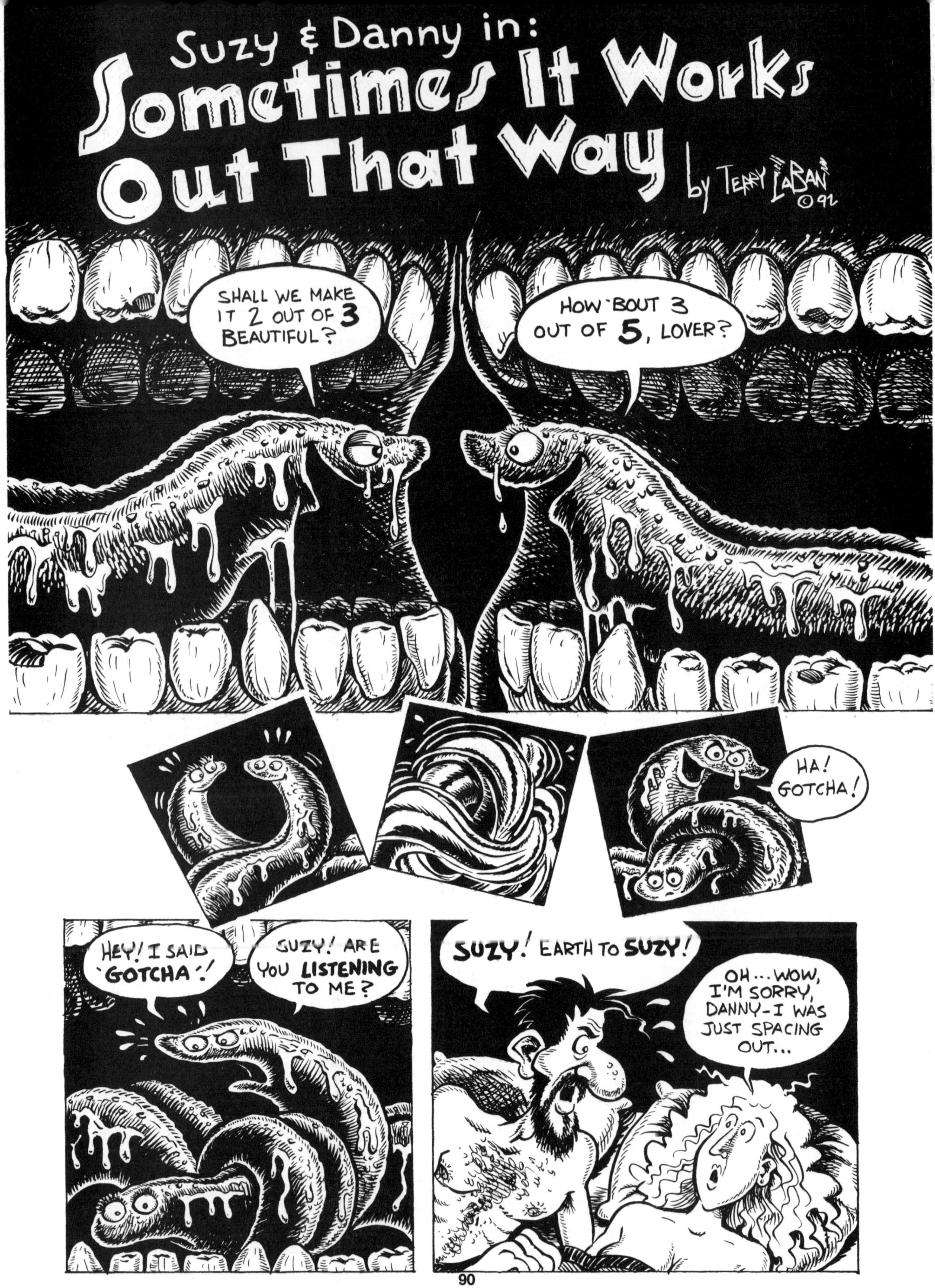
Suzy & Danny in:
Sometimes It Works Out That Way
by Terry LaBan ©92
SHALL WE MAKE IT 2 OUT OF 3 BEAUTIFUL?
HOW 'BOUT 3 OUT OF 5, LOVER?
HA! GOTCHA!
HEY! I SAID 'GOTCHA'!
SUZY! ARE YOU LISTENING TO ME?
SUZY! EARTH TO SUZY!
OH... WOW, I'M SORRY, DANNY-I WAS JUST SPACING OUT...

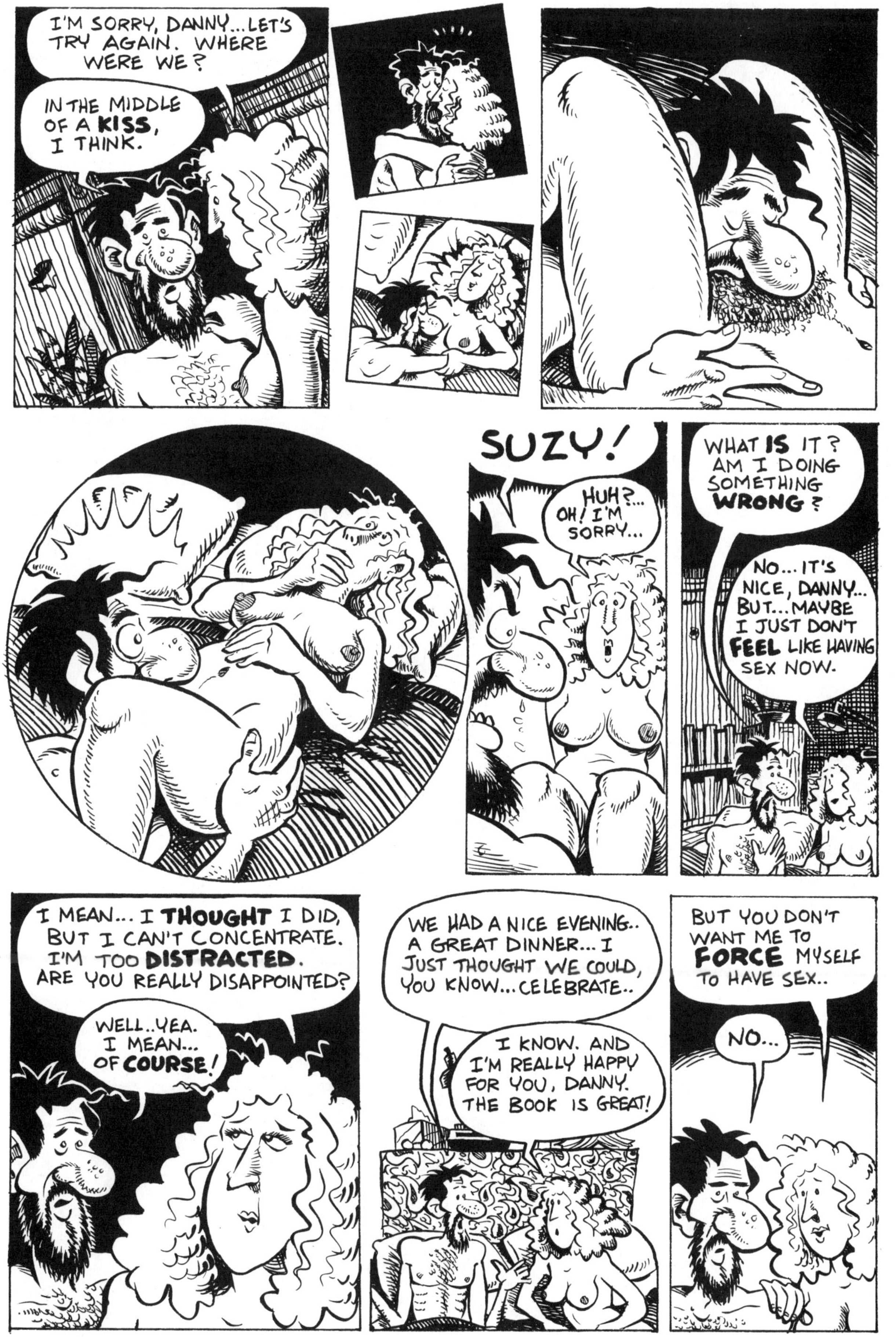
I'M SORRY, DANNY... LET'S TRY AGAIN. WHERE WERE WE?
IN THE MIDDLE OF A KISS, I THINK.
SUZY!
HUH?... OH! I'M SORRY...
WHAT IS IT? AM I DOING SOMETHING WRONG?
NO... IT'S NICE, DANNY... BUT... MAYBE I JUST DON'T FEEL LIKE HAVING SEX NOW.
I MEAN... I THOUGHT I DID, BUT I CAN'T CONCENTRATE. I'M TOO DISTRACTED. ARE YOU REALLY DISAPPOINTED?
WELL.. YEA. I MEAN... OF COURSE!
WE HAD A NICE EVENING.. A GREAT DINNER... I JUST THOUGHT WE COULD, YOU KNOW... CELEBRATE..
I KNOW. AND I'M REALLY HAPPY FOR YOU, DANNY. THE BOOK IS GREAT!
BUT YOU DON'T WANT ME TO FORCE MYSELF TO HAVE SEX..
NO...

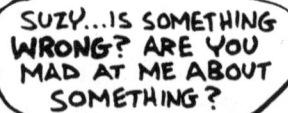

SUZY...IS SOMETHING **WRONG**? ARE YOU **MAD** AT ME ABOUT SOMETHING?

NO, DANNY! NOT AT **ALL**!

THEN WHY ARE YOU SO... **DISTRACTED** LATELY?

I'VE JUST BEEN **THINKING** A LOT SINCE I QUIT MY LAST JOB...ABOUT MY **FUTURE**.

WHAT **ABOUT** IT?

I JUST CAN'T BEAR THE THOUGHT OF GETTING **ANOTHER** CRUMMY **JOB**... I'M SMART... I'M ABLE...

...AND EVEN THOUGH I'M **LAZY**, I'M KIND OF AMBITIOUS.

SO?

SO... I'VE BEEN THINKING SERIOUSLY ABOUT GOING BACK TO **SCHOOL**.

OH-

DOES THAT FREAK YOU **OUT**?

NO...WHY SHOULD IT? I KIND OF THOUGHT YOU WOULD, ONE DAY...

I MEAN...THERE'S SOME **GREAT** UNIVERSITIES AROUND **HERE**.

UM...YEA... I.. DON'T KNOW IF IT'D **BE** AROUND HERE.

WADDAYA **MEAN**? WHERE **WOULD** IT BE?

I DON'T KNOW YET!... I'M JUST **THINKING** ABOUT IT!

LOOK... NOTHING'S EVEN **CLOSE** TO DECIDED! IT'S NOTHING TO **WORRY** ABOUT!

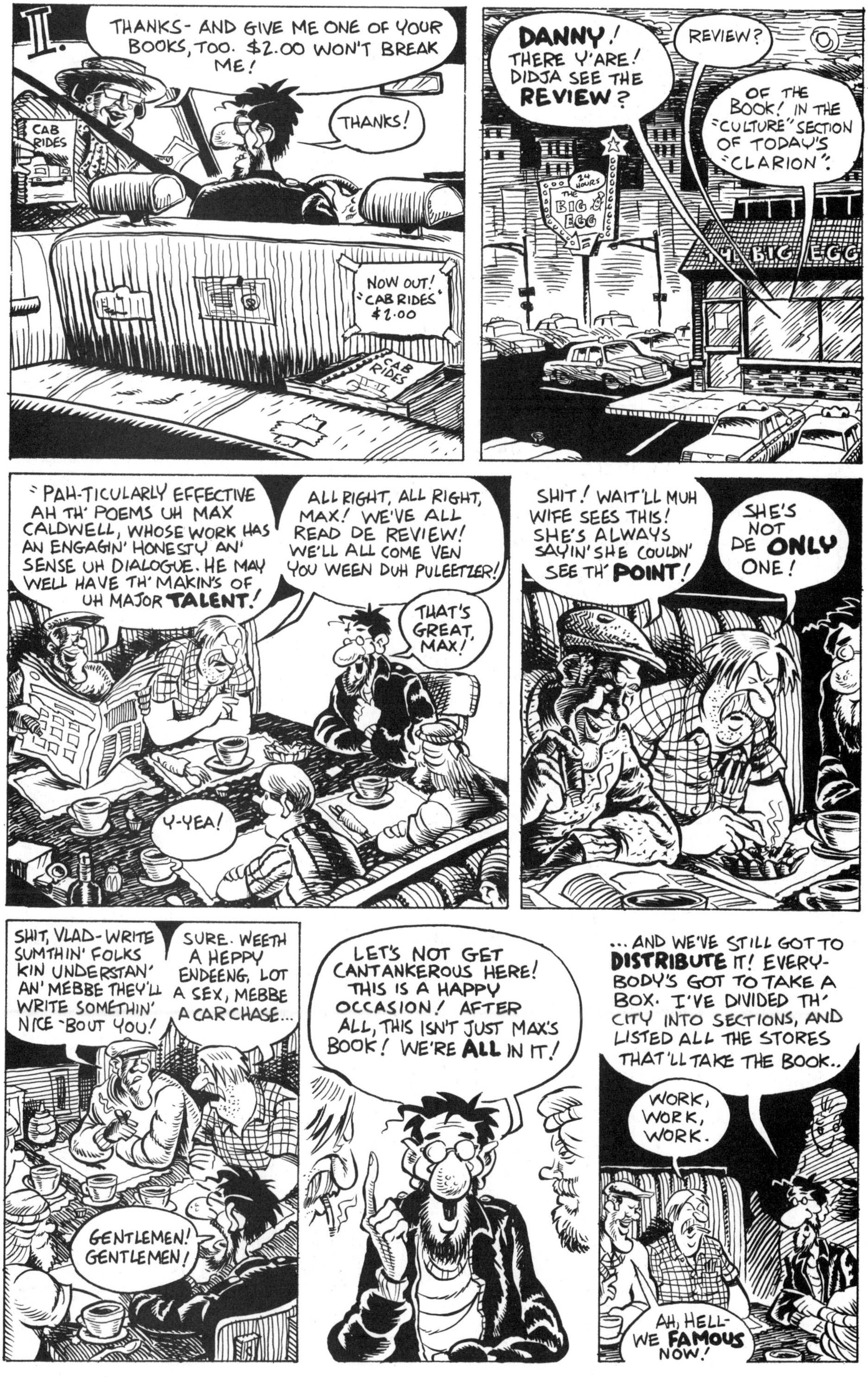
II.
THANKS- AND GIVE ME ONE OF YOUR BOOKS, TOO. $2.00 WON'T BREAK ME!
THANKS!
CAB RIDES
NOW OUT! "CAB RIDES" $2.00
CAB RIDES
DANNY! THERE Y'ARE! DIDJA SEE THE REVIEW?
REVIEW?
OF THE BOOK! IN THE "CULTURE" SECTION OF TODAY'S "CLARION"!
24 HOURS THE BIG EGG
THE BIG EGG
"PAH-TICULARLY EFFECTIVE AH TH' POEMS UH MAX CALDWELL, WHOSE WORK HAS AN ENGAGIN' HONESTY AN' SENSE UH DIALOGUE. HE MAY WELL HAVE TH' MAKIN'S OF UH MAJOR TALENT."
ALL RIGHT, ALL RIGHT, MAX! WE'VE ALL READ DE REVIEW! WE'LL ALL COME VEN YOU WEEN DUH PULEETZER!
THAT'S GREAT, MAX!
Y-YEA!
SHIT! WAIT'LL MUH WIFE SEES THIS! SHE'S ALWAYS SAYIN' SHE COULDN' SEE TH' POINT!
SHE'S NOT DE ONLY ONE!
SHIT, VLAD- WRITE SUMTHIN' FOLKS KIN UNDERSTAN' AN' MEBBE THEY'LL WRITE SOMETHIN' NICE 'BOUT YOU!
SURE. WEETH A HEPPY ENDEENG, LOT A SEX, MEBBE A CAR CHASE...
GENTLEMEN! GENTLEMEN!
LET'S NOT GET CANTANKEROUS HERE! THIS IS A HAPPY OCCASION! AFTER ALL, THIS ISN'T JUST MAX'S BOOK! WE'RE ALL IN IT!
...AND WE'VE STILL GOT TO DISTRIBUTE IT! EVERY-BODY'S GOT TO TAKE A BOX. I'VE DIVIDED TH' CITY INTO SECTIONS, AND LISTED ALL THE STORES THAT'LL TAKE THE BOOK..
WORK, WORK, WORK.
AH, HELL- WE FAMOUS NOW!

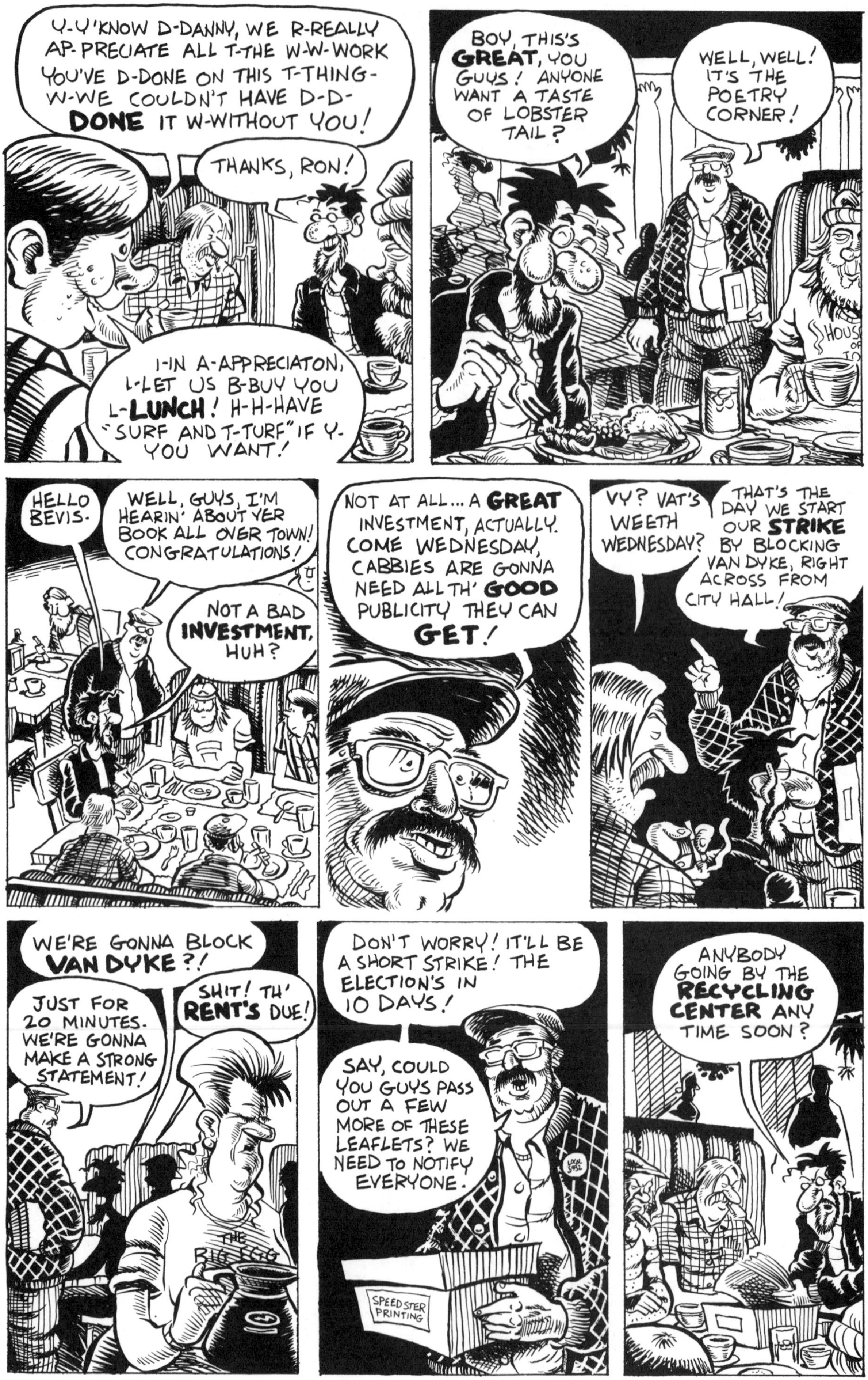
Y-Y'KNOW D-DANNY, WE R-REALLY AP-PRECIATE ALL T-THE W-W-WORK YOU'VE D-DONE ON THIS T-THING- W-WE COULDN'T HAVE D-D-DONE IT W-WITHOUT YOU!
THANKS, RON!
I-IN A-APPRECIATON, L-LET US B-BUY YOU L-LUNCH! H-H-HAVE "SURF AND T-TURF" IF Y-YOU WANT!
BOY, THIS'S GREAT, YOU GUYS! ANYONE WANT A TASTE OF LOBSTER TAIL?
WELL, WELL! IT'S THE POETRY CORNER!
HELLO BEVIS.
WELL, GUYS, I'M HEARIN' ABOUT YER BOOK ALL OVER TOWN! CONGRATULATIONS!
NOT A BAD INVESTMENT, HUH?
NOT AT ALL... A GREAT INVESTMENT, ACTUALLY. COME WEDNESDAY, CABBIES ARE GONNA NEED ALL TH' GOOD PUBLICITY THEY CAN GET!
VY? VAT'S WEETH WEDNESDAY?
THAT'S THE DAY WE START OUR STRIKE BY BLOCKING VAN DYKE, RIGHT ACROSS FROM CITY HALL!
WE'RE GONNA BLOCK VAN DYKE?!
JUST FOR 20 MINUTES. WE'RE GONNA MAKE A STRONG STATEMENT!
SHIT! TH' RENT'S DUE!
THE BIG EGG
DON'T WORRY! IT'LL BE A SHORT STRIKE! THE ELECTION'S IN 10 DAYS!
SAY, COULD YOU GUYS PASS OUT A FEW MORE OF THESE LEAFLETS? WE NEED TO NOTIFY EVERYONE.
SPEEDSTER PRINTING
ANYBODY GOING BY THE RECYCLING CENTER ANY TIME SOON?

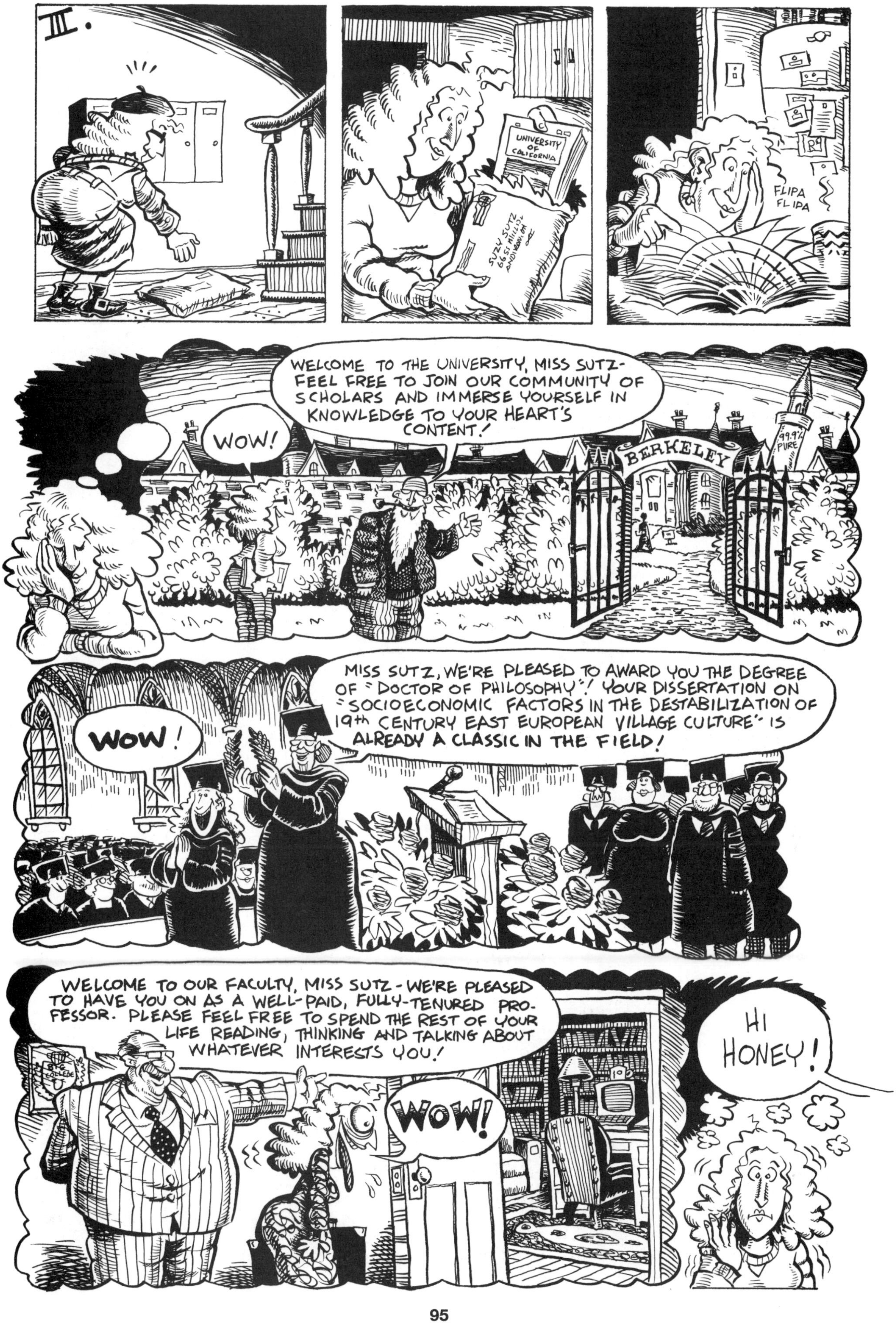
III.
UNIVERSITY OF CALIFORNIA
FLIPA FLIPA
WELCOME TO THE UNIVERSITY, MISS SUTZ- FEEL FREE TO JOIN OUR COMMUNITY OF SCHOLARS AND IMMERSE YOURSELF IN KNOWLEDGE TO YOUR HEART'S CONTENT!
WOW!
BERKELEY
99.9% PURE
MISS SUTZ, WE'RE PLEASED TO AWARD YOU THE DEGREE OF "DOCTOR OF PHILOSOPHY"! YOUR DISSERTATION ON "SOCIOECONOMIC FACTORS IN THE DESTABILIZATION OF 19th CENTURY EAST EUROPEAN VILLAGE CULTURE" IS ALREADY A CLASSIC IN THE FIELD!
WOW!
WELCOME TO OUR FACULTY, MISS SUTZ - WE'RE PLEASED TO HAVE YOU ON AS A WELL-PAID, FULLY-TENURED PRO-FESSOR. PLEASE FEEL FREE TO SPEND THE REST OF YOUR LIFE READING, THINKING AND TALKING ABOUT WHATEVER INTERESTS YOU!
WOW!
HI HONEY!

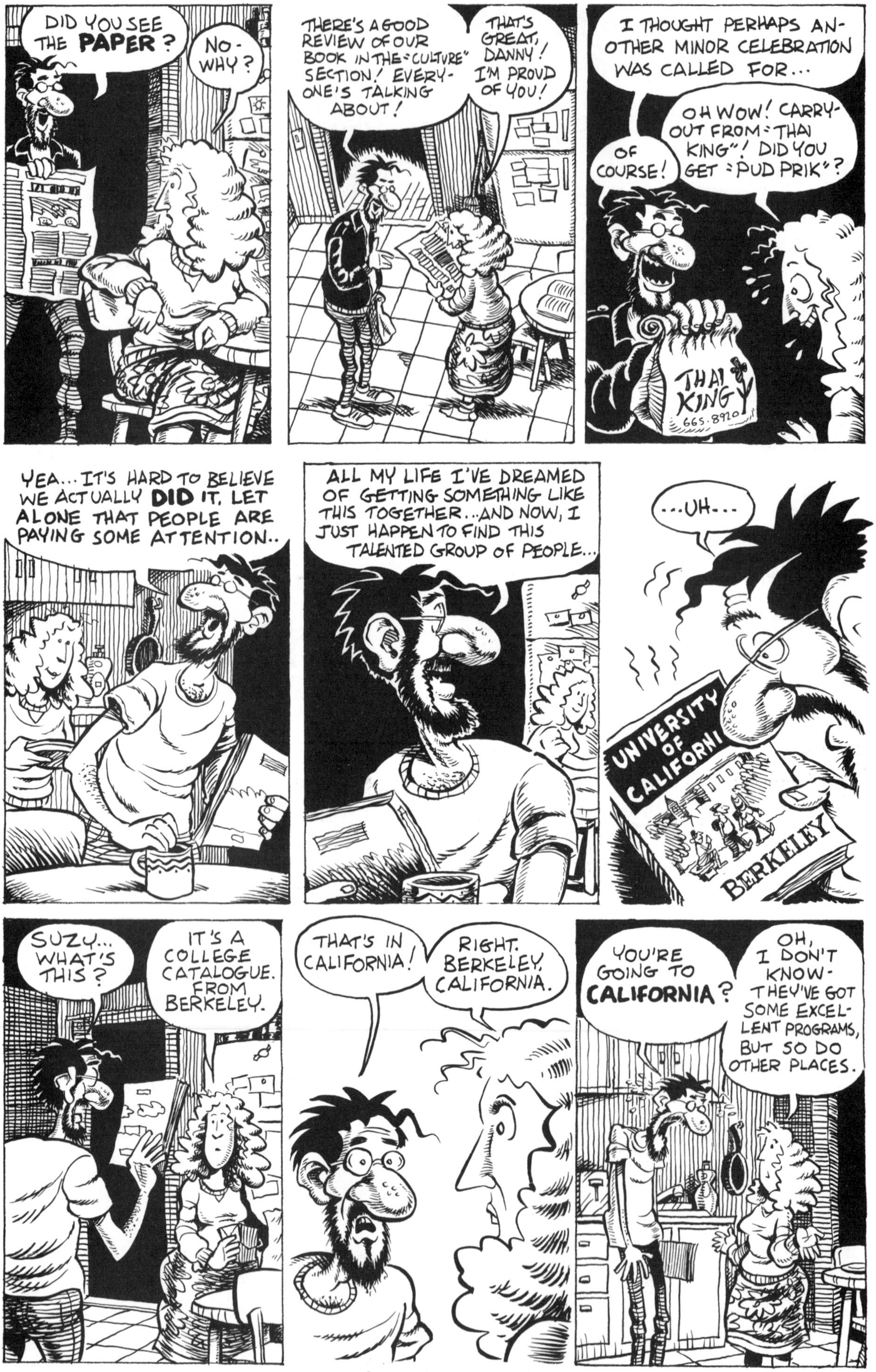
DID YOU SEE THE PAPER?
NO-WHY?
THERE'S A GOOD REVIEW OF OUR BOOK IN THE "CULTURE" SECTION! EVERY-ONE'S TALKING ABOUT!
THAT'S GREAT, DANNY! I'M PROUD OF YOU!
I THOUGHT PERHAPS AN-OTHER MINOR CELEBRATION WAS CALLED FOR...
OF COURSE!
OH WOW! CARRY-OUT FROM "THAI KING"! DID YOU GET "PUD PRIK"?
THAI KING
665-8920
YEA... IT'S HARD TO BELIEVE WE ACTUALLY DID IT, LET ALONE THAT PEOPLE ARE PAYING SOME ATTENTION..
ALL MY LIFE I'VE DREAMED OF GETTING SOMETHING LIKE THIS TOGETHER...AND NOW, I JUST HAPPEN TO FIND THIS TALENTED GROUP OF PEOPLE...
...UH...
UNIVERSITY OF CALIFORNI
BERKELEY
SUZY... WHAT'S THIS?
IT'S A COLLEGE CATALOGUE. FROM BERKELEY.
THAT'S IN CALIFORNIA!
RIGHT. BERKELEY, CALIFORNIA.
YOU'RE GOING TO CALIFORNIA?
OH, I DON'T KNOW- THEY'VE GOT SOME EXCEL-LENT PROGRAMS, BUT SO DO OTHER PLACES.

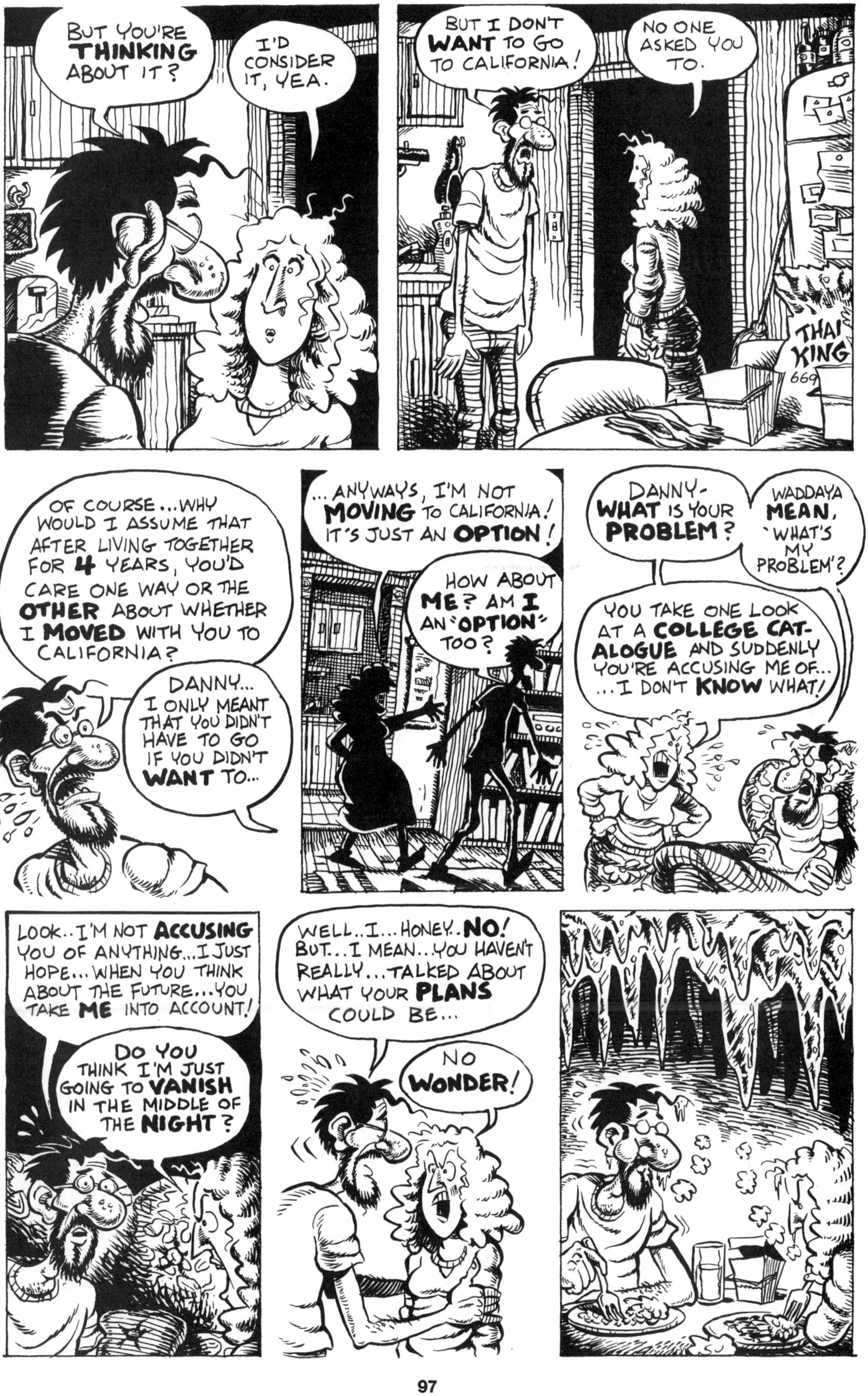
BUT YOU'RE THINKING ABOUT IT?
I'D CONSIDER IT, YEA.
BUT I DON'T WANT TO GO TO CALIFORNIA!
NO ONE ASKED YOU TO.
THAI KING 669
OF COURSE... WHY WOULD I ASSUME THAT AFTER LIVING TOGETHER FOR 4 YEARS, YOU'D CARE ONE WAY OR THE OTHER ABOUT WHETHER I MOVED WITH YOU TO CALIFORNIA?
DANNY... I ONLY MEANT THAT YOU DIDN'T HAVE TO GO IF YOU DIDN'T WANT TO...
...ANYWAYS, I'M NOT MOVING TO CALIFORNIA! IT'S JUST AN OPTION!
HOW ABOUT ME? AM I AN "OPTION" TOO?
DANNY- WHAT IS YOUR PROBLEM?
WADDAYA MEAN, 'WHAT'S MY PROBLEM'?
YOU TAKE ONE LOOK AT A COLLEGE CATALOGUE AND SUDDENLY YOU'RE ACCUSING ME OF... ...I DON'T KNOW WHAT!
LOOK.. I'M NOT ACCUSING YOU OF ANYTHING... I JUST HOPE... WHEN YOU THINK ABOUT THE FUTURE... YOU TAKE ME INTO ACCOUNT!
DO YOU THINK I'M JUST GOING TO VANISH IN THE MIDDLE OF THE NIGHT?
WELL.. I... HONEY.. NO! BUT... I MEAN... YOU HAVEN'T REALLY... TALKED ABOUT WHAT YOUR PLANS COULD BE...
NO WONDER!

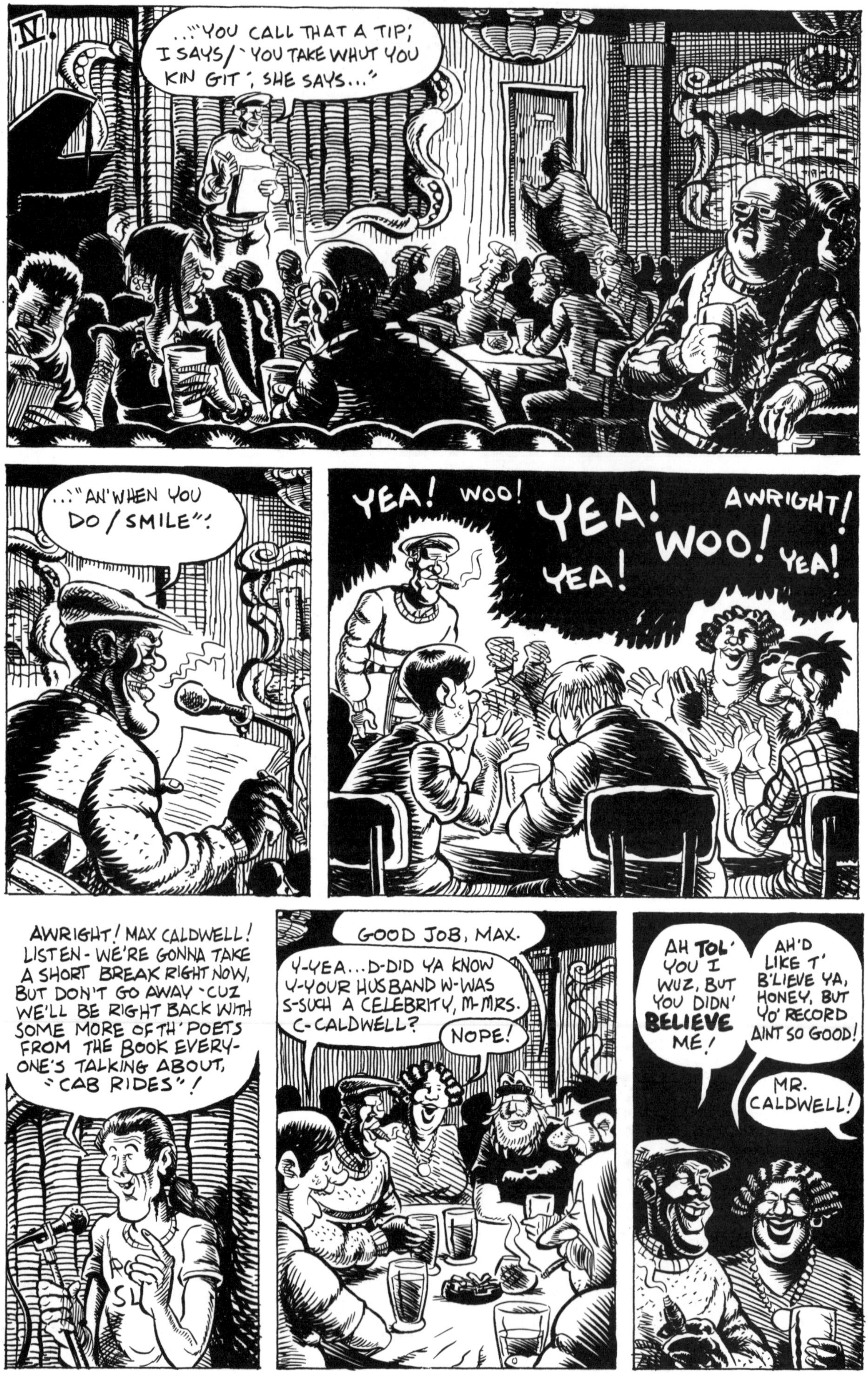

IV.
..."YOU CALL THAT A TIP," I SAYS / "YOU TAKE WHUT YOU KIN GIT", SHE SAYS..."
..."AN' WHEN YOU DO / SMILE"!
YEA! WOO! YEA! AWRIGHT! YEA! WOO! YEA!
AWRIGHT! MAX CALDWELL! LISTEN - WE'RE GONNA TAKE A SHORT BREAK RIGHT NOW, BUT DON'T GO AWAY 'CUZ WE'LL BE RIGHT BACK WITH SOME MORE OF TH' POETS FROM THE BOOK EVERYONE'S TALKING ABOUT, "CAB RIDES"!
GOOD JOB, MAX.
Y-YEA...D-DID YA KNOW Y-YOUR HUSBAND W-WAS S-SUCH A CELEBRITY, M-MRS. C-CALDWELL?
NOPE!
AH TOL' YOU I WUZ, BUT YOU DIDN' BELIEVE ME!
AH'D LIKE T' B'LIEVE YA, HONEY, BUT YO' RECORD AINT SO GOOD!
MR. CALDWELL!

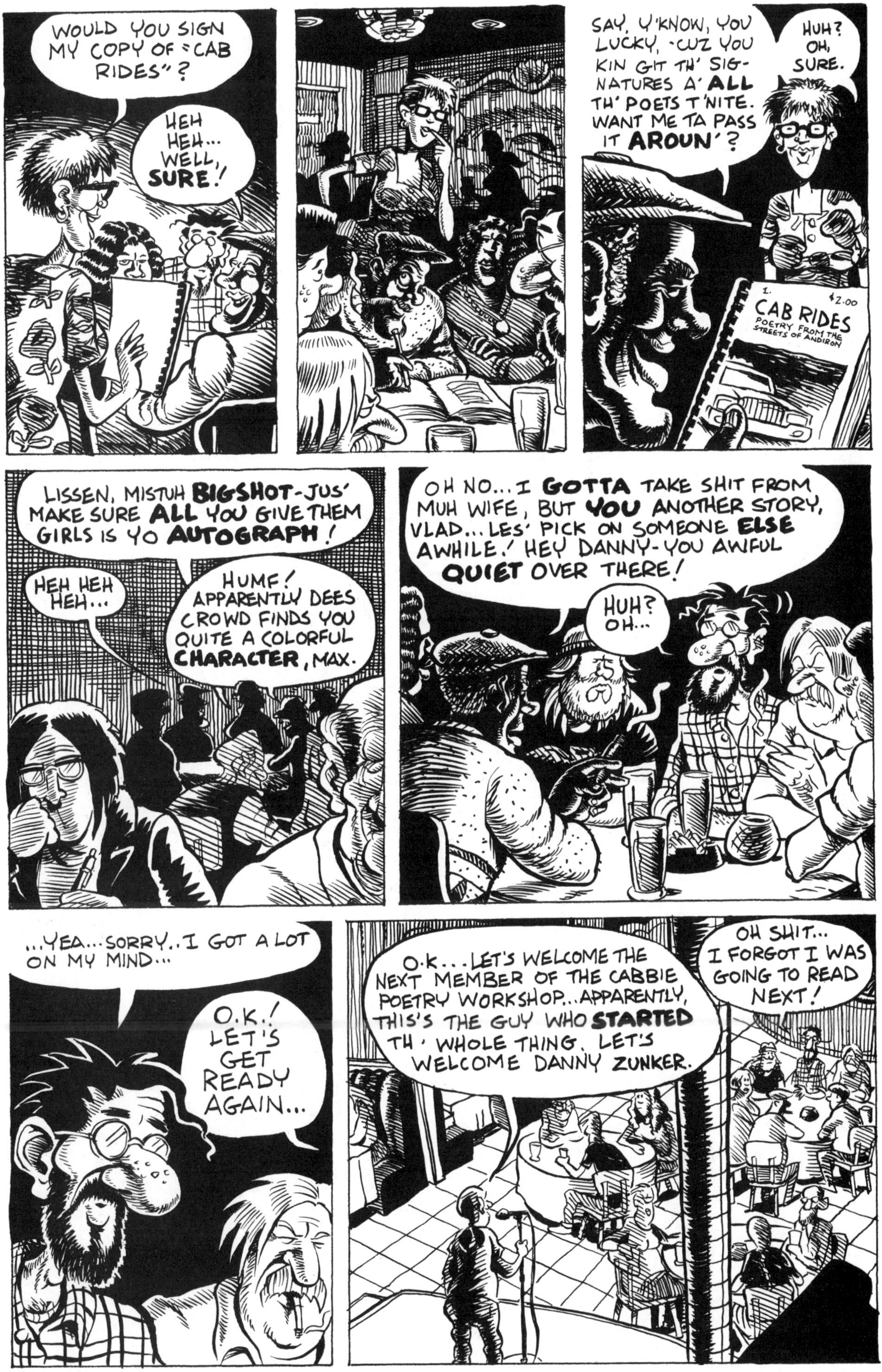

WOULD YOU SIGN MY COPY OF "CAB RIDES"?
HEH HEH... WELL, SURE!
SAY, Y'KNOW, YOU LUCKY, -CUZ YOU KIN GIT TH' SIGNATURES A' ALL TH' POETS T'NITE. WANT ME TA PASS IT AROUN'?
HUH? OH, SURE.
1. $2.00
CAB RIDES
POETRY FROM THE STREETS OF ANDIRON
LISSEN, MISTUH BIGSHOT-JUS' MAKE SURE ALL YOU GIVE THEM GIRLS IS YO AUTOGRAPH!
HEH HEH HEH...
HUMF! APPARENTLY DEES CROWD FINDS YOU QUITE A COLORFUL CHARACTER, MAX.
OH NO... I GOTTA TAKE SHIT FROM MUH WIFE, BUT YOU ANOTHER STORY, VLAD... LES' PICK ON SOMEONE ELSE AWHILE! HEY DANNY- YOU AWFUL QUIET OVER THERE!
HUH? OH...
...YEA...SORRY..I GOT A LOT ON MY MIND...
O.K.! LET'S GET READY AGAIN...
O.K... LET'S WELCOME THE NEXT MEMBER OF THE CABBIE POETRY WORKSHOP... APPARENTLY, THIS'S THE GUY WHO STARTED TH' WHOLE THING. LET'S WELCOME DANNY ZUNKER.
OH SHIT... I FORGOT I WAS GOING TO READ NEXT!

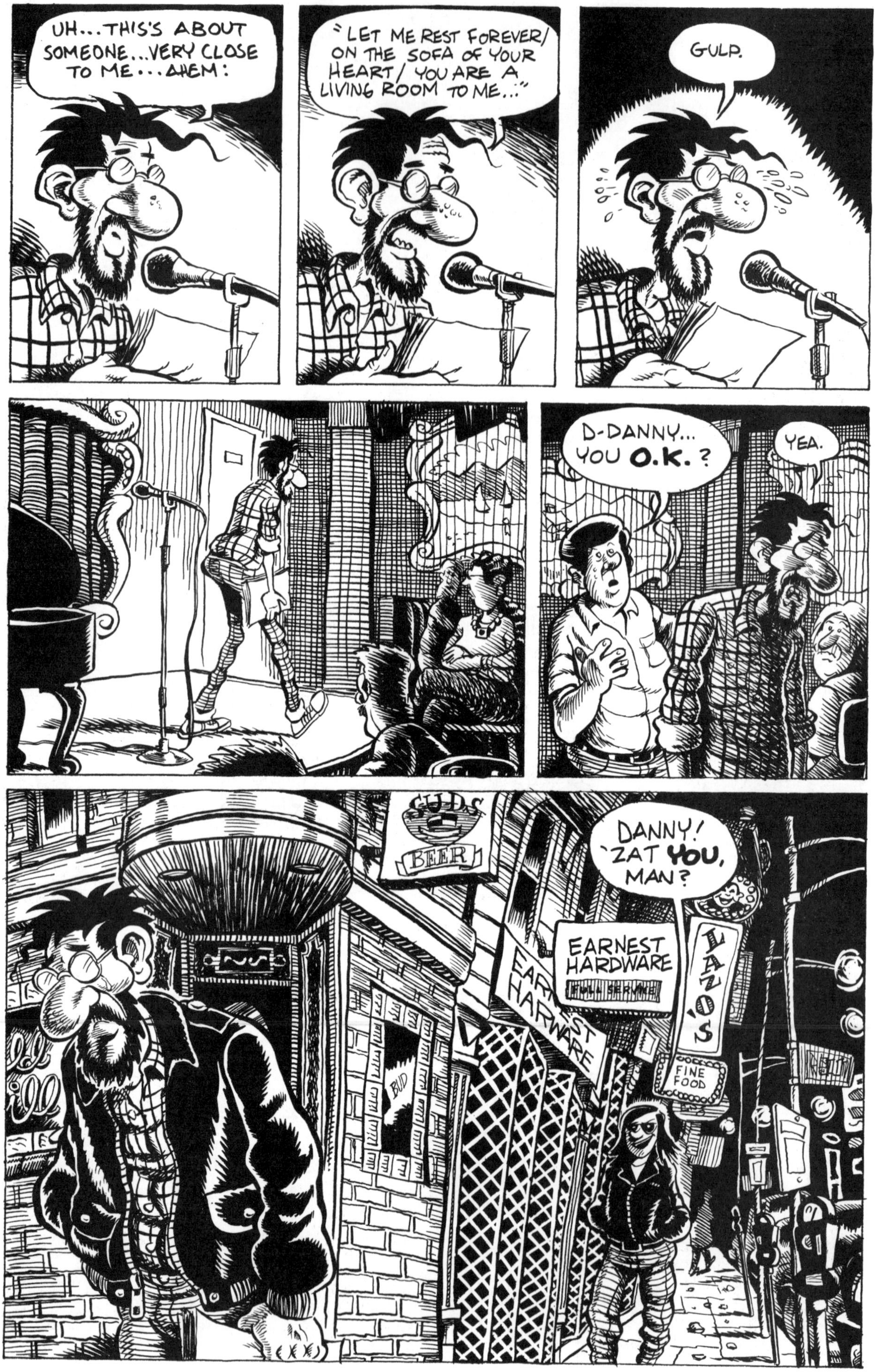
UH...THIS'S ABOUT SOMEONE...VERY CLOSE TO ME...AHEM:
"LET ME REST FOREVER/ ON THE SOFA OF YOUR HEART/ YOU ARE A LIVING ROOM TO ME...."
GULP.
D-DANNY... YOU O.K.?
YEA.
BEER
DANNY! 'ZAT YOU, MAN?
EARNEST HARDWARE
EARNEST HARWARE
FINE FOOD
BUD

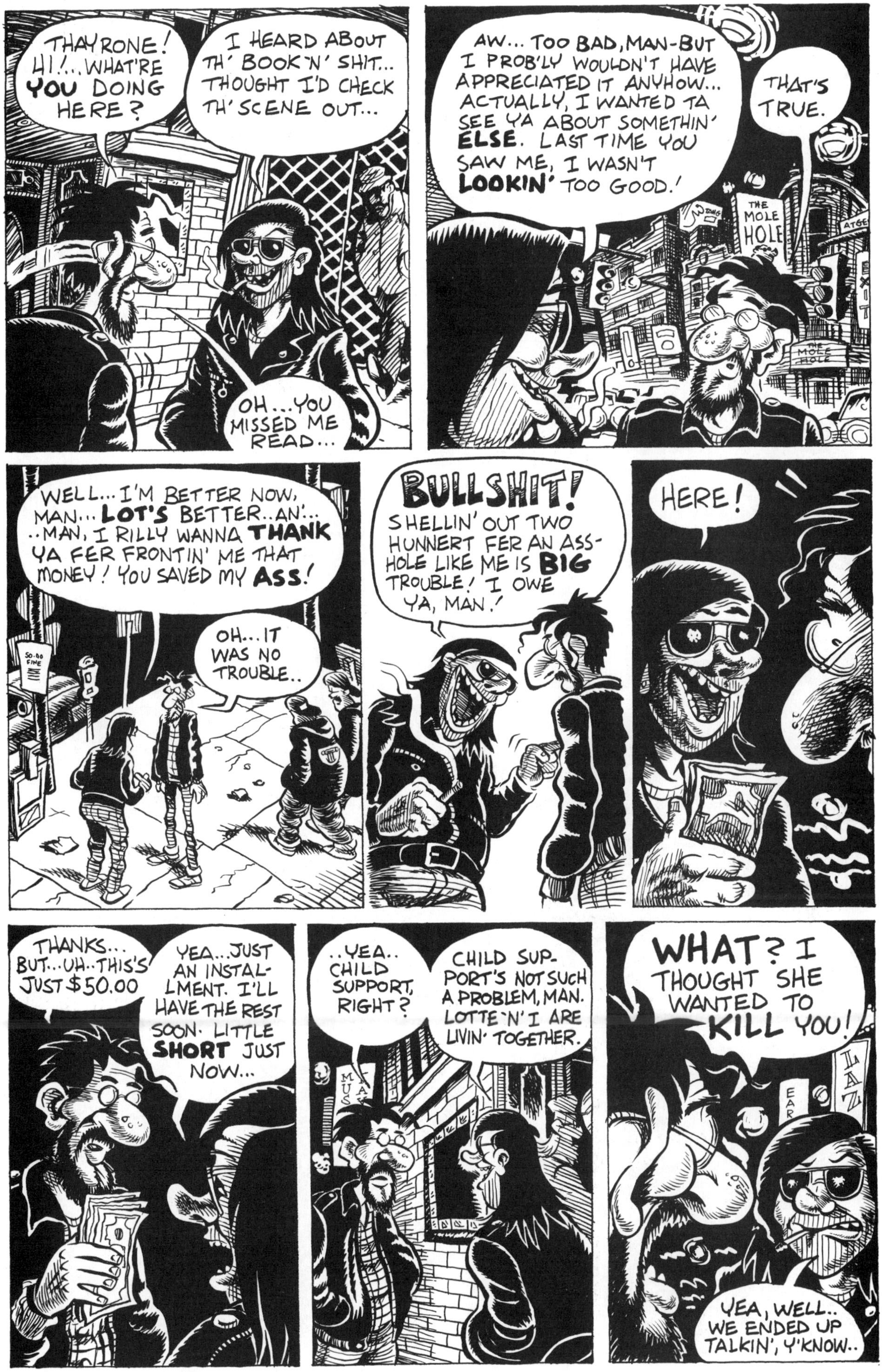

THAYRONE! HI!..WHAT'RE YOU DOING HERE?
I HEARD ABOUT TH' BOOK 'N' SHIT... THOUGHT I'D CHECK TH' SCENE OUT...
OH...YOU MISSED ME READ...
AW... TOO BAD, MAN-BUT I PROB'LY WOULDN'T HAVE APPRECIATED IT ANYHOW... ACTUALLY, I WANTED TA SEE YA ABOUT SOMETHIN' ELSE. LAST TIME YOU SAW ME, I WASN'T LOOKIN' TOO GOOD.!
THAT'S TRUE.
THE MOLE HOLE
WELL... I'M BETTER NOW, MAN... LOT'S BETTER..AN'.. ..MAN, I RILLY WANNA THANK YA FER FRONTIN' ME THAT MONEY! YOU SAVED MY ASS!
OH... IT WAS NO TROUBLE..
BULLSHIT! SHELLIN' OUT TWO HUNNERT FER AN ASS-HOLE LIKE ME IS BIG TROUBLE! I OWE YA, MAN.!
HERE!
THANKS... BUT...UH..THIS'S JUST $50.00
YEA..JUST AN INSTAL-LMENT. I'LL HAVE THE REST SOON. LITTLE SHORT JUST NOW...
..YEA.. CHILD SUPPORT, RIGHT?
CHILD SUP-PORT'S NOT SUCH A PROBLEM, MAN. LOTTE 'N' I ARE LIVIN' TOGETHER.
WHAT? I THOUGHT SHE WANTED TO KILL YOU!
YEA, WELL.. WE ENDED UP TALKIN', Y'KNOW..

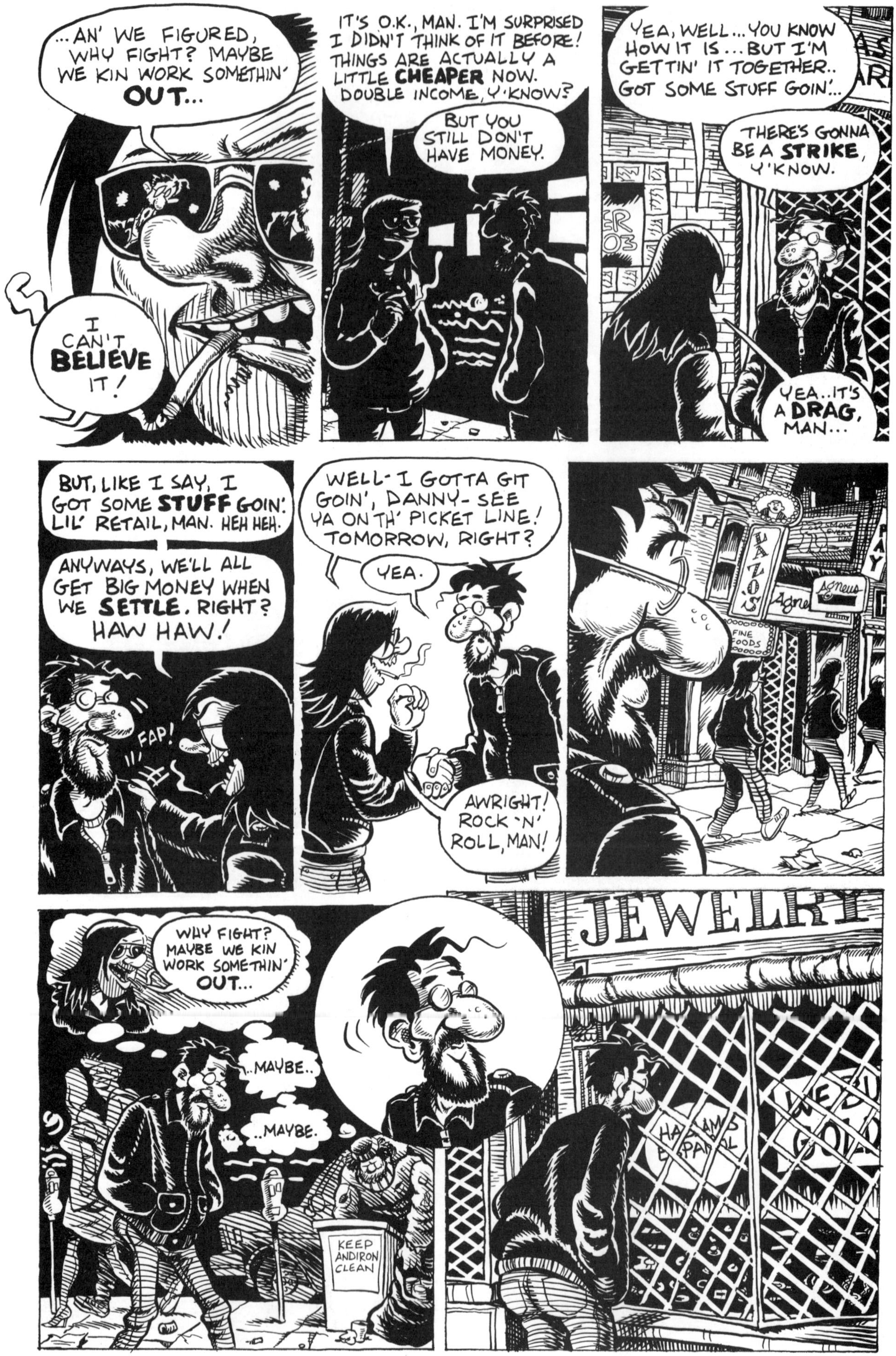

...AN' WE FIGURED, WHY FIGHT? MAYBE WE KIN WORK SOMETHIN' OUT...
I CAN'T BELIEVE IT!
IT'S O.K., MAN. I'M SURPRISED I DIDN'T THINK OF IT BEFORE! THINGS ARE ACTUALLY A LITTLE CHEAPER NOW. DOUBLE INCOME, Y'KNOW?
BUT YOU STILL DON'T HAVE MONEY.
YEA, WELL... YOU KNOW HOW IT IS... BUT I'M GETTIN' IT TOGETHER.. GOT SOME STUFF GOIN'...
THERE'S GONNA BE A STRIKE, Y'KNOW.
YEA.. IT'S A DRAG, MAN...
BUT, LIKE I SAY, I GOT SOME STUFF GOIN'. LIL' RETAIL, MAN. HEH HEH.
ANYWAYS, WE'LL ALL GET BIG MONEY WHEN WE SETTLE. RIGHT? HAW HAW!
FAP!
WELL- I GOTTA GIT GOIN', DANNY- SEE YA ON TH' PICKET LINE! TOMORROW, RIGHT?
YEA.
AWRIGHT! ROCK 'N' ROLL, MAN!
FINE FOODS
WHY FIGHT? MAYBE WE KIN WORK SOMETHIN' OUT...
..MAYBE..
..MAYBE.
KEEP ANDIRON CLEAN
JEWELRY

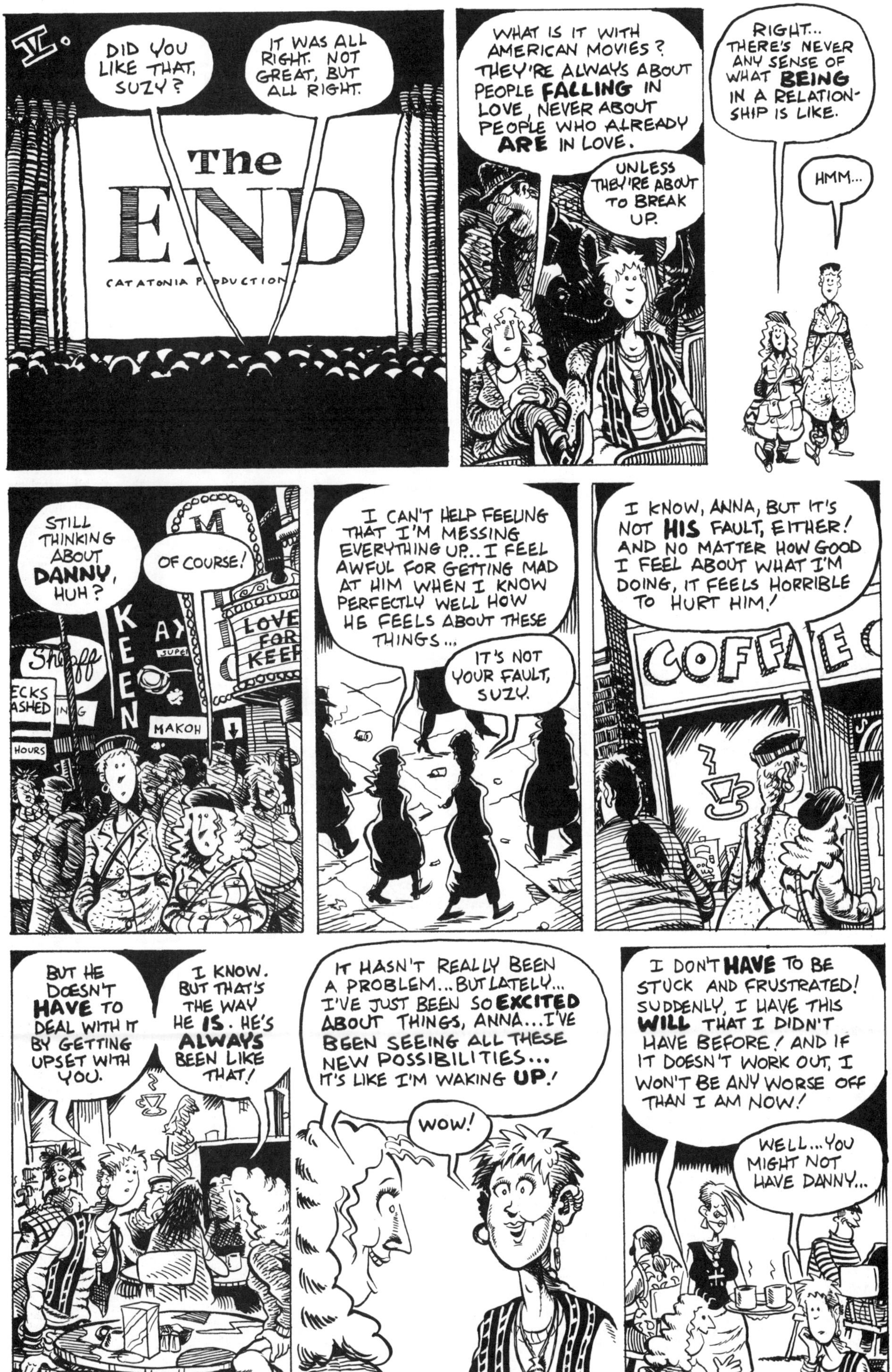
V.
DID YOU LIKE THAT, SUZY?
IT WAS ALL RIGHT. NOT GREAT, BUT ALL RIGHT.
The END
CATATONIA PRODUCTIONS
WHAT IS IT WITH AMERICAN MOVIES? THEY'RE ALWAYS ABOUT PEOPLE FALLING IN LOVE, NEVER ABOUT PEOPLE WHO ALREADY ARE IN LOVE.
UNLESS THEY'RE ABOUT TO BREAK UP.
RIGHT... THERE'S NEVER ANY SENSE OF WHAT BEING IN A RELATIONSHIP IS LIKE.
HMM...
STILL THINKING ABOUT DANNY, HUH?
OF COURSE!
I CAN'T HELP FEELING THAT I'M MESSING EVERYTHING UP... I FEEL AWFUL FOR GETTING MAD AT HIM WHEN I KNOW PERFECTLY WELL HOW HE FEELS ABOUT THESE THINGS...
IT'S NOT YOUR FAULT, SUZY.
I KNOW, ANNA, BUT IT'S NOT HIS FAULT, EITHER! AND NO MATTER HOW GOOD I FEEL ABOUT WHAT I'M DOING, IT FEELS HORRIBLE TO HURT HIM!
COFFEE
BUT HE DOESN'T HAVE TO DEAL WITH IT BY GETTING UPSET WITH YOU.
I KNOW. BUT THAT'S THE WAY HE IS. HE'S ALWAYS BEEN LIKE THAT!
IT HASN'T REALLY BEEN A PROBLEM... BUT LATELY... I'VE JUST BEEN SO EXCITED ABOUT THINGS, ANNA... I'VE BEEN SEEING ALL THESE NEW POSSIBILITIES... IT'S LIKE I'M WAKING UP!
WOW!
I DON'T HAVE TO BE STUCK AND FRUSTRATED! SUDDENLY, I HAVE THIS WILL THAT I DIDN'T HAVE BEFORE! AND IF IT DOESN'T WORK OUT, I WON'T BE ANY WORSE OFF THAN I AM NOW!
WELL... YOU MIGHT NOT HAVE DANNY...

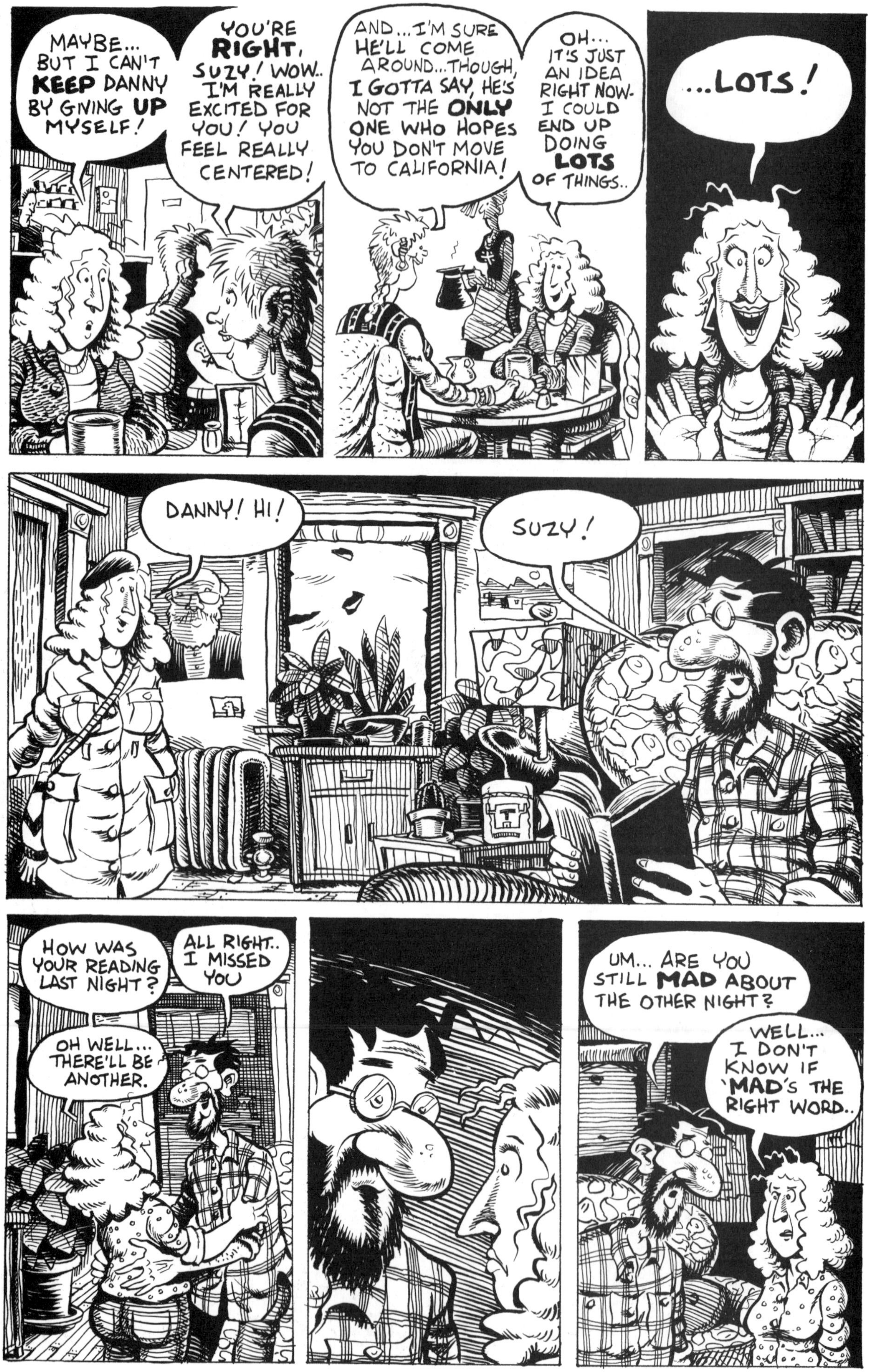
MAYBE... BUT I CAN'T KEEP DANNY BY GIVING UP MYSELF!
YOU'RE RIGHT, SUZY! WOW.. I'M REALLY EXCITED FOR YOU! YOU FEEL REALLY CENTERED!
AND... I'M SURE HE'LL COME AROUND... THOUGH, I GOTTA SAY, HE'S NOT THE ONLY ONE WHO HOPES YOU DON'T MOVE TO CALIFORNIA!
OH... IT'S JUST AN IDEA RIGHT NOW- I COULD END UP DOING LOTS OF THINGS..
...LOTS!
DANNY! HI!
SUZY!
HOW WAS YOUR READING LAST NIGHT?
ALL RIGHT.. I MISSED YOU
OH WELL... THERE'LL BE ANOTHER.
UM... ARE YOU STILL MAD ABOUT THE OTHER NIGHT?
WELL... I DON'T KNOW IF 'MAD'S THE RIGHT WORD..

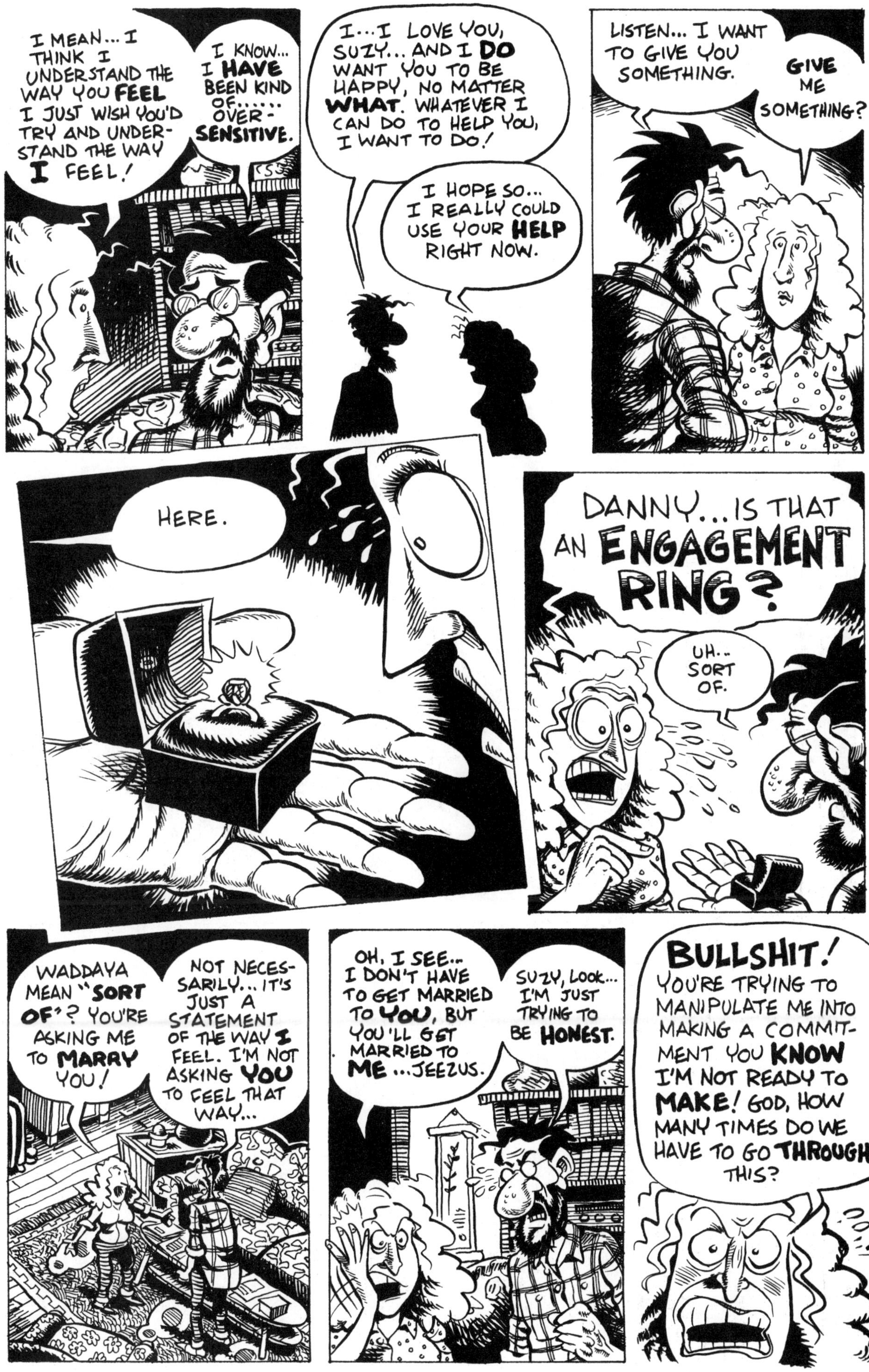
I MEAN... I THINK I UNDERSTAND THE WAY YOU FEEL I JUST WISH YOU'D TRY AND UNDERSTAND THE WAY I FEEL!
I KNOW... I HAVE BEEN KIND OF...... OVER-SENSITIVE.
I...I LOVE YOU, SUZY... AND I DO WANT YOU TO BE HAPPY, NO MATTER WHAT. WHATEVER I CAN DO TO HELP YOU, I WANT TO DO!
I HOPE SO... I REALLY COULD USE YOUR HELP RIGHT NOW.
LISTEN... I WANT TO GIVE YOU SOMETHING.
GIVE ME SOMETHING?
HERE.
DANNY... IS THAT AN ENGAGEMENT RING?
UH.. SORT OF.
WADDAYA MEAN "SORT OF"? YOU'RE ASKING ME TO MARRY YOU!
NOT NECES-SARILY... IT'S JUST A STATEMENT OF THE WAY I FEEL. I'M NOT ASKING YOU TO FEEL THAT WAY...
OH, I SEE.. I DON'T HAVE TO GET MARRIED TO YOU, BUT YOU'LL GET MARRIED TO ME ...JEEZUS.
SUZY, LOOK... I'M JUST TRYING TO BE HONEST.
BULLSHIT! YOU'RE TRYING TO MANIPULATE ME INTO MAKING A COMMIT-MENT YOU KNOW I'M NOT READY TO MAKE! GOD, HOW MANY TIMES DO WE HAVE TO GO THROUGH THIS?

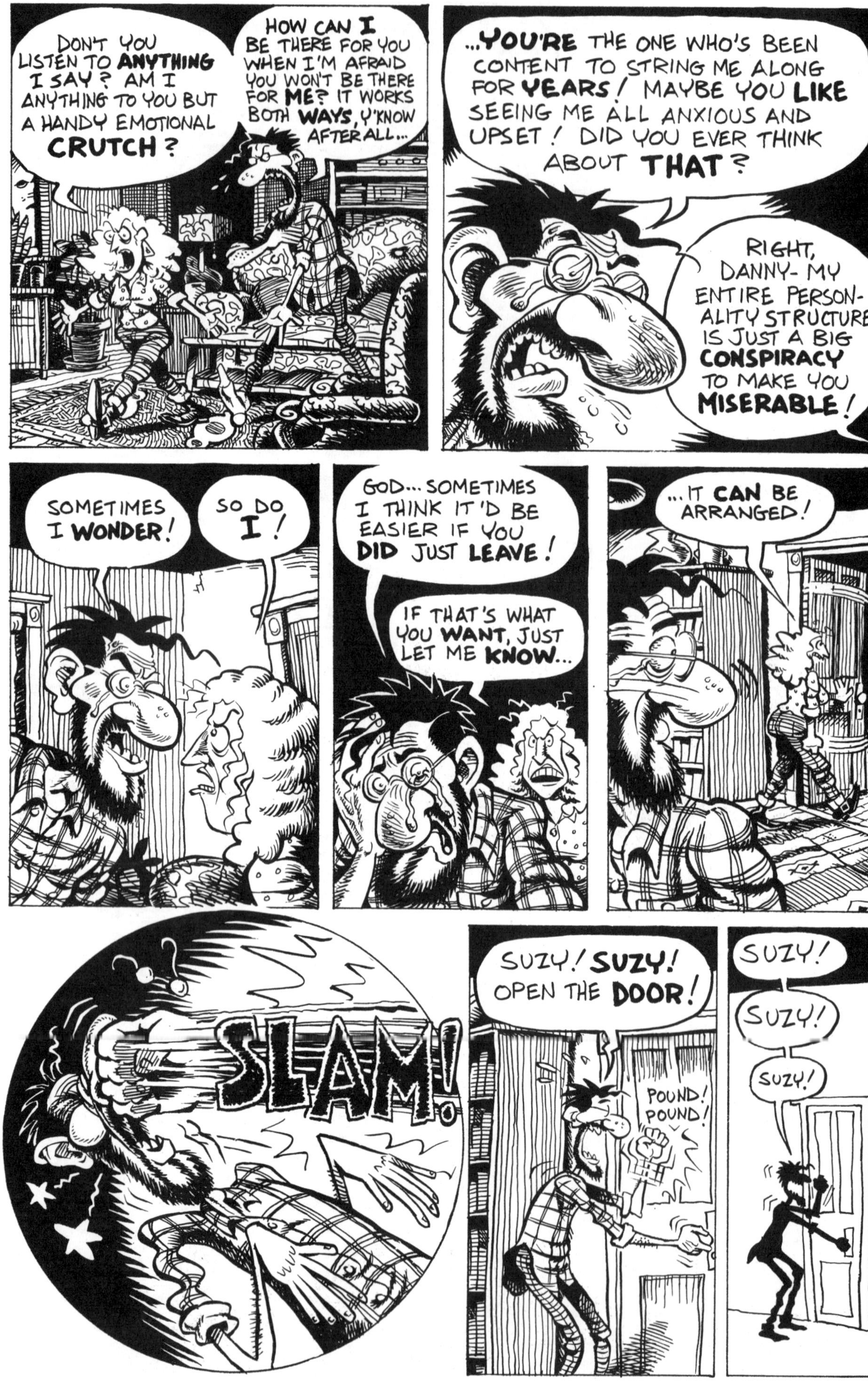
DON'T YOU LISTEN TO ANYTHING I SAY? AM I ANYTHING TO YOU BUT A HANDY EMOTIONAL CRUTCH?
HOW CAN I BE THERE FOR YOU WHEN I'M AFRAID YOU WON'T BE THERE FOR ME? IT WORKS BOTH WAYS, Y'KNOW AFTER ALL...
...YOU'RE THE ONE WHO'S BEEN CONTENT TO STRING ME ALONG FOR YEARS! MAYBE YOU LIKE SEEING ME ALL ANXIOUS AND UPSET! DID YOU EVER THINK ABOUT THAT?
RIGHT, DANNY- MY ENTIRE PERSON-ALITY STRUCTURE IS JUST A BIG CONSPIRACY TO MAKE YOU MISERABLE!
SOMETIMES I WONDER!
SO DO I!
GOD... SOMETIMES I THINK IT'D BE EASIER IF YOU DID JUST LEAVE!
IF THAT'S WHAT YOU WANT, JUST LET ME KNOW...
...IT CAN BE ARRANGED!
SLAM!
SUZY! SUZY! OPEN THE DOOR!
POUND! POUND!
SUZY!
SUZY!
SUZY!

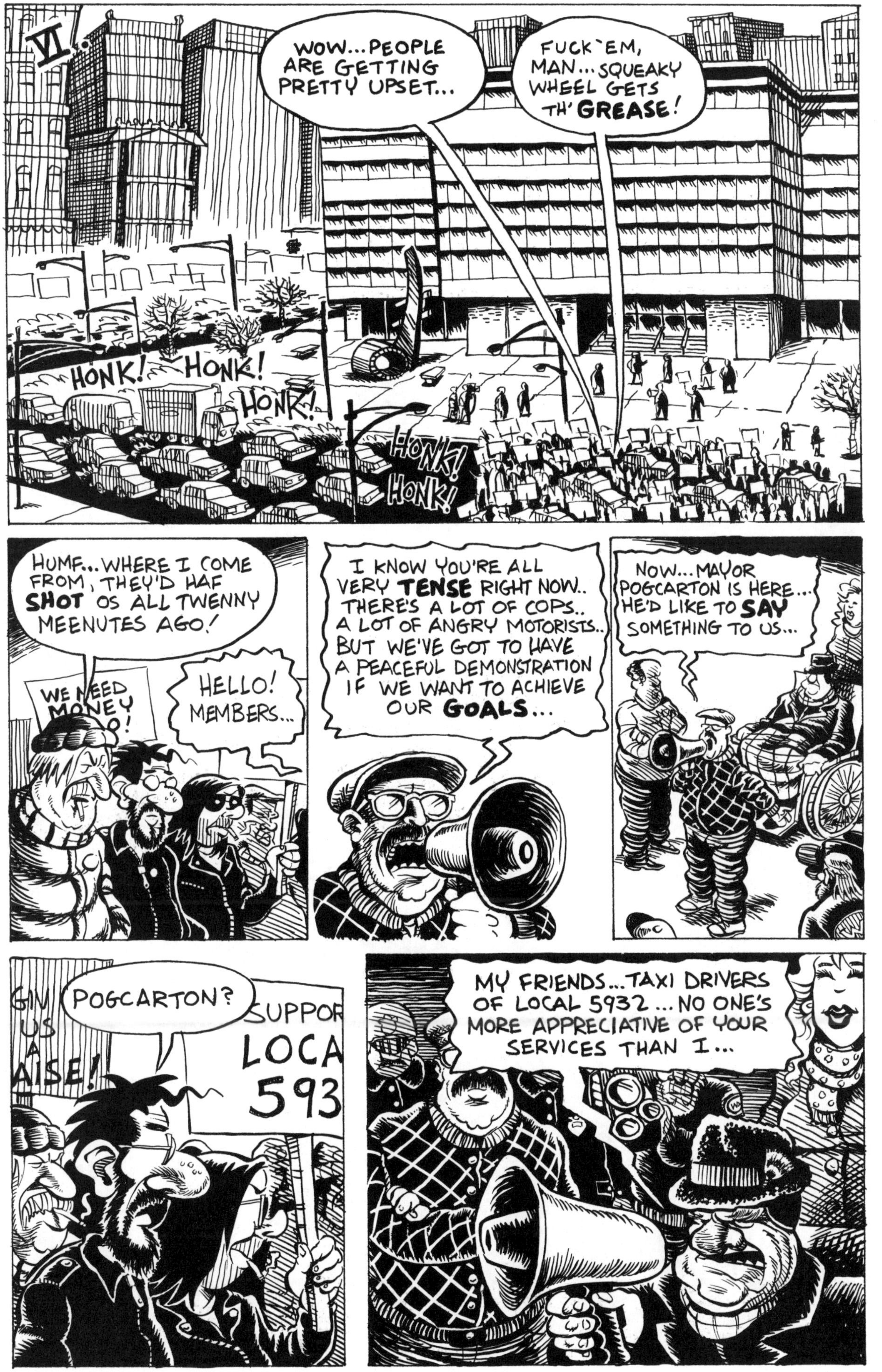
VI.
WOW... PEOPLE ARE GETTING PRETTY UPSET...
FUCK'EM, MAN... SQUEAKY WHEEL GETS TH' GREASE!
HONK! HONK! HONK! HONK! HONK!
HUMF... WHERE I COME FROM, THEY'D HAF SHOT OS ALL TWENNY MEENUTES AGO!
WE NEED MONEY
HELLO! MEMBERS...
I KNOW YOU'RE ALL VERY TENSE RIGHT NOW.. THERE'S A LOT OF COPS.. A LOT OF ANGRY MOTORISTS.. BUT WE'VE GOT TO HAVE A PEACEFUL DEMONSTRATION IF WE WANT TO ACHIEVE OUR GOALS...
NOW... MAYOR POGCARTON IS HERE... HE'D LIKE TO SAY SOMETHING TO US...
POGCARTON?
SUPPOR LOCA 593
MY FRIENDS... TAXI DRIVERS OF LOCAL 5932... NO ONE'S MORE APPRECIATIVE OF YOUR SERVICES THAN I...

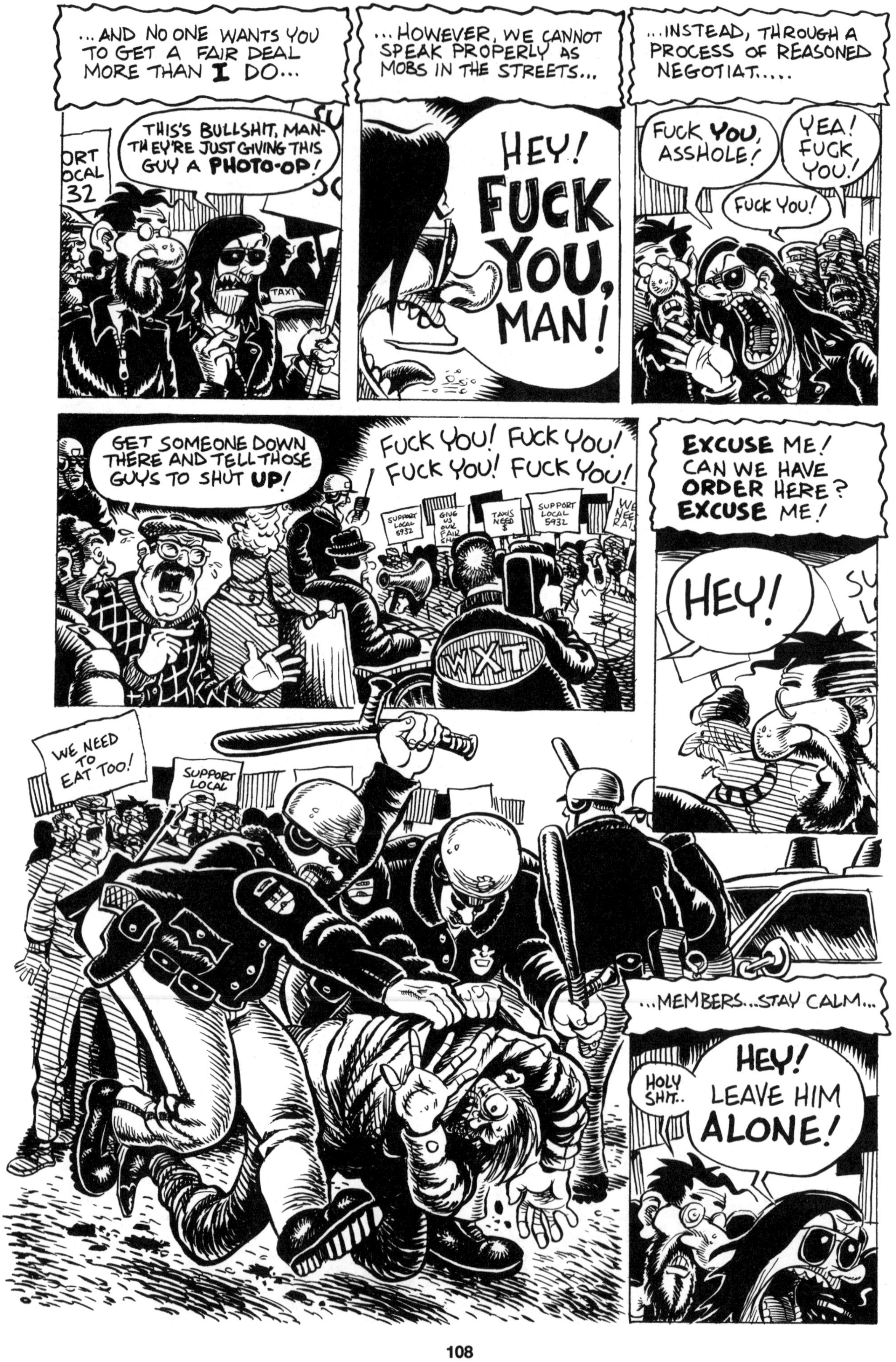
...AND NO ONE WANTS YOU TO GET A FAIR DEAL MORE THAN I DO...
THIS'S BULLSHIT, MAN- THEY'RE JUST GIVING THIS GUY A PHOTO-OP!
...HOWEVER, WE CANNOT SPEAK PROPERLY AS MOBS IN THE STREETS...
HEY! FUCK YOU, MAN!
...INSTEAD, THROUGH A PROCESS OF REASONED NEGOTIAT.....
FUCK YOU, ASSHOLE!
YEA! FUCK YOU!
FUCK YOU!
GET SOMEONE DOWN THERE AND TELL THOSE GUYS TO SHUT UP!
FUCK YOU! FUCK YOU! FUCK YOU! FUCK YOU!
SUPPORT LOCAL 5932
GIVE US OUR FAIR SHA
TAXIS NEED $
SUPPORT LOCAL 5932
WXT
EXCUSE ME! CAN WE HAVE ORDER HERE? EXCUSE ME!
HEY!
WE NEED TO EAT TOO!
SUPPORT LOCAL
...MEMBERS...STAY CALM...
HOLY SHIT..
HEY! LEAVE HIM ALONE!

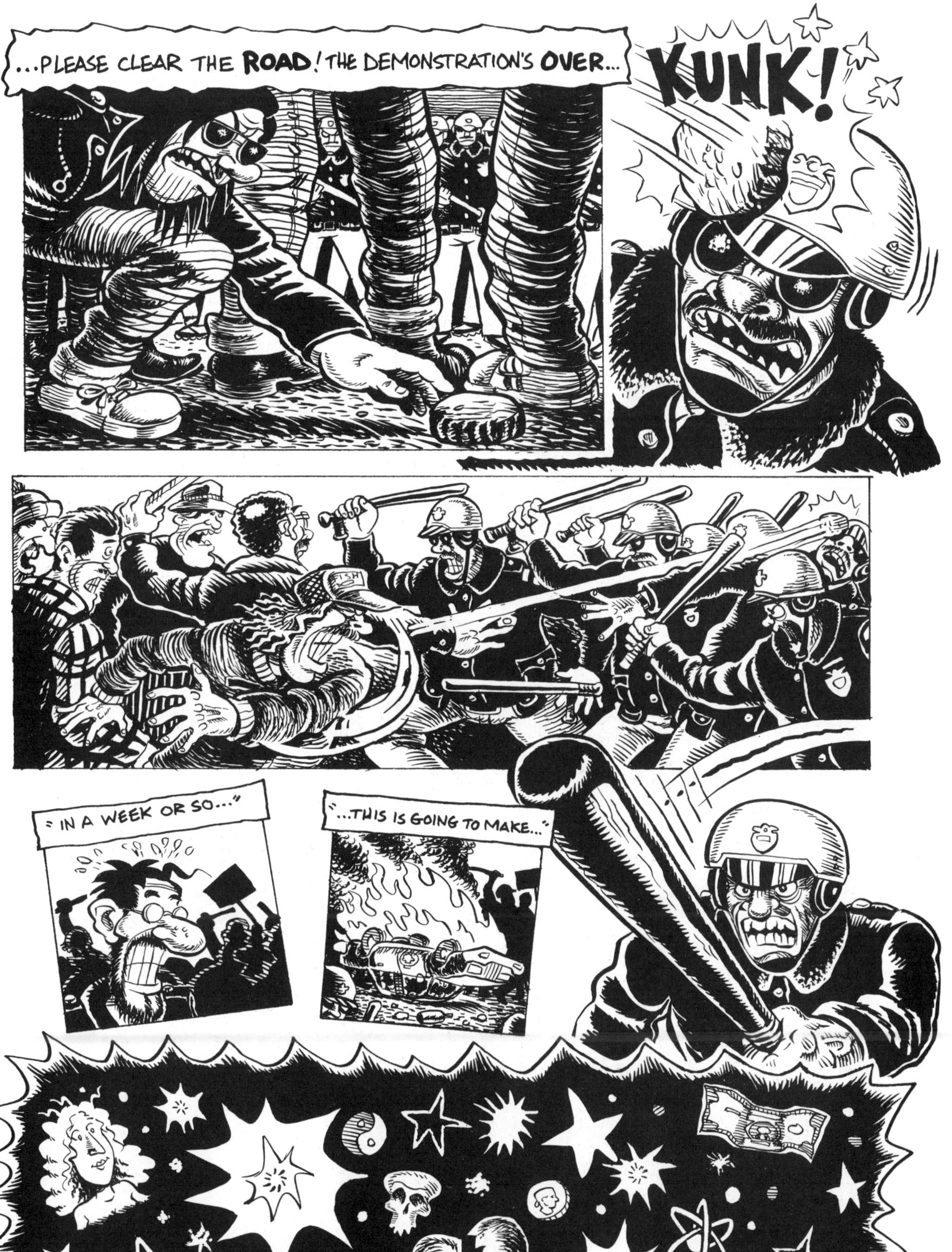
...PLEASE CLEAR THE **ROAD**! THE DEMONSTRATION'S **OVER**...
KUNK!
"IN A WEEK OR SO..."
"...THIS IS GOING TO MAKE..."
"...A GREAT POEM."

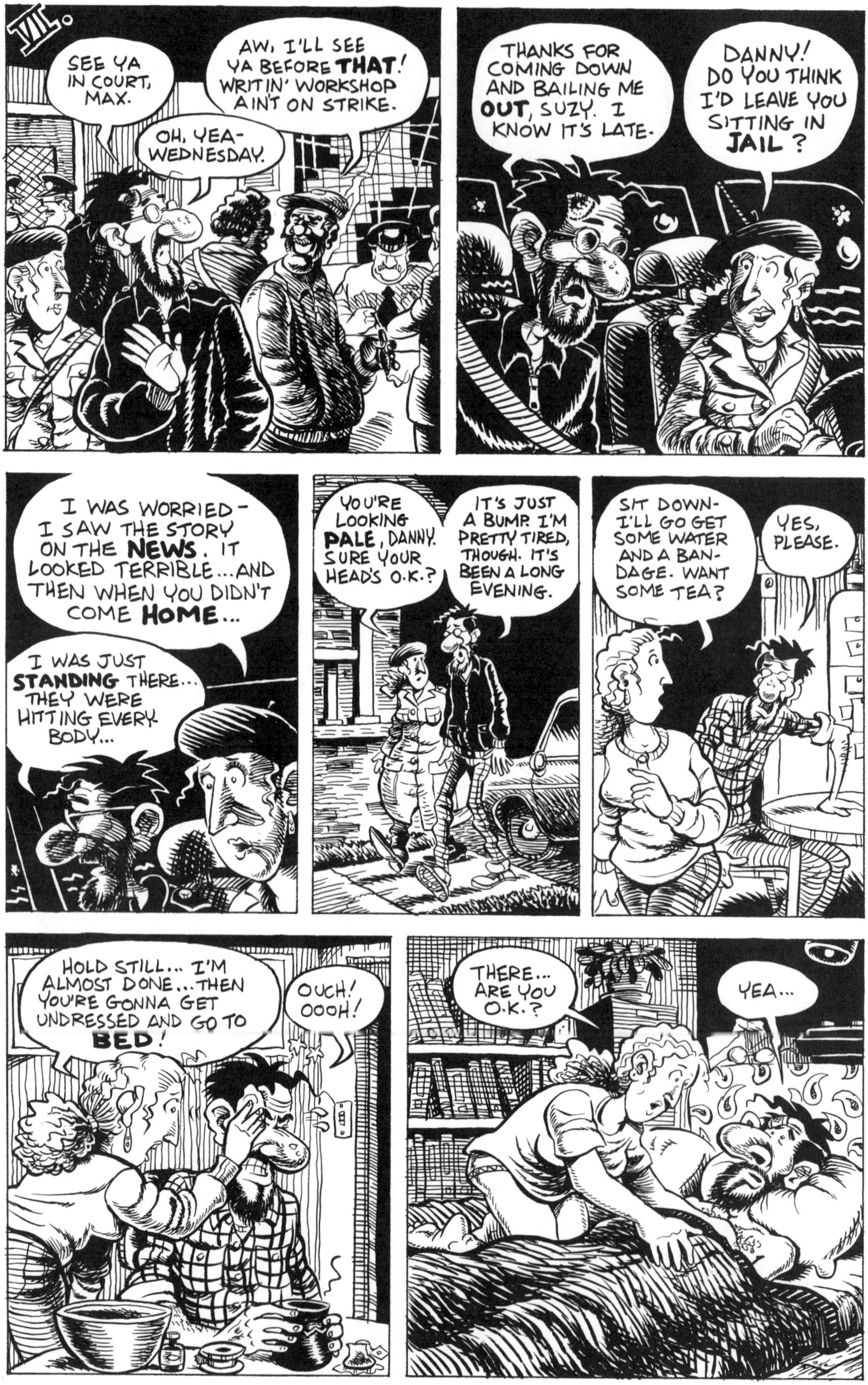
VII.
SEE YA IN COURT, MAX.
AW, I'LL SEE YA BEFORE THAT! WRITIN' WORKSHOP AIN'T ON STRIKE.
OH, YEA- WEDNESDAY.
THANKS FOR COMING DOWN AND BAILING ME OUT, SUZY. I KNOW IT'S LATE.
DANNY! DO YOU THINK I'D LEAVE YOU SITTING IN JAIL?
I WAS WORRIED - I SAW THE STORY ON THE NEWS. IT LOOKED TERRIBLE...AND THEN WHEN YOU DIDN'T COME HOME...
I WAS JUST STANDING THERE... THEY WERE HITTING EVERY-BODY...
YOU'RE LOOKING PALE, DANNY. SURE YOUR HEAD'S O.K.?
IT'S JUST A BUMP. I'M PRETTY TIRED, THOUGH. IT'S BEEN A LONG EVENING.
SIT DOWN- I'LL GO GET SOME WATER AND A BAN-DAGE. WANT SOME TEA?
YES, PLEASE.
HOLD STILL... I'M ALMOST DONE...THEN YOU'RE GONNA GET UNDRESSED AND GO TO BED!
OUCH! OOOH!
THERE... ARE YOU O.K.?
YEA...

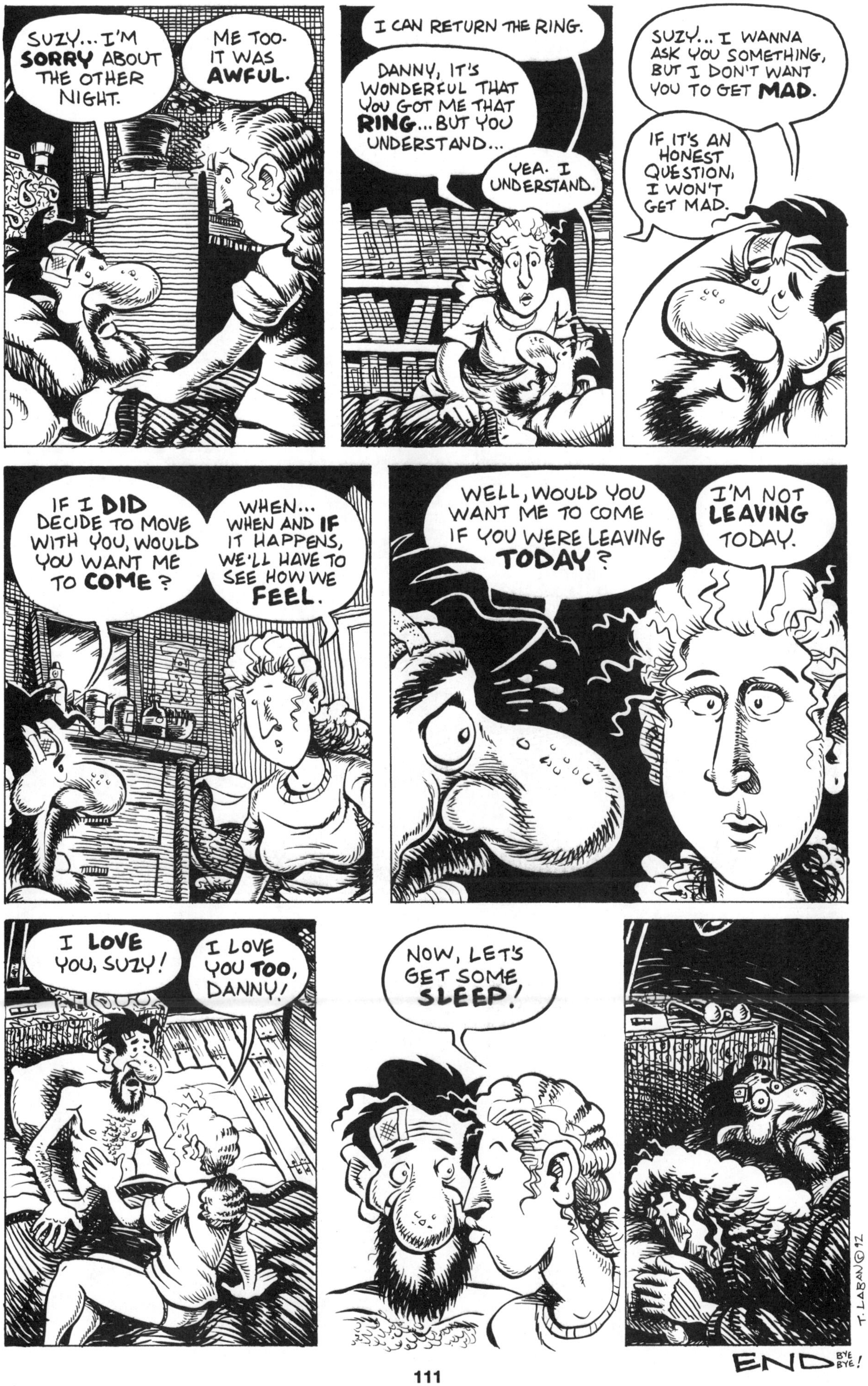
SUZY... I'M **SORRY** ABOUT THE OTHER NIGHT.
ME TOO. IT WAS **AWFUL**.
I CAN RETURN THE RING.
DANNY, IT'S WONDERFUL THAT YOU GOT ME THAT **RING**... BUT YOU UNDERSTAND...
YEA. I UNDERSTAND.
SUZY... I WANNA ASK YOU SOMETHING, BUT I DON'T WANT YOU TO GET **MAD**.
IF IT'S AN HONEST QUESTION, I WON'T GET MAD.
IF I **DID** DECIDE TO MOVE WITH YOU, WOULD YOU WANT ME TO **COME**?
WHEN... WHEN AND **IF** IT HAPPENS, WE'LL HAVE TO SEE HOW WE **FEEL**.
WELL, WOULD YOU WANT ME TO COME IF YOU WERE LEAVING **TODAY**?
I'M NOT **LEAVING** TODAY.
I **LOVE** YOU, SUZY!
I LOVE YOU **TOO**, DANNY!
NOW, LET'S GET SOME **SLEEP**!
T. LABAN ©92
END BYE BYE!

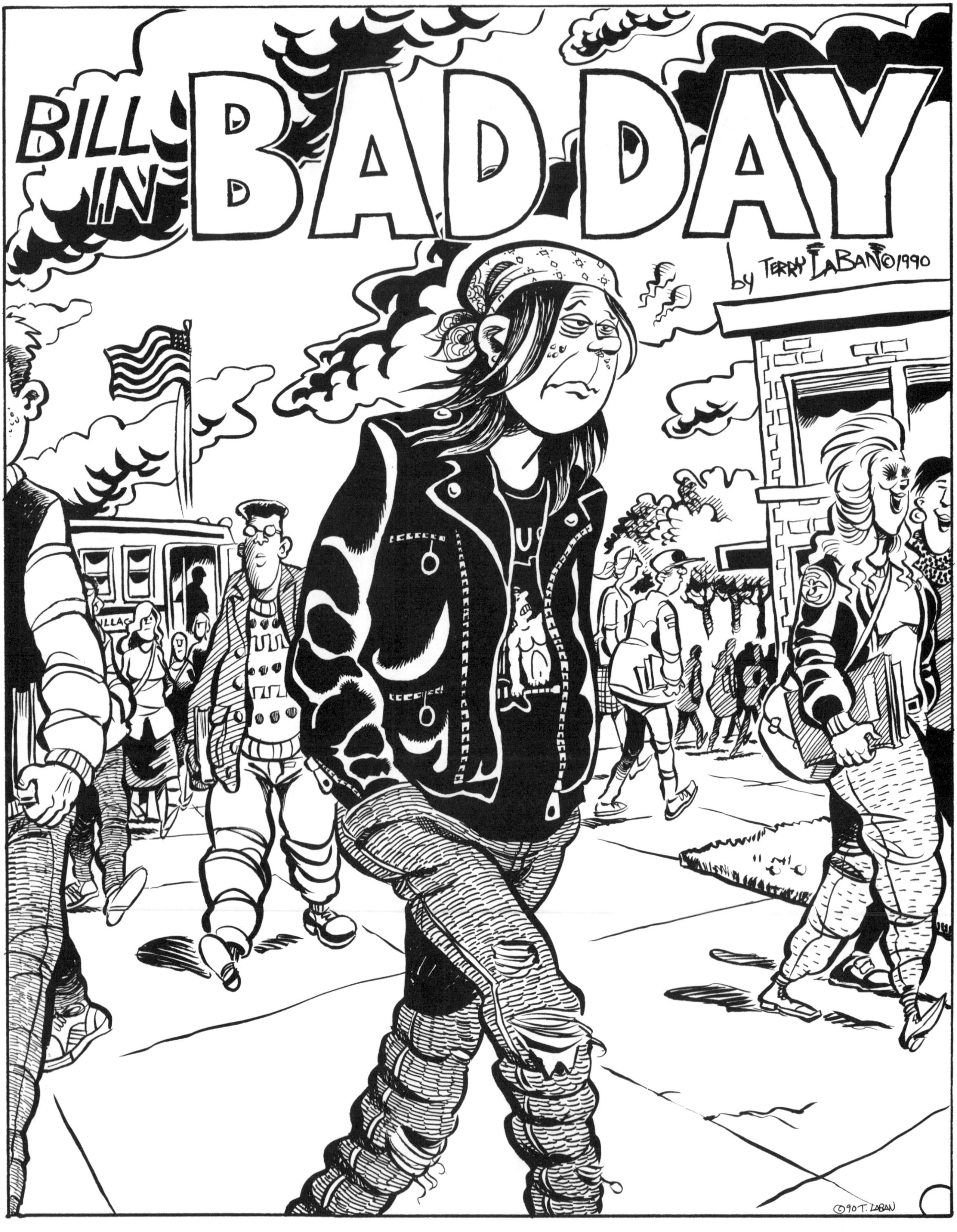
BILLY IN
BAD DAY
by TERRY LABAN ©1990
©90 T. LABAN

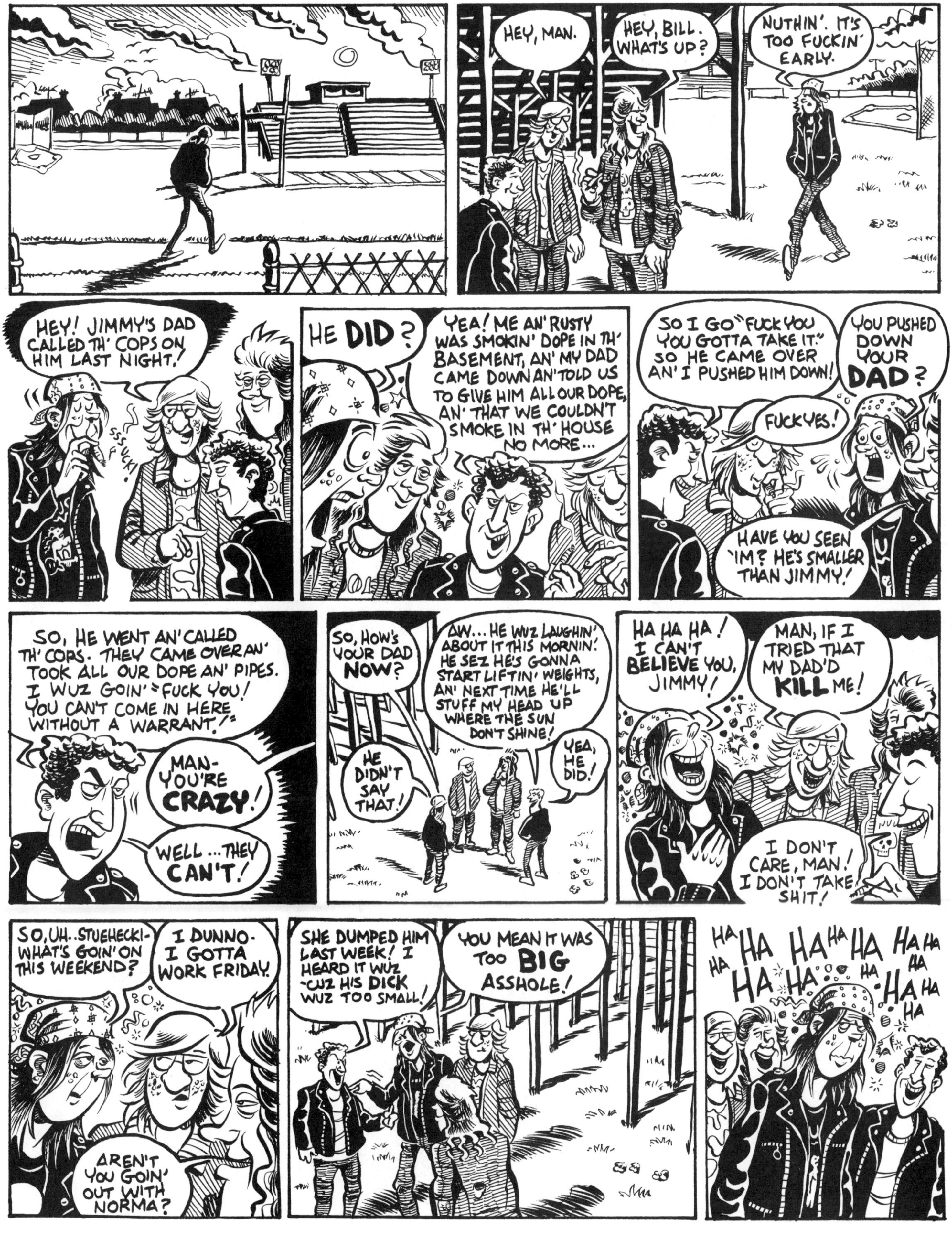

HEY, MAN.
HEY, BILL. WHAT'S UP?
NUTHIN'. IT'S TOO FUCKIN' EARLY.
HEY! JIMMY'S DAD CALLED TH' COPS ON HIM LAST NIGHT!
SSSUCK!
HE DID?
YEA! ME AN' RUSTY WAS SMOKIN' DOPE IN TH' BASEMENT, AN' MY DAD CAME DOWN AN' TOLD US TO GIVE HIM ALL OUR DOPE, AN' THAT WE COULDN'T SMOKE IN TH' HOUSE NO MORE...
SO I GO "FUCK YOU YOU GOTTA TAKE IT." SO HE CAME OVER AN' I PUSHED HIM DOWN!
YOU PUSHED DOWN YOUR DAD?
FUCK YES!
HAVE YOU SEEN 'IM? HE'S SMALLER THAN JIMMY!
SO, HE WENT AN' CALLED TH' COPS. THEY CAME OVER AN' TOOK ALL OUR DOPE AN' PIPES. I WUZ GOIN' "FUCK YOU! YOU CAN'T COME IN HERE WITHOUT A WARRANT!"
MAN- YOU'RE CRAZY!
WELL ... THEY CAN'T!
SO, HOW'S YOUR DAD NOW?
AW... HE WUZ LAUGHIN' ABOUT IT THIS MORNIN'. HE SEZ HE'S GONNA START LIFTIN' WEIGHTS, AN' NEXT TIME HE'LL STUFF MY HEAD UP WHERE THE SUN DON'T SHINE!
HE DIDN'T SAY THAT!
YEA, HE DID!
HA HA HA! I CAN'T BELIEVE YOU, JIMMY!
MAN, IF I TRIED THAT MY DAD'D KILL ME!
I DON'T CARE, MAN! I DON'T TAKE SHIT!
SO, UH.. STUEHECKI- WHAT'S GOIN' ON THIS WEEKEND?
I DUNNO- I GOTTA WORK FRIDAY.
AREN'T YOU GOIN' OUT WITH NORMA?
SHE DUMPED HIM LAST WEEK! I HEARD IT WUZ -CUZ HIS DICK WUZ TOO SMALL!
YOU MEAN IT WAS TOO BIG ASSHOLE!
HA HA HA HA HA HA HA HA HA HA HA HA HA HA HA HA HA

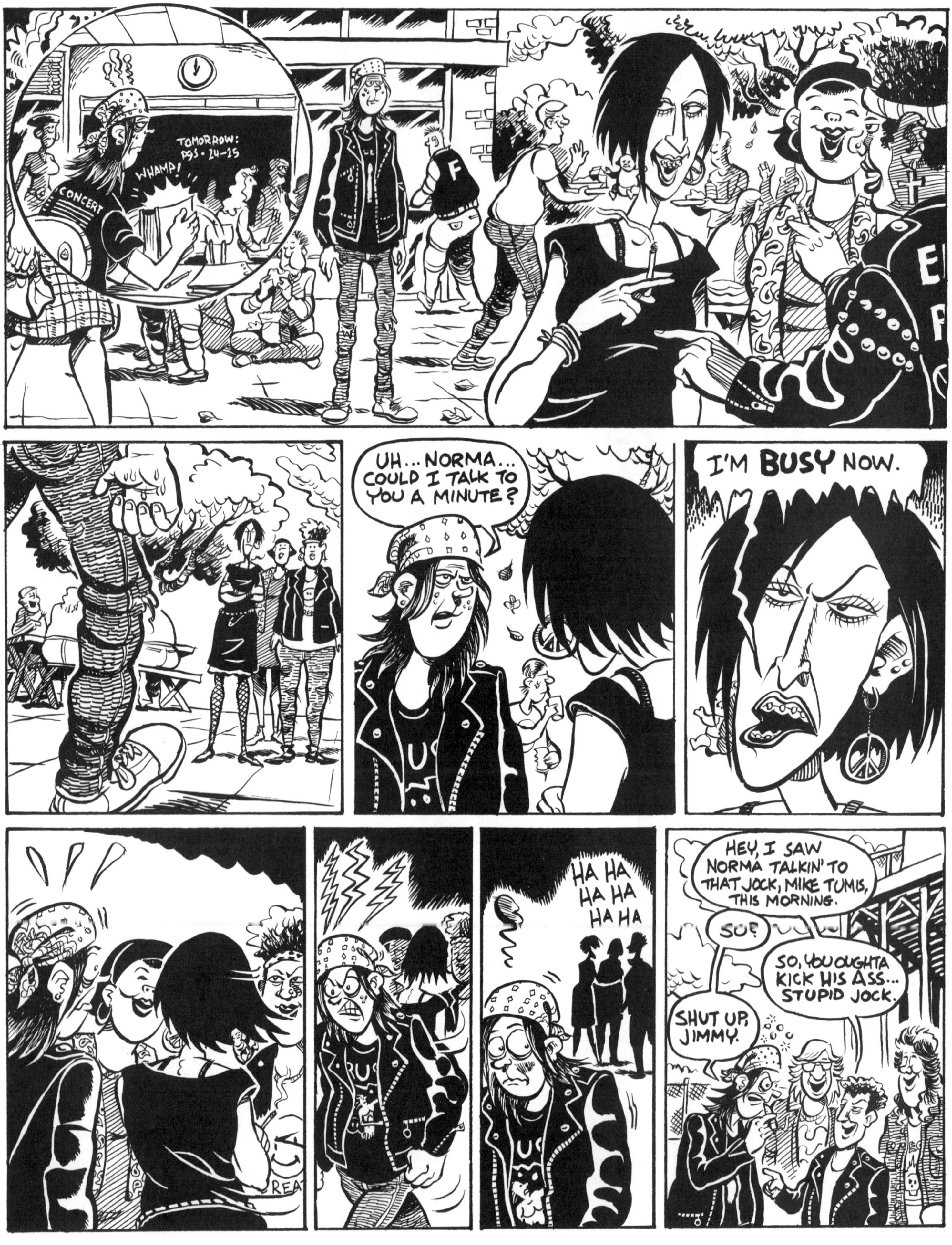
TOMORROW: PGS. 24-25
WHAMP!
CONCERT
UH... NORMA... COULD I TALK TO YOU A MINUTE?
I'M BUSY NOW.
HA HA HA HA HA HA
HEY, I SAW NORMA TALKIN' TO THAT JOCK, MIKE TUMIS, THIS MORNING.
SO?
SO, YOU OUGHTA KICK HIS ASS... STUPID JOCK.
SHUT UP, JIMMY.

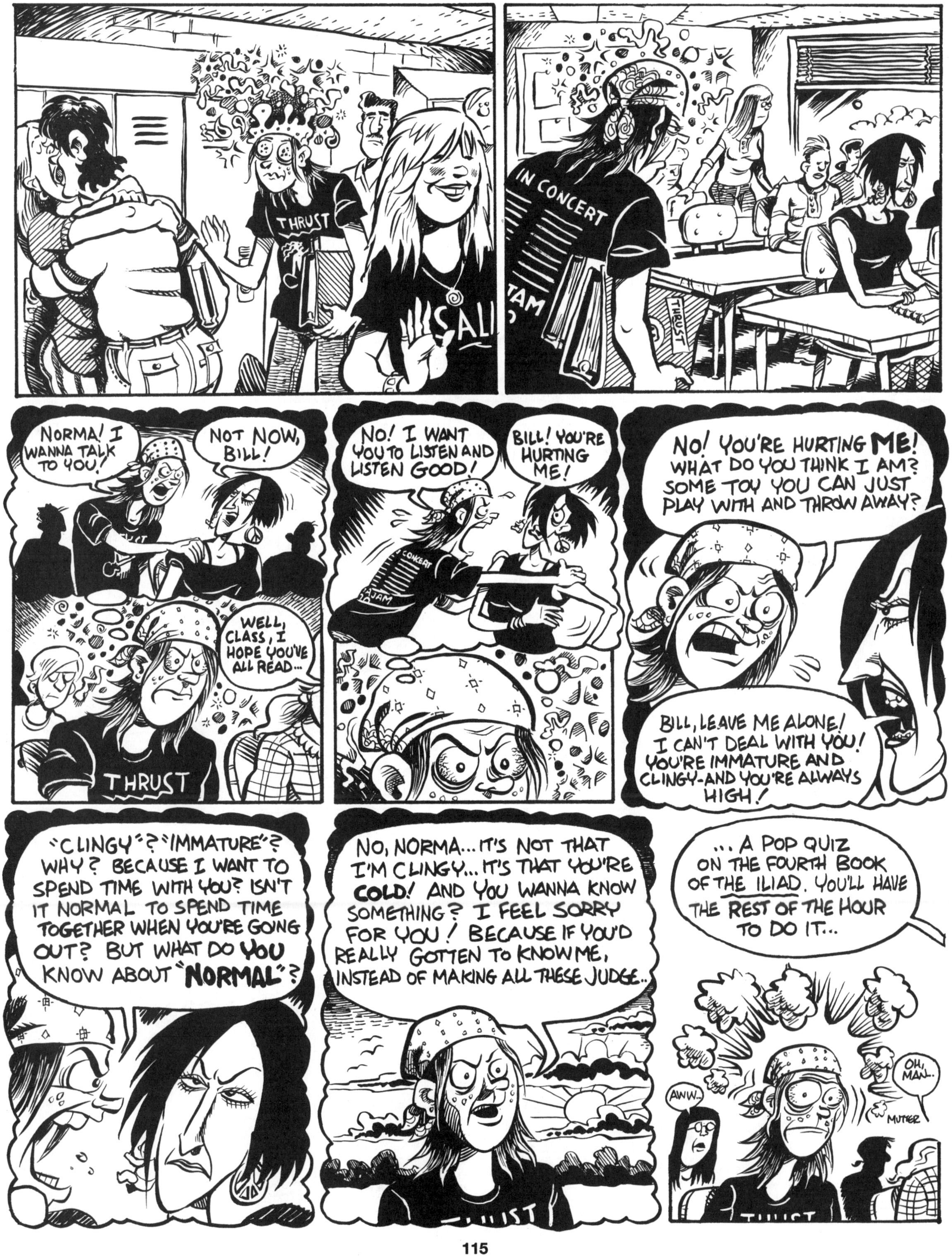
THRUST
SALI
IN CONCERT
TAM
THRUST
NORMA! I WANNA TALK TO YOU!
NOT NOW, BILL!
THRUST
WELL, CLASS, I HOPE YOU'VE ALL READ...
THRUST
NO! I WANT YOU TO LISTEN AND LISTEN GOOD!
BILL! YOU'RE HURTING ME!
CONCERT
NO! YOU'RE HURTING ME! WHAT DO YOU THINK I AM? SOME TOY YOU CAN JUST PLAY WITH AND THROW AWAY?
BILL, LEAVE ME ALONE! I CAN'T DEAL WITH YOU! YOU'RE IMMATURE AND CLINGY-AND YOU'RE ALWAYS HIGH!
"CLINGY"? "IMMATURE"? WHY? BECAUSE I WANT TO SPEND TIME WITH YOU? ISN'T IT NORMAL TO SPEND TIME TOGETHER WHEN YOU'RE GOING OUT? BUT WHAT DO YOU KNOW ABOUT "NORMAL"?
NO, NORMA... IT'S NOT THAT I'M CLINGY... IT'S THAT YOU'RE COLD! AND YOU WANNA KNOW SOMETHING? I FEEL SORRY FOR YOU! BECAUSE IF YOU'D REALLY GOTTEN TO KNOW ME, INSTEAD OF MAKING ALL THESE JUDGE...
... A POP QUIZ ON THE FOURTH BOOK OF THE ILIAD. YOU'LL HAVE THE REST OF THE HOUR TO DO IT...
AWW...
OH, MAN...
MUTTER

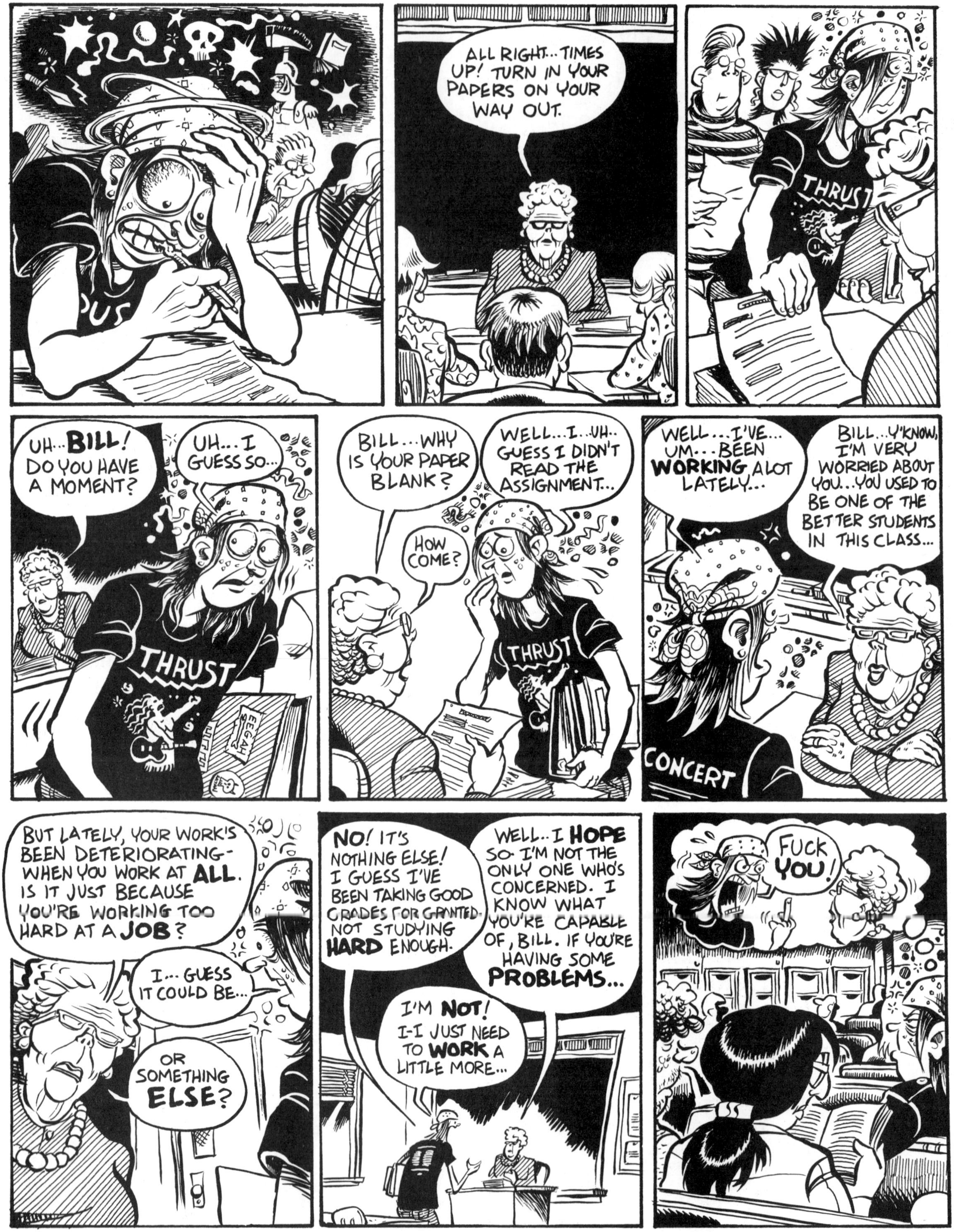
ALL RIGHT... TIMES UP! TURN IN YOUR PAPERS ON YOUR WAY OUT.
THRUST
UH... BILL! DO YOU HAVE A MOMENT?
UH... I GUESS SO...
THRUST
EEGAH
BILL... WHY IS YOUR PAPER BLANK?
WELL... I... UH.. GUESS I DIDN'T READ THE ASSIGNMENT...
HOW COME?
THRUST
WELL... I'VE... UM... BEEN WORKING A LOT LATELY...
BILL... Y'KNOW, I'M VERY WORRIED ABOUT YOU... YOU USED TO BE ONE OF THE BETTER STUDENTS IN THIS CLASS...
CONCERT
BUT LATELY, YOUR WORK'S BEEN DETERIORATING- WHEN YOU WORK AT ALL. IS IT JUST BECAUSE YOU'RE WORKING TOO HARD AT A JOB?
I... GUESS IT COULD BE...
OR SOMETHING ELSE?
NO! IT'S NOTHING ELSE! I GUESS I'VE BEEN TAKING GOOD GRADES FOR GRANTED- NOT STUDYING HARD ENOUGH.
WELL.. I HOPE SO. I'M NOT THE ONLY ONE WHO'S CONCERNED. I KNOW WHAT YOU'RE CAPABLE OF, BILL. IF YOU'RE HAVING SOME PROBLEMS...
I'M NOT! I-I JUST NEED TO WORK A LITTLE MORE...
FUCK YOU!

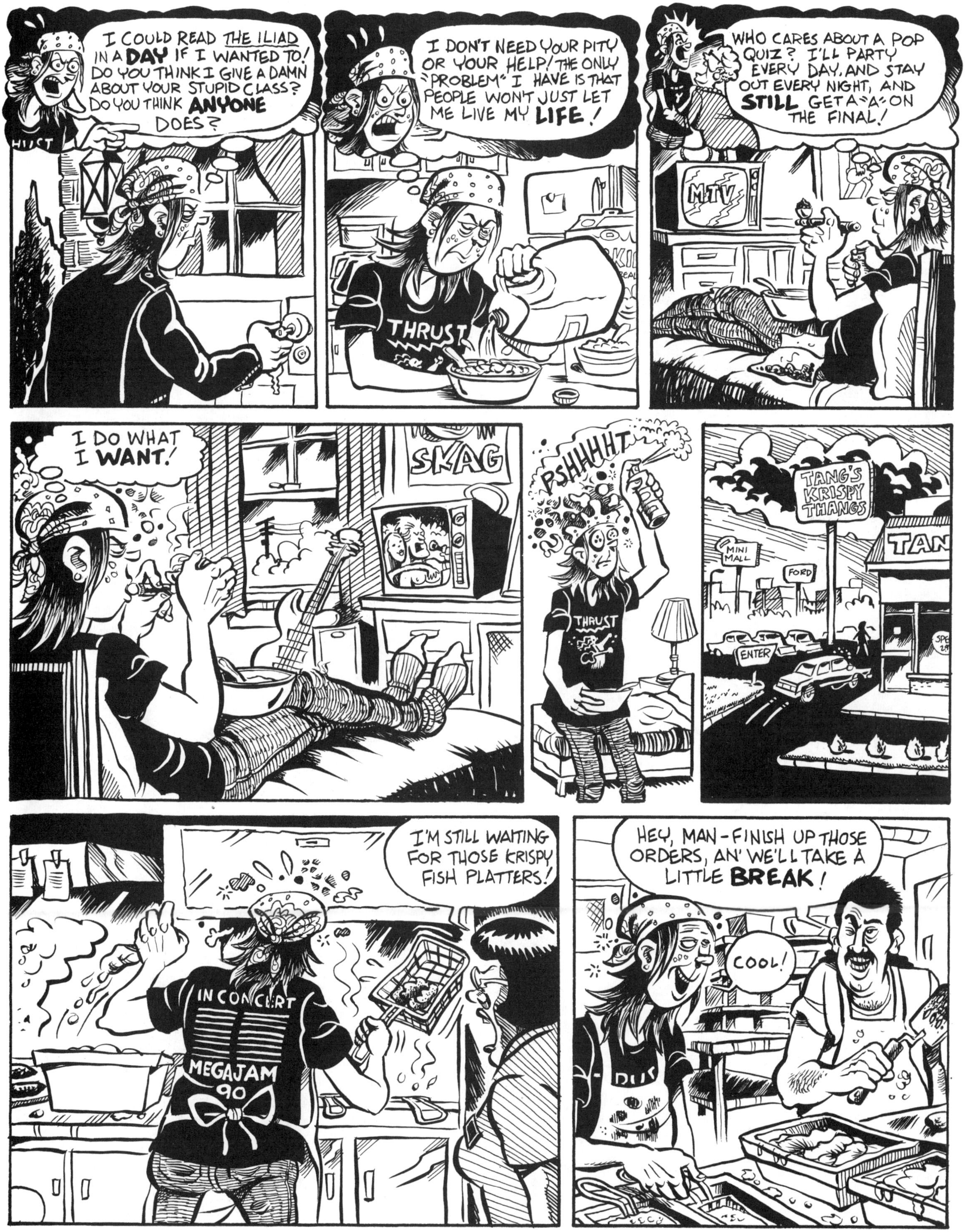
I COULD READ THE ILIAD IN A DAY IF I WANTED TO! DO YOU THINK I GIVE A DAMN ABOUT YOUR STUPID CLASS? DO YOU THINK ANYONE DOES?
I DON'T NEED YOUR PITY OR YOUR HELP! THE ONLY "PROBLEM" I HAVE IS THAT PEOPLE WON'T JUST LET ME LIVE MY LIFE!
THRUST
WHO CARES ABOUT A POP QUIZ? I'LL PARTY EVERY DAY, AND STAY OUT EVERY NIGHT, AND STILL GET A "A" ON THE FINAL!
MTV
I DO WHAT I WANT!
SKAG
PSHHHHT
THRUST
TANG'S KRISPY THANGS
MINI MALL
FORD
ENTER
I'M STILL WAITING FOR THOSE KRISPY FISH PLATTERS!
IN CONCERT
MEGAJAM 90
HEY, MAN - FINISH UP THOSE ORDERS, AN' WE'LL TAKE A LITTLE BREAK!
COOL!

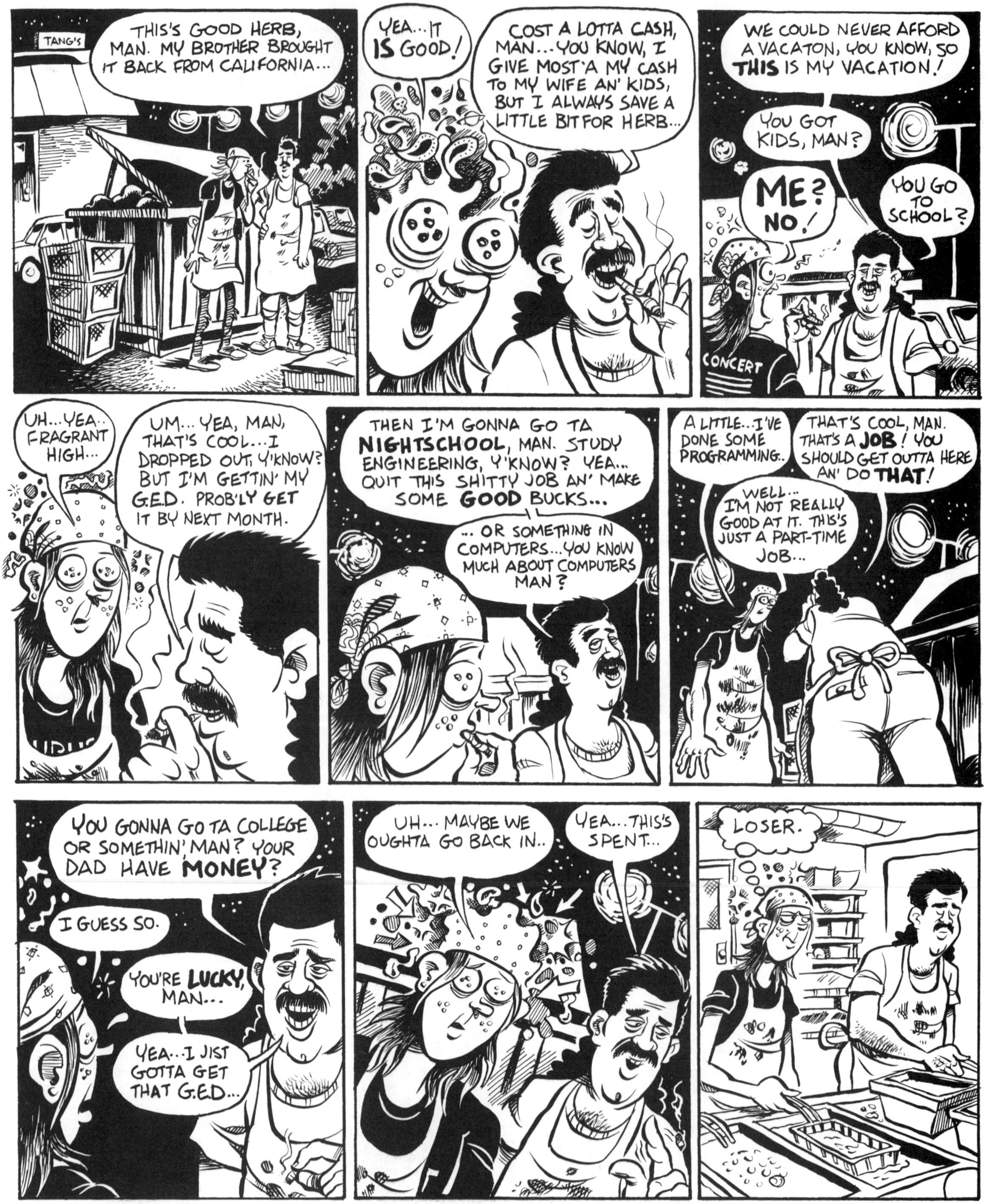

TANG'S
THIS'S GOOD HERB, MAN. MY BROTHER BROUGHT IT BACK FROM CALIFORNIA...
YEA... IT IS GOOD!
COST A LOTTA CASH, MAN... YOU KNOW, I GIVE MOST'A MY CASH TO MY WIFE AN' KIDS, BUT I ALWAYS SAVE A LITTLE BIT FOR HERB...
WE COULD NEVER AFFORD A VACATON, YOU KNOW, SO THIS IS MY VACATION!
YOU GOT KIDS, MAN?
ME? NO!
YOU GO TO SCHOOL?
CONCERT
UH... YEA.. FRAGRANT HIGH...
UM... YEA, MAN, THAT'S COOL... I DROPPED OUT, Y'KNOW? BUT I'M GETTIN' MY G.E.D. PROB'LY GET IT BY NEXT MONTH.
THEN I'M GONNA GO TA NIGHTSCHOOL, MAN. STUDY ENGINEERING, Y'KNOW? YEA... QUIT THIS SHITTY JOB AN' MAKE SOME GOOD BUCKS...
... OR SOMETHING IN COMPUTERS... YOU KNOW MUCH ABOUT COMPUTERS MAN?
A LITTLE.. I'VE DONE SOME PROGRAMMING..
THAT'S COOL, MAN. THAT'S A JOB! YOU SHOULD GET OUTTA HERE AN' DO THAT!
WELL... I'M NOT REALLY GOOD AT IT. THIS'S JUST A PART-TIME JOB...
YOU GONNA GO TA COLLEGE OR SOMETHIN' MAN? YOUR DAD HAVE MONEY?
I GUESS SO.
YOU'RE LUCKY, MAN...
YEA.. I JIST GOTTA GET THAT G.E.D...
UH... MAYBE WE OUGHTA GO BACK IN..
YEA... THIS'S SPENT...
LOSER.

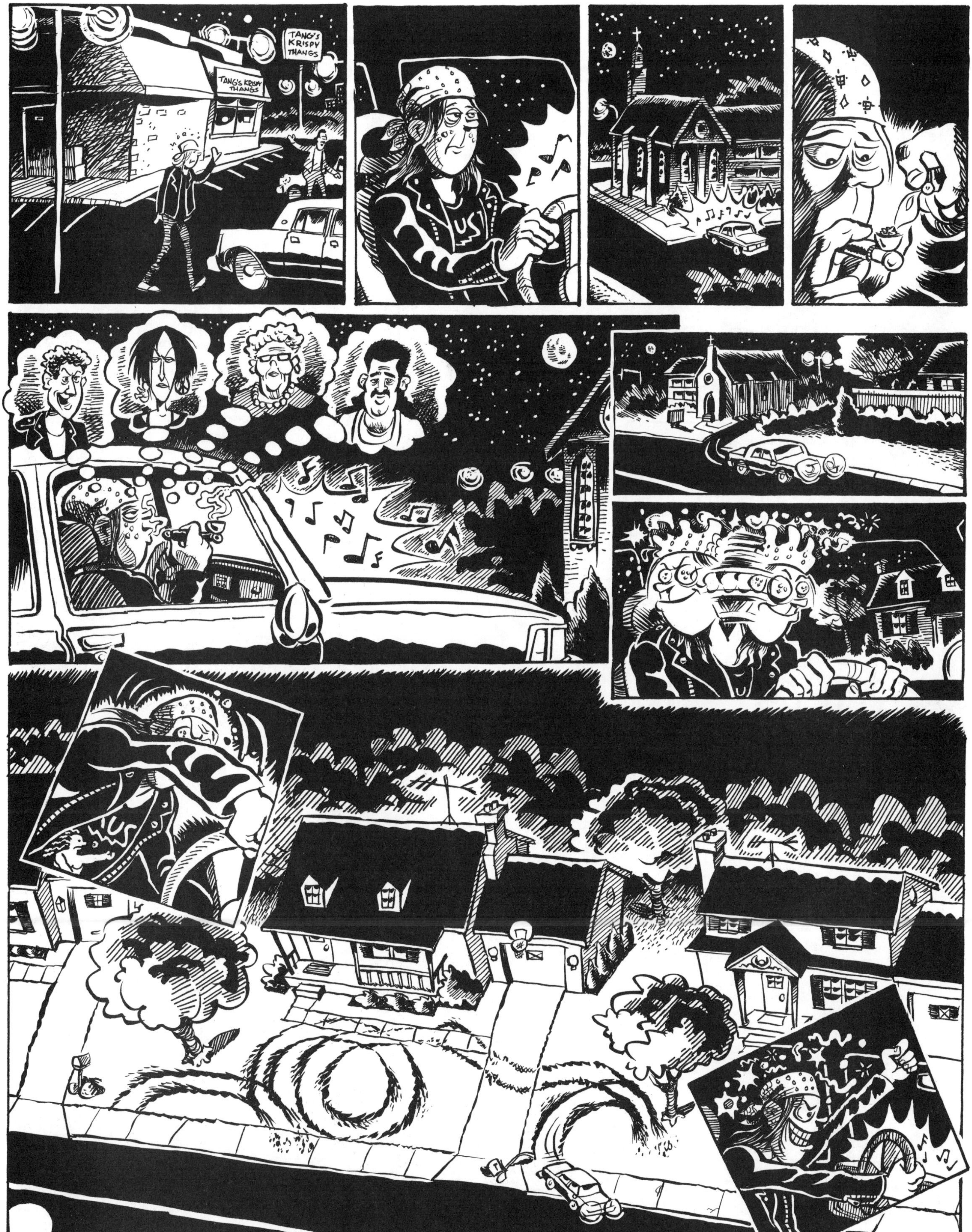
TANG'S KRISPY THANGS
TANG'S KRISPY THANGS

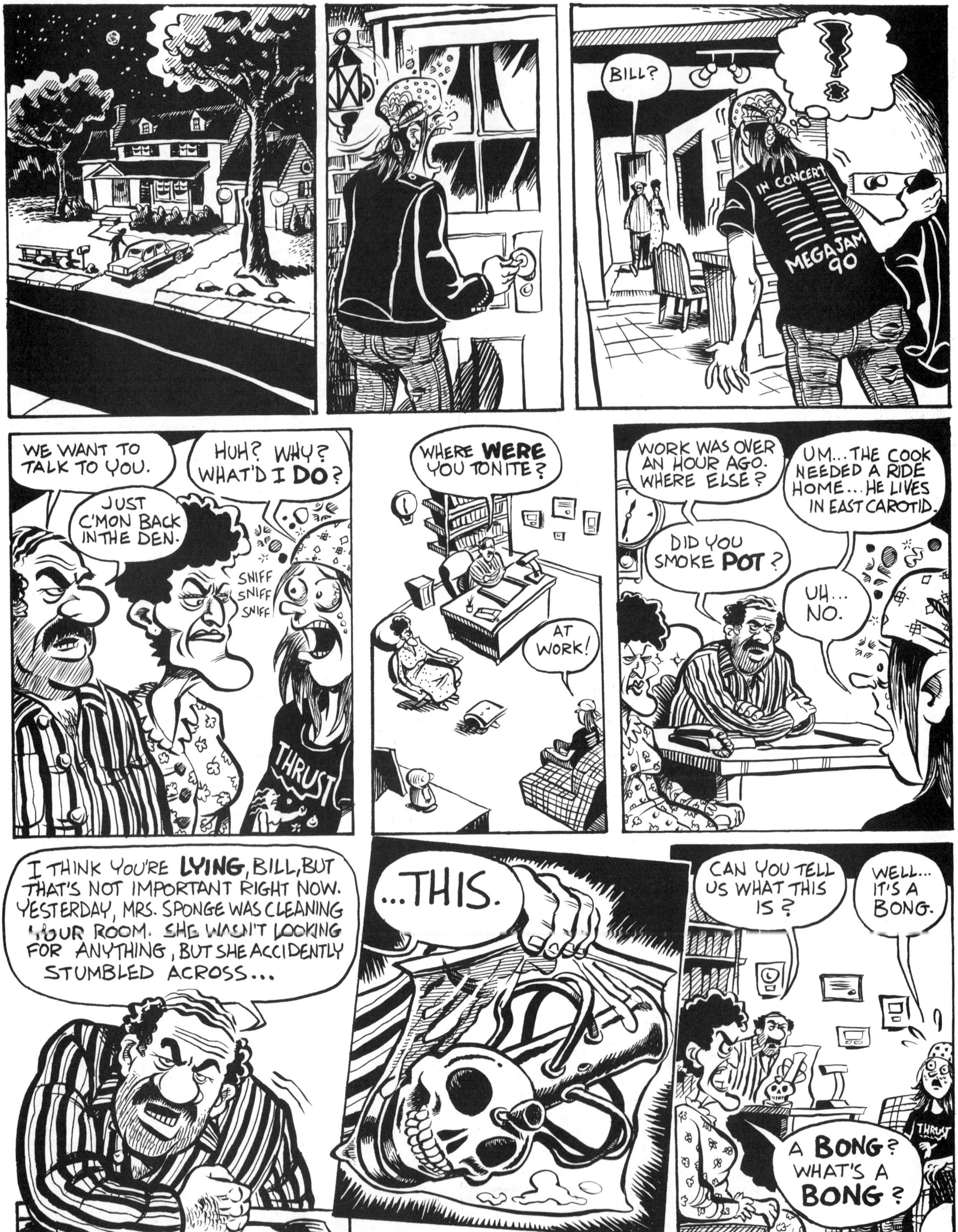
BILL?
WE WANT TO TALK TO YOU.
HUH? WHY? WHAT'D I DO?
JUST C'MON BACK IN THE DEN.
SNIFF SNIFF SNIFF
THRUST
WHERE WERE YOU TONITE?
AT WORK!
WORK WAS OVER AN HOUR AGO. WHERE ELSE?
UM... THE COOK NEEDED A RIDE HOME... HE LIVES IN EAST CAROTID.
DID YOU SMOKE POT?
UH... NO.
I THINK YOU'RE LYING, BILL, BUT THAT'S NOT IMPORTANT RIGHT NOW. YESTERDAY, MRS. SPONGE WAS CLEANING YOUR ROOM. SHE WASN'T LOOKING FOR ANYTHING, BUT SHE ACCIDENTLY STUMBLED ACROSS...
...THIS.
CAN YOU TELL US WHAT THIS IS?
WELL... IT'S A BONG.
A BONG? WHAT'S A BONG?

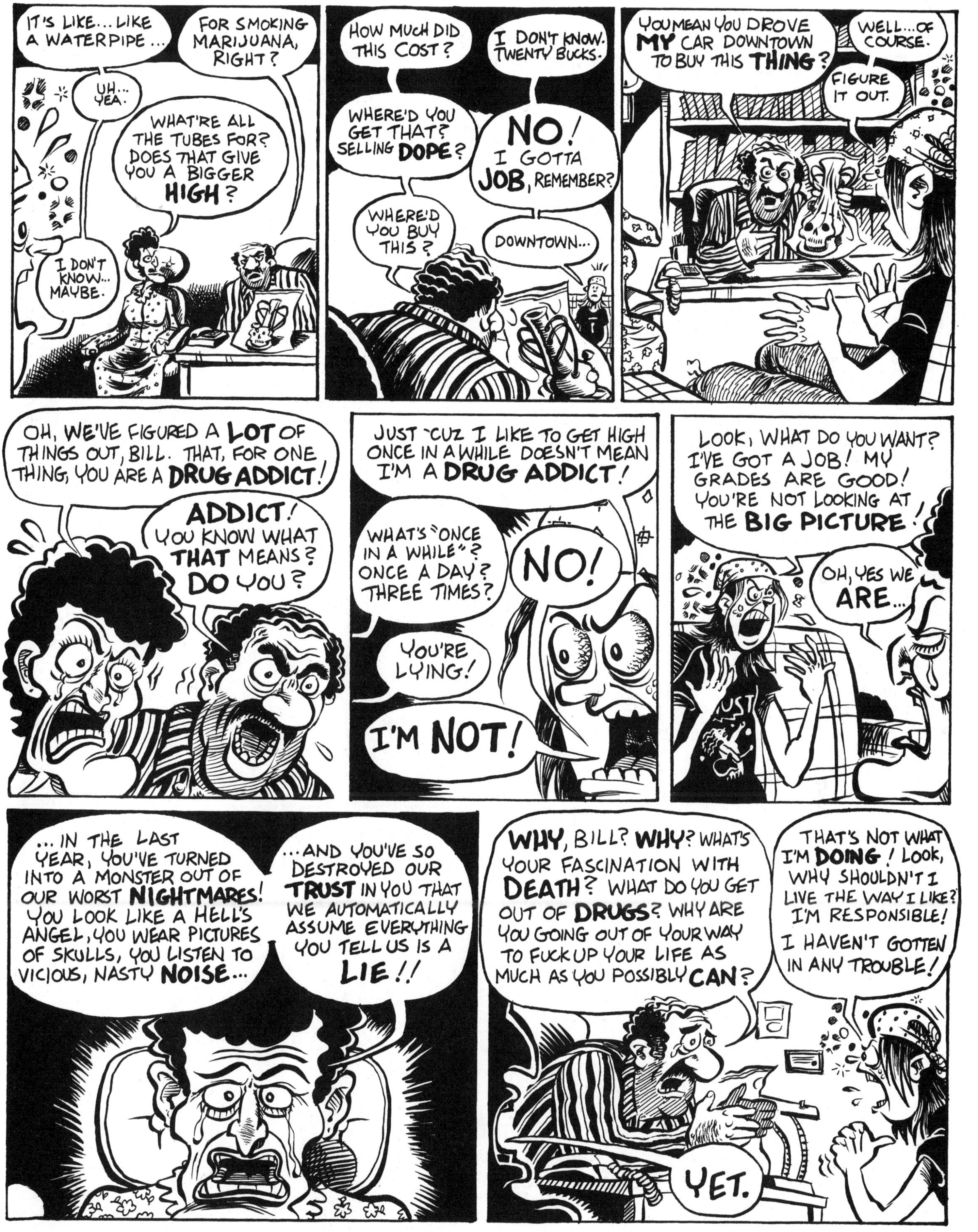
IT'S LIKE... LIKE A WATERPIPE...
FOR SMOKING MARIJUANA, RIGHT?
UH... YEA.
WHAT'RE ALL THE TUBES FOR? DOES THAT GIVE YOU A BIGGER HIGH?
I DON'T KNOW... MAYBE.
HOW MUCH DID THIS COST?
I DON'T KNOW. TWENTY BUCKS.
WHERE'D YOU GET THAT? SELLING DOPE?
NO! I GOTTA JOB, REMEMBER?
WHERE'D YOU BUY THIS?
DOWNTOWN...
YOU MEAN YOU DROVE MY CAR DOWNTOWN TO BUY THIS THING?
WELL... OF COURSE.
FIGURE IT OUT.
OH, WE'VE FIGURED A LOT OF THINGS OUT, BILL. THAT, FOR ONE THING, YOU ARE A DRUG ADDICT!
ADDICT! YOU KNOW WHAT THAT MEANS? DO YOU?
JUST 'CUZ I LIKE TO GET HIGH ONCE IN A WHILE DOESN'T MEAN I'M A DRUG ADDICT!
WHAT'S "ONCE IN A WHILE"? ONCE A DAY? THREE TIMES?
NO!
YOU'RE LYING!
I'M NOT!
LOOK, WHAT DO YOU WANT? I'VE GOT A JOB! MY GRADES ARE GOOD! YOU'RE NOT LOOKING AT THE BIG PICTURE!
OH, YES WE ARE...
... IN THE LAST YEAR, YOU'VE TURNED INTO A MONSTER OUT OF OUR WORST NIGHTMARES! YOU LOOK LIKE A HELL'S ANGEL, YOU WEAR PICTURES OF SKULLS, YOU LISTEN TO VICIOUS, NASTY NOISE...
...AND YOU'VE SO DESTROYED OUR TRUST IN YOU THAT WE AUTOMATICALLY ASSUME EVERYTHING YOU TELL US IS A LIE!!
WHY, BILL? WHY? WHAT'S YOUR FASCINATION WITH DEATH? WHAT DO YOU GET OUT OF DRUGS? WHY ARE YOU GOING OUT OF YOUR WAY TO FUCK UP YOUR LIFE AS MUCH AS YOU POSSIBLY CAN?
THAT'S NOT WHAT I'M DOING! LOOK, WHY SHOULDN'T I LIVE THE WAY I LIKE? I'M RESPONSIBLE! I HAVEN'T GOTTEN IN ANY TROUBLE!
YET.

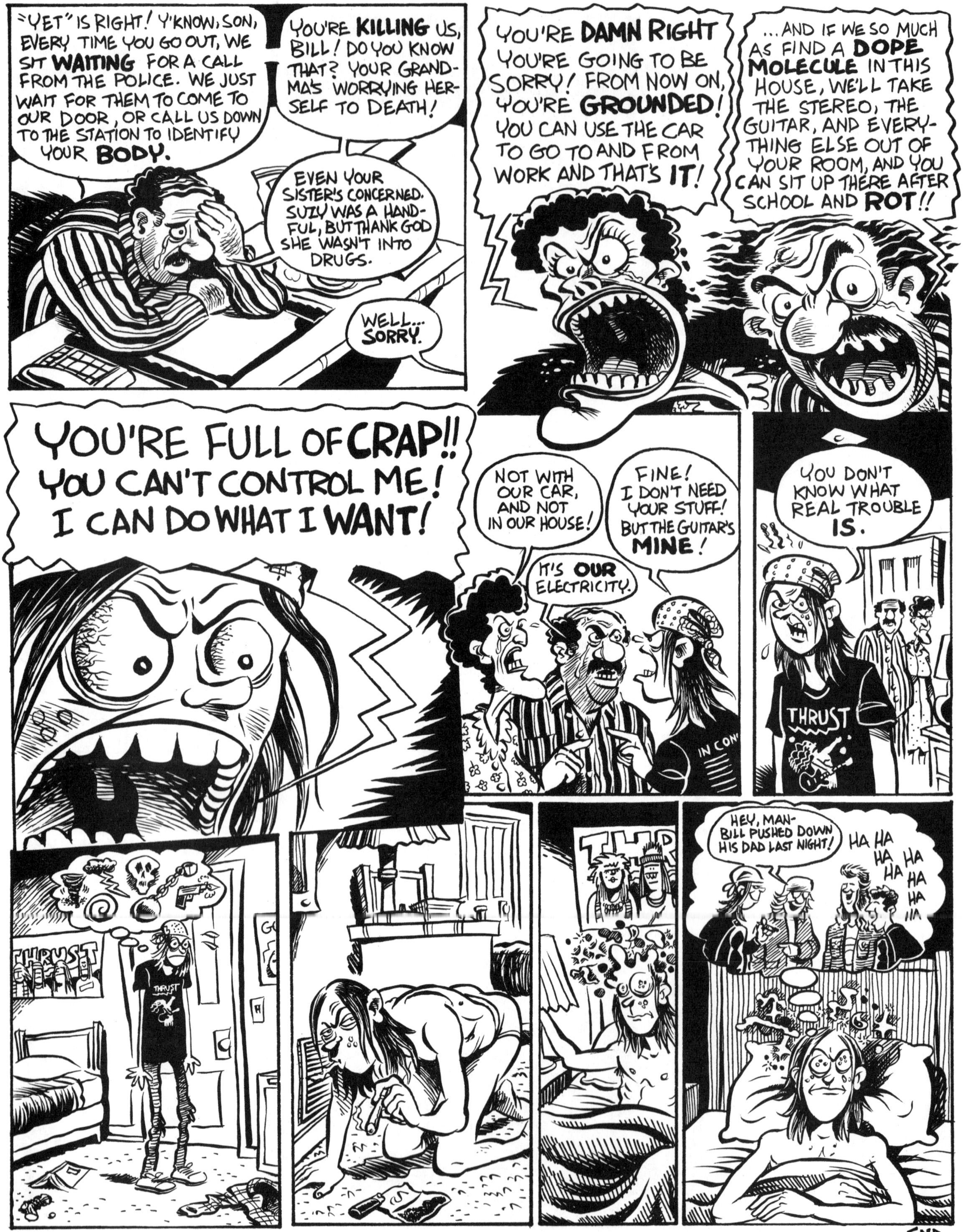
"YET" IS RIGHT! Y'KNOW, SON, EVERY TIME YOU GO OUT, WE SIT **WAITING** FOR A CALL FROM THE POLICE. WE JUST WAIT FOR THEM TO COME TO OUR DOOR, OR CALL US DOWN TO THE STATION TO IDENTIFY YOUR **BODY**.
YOU'RE **KILLING** US, BILL! DO YOU KNOW THAT? YOUR GRAND-MA'S WORRYING HER-SELF TO DEATH!
EVEN YOUR SISTER'S CONCERNED. SUZY WAS A HAND-FUL, BUT THANK GOD SHE WASN'T INTO DRUGS.
WELL... **SORRY**.
YOU'RE **DAMN RIGHT** YOU'RE GOING TO BE SORRY! FROM NOW ON, YOU'RE **GROUNDED**! YOU CAN USE THE CAR TO GO TO AND FROM WORK AND THAT'S **IT**!
...AND IF WE SO MUCH AS FIND A **DOPE MOLECULE** IN THIS HOUSE, WE'LL TAKE THE STEREO, THE GUITAR, AND EVERY-THING ELSE OUT OF YOUR ROOM, AND YOU CAN SIT UP THERE AFTER SCHOOL AND **ROT**!!
YOU'RE FULL OF **CRAP**!! YOU CAN'T CONTROL ME! I CAN DO WHAT I **WANT**!
NOT WITH OUR CAR, AND NOT IN OUR HOUSE!
FINE! I DON'T NEED YOUR STUFF! BUT THE GUITAR'S **MINE**!
IT'S **OUR** ELECTRICITY.
IN CON
YOU DON'T KNOW WHAT REAL TROUBLE **IS**.
THRUST
THRUST
THRUST
HEY, MAN-BILL PUSHED DOWN HIS DAD LAST NIGHT!
HA HA HA HA HA HA HA HA HA
END